Beneath the Same Heaven

A Novel

Anne Marie Ruff

Open Books

Published by Open Books

Copyright © 2018 by Anne Marie Ruff

Opening quote by Alexander Solzhenitsyn from
The Gulag Archipelago, licensed under CC via
https://en.wikiquote.org/wiki/Aleksandr_Solzhenitsyn

Author portrait by Nancy Hauck

ISBN-13: 978-1948598019

For my parents

"If only there were evil people somewhere insidiously committing evil deeds and it were necessary only to separate them from the rest of us and destroy them. But the line dividing good and evil cuts through the heart of every human being. And who is willing to destroy a piece of his own heart?"

— Alexander Solzhenitsyn
Novelist, Nobel laureate (1918-2008)

Prelude

Los Angeles, California.
The day of the bombing

"So you don't know where he is?" the man asks, with some urgency.

"What do you mean?" Kathryn answers into the phone, soap bubbles dripping off her hand into the kitchen sink. "*You* scheduled his offshore job. He told me he'd be gone for a week or so."

"You better call him, and find out where he's at," the man abruptly hangs up.

Kathryn dries her hands and calls her husband's phone number. She had just spoken to him yesterday. Without ringing, the phone immediately transfers to her husband's voicemail. "Hello, this is Rashid Siddique, please leave me a message."

She does not.

Irritated, she dials again. These oil platforms too far offshore for good phone reception always frustrate her. As her husband's voice again tells her to leave a message, she hears a knock at the door. He must be home already. "Did you forget your keys?" she shouts through the door. She smoothes an errant blonde hair, smells her wrists, clicks her tongue at her unperfumed skin.

She opens the door wide, only to find a man dressed in a suit, his expression humorless.

"Hello?" She closes the door back down to a few inches.

"Excuse me, ma'am," he checks the number on the outside of the door. "I'm looking for Mrs. Siddique."

"I *am* Mrs. Siddique."

He scans her face. "Yes. Mrs. Siddique, I'd like to ask you a few questions." He flashes her a badge. "Agent Roberts, FBI."

"Why are you here?" she closes the door a little more.

"Rashid Siddique is your husband?"

"You seem to know that already."

"Where is he right now?"

"Working."

When she fails to elaborate, he raises his hand, opening his fingers to reveal a ring, a yellow band of gold resting on his palm. She can just make out an inscription on the inside of the ring.

"I think you recognize this ring, Mrs. Siddique?"

The blood drains from her face. "Where did you get that?"

"At the site of the freeway bombing," he says.

"The freeway bombing?"

"I think you'd better let me come in."

Part One

The Book of Before

Chapter I

Dubai, United Arab Emirates.
Eight years before the bombing

"Zombie…zombie…zo..om..be..ee..ee," the lead singer belted out into the nightclub.

In the middle of the crowded dance floor a man locked eyes with a woman, her arms raised above her head, as they shouted out the refrain in unison; their voices drowned out by the band's percussion. Her blonde hair stood out to him, but their differing skin colors were unremarkable amidst the polyglot mix of revelers around them. "What are your plans?" he spoke directly into her ear. She smiled and shook her head.

As the band closed the last song of their set, Latvian cocktail waitresses hustled to settle all the open tabs. The lights came up and the still pulsating mass of bodies on the dance floor let out a collective groan of disappointment. The man repeated his question. "What are your plans?"

She paused, smiled flirtatiously and replied. "Same as yours." Perhaps the vodka fuelled her boldness.

He smiled, the answer easier than he expected. "What's your name?"

"Kathryn. Yours?"

"Rashid."

"*Robert?*" she asked. Could he possibly have a name as common as her father's?

"*Ra*shid" he said, emphasizing the first syllable.

"Rashid," she confirmed. "Arab?"

"No. Pakistani. Punjabi. We're from Lahore. You're…" he picked up her hand, provocatively brushed his fingers across her palm, "British?" For a split second he imagined how his father would react to a British girl, a descendent of the people who had caused the bloody partition of Pakistan from India.

She smiled, shook her head. "You'll figure it out," she laughed, allowed him to keep her hand in his as he led her out of the nightclub. Rashid nodded at the bouncers, burly Ethiopians who preserved the dividing line between the rigid local Muslim world outside and the permissive international bubble within.

Rashid stood behind her in the crowded elevator so he could press against her back even as he protectively stared down another man who tried to look at her. In the hotel lobby he held out his mobile phone. "Trade me," he said. With a curious expression, she offered her phone. He slid his phone into her back pocket. "Wait here. Only answer my phone if you see your number." And he walked to the hotel reception desk.

Kathryn walked past a security guard to sit on an ornately upholstered couch in the middle of the lobby. In her alcohol haze she watched the regular crowd spill out of the elevator and into the humid, still balmy air on the sidewalk. She did not recognize any as colleagues from her job at the American Chamber of Commerce.

Rashid negotiated with the South African hotel receptionist, exchanged cash for a room. Key in hand, Rashid walked past Kathryn, willing himself not to look at her, and went back up in the elevator.

After a few minutes, Rashid's phone vibrated in Kathryn's back pocket. She recognized the incoming number as her own and answered.

"Wait five minutes," Rashid said. "Then take the elevator up to the 7th floor and then take the stairs down to the 5th. I'm in room 505."

Kathryn followed his instructions, small acts of discretion in deference to the local sensibilities.

He could hear her footsteps. He stood behind the door and held it open for her. She came to him and he smiled. He loved Western women, how easily they submitted. How easily he had learned to act like a Western man in the nightclubs.

She smiled back as he leaned down to kiss her. Pressing into each other, just inside the door, she ran her fingers through his thick black hair, touched the exotically dark skin of his neck. He reached for the backs of her thighs to pick her up. Firm, strong, not like the soft flesh of educated Pakistani girls. She wrapped herself around his waist, allowing him to carry her to the bed. His ease and confidence surprised her, so unlike the deferential South Indian tea porters at her office. As he peeled his damp shirt up over his head, adrenaline surged through her system, her heart raced.

"Wait…this is not what I usually do," she said, her forehead wrinkling with anxiety. "I mean, not so fast."

"Don't worry." He sat back on his calves, bringing his hands to his lap. Maybe she was different from the British nurses who always drank too much in the clubs. "We don't have to." Maybe he would just talk with her. Maybe she would cry about her homesickness, the way Chechen prostitutes did. "I like you, but I won't force you." He closed his eyes, breathed deliberately, recalibrated, finding himself already seated as if for prayers.

She liked his sudden sincerity, how he dropped his dance floor swagger. She looked up at the ceiling and noticed the arrow pointing toward Mecca, the helpful hotel instruction directing guests to pray in the correct direction.

"*Mafi mushkala*," he said in Arabic, *no problem*.

She smiled. "Yeah, mafi mushkala." Slowly, she raised her legs, rewrapping them around his torso and pulled him toward her. "I'm not worried. I want to be here," she whispered into his ear.

He took his time taking off her clothes. She reached into his pocket and found a condom there, nodded her approval.

She reached out to turn on the light next to the bed. "I want to see you." What had her friend said about Arabic men? Something about how easily they could lead two lives if they had two wives? Was the same true for Pakistani men? She ran her fingers through the dark hair on his chest. "You have a wife back home?"

He shook his head, raised up his torso, enjoyed the movement of her breasts as he thrust. "Just my family, parents, brothers, sisters." She wasn't like the British or the Chechen women. He locked eyes with her again. She didn't look away, didn't pretend she wasn't doing this. He slowed his movements, wanted to please her. She pulled his hips against her, directed their pace with a determined intensity.

A whimper of pleasure escaped from her throat. She took a few deep breaths. "Pakistani," she said.

Somehow her voice softened all the hard sounds of the word. And he moved, driving quickly to climax. He collapsed with fatigue against her.

"American," he whispered in her ear. "You're American, yes?"

She smiled. "Yes."

———

The smoke curled around Rashid's face as he passed Kathryn the water pipe hose. She listened for the sound of the bubbles as she inhaled the sweet tobacco smoke. Rashid sipped sweet tea with fresh mint leaves from a small handleless tea cup.

"So tell me about your sisters, about their marriages," she spoke through her billowing exhale.

The waiter approached their table on the hotel patio, used small metal tongs to replace the coals on the *sheesha* and refilled their teacups.

"Not much to tell," he shrugged his shoulders. "Normal type arranged Pakistani marriages. They went to good families we've known for a long time."

"Did they want to go?"

"What do you mean?"

"I mean, didn't they want to choose their husbands for themselves? How can you make a marriage work with a total stranger?" She set the hose down on the table, the tobacco seemed to slow the world and the tea seemed to speed up her heart.

Rashid shrugged his shoulders. "We're raised to expect arranged marriages. It's not strange. People grow to love each other all the time."

"So, are your sisters in love with their husbands?" Kathryn brought the hose again to her lips, took a long aggressive draw.

"I think one is. The other one, maybe she isn't as happy with her husband. He likes to talk too much for her." Rashid reached out, ran his fingers across the coiled leather hose.

"So your parents made one good choice, one not so good choice. Doesn't seem like good odds to me. I wouldn't want to risk my parents' choice," Kathryn shuddered thinking about the kind of blonde haired, well-educated but boring man they would likely choose for their only daughter.

"Risk?" Rashid looked into the hotel lobby, watched local men dressed in crisp white *dish dashas* walk gracefully past the gilt and tile water fountain. "What is the divorce rate in America?"

Kathryn raised her teacup, let the decorative gold design rest against her lips. She sat silently for a minute thinking over the obvious statistic they both knew, half of all American marriages ended in divorce.

Rashid continued. "Who knows more about married life, you or your parents? Wouldn't your parents only want the best for you? A husband from a good family, a good earner, a good family to help you raise your children?"

She pulled up the corners of her mouth in a coy smile. "How do you do that?"

"Do what?"

"Show me the world I think I knew, but upside down. Making me understand that maybe what I had thought was right and wrong isn't so black and white."

Again he shrugged his shoulders. "Everybody has their own culture." He smiled the smile she loved, revealing white teeth, illuminating his whole face. "All the British people I knew in London always thought they were better than other cultures, especially Pakistani. But you're different."

"We're all different. But we all live beneath the same heaven. My father always taught me that."

"Wise man." Rashid grinned, "Maybe you should let him arrange your marriage."

Kathryn punched his arm teasingly. "And how about you? Is there an arranged marriage in your future?" She looked away to the swimming pool beyond the patio, trying to mask the seriousness of her question.

"No. For sure, no."

"Why?" Kathryn looked back at Rashid, relieved.

"Because I'm different."

"Yeah. Very different."

———

Kathryn heard the day's first *namaz*, the call to prayer. Saturday morning, before sunrise, she dimly registered in her sleep. After a year in the Gulf, the five daily calls to prayer broadcast from hundreds of mosques throughout the city had punctuated her days like the hourly calls of the shrill cuckoo clock her father purchased on his first diplomatic trip to Switzerland. The calls marked time, regularly reminding the faithful to turn their thoughts toward God. She felt Rashid disentangle himself from their now familiar embrace to rise from the bed. Whenever he returned from working offshore he would come to her apartment. Unlike any other woman he had known she filled the time between lovemaking with spirited questions, a generous understanding.

She heard him walk down the hall, assumed he would return in a few minutes from the bathroom. A half hour later she heard him again in the room. She opened one eye to see him remove his shirt and pants, tossing them on a chair.

"Where've you been?" she asked as he slid back into bed.

"To the mosque."

"The mosque?" she said surprised. "You never go to the mosque."

"My *chachaji*, my father's younger brother, is ill. My father said we should all pray for him at the mosque."

"But even before sunrise?"

"I'm happy to do it. I love my father the most. How can I ever refuse him anything he asks?"

"I thought you didn't believe in all of the organized prayer."

"I don't, but sometimes it's nice to be at the mosque. We all bow down shoulder to shoulder." He caressed her from neck to elbow. "For a moment we're allowed to stop everything else and do this thing we all know, this thing that makes us brothers. When I was studying in London, I used to go to the mosque whenever I felt homesick. I just liked to see all the men who reminded me of my father, to hear them speak Urdu when they rolled up their prayer rugs to leave the mosque."

"Hmm." She closed her eyes, wrapping her leg around his, "sounds kind of nice."

They drifted back to sleep.

Rashid set dates and a pitcher of water on the table. The smell of lamb *biryani* and vegetable curry permeated Kathryn's apartment. The late afternoon sun streamed through the windows. In scarcely a half hour, the sun would sink below the horizon and those observing *Ramadan* would break their first day of fasting.

He waited for her to come from the office, anxious that she might be irritable with hunger and thirst. He would never have dreamed to suggest that she fast with him. But she had simply told him she would join him in observing the Muslim holy month of Ramadan. At least this first year.

From the window he saw her step out of a taxi, her long skirt flowing elegantly against her leg in the breeze. Almost before she could close the car door, the taxi raced back into the flow of traffic.

Within ten minutes the streets would be empty, everyone with a family would be home to eat together. The taxi drivers would gather like bachelors at the mosque, finding community in other men who had left their wives and children in Pakistan in hopes of a better salary in the Gulf.

She opened the door, inhaled deeply, smiled. He embraced her, kissing her on the lips.

"I thought there's no sexual contact while you're fasting," she teased.

"I'm not that strict," he said, leading her by the hand to the table. As they sat down every mosque in the city broadcast the call to prayer at the moment the last molten bit of sun dipped below the horizon. Without ceremony he poured her a glass of water and passed her the small plate of dates.

"Don't you say something?" She hesitated to accept the plate. "A prayer or a blessing or something before you break the fast? I want to experience a traditional Ramadan."

He shook his head and bit into a date. "It's enough that all day long you feel hunger and thirst so you feel compassion for the poor." He watched her take a small sip and then a long draw of water. "But in my family, a traditional Ramadan evening would never be only two people. In Pakistan you always have your family with you—your aunties and uncles and cousins. We all stay up late eating and laughing and enjoying."

"So when will you take me to Pakistan to meet them all?"

"You want to go?" he said.

"Of course I want to go," she hungrily piled biryani on her plate, loved that he had spent the day cooking for her. "You know I'm always ready to travel anywhere. And it's even better to travel with someone who knows the country."

"Well I can't just go and bring my girlfriend. It's a traditional country."

"But your parents sent you to London for university. Do they really think you didn't have girlfriends there?"

"It's not something we talk about. They've been trying to arrange my marriage since I got this job three years ago. They know lots of families who want their girl to marry a good earner like me."

She paused mid-bite. "So, they're still trying to arrange your marriage?"

"They have girls for me to meet every time I go home. But I'm always sure those girls won't want to marry me."

"How? You're so handsome, and you have a good job. Why wouldn't they want to marry you?"

He looked up with a mischievous smile. "You always have a chance to talk to her, in private, for a little time after the families make the introduction. I just tell the girl I'll divorce any woman who gets fat."

"And?"

"And they always tell their parents that I'm not the right guy. We're Punjabis, we eat ghee, butter, in everything. Show me a Punjabi woman over 35 who's not fat." He tore a piece of bread and dipped it in the curry. "No girl wants to take that risk."

"I would."

He ate quietly, feeling the relief of warm food filling his stomach.

"So you really want to go to Pakistan?"

"Yeah, I really want to go to Pakistan."

"All right." Picking up his glass, he spoke into the water. "Then I'll tell them we will marry."

Stunned, she set her hands on the table. "Is that what you will tell them, just so they won't freak out, or do you really want to get married?"

"You tell me," he said, the mischievous smile returning, and popped a date in her mouth.

Chapter 2

Lahore, Pakistan.
Seven years before the bombing

Kathryn and Rashid bumped down the lane in a rickshaw. Since leaving the main road connecting Rashid's village with the bustling city of Lahore in northeastern Pakistan, she felt as if she were traveling back in time. The gritty, inelegant commercial buildings of the main road had given way to houses, rural compounds in varying degrees of disrepair. She leaned out the side of the rickshaw to get a better view of green fields of wheat and mustard, neat rows of dried cowpies stacked beside mounds of hay.

Her brilliant blue headscarf fluttered in the gentle breeze. So much more beautiful, Rashid mused, than the drab Arabic style headscarves she had bought trying to fit in to the culture she expected. Rashid surreptitiously slid a hand under the billowing cloth of the salwar kameeze. He had meticulously ordered these clothes from the Pakistani tailor in Dubai. In her apartment he had pulled the drawstring waist so the baggy pants dropped effortlessly to her ankles. He had made love to her standing up, a foreign woman in familiar Pakistani dress. But today she slapped his hand in mock scandal, hoping the rickshaw driver wouldn't see.

Rashid signaled the rickshaw driver to stop at a wrought iron gate. A man, whom Kathryn immediately recognized as Rashid's brother, opened the gate and ushered the couple into a large courtyard. A second rickshaw driver brought their luggage as people spilled out of the surrounding rooms.

Rashid hugged his brother, introducing him to Kathryn as Riaz. She barely greeted him before others called out Rashid's name, laughing and touching his head and his shoulders. Several women greeted Kathryn with shoulder to shoulder embraces, pats to her head, strokes to her hands. Everyone spoke Urdu with a smattering of English words. She felt the reception incomprehensible, simultaneously restrained and effusive.

Two women led Rashid and Kathryn through a set of open doors into a room with several charpoys, wooden bed frames with lattice strung seats big enough for both lounging and sleeping. An older man with a neatly trimmed grey beard and handsome shock of black hair sat beaming, a tiny girl nestled up against his side. He held out his arms to embrace Rashid, who stooped down and momentarily touched his father's feet in a display of deference. The older man set his hand atop his son's head then quickly pulled him up by the shoulders and affectionately thumped his back.

Rashid motioned for Kathryn to approach the older man. For an apprehensive moment, she realized Rashid hadn't prepared her to greet her future father-in-law. The whole family ceased their bustling, waited. The distance between the worldly American lover and the landed Pakistani patriarch took on an exaggerated dimension. Her breath caught in her throat. She searched Rashid's expression for any shred of guidance. As if in a vacuum, she raised her arms as if to hug Rashid's father. He did not reciprocate, blocked her gesture by awkwardly patting her wrists. She had blundered. They had all seen it. Then the patriarch's eyes warmed into a laughing smile. "Welcome, *beta*, welcome, child," he boomed, at which point the world resumed its spinning, the family returned to its musical chatter and Kathryn safely entered their familiar foreign world.

The family gathered in the courtyard for the evening meal,

11

dragging charpoys and stools into a circle. The unmarried women unceasingly offered *rotis*, round wheat flatbreads, fresh from the stovetop griddle in the kitchen and ladlefuls of curried gravies. Only after the elders had repeatedly refused more food did the young women sit to eat their own spicy *pallak gosh,* spinach and goat curry, never spilling a drop on their multi-colored clothes.

Rashid's female relatives surrounded Kathryn, talking and laughing with her, their headscarves brushing her shoulders when they readjusted them. The warmth of their bodies mingled with hers as they refilled her plate with creamy mustard greens and spicy lentil gravy.

Rashid sat between his parents, engaged in an animated conversation. Rashid's mother, a handsome woman with strong features and a substantial build, exuded an aura of control. She deferred neither to her husband in conversation, nor to the family members who came to ask her questions or refill her water glass.

Rashid looked up at Kathryn, winked at her conspiratorially. His parents also looked at her, obviously discussing something about her in Punjabi. Rashid's father raised his own roti toward her, smiling and nodding, encouraging her to eat more.

Rashid's younger sister leaned over and said to Kathryn, "Mummy and Daddy like you. They can see you have a good nature. And you know how to eat our food. When will you marry?" The girl wobbled her head, half nod, half shake, a gesture Kathryn had come to appreciate for its vague possibilities of mostly *yes* with the look of *no.*

Kathryn wobbled her head back and started to speak when someone somewhere in the house turned on a stereo and energetic *bangra* music filled the air. A couple of Rashid's *cousin brothers*—as he called them—shouted with delight, springing to their feet and shaking their shoulders to the beat. The whole family turned to watch. Light on their feet, they flew their hands in the air above their heads, lifted their knees high as they jumped with each step, their faces beginning to glow with the effort. Kathryn recognized the rhythm, Punjabi bangra remixes had been wildly popular in the nightclubs of Dubai. Almost involuntarily, she started to shake her shoulders. The women around her reached for her hands, pulled her to standing, urging her to dance. Kathryn looked to Rashid to gauge his reaction. Already on his feet, arms up, he strutted like a peacock, dancing, occupying a huge space in the courtyard with his relatives. Kathryn joined the group of women, repeating the moves he had taught her, *right hand up like you're screwing in a light bulb, left hand down like you're patting a child on the head.* Her shoulders bounced, her feet pounded the ground, filled with the sheer physical joy of dancing she and Rashid shared.

And everyone—young and old—was on their feet, moving, laughing. Kathryn watched two young girls cross their wrists and grasp each others' hands, spinning around an unseen point, faster and faster, the centrifugal force spinning their clothes away from them. They disengaged and one reached for Kathryn. She mimicked the spin, her feet close to her partner's, their shoulders leaning out away from each other. She saw only the delight on the other woman's face as the rest of the family and the courtyard disappeared into a blur of sound and color.

Just when she thought she might lose her balance, her partner stopped, released one hand and steadied her with the other. Kathryn hugged her and sat on the nearest charpoy to regain her balance, the stars swirling above her.

Kathryn brought her future father-in-law a glass of warm milk. After almost a week in his home she had become part of his nightly ritual. He motioned for her to sit across from him while he drank. He spoke to her in Punjabi. Sabeen, Rashid's eldest sister-in-law, translated.

"My mother and father chose my wife, and she has been a good woman for me," he said. "She is strong and smart, and she gave me three sons."

Kathryn nodded at the translation.

"My son is choosing you, that's very different for our family, for our clan. But I can see you are also strong and smart. You will have to compromise sometimes because our culture is so different, but even my wife and me, until now we compromise with each other."

When he had finished his milk, Kathryn reached out to take his empty glass. "You have all made me feel so welcome," she said. "Any compromise seems like a bargain to be part of your family."

Rashid's sister-in-law smiled and patted Kathryn's knee affectionately.

He continued, "My wife was not agreeing with my decision to split the family businesses between Rashid's two elder brothers. But they've done well here in Pakistan, they're happy here. The eldest runs our farms here in the village, and my middle son takes care of the trading companies in Lahore. Rashid though, always I saw he was different. He had a desire for adventure, the confidence to go abroad."

Kathryn smiled as she looked down, swirling the cup in her hands. New glass bangles jingled softly against the intricate henna designs on her skin.

"Today at your engagement ceremony, my relations asked me where you'll live after you are married. Of course, it's your choice, Dubai, London, America," he glanced heavenward with his palms upturned, "only God can be knowing for sure. But you will always be welcome here in Pakistan. We are Punjabis, we always have space for our families. And *insha'allah*, God-willing, you will bring sons here to know their father's country."

"Insha'allah," she repeated. "Thank you, Daddyji." They both smiled at the title, simultaneously intimate and respectful.

"*Sonja, beta*, sleep child," he said to her directly.

He stood up and walked to his room.

"Good night *didi*, sister," Sabeen said before heading in the opposite direction. Kathryn brought the cup to the kitchen, the *bhai* would come and wash everything in the morning.

Kathryn walked silently on bare feet out the door to the courtyard. The hinges squeaked. She looked for her shoes among the pile just outside the door. Moonlight glinted off the sequins sewn into ladies *juttis*. She stepped over the men's slippers with their upturned toes to slide one foot and then the other into the pair she thought Mummyji had bought for her. But rather than stiff new leather, these were soft, well worn. She allowed herself the comfort of walking in

14

someone else's shoes. She went to the single charpoy forgotten in the center of the courtyard, spooking one of the nameless family cats away as she rested on the latticed strings.

She looked up at the moon and tried to imagine her wedding here. She had heard of local Muslim weddings in Dubai. The husband would sign a ceremonial contract with the wife's father before the mullah, and the elaborate, but separate parties for the men and the women would follow. She knew nothing about Pakistani wedding customs, but she could not imagine her wedding would be nearly as somber, given the exuberant hospitality she had seen this week with Rashid's family. She tried to imagine her parents here. Would her mother be able to eat the spicy food and heavy sweets? Would her father be dismayed at the seemingly frivolous practicality of Rashid's family, the conversations devoid of intellectual debate or literary references?

She heard the door hinge squeak.

Sabeen appeared. "You are here alone, beta?" She slid onto the charpoy next to Kathryn, a gesture that would have seemed intrusive in Kathryn's family.

"I was just looking at the moon."

"Sometimes when it's too much hot for sleeping, Daddyji and my husband pull all the beds onto the roof so that we can feel any tiny breeze under the stars. On the worst nights Daddyji even will go down the lane and hire the *juice wallah* to bring us fresh lemonade."

"Daddy seems like a very sweet man."

"Oh, you are very lucky to marry into this family, not all men are like Daddyji."

"What do you mean?"

"He's very careful about the females in his family. He made sure all his daughters are educated, and he taught Mummyji everything about his business. When he goes traveling to the city she can go out to the farm and manage the workers and the business arrangements. Even me, when he arranged with my parents for my marriage with Rashid's eldest brother, I had one year of university left before I would complete my degree. Daddyji suggested we postpone the wedding for one year so I could finish, and he even paid my university fees for that year."

Kathryn turned to look at Sabeen, whom she had mistaken for a simple village girl. "What did you study?"

"Commerce and business administration. I wanted my parents to find me a boy in London to marry, so I could go abroad and have a career. But every boy we found, when we asked our relations abroad to call on him, we found out each and every boy was drinking and going to nightclubs."

"Like Rashid," Kathryn said.

"Mummy and Daddy worried about him a lot while he was in London. They thought he might go and run off with a *goree*, a white girl."

"You mean like me?"

"But you're different," Sabeen said without any embarrassment. "You're here with us. You came to our village, ate our food with us."

"And I can dance the bangra!" Kathryn giggled as she lifted her hands into the air and spun her wrists bangra style. Sabeen joined her, dancing to an imaginary beat.

The door hinges creaked again. "Hey, *bhabi,* sister-in-law," Rashid called out, "what are you doing with my wife?"

Sabeen, who answered to an entire constellation of words describing her relationships to her family members more often than she answered to her own name, sat up and laughed. "You brought her here, so now you have to share her with us. And she isn't your wife yet!"

She helped Kathryn to her feet and they both slipped their shoes back into the pile beside the door. Rashid took Kathryn's wrist as she walked past him in the doorway. The door hinges squeaked once more as Sabeen discreetly left. Rashid walked Kathryn to the room she had been sharing with one of his cousin sisters. The younger girl's clothes, even her handbag, were gone.

"What happened?" Kathryn asked.

"She moved to another room."

"Why?"

"I prayed for her father, my chachaji, when we were in Dubai. He's well now, so I asked her for a favor in return," Rashid smiled mischievously, closing the door behind them.

16

They made love quietly. The gentle breeze blowing through the open window, the sounds of crickets and distant dogs, the proximity of Rashid's family somehow altered their pleasure.

"What will your family say in the morning?" she said.

"Nothing."

"Really? You'll walk out of this room and Mummyji'll be drinking *chai*, and your nephews will be running around with biscuits, and she'll say nothing?"

"They know you're a Westerner. They know your culture is different and you don't follow our rules. Frankly, until now you've followed more of our rules than they expected."

"They don't seem very strict about Islamic rules. I mean, your uncles were drinking whiskey."

He turned his head to look at her. "In our culture, it's more important to follow the rules of our clan than the rules of Islam."

"What do you mean?"

"I mean we have to be loyal to each other first. Our allegiance to Islam comes from that. We see other Muslims like part of our greater clan."

"So how do you show your loyalty?"

He turned to look out the window. The moonlight reflected in his eyes. "When I was ten," he said, "Indian army tanks invaded the Golden Temple, the most holy place for Sikhs. Two years later, Prime Minister Indira Ghandi's Sikh body guards assassinated her."

"That's how you demonstrate loyalty?"

"No, that was a political action. But after that the Hindus in Delhi rioted. We watched it on the television news. Hindus killed Sikhs by the thousands, they threw gasoline on their turbans and burned them alive. We were seeing pictures of the burned bodies, the Hindu police did nothing," he practically spat out the word Hindu.

She shivered despite the warm air and pulled the sheet up over her shoulders.

"I remember my mother saying to my brothers and me that if a mob ever came to attack our home, the women in the house would take the gas cylinder for our cooking range and blow it up.

They would kill themselves, but also take out some of our attackers. Then my mother told me and my brothers, 'You boys will run away, survive however you can, and grow up to take revenge on those families that tried to kill us'."

"Your mother said that?" Kathryn, horrified, couldn't imagine her own mother delivering such deadly instructions to her as a young girl in their suburban home.

"My parents lived through Partition. In 1947, when the British pulled out and Pakistan was created, their families were living on what became the Indian side. Until now my father won't talk about the killings he saw when they crossed over to Pakistan."

"Was his own life in danger?"

"Of course," Rashid said, almost angrily. "Exactly when my grand-parents crossed the border, they were taken in and protected by two brothers, *Pashtuns* who worked as drivers for a rich family. They hid my father, his brother, and their parents in a car in a garage for three days, until they could move safely to relatives in Lahore."

"The Pashtuns were Muslims?"

"Yes."

"So they were showing loyalty to their greater clan."

"You understand."

She let out a long sigh. The heavy story crowded out the previous week's lightness, as if she had been playing jaxx at a funeral, a childish girl ignorant of the suffering around her.

"Hold me?" she asked quietly.

He put out his arm and she rested her head on his chest. He wrapped his arm around her shoulders and squeezed her to him.

"We won't live in Pakistan." He tried to reassure her. "This isn't your history, not your issue. Just respect my parents, that's the only loyalty they'll expect from you."

———————

Rashid's middle brother, Majid, opened the car door for Kathryn, and held out his forearm for support. She climbed into the seat, gathering up her flowing *kameeze* and *chunni*.

"Thank you," Kathryn said.

Majid's wife, Aisha, giggled. "Americans, always you're saying thank you. Are people in your country so selfish you must show gratitude for every tiny thing?"

Before Kathryn could answer, Rashid pushed in beside her. "Make space," he said as the driver started the engine. She scooted closer to Aisha as Sabeen and her husband Riaz piled into the front seat.

They lurched into the lane, the brothers continuing a spirited conversation. Unlike their sweaty bumpy rickshaw ride in, Kathryn now viewed the farms and farmhouses speeding by from air conditioned comfort.

"What are you talking about?" Kathryn asked Rashid.

He laughed, still gesturing to his brother Riaz. "I told him he has *crores* of rupees, he's rich, but still lives like a country boy. He loves his cows more than his cars."

"Shoukart, what is a car for?" Riaz asked the driver, who only shrugged. "A car is only a vehicle for bringing you from one destination to another. A cow? Now a cow makes you milk, makes you money, keeps you company, maybe even takes you from one place to another." He looked out the window. "Of course I care more about my cows than my cars." He turned the air conditioning down from full blast. "I'm not like our brother Majid," he said with finality.

"Why isn't Majid with us?" Kathryn asked.

"He took his new car because he has to stop by his office for some business," Aisha explained. "He'll meet us at the gold shop."

As they reached the outskirts of Lahore, the smells of charcoal and grilled meat, spices, rotting fruit, car exhaust, and incense all seeped into the car.

Kathryn could barely process the dizzying array of street vendors, small shops, apartment buildings they passed.

"Let's stop for *samosas*, or *pani poori*," Rashid told the driver.

Riaz shook his finger. "No snacks until after we arrive to the gold shop. I know you," he turned to look at his brother, "I have to impose the discipline or we'll never get everything done." He turned back to the driver, "Shoukart, to the gold shop directly."

"*Han ji,*" Shoukart affirmed.

They turned down a small lane and then another and another, seemingly lost. Then without warning, Shoukart stopped the car and everyone piled out.

Through a dingy door and up a set of old wooden stairs they arrived at the shop. Brightly lit glass cases sat atop marble tiled floors. Mirrors lined the walls and bright yellow gold jewelry sparkled from every surface. A man in a beautifully embroidered silk *kurta* greeted Riaz warmly. Majid stood up from where he had been drinking tea with the shop owner.

Riaz introduced Rashid to the shop owner, who turned to look at Kathryn. "And you beta, you are the lucky bride marrying into this family?"

Kathryn smiled. Rashid glanced proudly at Riaz.

Sabeen and Aisha moved toward the front of the store to inspect the ornate gold necklaces. Rashid thumped Majid on the shoulder. "You got here so quickly?"

"You know, younger brother," Majid said, "I like to drive my car, I don't waste any time."

Sabeen led Kathryn to a glass case, "Which styles do you like?"

Kathryn, overwhelmed by the sheer volume of gold, tried to discern the differences between them. "I guess the shorter ones." She pointed to a few studded with emerald and ruby colored stones.

"Don't go for stones," Aisha said quietly, "they sell the gold by the gram and the stones are never worth as much as the gold, so the value is not good."

"Can I ask to try them on?" Kathryn asked Sabeen.

"Of course madam," the shop owner said in a deeply resonant voice. "You should see what you will look like as a Pakistani bride." He motioned to a young man behind him who brought a tray with six small cups of tea, and then to a slightly round middle-aged man who joined them from behind the counter. He aimed a remote control at a wall mounted television, generating sound and color as if to make them feel at home.

"Which ones madam?"

Kathryn, teacup in hand, tentatively pointed to three different necklaces. Sabeen took each one in turn from the salesman and placed them around Kathryn's neck.

"I think I like this one best," Kathryn said, fingering the clusters of small gold beads clustered amidst the intricately filigreed designs. "How much is it?" she asked Aisha.

Aisha, the practiced wife of a businessman, motioned for the salesman to weigh the gold piece. "Today's gold price is a little lower than usual, and this shop's making charge is always fair." The salesman tapped his calculator and presented a price.

Kathryn gasped. "It's almost five thousand dollars!" she said to Aisha. She took Sabeen by the arm to whisper into her ear. "I don't need such expensive jewelry just for the wedding. Is there a gold set in the family that I could just borrow for the day?"

Sabeen stepped back and looked at Kathryn as if she had asked to wear fur in the middle of a sweltering Lahore summer. "Someone else's gold? But you must have your own gold. It isn't just for your wedding day. It's your insurance. If your husband dies or you need money for an emergency you can sell your gold. No, you can't borrow it, and you should choose as heavy a piece as Rashid is willing to buy."

Kathryn looked up toward Rashid, saw his face light up. "Samosas!" Shoukart, the driver, handed him a little bag fashioned from last week's newspaper, the contents already making big greasy spots over the photos of local politicians. He turned to Kathryn. "We have snacks. Now you can shop as long as you like."

The television blared a Pakistani film song—a young man crooning wistfully, intercut with shots of a girl seen through a soft filter.

The store attendant appeared with small plates and paper napkins and the three brothers gathered around the snacks, greedily dipping the deep fried potato dumplings into sweet tamarind sauce. Rashid raised his hand, calling over to Shoukart to join them. "*Aja virji*, come brother, you were clever to buy so many." The Pashtun driver who had stood quietly deferential, easily joined and engaged in their banter.

Rashid watched the television distractedly. The song had ended and a newscaster described the American military presence in Afghanistan, with footage of Bagram Air Base. American soldiers had been accused of forcibly searching Afghan homes, aggressively touching women, even shooting a man when he brandished a dagger in his own home. Shoukart shook his head. "How do they think they can occupy Afghanistan like that?" he spoke in Urdu. "The Americans don't understand us Pathans, they will never escape our *badan*, our justice." Rashid's brothers nodded in sympathy. "Every one of us knows the *Pashtunwali*, we are bound like brothers to take revenge."

At the jewelry counter Aisha turned her back to the salesmen, spoke in low tones to Kathryn. "You should tell me what you like, but don't let the shop owner hear. We won't buy today, you can tell him you're not fond of his designs. Then I'll ask Majid to bargain with him later, on a day when the gold price is more down."

Kathryn discreetly reached toward the necklace still on the gram scale and nodded to Aisha.

"And the matching bangles and earrings, they are fine for you?"

Kathryn wobbled her head affirmatively. "Sir," Kathryn asked the salesman, "can you show me plain gold bands for my husband? The jewelry set is your tradition," she smiled to her future sisters-in-law. "A ring is my tradition."

She picked up a simple, wide band. "Can you engrave the inside?"

"Of course," the salesman said. "Whatever you like." He offered her a piece of paper and a pen.

She wrote, *Beneath the Same Heaven*.

Chapter 3

Dubai, United Arab Emirates.
Six years before the bombing

Kathryn raised a glass of dark beer to toast Sameh, a colleague at the Chamber who translated all of her articles into Arabic. "To your mother's visa."

"To my mother's visa," he raised his glass to hers, thick drops of condensation falling in the hot evening air of the outdoor beer garden. "You can't imagine how many hours, how many days I spent going from one ministry to another here. The Emirati officials wanted so many papers, everything from Iraq, birth certificates, death certificates, marriage certificates, property certificates. After two wars, those papers don't even exist any more in my country, or if they do, no one can find them. But finally, I convinced them to let her come. So soon you'll meet her."

"*Al-hamda'allah,*" Kathryn said, smiling at the irony of thanking Allah, in a Muslim country, while drinking a beer with an Iraqi man, now working in the UAE as a naturalized citizen of a distant Nordic country. "When will she arrive?"

"My younger brother is traveling from Sweden to Baghdad to help her and my youngest sister pack their things. Then I have to arrange for a bigger flat here so they'll be comfortable. I think maybe three or four months until they are here."

"But at least she knows it will happen."

"Yes, she tells me everything's fine and not to worry. But I hear news from their neighbors; a bomb landed down the street, or someone's uncle was kidnapped, or their sister-in-law raped."

Kathryn wrapped her hands around her glass, uncomfortably. "I can't help but feel some responsibility for what's happening in your country."

He looked in her eyes, leaned back in his chair and laughed with surprising force. "Responsible? How are you responsible?"

"Well, we elect our leaders and they have invaded your country—again—causing this chaos."

"Do you really think you have any influence on any of that? You Americans, sometimes you really do believe you are powerful. My friend, governments are governments, people are people. You're not responsible. I worked as a government translator during Saddam's time. But I certainly don't feel any responsibility for what Saddam Hussein did when he was in power."

She raised an eyebrow, nodded her head in concession, a shade of embarrassment rising in her cheeks. "Perhaps it's all just an illusion that we have any influence on our leaders, but we are raised in America to believe we do. So, how about this? I'm terribly sad for what my country has done in your country."

"Me too," Sameh sighed, "me too."

A waitress arrived, asked, "Anozher beer?" with an Eastern European accent.

"Not yet, but soon," Sameh said with renewed enthusiasm. "But please—French fries." He drank again. "Now, let's talk of something happier, you just returned from Pakistan, now you're married."

"Oh, the wedding," Kathryn smiled broadly. "I don't think I've ever had so much fun in my life. When Rashid comes back onshore, you should come over and look at the wedding album. The whole event was just so big, so over the top," she gestured widely with her hands, forty red and white bangles that marked her as a new bride jingling along her forearms.

"And your parents came?"

"Yes, I was so proud of them. Especially my mother, she never once complained about the heat or the filth, she just danced and ate and laughed with Rashid's family like she had known them all her life. My father tried a couple of times to talk foreign relations with Rashid's brothers, but they were always interrupted by some fun before it got serious. And the *mehendi*," she rubbed the faded henna designs on the backs of her hands, "the henna party was so fun. The mehendi artist worked for almost eight hours straight covering all the women's hands, even my mom. He didn't realize until almost midnight that I was the bride. By the time he finished almost everyone was asleep, there were people on blankets and little sleeping mats everywhere."

The fries arrived, Sameh chuckled.

"And the extended family…Rashid was the last son to be married in his family, so relatives came from all over, even some cousins from London, and an uncle who had been estranged from Rashid's father over some business issue. And the most amazing to me, a Pashtun man came all the way from the frontier territories near Afghanistan. He was their driver's father, he'd helped Rashid's father to safety when they crossed from India during Partition."

"Why was that amazing to you?"

"I guess because he hardly knew Rashid, and he certainly didn't know me."

Sameh grinned, "But a wedding in this part of the world isn't really about you." He took a long swig of his beer, "It's about the extended family, the clan, affirming alliances. That Pashtun man wasn't coming for you or Rashid, he came out of loyalty to your father-in-law and his clan. And you know the Pashtuns, they are the most loyal people in the world."

She reached for a few fries. "I guess that makes sense, it's just such a different way of thinking than how I grew up."

"Well, you should get used to it. You've married into that world now."

"Yes, but I have the benefit of being the outsider. I can sort of pick and choose about how much their norms apply to me. And Rashid's company will transfer him to the U.S., so by next year we're planning to leave this part of the world."

"Maybe," he fiddled with his coaster, a cardboard disc with a beer logo and a promise of a better time, "but lots of things in life are our *naseeb*, they are written, already chosen for us." He drew his finger across his forehead.

Chapter 4

Los Angeles, California.
Five years before the bombing

"Dinner's ready, Kathy," her mother called out. "Do you want us to start, or should we wait for Rashid?"

"Let's wait," Kathryn said. "He said he'd just pick up coffee and cereal, I don't know what's taking him so long." She carried a couple of moving boxes from the living room of their newly rented apartment to their bedroom, and sat down on the bed, letting out a long sigh.

The front door opened with a bang.

"Amazing!" Rashid said. "All of this stuff from Walmart for less than a hundred dollars."

"You were gone a long time, we've moved all the boxes into the other rooms so you and Kathryn can unpack them. Everything all right?" Kathryn's mother asked.

"Great. Everything is better than all right." Rashid set his shopping bags down on the counter. "The place is huge. They have everything. I was looking at watches, and camping equipment. I spent an hour just to find the coffee. I have more bags in the car."

"Robert," Kathryn's mother called to her husband, "can you help Rashid with the bags?"

"Coming," Robert called back from the hallway as the front door slammed again. "Kathryn," he stopped at the bedroom door, "are you all right?"

"I guess," she looked up from the bed. "I just feel like Rashid is different here."

Kathryn's father took a step into the room. "How so?"

"I mean, he's clean-shaven, he's wearing a baseball cap and jeans. You heard him going on about Walmart. He seems so...so American," she picked up a framed wedding photo from one of the open boxes. "Hard to believe we are the same people." From behind the frame Rashid smiled in his starched silk kurta pajama, she looked irrepressibly happy in a traditional red wedding dress and chunni, light glinting off the gold thread and beadwork along the border.

"Life changes," her father said simply.

"It's so strange, I feel almost homesick, but I am back in my own country."

He smiled, "Not strange, that's just reverse culture shock."

"Really?"

"Of course. I felt it when I came back from diplomatic postings."

"Does it pass?" she asked.

The front door banged again.

Her father smiled ruefully, "Everything passes. But for now let Rashid try out being American. He's just doing what you did in Pakistan."

Kathryn looked at the photo again. She just wanted to cry, to lay down in the bed, and wake up back in Dubai, back in the international life they had made for themselves.

"Kathy, Robert, come for dinner," Margaret called out.

"Come, let's eat," he said and walked out.

At the dinner table Kathryn's father raised his wine glass, looked from his daughter to his son-in-law, "Welcome home, welcome to our country. I hope you'll both find comfort, opportunity, and prosperity here."

"And happiness," her mother added.

"I hope so too," said Rashid.

"Insha'allah," Kathryn said out of habit as she raised her glass.

"Kathryn," Rashid said, amused, "we're not in an Islamic country anymore. You Americans don't wait for Allah, *you* make things happen. Is Walmart successful because of Allah? No, somebody hustled, somebody worked hard, and the system is set up for business like this. I can only imagine what my father's business would have looked like if he had started it here with this kind of big capitalism."

Kathryn's stomach turned as she brought her glass to her lips, hoping to conceal the tears welling up in her eyes. This was not the Rashid she had fallen in love with.

"Rashid, have you checked in with your company yet?" Margaret changed the subject. "When will you start?"

"I called my manager yesterday, and he'd like me to start as soon as possible, but I can't until I complete the test for my hazardous materials license and my FBI clearance comes."

"FBI clearance?" Kathryn's father asked, "What for?"

"Some of our tools use radioactive materials to take measurements in the well," he explained.

Kathryn shoved her chair back and rushed to the bathroom. Rashid tried not to look irritated, Kathryn had been so moody since they had moved to America.

Kathryn heard only muffled voices as she knelt over the toilet, retching. As the nausea passed, she sat on the chilly tiled floor and tried to cry, to express some nameless shapeless grief, but the tears would not come.

That night, after her parents had gone to their hotel, Kathryn and Rashid lay in bed, willing their bodies to synchronize with the local time zone. He wrapped his arm around her. Wordlessly, she turned her back to him so they fit together like two spoons.

He caressed her belly, her hips, the curve of her backside. He touched her breasts, discovering an unexpected fullness in one and then the other. She startled him with a little cry of pain as he squeezed her nipple. He smiled to himself, turned her over so he could place his head on her belly.

"What are you doing?" she asked.

He lifted his head to look at her, laughed a little and said, "You're pregnant, yes?"

———

The next day a home pregnancy test kit, blinking a little blue plus sign, confirmed his intuition. He laughed and embraced her, picked her up and spun around. "Let's call my family in Pakistan, my father will be too happy!"

"No, not yet. You're not supposed to tell people so early. You have to make sure the pregnancy continues without a miscarriage."

"Are you sure? How long?"

"I don't know," she placed a hand tentatively on her belly, trying to feel what might be happening inside. "I'll ask my mother."

"You just said we shouldn't tell anyone."

"Oh, you're right," she sat down wearily. "I guess I'll have to get a book about pregnancy." She looked up at him. "Do you want to have a baby?"

He responded to the fear in her expression by wrapping his arms around her shoulders, leaning down to kiss her head. "Of course I want a baby, especially with you."

"But we've been arguing about everything since we came to America."

"*Habibti*," the Arabic term of endearment always made her smile, "we are arguing about politics, economics. This, this is family."

She smiled, fleetingly. "You know, everything will change once the baby comes."

"Everything always changes. That's life. Imagine, I was in Pakistan, then in London, then in Dubai. Now I am here in America, with my American wife. Until now I have wanted my life to change. This change is a blessing."

She looked up at the playful sparkle in his eye. She tilted her head, ready to kiss him.

He leaned down, close enough that she could feel his breath on her lips and said, "Now can I call Pakistan and tell them?"

"No!" she slapped him with mock force. He allowed her to wrestle him to the floor, laughing and shrieking, moving between the furniture and the boxes, until, panting, she stopped resisting. He rolled her onto her back, unbuttoned her shirt so he could kiss her just below her belly button, paused and unzipped her jeans.

She watched him undress himself, as she had so many times now, admiring his strong frame, his deliberate, confident movements. She opened her legs to allow him in, feeling the presence of this man, who had been her lover, was now her husband, would be the father of their child.

He moved gently with her, shyly almost, feeling they were not alone. He responded to the pressure of her hip turning him over so she could straddle him. The late morning sunlight coming through the window cast diagonals of light and shadow across her face and torso. He held her breasts with something like awe. She closed her eyes in pleasure and he noticed a radiance in her skin, independent of the light, impervious to the shadow. From deep within he felt a swirl of passion; pride, protectiveness, as he thought about the life inside her.

She rode him with increasing intensity, feeling herself approaching some precipice. As she let go, she moved in suspension, tentacles of warmth unfurling from her pelvis.

He waited until her movements slowed, like a receding tide, before rolling back above her. He finished quickly, then rolled off and lay next to her on the floor, breathing heavily.

"If the child is born here, he'll be an American," she said.

"He or she," Rashid said.

"He or she will be American by nationality," she continued, "but also Pakistani by heritage. We'll have to make sure the child is both, not half and half, and not neither."

"Of course."

———

A stack of books about pregnancy, birth, and babies grew on

Kathryn's bedside table faster than her expanding belly. Rashid teased her one night as she opened yet another book. "Do you really need to read more? What else is there to know?"

The pregnancy had brought about a truce in their political debates, so she tried not to take offense.

"I want to be prepared." She fluffed the pillow behind her. "And you're gone all the time working, so what's the harm in reading?"

"In Pakistan, no one reads books about pregnancy and birth. Is it so much more complicated in America?" He sat next to her on the bed.

"In Pakistan your sisters-in-law have your mother around, their aunties, all their female relatives probably explain everything to them. My mother is three hundred miles away and none of my close friends have been pregnant while I was around them."

"OK," he said playfully turning her book upside down.

"And in some ways it *is* more complicated in America," she righted the book. "The obstetricians are so quick to cut women open."

"What do you mean?"

"Cesarean sections. In the last three weeks, every single woman I've met in the park or the grocery store who talks to me about pregnancy has had a caesarian section."

"What for?"

"Maybe because the doctors are impatient with a slow labor, or women get scared about how long things take because they've never seen a birth before. In Los Angeles the c-section rate is almost thirty percent."

He thought for a moment, perplexed. "So why don't you go to Pakistan to have the baby? Mummyji will take care of you. I've only heard of surgeries in Pakistan for emergencies."

She closed her book thoughtfully. "But she's not my mother. Maybe my mom could come for the birth."

"Our girls always go to their mothers in the last month of their pregnancy. They leave their husband's family until the baby is a month or two old."

"I'm thinking," she said tentatively, grasping the book protectively,

"I'm thinking the surest way to keep a doctor from cutting me open is not to be in the hospital, to have the baby at home." She braced herself for his reaction. "With a professional midwife of course."

He shrugged his shoulders, "Sure, why not? My parents were both born at home."

She felt the baby move, and pulled Rashid's hand over her belly. Rashid curled up next to her, waiting.

"That's it?" she said incredulously. "You agree that we can have the baby at home? You aren't going to argue with me about it?"

"No. Do you want me to?" he said with a grin.

Chapter 5

Los Angeles, California.
The year of the bombing

Kathryn led Michael into his kindergarten classroom for his first day of school. He joined other kids sitting cross legged in a circle on the floor, looking eagerly at each other.

"Michael, say goodbye to baby Andrew," she patted the newborn in the sling across her breast.

Michael gave a distracted wave. Reluctantly, she turned to go, looked back to blow him a kiss, and then determinedly walked out of the classroom.

As she turned the key in the ignition, the radio sprung to life. A newscaster gave the usual litany of bad news, falling stock prices, acrimony in Congress, pirates off the coast of Somalia, U.S. forces killed a dozen Taliban near Afghanistan's eastern border. She cut off the monotony of the daily news, with the press of a button. Instantly, the car filled with the familiar words of a singer, a melody she had memorized as a teenager. She relaxed, turned into the parking garage. As she pulled the key out of the ignition the radio went dead and a tiny cry from the baby echoed the last note of the song.

She hurried up two flights of stairs, the carseat—with the baby still buckled in—knocked against her leg with each rising step. She felt her milk coming into her breasts even before he cried for it. By the time she locked the front door behind her, two dark circles of milk had soaked through her Pakistani kurta. Irritated, she pulled the kurta off and dropped it on top of a pile of neglected dirty laundry. She didn't bother to find another. She just might be able to finish her cold coffee and feed herself something before she nursed. The phone rang. The baby cried, an angry, hungry cry. The ringing continued as she fumbled with the car seat buckles and the baby's kicking legs. She tried to ignore the ringing as she maneuvered the baby into position. She saw Andrew's eyes open widely, wildly. Her coffee would have to wait. He latched on to her, relaxing almost immediately into the safety and pleasure of her milk.

The phone rang again. Irritated, she tried to ignore it. She exhaled as the ringing gave way to silence, only to begin again in another second. She swore under her breath and awkwardly pushed herself up.

"Hello?" she said into the phone. When no one responded, she repeated herself, preparing to hang up in frustration.

"Kathryn?" a man's voice said unsteadily.

"Yes?"

"Kathryn? It's me, Rashid."

"What do you need? Why do you sound so strange?"

"Kathryn, have you seen the news?"

"I heard a bit on the way home from the school. Nothing new, why?"

"Did you hear about the attack? The U.S. Government is saying Taliban were killed."

"OK. Look, Rashid, I'm trying to feed the baby. What do you need?"

"The attack, it wasn't Taliban, it was a wedding…"

"So…?"

"They…he…the…" he could not find the words to start. "It was a wedding in the northwestern territories. It wasn't in Afghanistan, it was on the Pakistan side of the border. It was a drone attack… and my father…was there."

The baby pulled away from her breast, blissfully contented.

"Your father?" she asked.

"My father was a guest…he was killed. My father's dead."

She could not speak. Could not reconcile the comfort of this maternal moment with the horror of the words coming through the phone. She touched the baby—a half Pakistani baby. She closed her eyes hoping to shut out everything beyond her body and this baby.

"Kathryn, are you there?" he was almost pleading.

She sat down on the couch, slowly exhaling. "Are you sure? How do you know?"

"My brothers called me."

"From Lahore?"

"Yes."

"Then they weren't at the wedding. How would they know? Maybe there's a mistake."

"My uncle called them. Not my real uncle, Shoukart's father, the Pashtun man who protected my father during Partition. My father went for the youngest son's wedding."

"Oh God. Where's your mother, was she with him?"

"No, she's at home, only my father traveled for the wedding."

She began to tremble. The pieces of his story slowly assembled in her mind. His father—dead, the killer—her country. She felt exposed, reached for a blanket to cover her breasts, the baby, her distant sense of culpability.

"Where are you? Can you come home?"

"I'm offshore on a rig. I told you I had a job in Ventura today. I'll have to wait for the next ferry."

She heard the helpless edge in his voice.

"Come home," she said. "We'll all be waiting."

———

Rashid hung up the phone, clenched his fists until his fingernails dug into his flesh. His brothers had reached him so easily by phone, delivering the news with unbearable efficiency. For him to reach his mother would take long days, anxious nights.

He unzipped his coveralls, stepped out, letting them crumple on the rig floor. Out of habit he reached to make sure his plastic radiation exposure badge was in place on the waistband of his jeans.

He ignored the shouts of his rig team calling him back to his work. The series of small explosions they had meticulously planned to perforate the oil well no longer mattered. He could only think of getting to Pakistan. Should he bring Michael? Kathryn and the baby were out of the question. Even though they had traveled to Lahore with Michael when he was still an infant—had presented his father with the only male heir to carry the family name—he couldn't bear to overlap the birth of his second son with the death of his father.

He looked at his watch, at least two hours until the noon ferry would deliver him to shore. He paced back and forth along the edge of the rig dock like a caged lion, spat into the water. The ocean accepted his bitter expression. He remembered his father—once he had failed to react when Rashid hit him in anger over the slaughter of a beloved goat for the *Eid* feast marking the end of Ramadan. "Our emotions come and go, beta," his father had said with infinite patience to his young son, "what matters is action, how those emotions take form in action that others can see. That goat is dead now. But you can make sure it is cooked with reverence, the meat shared, so the goat's sacrifice has meaning."

Angrily, Rashid punched at the tiny keypad on his phone, brusquely asked the operator to connect him with the international airlines that would carry him to the land of his birth. "I need the next flight to Islamabad, and a connection to Lahore. I must arrive as soon as possible."

"Let me check, sir…" the agent spoke with a South Asian accent. "We have one flight a day to Islamabad, through Dubai. Today's flight has just departed. Can I reserve a seat on tomorrow's flight for you?"

"My father's body will already be in the ground by the time I get there," Rashid said quietly.

"I'm sorry, sir?"

"My father was killed last night. I need to get to my mother, my family. But I'll miss the burial."

The agent let out a sigh, "Oh, I am so sorry, brother." He spoked quietly now, "I missed my own father's funeral. I was working in Dubai. My employer held my passport and wouldn't interrupt his holiday weekend to retrieve it so I could fly back to Karachi."

"Really?" Rashid asked indignantly.

"How could I ever forgive my employer? I quit, full stop. I'll make sure you're on tomorrow's flight, sir."

———————

Rashid knocked. Kathryn opened the door almost immediately. When he saw her, the baby content in her arms, Michael, looking so grown up at her side with his expression of serious concern, Rashid could no longer contain his emotions. He reached for his family. They embraced him before the door slid closed behind him. He wept. Michael wrapped his arms around his father's waist. "I'm sorry Baba, don't be too sad. We're all sorry, even baby Andrew's sorry."

Rashid pulled back from Kathryn, knelt down to look at his elder son. He stroked Michael's hair, laid his hands on his shoulders. "You don't need to be sorry, beta. It's not your fault. But we're all sorry, we'll miss Babu."

"Can we see him again?" Michael asked.

"No, not in this world. He's gone, no one can bring back my father."

Kathryn bit her lip, let the tears roll down her face.

"I need to go to my mother now, to help her and be close to my brothers."

"In Pakistan?" Michael pronounced it just the way his father did.

"Yes, in Pakistan."

"Then I'll need to be with my mother here, to help her and to be close to my baby brother."

Rashid embraced the boy, marveling at how the infant he had seen enter the world had become a little man, a son already aware of his role in the family.

"You'll come back, right?"

Rashid felt his son's question, the vibrations of the boy's anxious voice pressing into his chest, as much as he heard the question.

"Of course," he held Michael's head with one hand, reached out for Kathryn with the other, "of course."

Chapter 6

Lahore, Pakistan.
Months before the bombing

Rashid emerged from the air conditioned chill of the flight, felt the warm air of Lahore envelope him. The world appeared to him as if through a scrim. The blazing afternoon light only revealed the ugly surfaces around him, the cracked asphalt of the runway, the crumbling concrete surrounding the airport. The light did not penetrate to reveal anything of the city he had loved. He urged the taxi driver to speed him to his mother. This was no longer his country. Without his father to bless him on his arrival, this was now barren land.

Rashid paid the driver with an American $20 bill. The driver raised his eyebrows in surprise, held the bill to his heart in gratitude. Rashid, oblivious to his overpayment, looked to the locked gate, the silent courtyard of his father's house. As the taxi returned down the gravel road, Rashid banged the metal latch against the gate, called out for his mother.

After a few moments, his mother's elder sister, his *apa* walked to him, wordlessly opened the gate. Instinctively, he reached down to touch her feet in respect, she set her hand on his head in blessing.

"Come, beta," she said, "your mother's waiting."

He followed his aunt, the white salwar kameeze that marked her grief hung limp around her flesh. No breeze animated her tunic, nor the sheer cloth of the chunni covering her head. Rashid stepped out of his shoes on the steps before the door, left his single bag in the courtyard.

As his eyes adjusted to the shadows inside he did not recognize the woman hunched on the charpoy before him. Without the bustle of the family around her, in the absence of her husband, Rashid saw his mother for the first time as a little old woman.

Rashid's apa said quietly, "Didi, Rashid *puta* is here."

His mother lifted her head. Her steely gaze caught him off guard, he stood momentarily paralyzed. After a long moment she inhaled, lifting her shoulders, raising her chin until she appeared again as he had known her, her spine erect with pride and power.

She nodded her head, motioned with her hand for him to come to her. He obeyed quickly, touching her feet to seek her blessing. He then lifted his arms to embrace her, to offer her comfort. But before he could draw himself close, she reached out for his shoulders. She held him at arm's length.

"It's good you've come, you are the one we're depending on."

"Yes, Mummyji, I came as fast as I could. I'll stay as long as you need me. Tell me, what do you need?"

She let her hands drop into her lap. "You are the one, you will take action to relieve our grief. We will be avenged."

He had known she would remind him of his responsibility. But the smell of his American wife still lingered in his clothes, the image of his American sons hovered in his mind. They would discuss it later. There was much to know before he had to face it.

"Where are my brothers?" he asked to change the topic.

"Your brothers have gone to be with Shoukart's father to bury the bodies."

"Bodies?" Rashid held his hand to his breast. "How many were killed?"

"At least a dozen, more were injured. Even Shoukart is gone, and the younger son's bride. Not even a day together as husband and wife."

"Shoukart is gone?" Rashid raised himself to sit next to his mother. His apa came from the kitchen carrying a tray with tea cups. Distractedly, Rashid reached out for the hot tea, thinking over the years he has spent with Shoukart. The same age as Rashid's eldest brother, Riaz, Shoukart had often restrained Rashid from mischief. They had shared tea and snacks on countless occasions.

The house was eerily calm. "Where is everyone else?" he asked.

"I sent them to the *masjid*, the mosque to pray," his mother said.

"So only you and apa are here? It's not safe for you two women to be alone here, especially when people learn that Daddyji's... not here."

"It's fine, I knew you were coming." She reached out and patted his hand, looked in his eyes for a long time, as if searching for something, perhaps some trace of her husband, perhaps some strength on which she could draw. He held her gaze.

"Well, let's not waste our time here, we need to go. I was waiting for you to travel."

"Where?"

"To the *Lak-e-Gar*, to the Northwest Territories. I need to see for myself where our family was attacked."

Chapter 7

Los Angeles, California.
Months before the bombing

Rashid turned the key in the lock, expected Kathryn and the boys to be sleeping at this early hour. The smell in the apartment, a combination of coffee and baby's skin, mother's milk and laundry detergent, struck him as impossibly innocent, naïve, in contrast to the smells of the Lak-e-Gar; dust and cooking fires, grilled meat, death. He closed his eyes, covered his nose, trying to hold onto the memory of those smells.

He set down his bag, took off his shoes and walked across the Persian carpet to the bedroom. He heard a faint rustle as he opened the door. Kathryn lay in the middle of the bed, her breathing regular. Michael slept curled up next to her. The baby blinked as a shaft of morning light sent a long finger of brilliance over the bed. Andrew's little feet and hands moved whimsically in uncoordinated directions. Occasionally a smile passed over his tiny face. Rashid knelt down to lay his head next to the baby. The baby turned as if to look his father in the eye. Rashid smiled, a rueful smile of gratitude and sorrow. His father would never know this child. And this child might never understand his place in the family, Rashid's responsibility to their clan.

The baby whimpered, his little forehead wrinkling in discomfort. Kathryn stirred, turned on her side and reached for the baby with her eyes still closed. Rashid watched as she pulled open her night shirt, revealing the curve of her breast and her nipple which disappeared into the baby's mouth.

Rashid raised himself onto the bed, finding just enough space to lie next to the baby. He reached out to stroke Kathryn's other breast, to reach across her body and lay his hand on Michael's head. But the seed his mother had planted in his heart had already taken root. He closed his eyes and saw the rubble of the wedding, the stains of blood on the bricks. The pain returned just as powerfully as when he had first seen the evidence of the killings. He pulled his hand back, closed his eyes on his American family.

Rashid shot up to sitting in the bed, disoriented, sweaty, painfully hungry. Kathryn had closed the drapes to keep the daylight out, but the afternoon heat penetrated. Perhaps only a dream had awakened him. Persisting at the fringes of his consciousness he heard the cries of children, of old women and helpless young men. He saw an explosion and rather than shrapnel hurtling away from the point of impact, the gold and brilliant red of a bride's clothes seemed to hang, suspended in the air, shattered into a thousand distorted shapes.

He stepped out of the bed, angrily pulled the drapes open. Across the street a woman walked a dog dressed in a green sweater and a rhinestone collar. He resisted the urge to bang on the window and curse at her for her unholy affection for the dog, and then he remembered, here in America dogs are like children, free to enjoy luxuries undreamed of in Pakistan.

Slowly, stepping back from the window, he sought out some relief, something to tame his anger. He went to the bathroom, ran cool water over his hands, splashed his face, breathed deeply into the towel.

He paused before stepping out in the living room, tried to create some wall of separation in his mind, some sense that this American fantasy could be held in suspension away from what he knew he had to do. Rashid watched Kathryn preparing food in the kitchen, pulling square packages from the freezer and pressing the buttons on the microwave oven. When Michael saw Rashid, he ran to his father, abandoning his complicated plastic building blocks. Rashid opened his arms, received the boy who held him in a vice-like grip. Michael unleashed a flurry of questions about Pakistan, followed, without pause, by a flurry of statements about what had happened at kindergarten during Rashid's absence. When the child finally stopped, he thumped his father on the shoulder and demanded: "So? Tell me!"

Rashid carried Michael to the kitchen and reached out to embrace Kathryn with his free arm.

She looked up at him, fatigue had darkened the pale skin around her blue eyes. "It's good you slept," she said. "Let me get some food ready for us and then we can talk about it."

Rashid, grateful to remain silent, walked to the sofa where Andrew slept on an impossibly soft baby blanket.

"Please don't wake the baby," Kathryn called from the kitchen. "I want to at least feed you before I have to nurse him again."

"Daddy, Daddy," Michael peppered the air with requests and retellings that Rashid could barely decipher.

"Beta," Rashid said wearily to Michael, "please just sit quietly with me. It was a long journey and I'm not completely here."

Michael's expression grew serious and he put his hand on top of Rashid's. "Where are you then? Still in Pakistan?"

His son's sensitivity gave him pause. He put his other hand to his heart. "Exactly, beta. Part of me is still in Pakistan, with my family. I don't know, maybe part of me will always be there."

"Well, can we bring that part of Pakistan here, so all parts of you can be here with us?"

Rashid gently placed a hand on Andrew's back, felt the baby's lungs expand and contract. "I don't think it's possible, but maybe we can figure out something else."

Kathryn set plates on the table—simple, unspiced dishes of vegetables and chicken—that struck Rashid as ingredients for a curry she had yet to prepare. "Come, let's eat," she said. "You can start to get back to a regular schedule at least with your meals."

She placed a few vegetables and a bit of chicken on Michael's plate. "Sit up. Roll up your sleeves before you eat." Michael did as he was told. She scooped larger quantities onto Rashid's plate. "Tell me, how is your mother? How was the trip?"

Rashid looked up at Kathryn, shook his head, poked at the food with his fork. "How can I tell you? It was awful. Worse than I expected."

"In what way?" she felt her chest tighten.

"The attack was horrible. It wasn't just my father, but the bride, old women, children, even Shoukart, our driver. Fifteen people dead, sixty wounded. Only worth a few seconds on the news here. But the village, the families of the dead, my mother, how can they ever forget that attack?"

Kathryn glanced at Michael, concerned about upsetting him. "How is your mother coping?"

He paused, how could he possibly translate his mother's reaction into a language that Kathryn would understand? "She responded how every Pakistani woman would. She's strong. Too strong."

"What do you mean? Are there any rituals, a way that Islam helps her get through her grief?"

"There are codes," he said vaguely, "but they're not really about Islam, they're based on our families, the way we protect ourselves." He reached for a glass of water, his throat constricted.

As Kathryn cocked her head and began to ask a question, Andrew let out a low pitched cry, almost a growl. "Hold that thought," she said to Rashid as she stood up from the table and whisked Andrew from the sofa to the bedroom.

"What's your code, Daddy? You mean like a secret code that helps you get the bad guys? I saw a movie where they used a secret code to blow up a building with bad guys in it."

Rashid stabbed a piece of broccoli with his fork. "No, our code is like a set of rules that a family should follow. We call it *izzat* or *badan*. It might have to do with bad guys, but it isn't secret." He slowly bit into the broccoli. "When you're older, you'll understand it better."

Kathryn returned to the table holding the baby and attempted to feed herself with her free hand. "I'm thinking about calling my contact at the International Human Rights Commission, or maybe the ACLU. Something. We have to bring a lawsuit or lodge an international complaint about the bombing." The baby kicked his feet, nearly knocking her plate over. She reached down, irritated, and restrained him. "I just haven't had time to do anything, but we can't keep quiet about this, we have to do something."

He raised his eyebrows skeptically, "You think the U.S. military listens to the ACLU or the international organizations? What do they care about an old man in Pakistan?"

"It's not just one man, not just your father, we're continually launching these drones, predators, whatever they are, and attacking Pakistan, a country that's supposedly our ally."

"We?" Rashid shoved his chair away from the table. "For sure I didn't do this. I didn't vote for this president, ask for this fucking government." He stood up and walked out of the room, leaving a chill to settle over the table.

Michael looked from his mother to the empty seat and back. "Mommy, we did this? What's an ally?"

She brought her free hand to her head, pressed her fingers into her temples. "No, of course we didn't do this." Any possible reply to his second question disappeared in her long low sob. Kathryn's expression of pain silenced the little boy into fear.

———

Kathryn woke with the first light, next to an empty space in the bed. "Jet lag?" she called out as she walked into the kitchen. But Rashid was not there. Nor was he in the bathroom, nor anywhere else in their home. She stood still in the middle of the room, wrapped one arm and then the other around her torso, a lonely, one-person embrace. She picked up the phone off the kitchen counter and dialed his number.

The phone vibrated silently in Rashid's pocket. He didn't answer it, tried to focus his thoughts on his prayers as he raised his prostrate torso back to upright. The inside of the mosque retained the night's darkness in the grey early morning light, the unmistakable rumble of the freeway coming from just beyond the building's walls. The few men around him demonstrated the same quiet, humble demeanor as those in Pakistan who typically rose before dawn for the first of the daily prayers. In unison they held up their hands in supplication. In unison, they repeated their holy words. Rashid very carefully attuned his heart, trying to perceive the presence of his father. He searched vainly in their collective breath, for the familiar sound of his father's contented exhale.

"What happened?" Rashid said, opening the door to see Kathryn sitting on the sofa.

"You tell me what happened," she said, letting her hands fall limply into her lap. "You leave without saying anything, and then you don't answer your phone. Where have you been? How long do I have to handle all this by myself?"

"I was at the mosque," he said simply.

"The mosque?" She paused at his unexpected statement. "What for? You haven't been to the mosque since we came to America."

"I miss my father. I'm trying to sort out some things in my head. I don't expect you to understand."

"Of course I won't understand if you don't even talk to me."

He sat down next to her, hands in his lap.

"And what, you won't even touch me? I'm your wife. What's happened to you? I'm so sorry your father is dead, but the boys and I…we're alive."

He looked up, as if seeing her for the first time since he had returned. He gently drew her into an embrace until he felt her shoulders release their tension. He ran his fingers down her hair and allowed her to weep. She spoke through her tears, a tumble of clipped and muffled words.

"I'm sorry," he said.

"You are?" she drew back to look at him, incredulous.

He pulled her back in, unable to speak. He let his body take over from where language failed him. He enveloped this woman, holding onto the body that had given him his children. He kissed the face that years ago had attracted him. He caressed the breasts that continued to inspire him.

"Rashid, the children," she started to protest.

He walked to the bedroom doorway, inside both boys slept peacefully on the big bed, so much bigger than the bed where he had slept with his parents as a child. He closed the door, already reaching for his belt buckle, and returned to her.

She submitted to him, unable to resist his touch, his smell, the generosity of his movements. They made love wordlessly, the physical overpowering the contradictions of their minds. She felt each moment a respite from the roles and responsibilities to which her life had been reduced. She relished the process, even as she rushed to finish before the children might interrupt them.

When he separated from her she simply watched as he walked to the bathroom, washed himself as he always did immediately after sex. She felt as if she had just witnessed some natural phenomena, a storm passing through their home, a perplexing sun shower that somehow makes no sense, brings relief and foreboding in equal measure.

Chapter 8

Rashid inspected the contents of his bag again: his fire retardant coveralls, his steel-toed boots, his radiation exposure badge, the company's security identification card, and the necessary toiletries—industrial strength soap, toothpaste.

"Glad to be going back to work?" Kathryn asked from the bed.

"It's a small job, shouldn't be difficult." He slipped a bottle of men's perfume into the bag. His perfumes always surprised her, the incongruous luxury of the complex masculine fragrance amidst the austerity; the perfume a legacy of his time among Arabs who never left their homes unperfumed.

He zipped up the bag, picked it up, checking the weight. The work would be a relief, a reassurance that everything was normal, that he could just continue in this American life, that the people he met in Pakistan and their plans were no more than a dream. He climbed into bed next to her. They entwined their limbs as they had done for years—he was unable to sleep in their bed without touching her—and she quickly succumbed to her exhaustion. He lay there, unable to sleep for his swirling thoughts, listened to her regular breathing, inhaled her sweet maternal smell. He watched the rise and fall of her delicately beautiful chest next to his, and tried not to think about her origins, her allegiances, her identity.

———————

Kathryn shifted the car into neutral just outside the school. Andrew made happy gurgling noises from his car seat behind her. Occasionally she made a noise in reply or chirped out a happy string of words just to reassure him she was there. She did not rush through this errand today. She relished this brief opportunity to wait for Michael in the middle of the day. In a few days she would be back at her office, Michael would stay in the afterschool program, and Andrew, her beloved baby, would spend the day in the nurturing care of professionally trained strangers.

The school bell rang and moments later the double doors at the front of the school burst open. She scanned the children—little girls in pink t-shirts, boys jumping in mock karate poses—for Michael. Only after nearly every car had pulled away, their young charges safely collected, did she see the familiar beige skin and dark hair of her son—his gait uncharacteristically slow, his expression glum.

She opened the door and stepped out, meeting her son as he reached the sidewalk. She knelt down and hugged him, his arms hung limp at his sides.

"What's wrong?" her voice pitched with concern.

He looked up at her and then looked away into the distance. "Nothing."

She hugged him again, guilt rising, certain he was already sad knowing she would soon be back at work. "Come," she held his hand, "say hello to your baby brother, he's so happy right now."

Michael dutifully climbed into his car seat, allowed his mother to fasten the buckles he could easily handle himself.

"Would you like to have some ice cream? We can stop at the grocery store on the way home."

Michael nodded.

She returned to the driver's seat, looked back. "What flavor? You choose."

"Rocky road," he looked up at her expectant expression and promptly added, "please."

———————

Michael ate his ice cream with gusto, while the baby lay in the middle of the carpet and played with his fingers and toes. Kathryn unloaded the groceries. The phone rang. She set it on speakerphone so she could keep working.

"Hi darling," she said.

"Hey. What's happening?" Rashid asked perfunctorily. They discussed the status of his job, the errands of her day. He had a habit of divulging very little over the phone, he had grown up requiring face-to-face conversations for almost every purpose, no matter how trivial. But after a day or so on a rig, he always missed the sound of her voice, the reassurance of her domestic activity, so he called, usually every day.

Michael licked the last bit of Rocky Road from his bowl and then picked up the phone. "Hi Daddy."

"Hi Michael, how was school today?"

With a melodramatic frown he said, "Bad."

"Bad? Why?"

"Somebody hit me."

Kathryn looked up, surprised. "Hit you? Who?"

"One of the bigger kindergartners. He wanted to play with my ball and I wouldn't give it to him."

From the other end of the phone line Rashid wished he could summon up his son's face. "Did you hit him back?"

"No," came the tiny voice through Rashid's phone, sounding so much younger than Michael did in person.

"You need to hit him back, nobody can disrespect you that way," Rashid said matter-of-factly.

"Rashid!" Kathryn's scandalized voice cut through. "You can't tell him that."

"Why? That's what my father taught me. After the first time I hit

52

the bully in my school, he didn't dare touch me again."

"But if he does that here he'll be punished by the teachers."

Rashid sighed, recalibrated. "All right Michael, listen. If that happens again, first you tell the kid never to hit you again. If he doesn't stop, next you tell your teacher. If he still doesn't stop, next you tell us. If we can't stop him, then...you hit him."

"You hear that?" Kathryn asked Michael. "You do everything you can and get the grownups to help you before you even dream of hitting someone back."

Silence.

"Don't just nod your head, tell your father you understand."

"Yes Daddyji," came the dutiful response.

"Ok, beta. I've been up for thirty hours on this job. I'm going to get some sleep now. I love you."

"Love you too, Daddy."

"I love you, darling," Kathryn's voice was warm and full, she must have moved the phone next to her ear.

"You too." He closed his phone and dropped it in his pocket. He walked under the bright afternoon sun to the metal box structure that served as crew housing on the rig. He lay down in the bed in the tiny cell-like room and stared at the ceiling, a bit of rust eating away at one corner where the welding had proved pervious. The effects of the caffeinated energy drinks that powered his erratic work schedule would take some time to dissipate. He heard crew mates in the break room across the walkway playing video games and watching pornos.

He lay down on the bed and dialed a long series of numbers and waited.

"Majid...yes, it's Rashid....Fine. And you?"

He fidgeted with the zipper on his coveralls, listening to his brother's questions in Urdu. "Well, that's what I wanted to talk about," he said in English and then slipped into Urdu. "I think I can't follow through with...with...with what we had discussed with those people. My life is here now. Kathryn. The boys. My job. Everything is fine for me."

Nervously, he pulled the zipper up and down, again and again. "No, not nothing. I *will* do something, something better. We know some people here who can bring revenge through the courts."

He held the phone away from his ear as his brother's voice rose loudly.

"It's not the same here. There are better ways. You have to trust that I know what I'm doing."

He moved the zipper faster. Listened. Disconnected the phone without saying goodbye.

He stood up, agitated and walked back outside, wanting some distraction. Maybe he should eat. Maybe he should join the other men with their videogames and porn. His feet followed the steel railing and he looked out at the blankness of the water. He stood, tapping the railing, humming, trying to block out thoughts of Majid's words. A familiar melody from his childhood came easily to his ear. The words drifted through his mind several times, unsung, before he realized his brother's words had triggered this melody, this memory. *Jay na Doger mareya, Maura rehna nakk nahin. Duniya uttey rehan da fer sadda haqq nahin.* If Doger, our traitor, is not killed for revenge then our pride is tarnished, and without pride we have no right to live.

He shook his head, trying to break the loop of his thoughts. He dialed Kathryn again.

"Hi…yeah, I'm OK. So…I'm thinking…I want to talk with you about the lawyer you mentioned, the one who could bring a lawsuit…yes, it should be big… OK, let's talk more when I get home."

Kathryn set three bags next to the door. In the morning she would drop off one bag with each child and then take the last one with her as she returned to her job. She looked forward to returning to the journal. Editing the chronicles of politicians, economic trends, and the upheavals of places distant—but familiar in the abstract—seemed easily comprehensible.

Michael startled her, appearing like an apparition in the middle of the room, pajama-clad, but clear-eyed.

She knelt down in front of him, held his arms and looked into his eyes. "What is it, beta?" the Urdu word for child now part of her native tongue.

"I'm thinking about Babu."

"What are you thinking about him?"

"I'm thinking about if he is angry with us."

Kathryn inhaled deeply, took Michael's hand and walked to the couch sitting him next to her. "Why would he be angry with us?"

"Because our country killed him. Do people feel angry after they die?"

Her mind skipped over a dozen possible answers, knowing Michael would remember and likely repeat her words. "I think when people die, they're freed from having to feel anything. They go beyond anger and pain and happiness. They experience something like peace, freedom."

"Really?" Michael wrinkled up his forehead. "If dying is so wonderful, how come nobody wants to do it? And why does Daddy feel so angry that Babu died?"

"Did Daddy tell you he's angry? Is he angry with us?" She felt a tightening in her chest.

"No."

"Then how do you know he's angry?"

Michael looked down at his hands, looked back into his mother's pale eyes. "I heard him on the phone, talking in that language," he hesitated.

"Urdu?"

"Yeah, Urdu. And he sounded angry and I heard him say Babu a bunch of times." He pursed his lips, picked at the cartoon fire trucks printed on his pajamas. "I'm afraid about what Babu might do from heaven if he's angry with you because you're American," he blurted.

"Oh beta," she said, pulling him tightly to her. "Babu won't do anything from heaven, and he was a very wise man, wise enough to know that I didn't have anything to do with his death." She held Michael again at arm's length and looked into his eyes. "You know,

I'm also sorry about what happened to Babu."

"I know, but what if Babu doesn't know?"

"Do you think we should tell him?"

Michael nodded his head earnestly.

"All right," she held Michael's hands in hers, "let's close our eyes and imagine he's here and talk to him."

They sat, the room silent, save the hum of the refrigerator.

"Do you want to start?" she said.

"What should I say?"

"Whatever you think he should know, whatever you want to say."

He inhaled, sat up straighter. "Babu, we're all very sorry about what happened, even baby Andrew, but he can't say anything. Please don't be angry, and tell Daddy not to be angry. It's not Mommy's fault about the bomb. She's really nice, and makes good Pakistani food, even if it's not perfect." He looked at her, eyebrows raised in question. "What else should I say," he whispered, as if Babu might not hear.

With eyes closed, as if in prayer, she whispered back, "How about, we send out our best prayers and thoughts to your wife, our *Biji*, and to the rest of the family." She hesitated, waiting for Michael to repeat her words. When he didn't she added more loudly, "especially Rashid, who means the world to me."

Kathryn opened her eyes to see Michael staring intently at her. He smiled and nodded. "Do you think he heard us, Mummy?"

"I think so."

He threw his little arms around her waist and nestled his head in her chest. She stroked his hair and looked around the room. Everything appeared the same as it did just a few months ago; a blend of Eastern and Western photos, music, paintings.

Yet as she and Michael walked to the bedroom across the Persian carpet—Rashid had haggled over it with an Iranian trader on a bright winter afternoon in Dubai—she hesitated over each step as if any of the stylized flowers beneath her feet might explode like an unseen landmine.

Chapter 9

"Fuck, I'm hungry," Rashid's crewmate, Jerry, complained from the passenger seat as Rashid inserted his security card in the truck's dashboard tracking system. "Let's stop at Dos Amigos and get a dozen tacos and some margaritas."

"Can't," Rashid said.

"Oh that's right, you fuckin' sand niggers don't drink."

"Fuck you," Rashid said casually, "bastard, you know I'm Pakistani not Arab."

"Same shit. At least let me buy us some tacos. That rig food always sucks." Jerry pulled off his grimy company cap and ran his hand across his forehead.

"Can't. We got the source on this truck." Rashid pointed up, to the ends of the 20-foot cylindrical tools just visible over the truck cab. "Gotta go directly back to the base or they'll fuckin' write me up for a diversion."

"Like whadda they think we're gonna do with a thimbleful of radioactive shit at a taco place anyway?" Jerry grabbed his stomach as it growled.

Rashid envisioned the source safely ensconced in its long pipe-like tool, lowered into a well, sending out energy to map the surrounding geological formations like an upside down periscope. Rashid marveled at the mind that engineered a tool like that. "Jerry, go buy yourself an imagination."

"What the fuck for? Least drive fast and then we can get tacos after we drop the tools in the base." Jerry set the cap back on his head, pulled it low to cover his eyes so he could nap.

Rashid drove precisely the speed limit, scanned his rear view mirrors every few seconds, just as he had learned from the Department of Transportation commercial driving safety course. He checked the odometer, estimated an hour and a half until they would reach the base.

The rocket launcher—as they fondly referred to their truck—followed the curves of the freeway climbing into the mountains north of Los Angeles. An endless parade of big cars, trucks, and even big rigs passed him, barreling along at gas-guzzling speeds.

As the monotony of the drive wore on, Rashid craved spicy food, sex, and a good sleep in their big bed. He checked the date on his watch. Almost forty days since his father had been killed. His brother had said they should take action within six months, not to wait too long. Majid had never been to America, what did he know of life here, of how much Rashid could enjoy, how much he could lose?

As he passed a sign displaying food, fuel, and lodging available at the next exit, he wondered if Kathryn would have any spicy food ready in the refrigerator, or if he would have to settle for hot sauce on whatever he could find.

From a billboard, a woman, grotesquely feminine, displayed her barely covered breasts to advertise a nearby casino. The West knows nothing of the value of the hidden, the power of mystery he thought.

Against the backdrop of the hillsides beyond his windshield, he saw Kathryn. He saw her learning to make rotis in his mother's kitchen, slapping the dough back and forth in her hands, the way Mexican women here made tortillas. He saw her slipping into the all-black costume of the women in the Gulf, wearing the *abaya* and *shela* as an experiment, so she could know directly how it felt to be a covered woman. He saw her hailing a taxi to take her to her office, saw her dancing in nightclubs, saw her observing Ramadan with friends in their parents' village in Oman. She could do anything.

Why couldn't she also help him take his revenge, in the American way? She would call her contacts.

————————

"We need an international perspective for this piece," Kathryn said. She doodled in her notebook as one of the journal's contributors responded through the phone. "Yes, I know there's the comment from the professor at the American University in Beirut. But can you find someone who might have a more contrasting opinion? Maybe a Persian intellectual or what about some of the young thought leaders in the Gulf?" She paused, clicked at her computer. "Let me see if we have someone in Iran in the database. And see if you can get some leads from the energy policy guy at the Center for Near East Policy or even the Farsi language department at Georgetown." She picked up the pen again as she listened. "OK, cool, we need to make sure we aren't just quoting expat American intellectuals. See what you can get in the next twenty-four hours, otherwise we may have to hold the piece for the next issue."

She hung up and turned around at the sound of the Asia editor's voice. He stepped into her office.

"Now that you're back," he did not bother to welcome her back from maternity leave, "I'm thinking we can move ahead on the series about the Saudis funding Islamic schools in Asia." He pulled at his mouse-like chin.

"What's your angle?"

"I wanted to focus on Indonesia, start with Jakarta and the Saudis' interest in East Timor. Some of my old Bangkok friends have been checking out the schools." He pushed up his sweater sleeve to glance at his watch. "But let's talk more after the Thursday deadline," and he darted back into the corridor.

Kathryn stood up and stretched her arms as she walked out to the secretary's desk.

"…and then the parking cop won't even look at me as she's writing up the ticket. I mean the dog's in the backseat barking like crazy…" the secretary prattled on about her crisis du jour to the Korean-American Pacific Rim freelancer.

"Welcome back," the freelancer greeted her warmly. "How are the babies?"

"Good, the older one doesn't seem like a baby anymore."

The Europe editor glanced up from his desk as Kathryn passed on her way to the bathroom. He smiled, raised a hand in greeting.

The bathroom door squeaked open in exactly the same way it had before Andrew was born. The exchanges with her colleagues could have been prerecorded, not a single person paused in their work to ask about her father-in-law. We are all intelligent, well-traveled, well-intentioned professionals, endeavoring to educate influential policymakers, she thought, could it be that no one here knows what has happened in my family?

———

Rashid repeated his prayers at the mosque. How hollow they seemed with no one else who knew they signified the passing of forty days of mourning. *Baba,* he asked silently, *what should I do? You were proud of me, loved my wife, our family. Be patient, we will take our justice.* He touched his head again to the floor and stood up, prayers finished, and walked back to his shoes with a dozen other men.

"You are thinking of your father?" a young man asked over his shoulder.

Startled, Rashid looked up, questioning.

"I think of my father too when I come to the mosque. He was killed. The Americans and their Israeli lapdogs bombed our neighborhood."

Rashid put his hand to his heart in sympathy. "I'm sorry."

The man looked at Rashid intently. Without a word, he seemed to look not just at Rashid's appearance, but through him, into his thoughts, into the confusion in his heart.

Rashid shifted his weight uncomfortably, stepped back on the carpeted floor.

"I'm Ali," the younger man finally smiled, offering his hand.

Rashid heard Ali's Palestinian accent, unusual among the south Asians who usually came to this mosque. "I'm Rashid." He took Ali's hand.

"Yes," Ali pumped his hand up and down. "Pakistani, yes?"

Rashid nodded.

"Good. And your father?"

"He was killed by the Americans too."

Ali clenched his fist, inhaled deeply. "Come, let us have tea, we have many things in common."

Rashid looked up from the refrigerator drawer as Kathryn came in. "You let these vegetables rot while I was offshore?"

She walked in with Michael clutching at her thigh. "Hello," she reached out to kiss Rashid, determined to ignore his comment. Michael laughed and ran into the living room, jumping into a pile of laundry on the floor. "Michael," she scolded.

"I washed the fucking clothes."

"Rashid, we're not rig workers, you don't need to swear."

"Anyway," he said, "they're clean." He threw the rotten vegetables in the trash with a disgusted snort.

"Remember the ACLU guy I told you about?" she asked. "He's got some ideas about organizations that are following the drone issue."

"So?" He brought a pan of scrambled eggs and store-bought rotis to the table. Michael came to his side, freshly laundered adult socks on his hands, each attempting to eat the other amidst a series of childish roars.

"He wrote about Guantanamo Bay for the journal last year," Kathryn said setting Michael in his chair, baby Andrew in his swing.

"What's Guantanamo?" Michael asked, holding his roti up with both hands, flapping it back and forth against his forehead.

"Michael, don't play with your food." She poured herself a glass of water. "It's a place in Cuba where the U.S. is holding people from other countries that our government thinks are dangerous."

"The guy from San Francisco?" Rashid asked, eating his dinner.

"Yeah." She took a big gulp of water.

"So what?" Rashid said indifferently.

Michael had set his roti on top of his eggs, obscuring them completely. "Why Cuba? Is Cuba far away from the U.S. so we'll be safe?"

"Michael, *please*. I'm trying to talk to your father, we'll talk about Cuba later."

"Why can't *we* talk about the ACLU later?" Rashid's food was already half eaten, his father had always taught them to eat first, talk later.

"I want to tell you before they call you for another job."

"Tell me what?"

"The ACLU's director might bring a suit in the International Court of Justice in the Hague."

"So what?" he said again.

"So what?" she said stunned. "Have you forgotten what we've been trying to do? Somebody has to take a stand against this undeclared war we're waging along the border in Pakistan."

"Stop fucking saying 'we'."

"Well it's our country. Like during the Vietnam War, we were secretly bombing Cambodia. Students protested at universities across the U.S., Kent State in Ohio."

"And did the protests stop the war, or the secret bombing?" Rashid sounded almost belligerent.

"Not immediately. But they were pivotal. If we could be named plaintiffs we could be involved in the suit." She felt the burn of the green chilies in the eggs.

Rashid inhaled, shook his head. "A waste of time, this will take years. Even if you can bring a suit, who says you'll win?"

"But the government needs to be held accountable for its actions. Thousands of predator drone attacks in Pakistan since 2001 have killed more than thirty-thousand people." She looked away from Rashid, noticed Michael sitting still in his chair. "Michael, finish your dinner."

"Do as your mother says," Rashid scolded.

"If we're involved in some kind of litigation, we can show that this military action isn't just unconstitutional, without the approval of Congress, but effects U.S. citizens directly."

"Kathryn," he sighed, "since when has the U.S. government cared about what the International Criminal Court says? It hasn't changed the U.S. policy in Israel and Palestine."

"Why are you fighting me on this? I thought you agreed with me."

"Go ahead. Call those people if you want." Rashid picked up his plate, set it on the counter with a bang, and walked out of the room.

Kathryn exhaled, suddenly exhausted. "At least I am trying to do something," she muttered to herself.

"Mummy, can a language make you angry?"

"What do you mean?"

"I mean when I hear Daddy on the phone speaking that other language he sounds angry. Can it do that?"

"When did he sound angry?"

"Today." Michael picked at his food.

"Someone called him?"

Michael nodded.

"Who?"

Michael shrugged.

"Words can make you angry, not just a language, but words… for sure."

Once the children were asleep, Rashid surprised Kathryn with a bottle of Scotch. He poured himself a small glass of the golden liquid and slowly sipped. He motioned for her to sit next to him.

"You want me to drink with you?" she asked.

"Yes, please. You won't nurse until morning. I need to relax, it's all so serious." He smiled, and for a moment she glimpsed the old Rashid of the discos.

"OK, just a minute." She pressed her hands into his shoulders, squeezing him into waiting. In the bathroom she combed her hair, removed the cloth diaper over her shoulder that had become a permanent fixture of her wardrobe and even sprayed perfume. She raised an eyebrow, smiled at herself in the mirror, and turned sideways trying to smooth her belly into pre-pregnancy form.

She returned to him, he smiled at her fragrance. He pulled out a chair for her and offered her a drink.

"Cheers," she said as they toasted. Kathryn felt the Scotch burn, the gentle buzz strangely out of place without the thumping beats of their night-clubbing life. She reached out to him, running her hands up the length of his thighs. The same pleasure in his form, his strength, that she had initially felt, flickered back into flame in her body.

He met her hands with his, interlacing their fingers. Silently confirming he loved her, he stopped her overture.

She raised an eyebrow in question.

"I just wish I wasn't in this position," he said, as if picking up the thread of some previous conversation.

When he didn't elaborate, she asked, "What position? Sitting in this chair?"

"No, in this position of obligation."

"Obligation to who?"

"To my family, actually, to my mother."

"We're all obligated to our families. That's the nature of the relationship."

"Yes, but this obligation feels so big, like it fills my whole sky, my whole future," he looked directly into her eyes, trying to gauge her understanding, then consumed the rest of his glass in a single gulp, grimacing in pain.

"What are you talking about?" Her voice trembled briefly.

He stood up and walked to the window, looked out into the impotent darkness of the city with its perpetually bright streetlights. "What happens in this country to a man when he kills another man?"

Caught off guard, she hesitated. "He's put on trial. If the jury finds him guilty he goes to jail."

"And?"

"And what?"

He tapped on the window, as if punctuating some idea beyond the glass. "And then the state takes its revenge, by taking the life of the murderer."

"No, that's not revenge, that's a deterrent, a lesson to other would-be murderers not to do the same thing."

"OK, call it a deterrent. But it's a punishment, a price that the responsible party has to pay, isn't it?"

"I guess. What does this have to do with anything?"

"It has to do with everything. Just listen." He mapped out with his hands two different territories. "What happens in America when another country attacks and kills people, murders Americans?" With a fist, he smacked into the palm of the other territory.

"Well, after Pearl Harbor, we joined the war against Japan and the Germans."

"And American soldiers did what?"

"Went to war…"

"And killed people, they took revenge for those murders, in other countries."

An unfamiliar defensiveness crept into her voice. "Why would you call that revenge? That's war. We had to make them stop. You can't just go into another country and attack their people."

"And how did the Americans eventually make it stop? How does a country take its revenge?"

She paused, uncomfortable with the reality of the answer she had to acknowledge.

He answered for her. "The Americans made it stop by attacking Japan, by killing millions of people in Japan, innocent people, dropping an atomic bomb."

She looked up, stricken.

"I'm not saying it was wrong. The Americans had to do it, they were attacked, they had to take revenge. It's human. Revenge satisfies the anger of grieving people, it's inevitable."

Adrenaline shot through her body at some nebulous danger. "No." She stood up, stepped unsteadily toward him. "Revenge just perpetuates a cycle of killing, we didn't go to war for revenge. We're not that kind of people. We went to war on principle, to stop a greater evil."

He inclined his head, as if to consider her position as he returned to his chair, sat down and poured himself another drink.

"And tell me, Kathryn, tell me how much the killing has stopped because of the Americans' actions? Because of wars of principle?"

She felt a chill in her veins.

"Vietnam. Cambodia. Iraq. Afghanistan." He paused and said one more word with infinite tenderness. "Pakistan."

"We're not at war with Pakistan, Rashid."

He looked up at her, raising an incredulous eyebrow. "Tell that to my mother, to my brothers."

She suddenly perceived a border between them, where before there had been none. "It's not my fault. There was nothing I could've done to prevent your father's death." She tried to reach across the divide with some reason, some idea that would comfort them, unite them. "America's trying to eliminate the camps that train terrorists."

"I never said it was your fault. This kind of killing, it is written," he drew his index finger across his forehead in the habit of Muslims referring to fate. "It is written," he said again drawing his finger across her forehead, causing a shiver along her spine.

"Nothing is written, Rashid. Revenge wouldn't make your father come back. Understand what happened…was an accident."

He pulled his hand away, his eyes grew wide with anger. "An accident!? Fucking hell."

She flinched, tears dropped on her cheeks.

"In my culture, revenge is a personal thing," he said, beginning to slur his words. "When a man kills, he knows that he may look the dead man's family in the eye, just before they kill him. That's a deterrent."

"What are you saying?" she whispered. "What do you mean?"

"My family expects revenge."

"We," she paused, flaring her nostrils, "we are your family."

He looked at her, his eyes roving over every point on her face.

He nodded, almost imperceptibly. "But how can I accept that this is my country?"

———————

In the morning he did not wake as the sun stretched across the bed. She turned to see him, both boys held fast in his embrace, one in each arm.

She ran her fingers along the contours of his arms. She marveled at their mutual connection. Maybe everything would be fine. She willed herself not to replay their words from the previous night.

She rose stiffly, went to the kitchen. Defiantly, she broke eggs into a bowl, chopped chilies and onions and tomatoes. She kneaded flour and water into dough, struggling to roll out round rotis, a skill she still had yet to master. She prepared his breakfast, Pakistani style.

As she chopped the cilantro, Rashid emerged from the bedroom, groggy and grumpy, grey from the previous night's alcohol.

The chai. She had forgotten the chai. No Pakistani breakfast would be complete without the sweet milky tea. She poured him a big glass of water. "Sit, wait while I boil the milk for tea." He did not speak, capitulated to her instructions.

Just as the milk nearly boiled over the rim of the pot, Michael padded into the room, his hair tumbling over his forehead. "What's that smell?"

"Breakfast," Kathryn said and kissed him on the forehead, a wooden spoon still in her hand.

"What kind of breakfast?" He walked to Rashid, struggled to climb into his father's lap.

Rashid leaned back, allowed the boy up. He closed his eyes and inhaled deeply. "Breakfast like I ate when I was a boy like you," he said. But the aromas, incomplete without the smell of burning cow dung, exhaust from the generator down the street, the rose smell of his mother's hair oil, only heightened his sense of dislocation. No matter how she tried, Kathryn could only produce a simulacrum of the land still embedded in his heart.

The baby whimpered, then let out a full fledged cry. Rashid slid Michael off his lap and they walked hand-in-hand to the bedroom. They emerged a moment later, Rashid quieting the baby in his arms and Michael tickling his brother's feet.

They all sat down together before this unusually elaborate breakfast. Kathryn told Rashid and Michael to eat as she tucked the baby's head under her shirt to suckle. For an instant all was right in her world, her entire family's needs met. What more could be required of her? What more could she possibly do?

Chapter 10

With no client jobs listed on the schedule board, Rashid's day would be filled with routine maintenance around the base. He fished his phone out of the pocket of his coveralls, dialed Ali's number. "*Salaam aleikum*," he said perfunctorily. "Ali, did I see you at my house yesterday?" He looked around to be sure he was alone. "How do you know where I live?" He fiddled nervously with the spare rubber o-rings in his pocket as he listened. "My brother?... Look I don't understand what you're doing, but I don't want you anywhere near my wife and children." He listened for a long time and restlessly kicked his steel-toed boots against the floor. Finally he spoke again. "Whatever I decide to do, you don't ever mention my family again... Yes, it *is* still my decision."

Kathryn returned to her desk, skimmed through the latest updates from Jane's Defense Weekly, the Economist Intelligence Unit. These might have included a mention of a drone attack, but foreign names would be included only if they controlled ministries, wielded power with opposition forces or invested significantly in industry or technology. She discretely felt her breasts. Four hours had passed since she nursed Andrew. She would have to pump. She stood up and closed her door, turned off her computer screen, so she could ignore the news of distant conflicts. A quick swivel of her chair allowed her a view of the small courtyard where colleagues sometimes went to smoke amidst the giant planters of well-tended shrubs and flowers.

She lifted her sweater and began the familiar process. Tiny jets of milk filled the baby bottle in her hand. She gazed out the window. No one had ever explained to her the slavish commitment required to feed a baby. Without fail, she had produced milk at regular intervals—never more than six hours apart—to a being who could not even form a single word to ask for it.

The phone on her desk rang, and she paused for a minute, irritated at the disturbance. She hit the little orange button. "Hello, this is Kathryn Siddique," she said mustering up her most professional demeanor.

"Kathryn, it's me. Rashid," his words sounded clipped, rushed.

"Rashid," she said relieved, "Where are you?"

"Where are *you*?"

"What do you mean? You called me at my office." She screwed the top on the bottle of milk—still warm from her body—and pulled her sweater down. "What's happening?

"Are you pumping?"

"Yeah, why?"

"In your office?"

"Rashid," her tone rose, "I always pump in my office."

"Why is your fucking shade open?" he sounded almost panicked.

Kathryn looked at the blinds she never closed. Beyond the window a young man picked at leaves from the shrub next to him, seemed to look directly at her. She pulled the little metal chain to draw the blinds across the window. "Why are you asking me this Rashid?"

"Goddammit, Kathryn, you don't have to do everything out in the open."

"Don't start," she lowered her voice to an angry whisper, "don't lecture me, I'm at the office, doing my job, and being a mother, and trying to handle what's going on with you. What more do you want from me?"

He exhaled, thinking angrily of the text Ali had just sent him.

How dare he mention his son's mother's milk? "Just keep your blinds closed. Be careful Kathryn."

"Of what?" She pulled back the blinds, on the now empty courtyard.

"Kathryn, I love you."

"I love you too," she said, puzzled. "That's not the point here."

"I'll see you at home."

With a jagged sense of incompleteness she zipped up the thermal lunch bag with the bottles of her milk inside.

Rashid pressed the buzzer on the intercom outside Michael's school, grateful for the locked door protecting his son. He looked into the security camera, heard the buzz as the door unlocked. He practically bolted inside the school.

He looked anxiously around Michael's classroom until he recognized his dark-haired son. "Michael," he called out, oblivious about whether or not he was interrupting. Michael hesitated, surprised to see his father before the end of the school day. "Why are you here?" he asked.

"To…pick you up," Rashid sounded unconvinced of his own reason. He gestured with his hands to coax Michael toward him. "We're letting your Mummy finish her work. *Chelo* beta, come, hurry. Let's get your things and go and pick up your baby brother."

"And Mummy will come home?"

"Of course." Michael ran into his father's arms and wouldn't let go. Rashid held Michael tightly, relieved.

"I like it best when we're all together," Michael said, pulling on his father's earlobe, smelling his familiar musky perfume.

"Hmm," Rashid affirmed. "Family's the most important thing. We all feel better when we're with our parents, isn't it?"

"Hi," Kathryn said cheerfully into her phone. "What's up?"

"Um…the client has called in a big offshore job," Rashid said. "It could be five or six days that I'm away."

"Again?" she groaned. "You'll miss the parent-teacher conferences on Tuesday."

"Can you go by yourself?"

"I don't have a choice, do I?"

"This is a big job, the bonus should be good," he didn't sound convinced.

She sighed with resignation. "I'll miss you."

"Wish me luck," he said distractedly. And with a businesslike tone, "I have to come home for extra coveralls. I can stop at the store first, do you need anything? Milk, eggs, anything?"

She rattled off a handful of items. "Thanks for taking care of that, for taking care of us," she said.

"Oh God," he sighed, "I'm trying."

Chapter II

The day of the bombing

The next morning Kathryn walked out of the daycare, feeling the lightness of moving without a child in her arms.

A helicopter flew overhead, traveling west over the freeway. Inside the car she turned up the radio. "...with traffic backed up in both east and westbound lanes on the 10 from Santa Monica to Hollywood. The 405 interchange has been closed as emergency vehicles are clearing debris..."

She reached into her purse for her sunglasses, realized she had forgotten the empty baby bottles she would need to pump later in the day. Shit. Every day she overlooked one thing; the laundry still damp in the machine, the call to building maintenance to fix the disposal, the permission slip for Michael's field trip. How could she be expected to remember everything? She checked her watch. She would still have enough time to swing by home and pick up the bottles before her scheduled call with the managing editor.

"...live reports confirm that the problem on the 10 and 405 freeways was caused by a major explosion in an SUV early this morning. We have no information yet on whether the explosion was intentional, or if so, who caused it..."

She was grateful she wouldn't have to drive anywhere near the traffic.

"…CHP reports at least four confirmed fatalities…"

She was relieved to turn off the car in the parking garage and stop the news.

In the kitchen, she realized why she had forgotten the bottles, she had neglected to wash the used ones from the day before, so they weren't ready in the dish rack for her. Just as the bubbles from the dish soap were overflowing out of the bottle, the phone rang. She fished it out of her purse, craned her neck so she could hold it between her ear and her shoulder and attempted to finish the washing.

"Hello," she said curtly. Her husband's manager identified himself and after a moment she paused in her washing, trying to understand the meaning of his words.

"So you don't know where he is?" the man repeated, with some urgency.

"What do you mean?" Kathryn answered into the phone, soap bubbles dripping off her hand into the kitchen sink. "*You* scheduled his offshore job. He told me he'd be gone for a week or so."

Kathryn dried her hands and called her husband's phone number. She listened. Hung up and dialed again, irritated. She heard a knock at the door.

She opened the door wide to reveal a Caucasian man dressed in a suit.

"Hello?" She closed the door back down to a few inches.

"Excuse me, ma'am," he checked the number on the outside of the door. "I'm looking for Mrs. Siddique."

"I *am* Mrs. Siddique."

He scanned her face. "Yes. Mrs. Siddique, I'd like to ask you a few questions." He flashed a badge, "Agent Roberts, Federal Bureau of Investigation."

"Why are you here?" she closed the door a little more.

"Rashid Siddique is your husband?"

"You seem to know that already."

"Where is he right now?"

"Working."

Silence.

He raised his hand, opened his fingers to reveal a ring, a yellow gold band resting on his palm.

"I think you recognize this ring Mrs. Siddique?"

The blood drained from her face. "Where did you get that? Is Rashid all right?"

"I think you'd better let me come in."

She stepped aside, motioning for the man to come inside and sit on the couch. She would miss the scheduled call with her managing editor. As the stranger sat down, the room appeared suddenly unfamiliar, unfriendly. She sat across from him in a chair, unable to sit back.

"This ring was found early this morning, inside the remains of an SUV at the scene of the bombing."

"The bombing…?" she echoed

"Yes, the bombing on the 10 freeway."

"The accident?"

"It was no accident. An SUV packed with fertilizer bombs exploded canisters of nails and ball bearings. A cell phone set off a detonator, a type of detonator common in the petroleum industry. Mrs. Siddique, your husband is dead. I need to understand how he was involved."

Part Two

The Book of Kathryn

Chapter I

The day of the bombing

I refuse to believe this man. He is not welcome here, he does not speak any truth I understand.

"Where was your husband in the last few days?"

"Offshore. On a rig, an oil rig. It's his job."

"When was the last time you spoke with him?"

"Yesterday."

"Do you know if your husband was associating with Islamic radicals?"

"What? What are you insinuating? Just because someone is a Muslim doesn't mean he's a terrorist."

I look again at the ring in my palm and see the gold shop where I bought it, remember writing down on a piece of paper *Beneath the Same Heaven*. I think I am going to vomit. "Excuse me," I say to the man who has thankfully stopped talking. I leave the ring on the arm of the sofa. I barely make it to the bathroom before the heaving starts. Tears are running down my face from the effort. He knocks on the door.

"Mrs. Siddique, are you all right?"

My God, what a question.

"I'm sorry Mrs. Siddique, but I'll need to bring you in for questioning."

"Give me a minute." I rinse my mouth, wash my face. I don't

even recognize the contorted face in the mirror, the trembling hand opening the door.

The man is sitting again on the edge of the couch. "I'll go with you," I tell him. "But I have to get something from the kitchen first." I return to the baby bottles in the sink, carefully rinsing off every tiny bubble, trying to buy myself some time to think. I return to the living room, a bottle in each hand. The man, he is really very ugly with his pasty skin and balding head, looks at me strangely. "I have a baby," I explain. "He'll need his milk."

Hours later, in the afternoon light, I close the car door and scream, not the scream of childbirth, not the scream of nightclub frenzy; but the scream of a woman becoming a widow.

The bomb has exploded in my life. The buildings I see are intact, the traffic still stops and starts on the streets around me, my skin and bones are unharmed, but the very fibers that held my life together— the threads of love and trust that bound me—have all been rent today.

The shrill ring of the phone rattles the charged silence in the car. I can see my mother's number on the screen. I am paralyzed, cannot possibly speak to her now. I will have to hurry to pick up the children in time. Michael's school will cancel his afterschool enrollment if I'm late three times.

I take a deep breath, blow my nose and wipe my eyes, and turn the key in the ignition. The radio blares to life. "...at this point, we cannot be certain that the bombers are affiliated with Al-Qaeda, or if they are homegrown terrorists. But we do know that both men, identified as Ali Al-Hassam and Rashid Siddique were both Muslim immigrants..." I slam my fist into the radio, turn it off. I power down the phone before I shift the car into gear.

Clutching Michael's hand, we walk down the hall of the daycare and a couple of mothers greet me warmly, balancing babies and diaper bags. The late-shift caregivers in the infant room are wiping the counter clear and straightening up the empty play area. I see no babies.

"Don't worry, Andrew's sleeping in the crib room," one of the caregivers responds to my alarmed look. "Hi Michael," she rustles his hair. She doesn't know yet. She still sees me as the woman I was yesterday. I take off my shoes and pad across the carpet to retrieve my beloved sleeping baby from his assigned crib.

I inhale his smell and resist my tears. The caregivers are waiting for me so they can go home. I return and retrieve from my purse the single bottle I was able to pump today. I take two empty bottles from Andrew's designated space in the refrigerator. "Stressful day," I explain to the caregiver. She nods kindly.

Back at home, I move ceaselessly. As long as I can keep moving, as long as the children are happy and the food is on the table and the laundry is in the dryer and the bottles are washed and my hair is washed and the diaper bag is emptied and the bills are opened and sorted...the day didn't really happen. Just before I sleep, I turn the phone back on and check my messages. I sit down with a pen and paper. The first is from my managing editor wondering if I will be able to make the call we had scheduled for ten minutes prior to his message, then another suggesting a time tomorrow to reschedule. I write down the time he suggests as a reminder.

The next is from my mother. "Kathryn?" I can hear the concern in her voice. "I'm just calling to see how you're doing, and the children. We haven't heard from you this week. Please give me a call as soon as you're able."

With each new message, I hope that it will be Rashid's voice, I hope that somehow, some digital representation of my husband will come through this little plastic device and restore my world to me.

Next is a friend I have known for more than a decade, but have hardly had a chance to speak to since Andrew was born. She asks how I am doing, trying to sound interested but not alarmed. She knows.

The next message is a reminder from the car dealership to schedule an oil change.

Then my mother again, "Kathryn, please call. We, uh, we've seen the news, and we're worried about you. Please call as soon as you can. We love you."

I don't need to turn on the news to know where I fit in the 24-hour news channels and the conflict-fuelled talk shows. The misguided victim wife, the naïve innocent abroad who was deceived into marriage and unwittingly helped facilitate this monstrous act.

And a final message, "Kathryn, your father and I would feel better if we know you're not alone. We've booked the first flight in the morning. We'll take a taxi from the airport. Please call as soon as you can."

I check the clock, past midnight. I pour myself a scotch trying to calm my nerves. I pour myself a second and then unplug the television and turn off the lights. I pull back the covers and am overwhelmed with feeling for my two sons who will grow up into men in this complicated, critical, cryptic world. I wiggle in between them, feeling their bodies on both sides of me. I hold their tiny hands for protection—whether for their protection or my own I am not sure.

The phone alarm trills again in the morning at the usual hour. I wake, and for one delicious moment, I experience the hope and freshness that accompany new beginnings the world over. I look at the boys, curled up against me, their skin radiant, their expressions peaceful. The bed is so spacious when Rashid is away on a job. And then I remember. The memory of the previous day's events comes crashing down like a guillotine, severing my future from my past.

I hear the birds outside the window, I hear the cars on the street. The world outside remains unchanged, but for the life of my husband. And the lives of the others who were killed. The thought of the others is too much for me to bear. I don't know them, I have not seen their faces, have not loved them, have not built a family with them.

Andrew stirs. His eyes open and I see them so clearly. They turn immediately to me and seem to reflect some deep understanding. This disturbs me, as if this baby, who has no language, no knowledge of how the world works, of how we deceive ourselves, has comprehended what has happened in our lives. His lips quiver and before the cry comes I move to him so he can nurse. I feel the milk come in, the relief that always comes with this transaction. But the relief reaches only to my stomach where it confronts a mass, a hardness, tightness in the muscles, pain. I resist the pain, try to divert my attention by thinking ahead. I have a lot to do today, I will get up and make my list even before I go to the office, so I won't forget anything. I wish Andrew would hurry up and finish.

The phone rings, triggering a surge of adrenaline. I pick it up, hoping for some good news. An unfamiliar number appears on the screen. Without pausing, I answer, thinking maybe, by some miracle, Rashid is calling me from a payphone somewhere. "Hello?" I say quietly, so I won't wake Michael.

"Hello, is this Mrs. Siddique?" a man says. The man is not Rashid.

"Who is this?"

"My name is John Carter, I'm a reporter with the *New York Times*, and I'm trying to reach the wife of Rashid Siddique."

My heart beats furiously. My mind races for an answer.

"Hello? Is this Mrs. Siddique?"

"It…you…this…you have the wrong number." I hang up the phone. My eyes scan the room. The phone rings again. The same number appears on the screen. I do not answer it. I realize with a sinking feeling that after enough rings my recorded voice will confidently confirm he has reached the line of Kathryn Siddique and I would like him to please leave a message. Silence. Andrew tugs at his toes and his sleeves. Michael groans and stretches his legs long. The phone rings again. I power down the phone. I lay there, imagining how many other reporters, law enforcement officials, gawkers will hunt me down, will press me for information, vent their outrage and confusion and grief at me.

Someone knocks on the door. Finally, I leave the bed. Pulling back the kitchen blinds, I see three television news vans parked on the street, neighbors talking into reporters' microphones. I shut the blinds. I check both door locks are turned, the shades are pulled. And then I pretend. I wash the baby's face and bottom, I dress him in clean clothes. The knocking continues. "Just ignore it," I tell Michael, hugging him and helping him dress himself. He chatters away about the lives of his toys, the shoes he wants that light up when you jump.

I set Michael in front of a bowl of Cheerios, Andrew into his swing with an assortment of toys before I shower. With only the usual interruptions of spilled juice and frustrated cries over dropped toys, I dress myself as if we were preparing for any other day. The knocking continues.

"Kathryn?" a woman's voice calls. "Kathryn, it's your parents."

Michael jumps down from his chair, turns the knobs and dead-bolts in the incorrect order, hopping with excitement. "It sounds like Grandma. Did you know Grandma was coming?"

"Go back," I command him. I slowly turn the locks, open the door just wide enough to allow my parents in. I hide from the cameras pointed in my direction.

Michael jumps at my father, who stoically hugs my son. Andrew squeals from the swing for attention. And I burst into tears. How fragile are my defenses. How ill equipped I am to handle any of this.

My mother reaches her arms round me, worry wrinkles her face, ages her. And I am a child again, wishing that she could cure all of this with a band aid and a kiss. She holds me for a long time, practically holds me up as I sink my weight against her. She says quietly into my ear, "What have you told Michael?"

"Nothing," I whisper. "He thinks Rashid is away on a long job." I pull back and wipe my tears. Michael, at my side, looks perplexed, seeks clues from the three of us adults about how he should feel.

"OK Michael, let's brush your teeth," I say. "We don't want to be late for school."

"But Mom, Grandma and Grandpa just got here."

"They'll be here when you get home from school. Don't worry," I say for my benefit as much as his.

My mother takes his hand. "I will help you," his face lights up. "You show me which toothbrush is yours."

My father kneels down to kiss Andrew on the head. Habitually, I push the swing back and forth and wonder what to say. My father puts his arms around me, quickly hugs me as if to confirm he is in my corner, and immediately launches into questions over the baby's head with a businesslike efficiency.

"Do you have a lawyer?"

"No, what for? Do I need a lawyer?"

"OK, I have a friend I'll contact. Make sure you don't say anything to those news reporters gathering outside. What's your financial situation? Did Rashid have a life insurance policy?"

"Uh, I think so, maybe through his company." I am off guard. "Dad, I'm still not sure he is dead."

"Really, why do you say that? What do you know? What did you know?"

"I didn't know, I don't know anything. I haven't seen a body. Only his wedding ring that the FBI showed me."

"What did you say to the FBI? What kinds of questions did they ask you?"

For a moment I feel something like pride. "I didn't tell them anything they couldn't have found out from public records. I told them how we met, that I visited his family in Pakistan. I told them that we had a wedding in Lahore and that you and Mom and Ted were there. They insisted that…"

"You told them I was in Pakistan?"

"Yes. Why wouldn't I?"

He looks down and runs his fingers through his hair, letting out a long exhale. "People in certain policy circles might think it not so wise that I was in Pakistan at that time in our relationship with them."

"Dad," my voice rises, suddenly defensive, "they would be able to see that in your passport. The American Chamber ran a little blurb in their newsletter. It was hardly confidential."

The baby's swing has stilled.

"All right, never mind about that. What about your finances, do you have enough to live on for a while?"

"Rashid is always very careful about the money, so I think I have enough for about six months, longer if I keep working."

Michael returns with a big smile, my mother's hand protectively on his shoulder. "Are you ready to take Michael to school?" she asks.

"Yes, thanks for helping with his teeth." I gather up the children's bags, grateful for a mundane task.

"I'll go with you," my father says decisively. "Margaret, you stay here."

"Can't Grandma come with us too?" Michael complains.

"No beta…no Michael," I tell him, the Urdu word suddenly foreign in my mouth, "it will be too crowded with all of us in the car."

In the car, my father, eerily reserved, responds only occasionally to the questions Michael asks. We all walk together into the day care center, me, a woman sandwiched between two generations of family. Once I point down the hall to direct my father, he takes the lead, walking at a dignified pace, chin up, the hard leather of his heels clicking precisely on the linoleum floor. I don't look at the other mother who passes me, she hardly notices me behind the unfamiliar man. He opens the door to the infant room for me, bright tissue paper flowers rustle against his shoulder as he makes way for me. The caregiver looks up, I see a smile flicker over her face before she recognizes me, and her expression goes cold. She makes no conversation as she takes the baby. I introduce the man behind me as my father. They nod at each other, but do not speak. She looks in the baby's eyes so she need not face me again. She has seen the news. I am now the woman from the news, a woman to be feared or pitied, but not a woman to talk with or joke with, not the woman I was before.

I walk back the way I came in, protected by my father. In the car my father still does not speak. I pretend again. I cheerfully walk Michael to the door of the school, kneel down to give him a hug. He smiles, turns to join his classmates. Will they know? Will his teachers know? Will they see him differently as well? I have to tell him something. What? By tonight.

My father has moved to the drivers' seat. He waits until he has pulled away from the school, the car seats both empty behind us, before he speaks. "You do understand how serious this is, don't you?"

I only nod.

"The FBI may give you a day or so of freedom, may seem to be leaving you alone. But they will be watching your every move, they will tap every call, they will monitor every email. You are now a terrorist's wife."

My throat constricts, my breathing nearly stops.

He looks in the rearview mirror, quickly turns down a side street and pulls up alongside a bank with a courtyard. The fountain in the center perpetually spouts a great column of water that falls back on itself in predictably chaotic forms. He parks the car.

"Come and sit with me."

I sit stunned, my father politely opens the door for me, helps me out. I am embarrassed by his chivalry. We walk and he motions for me to sit on a public bench with a view of the fountain.

He smoothes his hair, then sits with his hands in his lap. "Perhaps they have already placed a microphone in your car. I want to be sure we won't be overheard."

I look back at the car, pull my purse protectively onto my lap.

"Listen Kathryn, you know how much we love you. I'll do whatever's in my power to help you. I'll call in every favor, contact any person I know, go to any lengths to protect you. But I need to know exactly how you're involved. I need to know exactly what you know. You need to tell me anything Rashid said to you in the last weeks and months."

I clench my fists to hold the tears back. The water splashes, sounding like flesh hitting flesh. I let my breath out silently.

"Now don't cry, we're just having a conversation here. Just look at the fountain if you need to, and tell me what you know."

"Rashid had talked about revenge," I say slowly, wondering if I am betraying him. "He talked about the way a country takes revenge when its people are killed."

"When did he talk about that?"

"After his father was killed. He'd been quiet for weeks, been visiting the mosque in the mornings. I thought it was his process of mourning."

"Which mosque?"

"I didn't ask. I assumed the Pakistani mosque in Artesia. Michael went with him once."

My father presses his palms together. He almost looks like he is going to pray. "Did he have any new friends he spoke of, any people he went to see in the mosque?"

I feel my muscles tighten at this second interrogation.

"I need to understand how they'll accuse him, how you'll be implicated."

"He never mentioned anyone. Only Michael told me he saw Rashid speaking angrily with another man when he went with his father." I look at my father, alarmed. "Don't let them question Michael. He doesn't know anything. He's just a child."

"Don't worry. No one can talk to Michael without your permission. And how did Rashid treat you and the children? Did he act strangely? Was he gone at unusual times?"

"He's always gone at unusual times. That's the nature of his job." My voice grows shrill.

"And how was he around you and the children?"

I am silent remembering warmth, the feel of his skin, the heft of his limbs, the darkness of his hair. And then a stone cold numbness.

My father holds my hand. "I'm so sorry," he says offering me a handkerchief from his breast pocket.

I can't match my father's stoicism. I bury my face against his chest. He places an arm around me in a rigid gesture of comfort. He smells like wool and starched cotton. "How could he do something like this?" I sob, then catch myself, pull away, smooth the handkerchief in my hands. "Perhaps he has done nothing."

"Kathryn, unfortunately, this is not an unusual story for a Pakistani man."

I look away.

"I lived around these kinds of cultures long enough to know about revenge. When a man's family member is killed, he's obligated. The events that can unfold from that death are inexorable. What's unusual, he was a Pakistani man in America, with an American wife. But he was Muslim, went to the mosque, it will be understood here as Islamic terrorism. Plays right into the story that we understand… Islamic cultures are barbaric. Muslims are heartless. They're not like us, we're justified in invading and bombing their countries."

I look at my watch. "I have to call my editor," I'm suddenly rushing. "I have a meeting." My father sits quietly while I dial the number. I fish a notebook and my pen out of my bag.

"Hi Jerome, it's Kathryn. Sorry I wasn't able to make our call yesterday…Yes, I'm fine," I say stiffly. "…But Rashid has no role with the journal. *I* work for the journal…What do you mean, problematic?…Administrative leave?"

I let the phone drop to my lap. It remains illuminated for a few seconds before going dark.

My father looks at me. "The journal is letting you go?"

I shake my head, looking down at my feet. Then slowly, queasily, I flip my notebook shut, slide my pen into the spiral binding and return it to my purse. "No one will assume I am innocent, will they, Dad?"

"You don't need me to tell you terrorism has united us as Americans."

Terrorism. The word. I hate it. I hear it come from my father's mouth, I know it is somehow linked to my husband's actions, I feel it beginning to shred the fibers of my heart.

"And I'm afraid, Kathryn, you cannot expect that anyone will treat you generously in this situation."

I am sitting next to this man, but he is completely separate from me. I am alone, an island, no longer connected to the people and things that once held me in place. Only my children will anchor me now. What do I call them now? If I am widowed, are they orphaned? Half-orphaned?

"What should I do? What about the children?" I ask.

He looks past the fountain as if trying to divine a path to safety. Two starlings dive past each other, darting back up at the last minute, startling a few sparrows that have come to dip their beaks in the edge of the fountain.

He helps me stand, a protective arm around my shoulder. He has no answer.

My father navigates through the thicket of reporters that have gathered outside the parking garage. My mother opens the door before we even reach it as if pulling us to safety. She has found the one apron I own—she must have looked through every cupboard. She looks up and down the hall.

"I thought you might be Ted." My mother smiles at me as if I were just coming home from school and she had been expecting me with an afternoon snack.

"Ted?" I haven't thought of my older brother since my world capsized.

"I called him," my mother says gathering three coffee cups. "I asked him to come up from San Diego, because I thought we should all be together." She pours the coffee, the milk, and the sugar, remembering the exact proportions my father and I prefer.

I wrap my hands around the mug, trying to absorb some comfort through the ceramic. She rests her hand on mine, looks into my eyes. "Michael needs to know, Kathy."

I nod, I know that this is as important as the legal and logistical questions my father has asked, maybe even more so. I swirl the coffee in the cup.

"No good can come from keeping this from them."

"But what can I say? Michael won't understand what's happened, why his father's done this. *If* he's done this."

"You need to explain why his father's not coming home. Better he hears something from you than something from his classmates or his teachers."

There is a knock on the door. My mother calmly moves to the door, and calls out before opening it. "Who's there?" as if a neighbor might be coming asking to borrow a cup of sugar.

"It's Ted."

I exhale as the door opens.

My brother now has a few grey hairs in his goatee, a few more pounds around his middle than when I last saw him. Why do I feel disappointed when others age? Why do I wish for some impossible immortal stability?

He hugs my mother and then my father perfunctorily before taking three strides with his long legs and sitting down opposite me. "So…what kind of clusterfuck do we have going on here?"

He is so without angst, so-matter-of-fact that I let out a guffaw, part laugh, part sob.

"So, I know that Rashid went back to Pakistan to bury his old man. Thank you, American-military-industrial complex. And then, what, he decides to repay the favor? Avenging hero? And in the process my little sister and their kids are gonna get screwed."

My parents know Ted's irreverence well enough not to contradict him. Our mother speaks first, "We were talking about what she should tell Michael."

"Oh man," Ted says, accepting a cup of coffee from our mother. "I'm so sorry. This is such a shitty situation for you. Your husband tries to blow up a freeway—wouldn't we all love to do that sometimes—but it's not only really stupid, but by the way illegal and morally reprehensible, and now you get to figure out how to explain that to a kid."

He takes a sip of coffee and nods at our mother. "Where does Michael think he is now?"

"Rashid told us he had a big offshore job in Ventura. I expected he'd be gone about a week," I say.

"And Michael's cool with that? He doesn't think anything's up?"

I sip my coffee. "Maybe."

Ted pauses. "Just tell him there was an accident on the oil platform and his father's been blasted to smithereens." He narrates my situation as if it were a cartoon.

I see my mother glance to my father for his reaction.

"I can't do that. I can't make up such a lie," I protest.

"Why not? It's not so far fetched, oil is dangerous business. Explosives, pressure, radioactive tools, poisonous sulfur gas in the wells. Tell the story so it has shades of truth. Maybe say he was coming back from a job and he made a mistake, got into a car accident and the explosives in the truck blew up and killed him and his co-worker."

I look from my brother to my parents—who taught me never to lie—to gauge their reaction.

"That's not such a bad idea," my mother says.

"Really?"

"Think about how Michael will grow up," she says. "It'll be hard enough that his father's been killed suddenly. But to grow up knowing that his father was a terrorist and killed other people."

Again, I flinch at the word. *Terrorist.* Hearing it from my mother feels like a betrayal.

"And how can he possibly understand that some culture might think this logical, justified. Better to disconnect him from that, to protect the good memories he has of his father," she says.

"But even if I tell him that, the whole world knows a different story. How do I maintain my story in the face of that?" I gesture toward the news vans gathered outside.

We are all silent.

Ted slides his hand across the table, as if turning the page in an imaginary comic book. "A whole new life for you," he concentrates, teasing out each word, each new thought as he goes. "You should move, leave your job, go back to your maiden name, for the children also. They can't stay at their school, the day care. You'll need to start fresh."

"How do I do that? You mean like a witness protection plan?"

My father raises an eyebrow, "Maybe the FBI would be willing to help you make those kinds of arrangements. I could call some friends at the Bureau."

"Fuck the FBI, Dad. Sorry, I just mean Kathy doesn't need the government to give her permission to start over. She can just do what she needs to do. She can move with the boys to San Diego, they can even crash in our guest house until she finds a place. She can find a new job, using her references that knew her with her maiden name. When people try to talk to the boys about Rashid Siddique, you can all just say he was not their father, they'll have different last names."

I turn his words over in my mind, feeling the hope they offer, a path forward out of this morass. I simply shed this life, like a snake shedding its skin, there is no shame in that change for the snake, it is simply growth, regeneration. I look up at Ted, who sits almost smugly waiting for an answer from me. All I want is to be alone, to sit with myself, with this absence, examine the gaping wound I feel. I leave the table and lock myself in the bathroom.

I use the toilet, wash my hands, look at myself in the mirror. I see the woman reflected there, and wonder who she is. I remember the younger me, the woman laughing and dancing in the nightclub, the woman who fell in love, the woman who went to Pakistan, who embraced, trusted, loved. I see myself rounded, glowing with the prospect of a new baby. I see the woman at a desk, making calls, questioning intellectuals, politicians, businessmen. What other woman is waiting inside this body? I run my fingers through my long hair. What is it worth to me now? I follow the lines of my eyebrows, the wrinkles that spread out from the corners of my eyes, proof of abundant past happiness in my life. I watch my lips, draw them up in a smile, down in a frown. I run my hand down my chin, and over my neck, my sternum. I slide my fingers down between my breasts, over the softness of my belly and continuing past my pelvis, to my pubis. I pause, almost holding myself up, supporting this place, the locus of my family. Rashid entered me here and from here the boys emerged into the world. Who will know it now? What will it mean? How could the man who knew this place have abandoned this marriage, his children, me? I open my mouth and scream. I draw my hands up to cover my face. I feel a void spreading out from my center and then everything goes dark and silent.

———————

"Mommy?" I hear a tiny voice, sad, frightened. "Mommy?" I feel a tiny hand stroke my forehead.

I open my eyes to silhouettes. Michael stands beside my bed, his little shoulders so straight, so perfectly proportioned. Behind him my mother, light suffusing through the grey hairs coiffed above her head. She holds Andrew in her arms.

I am disoriented. The room seems too dark. A line of pale light seeps in at the edge of the drawn curtains. I reach out for Michael's shoulder and draw him to me. He comes closer and rests his head on my chest, while I stroke his hair. My head throbs dully with every beat of my heart.

"What happened?" I question my mother over his head.

"You fainted in the bathroom." She sits on the edge of my bed. "Ted managed to walk you in here, we figured if you could sleep…"

Michael climbs to the inside of the bed, holding my hand. "Are you feeling better, Mommy? Grandma said you were sick, that's why you couldn't come to pick me up from school."

I push myself up to sitting, feeling the milk pressing in my breasts. "Mom, give me the baby, he must be hungry."

"I gave him a bottle about a half hour ago," she says.

Guilt. I have failed both of my children.

"Mommy, where is Daddyji? Grandma said I should talk to you about it."

I look from my mother to my father to Ted. I draw in a deep breath. And I lie. "Your father was in a terrible accident," I repeat the story my brother has told me. "He had been offshore on a job and there was a terrible explosion in the vehicle he was driving." A small lie, a sin of omission really, I did not actually utter any false statements.

Michael looks up at me, eyebrows raised in alarm. "Is he all right? When will I see him?"

I shut my eyes tight, seeing Rashid in my mind's eye as I last saw

94

him, the night before he left on the job. I open my eyes and look at my son, this beautiful creature who carries Rashid's DNA. And I tell him the truth. "Michael, your father has been killed." His eyebrows rise even higher. "I'm so sorry my child." Yet more pressure, tears behind my eyes. "We will not see him again."

"You mean he's gone forever? Like Babu?"

He has no idea just how the two events are linked, only that the outcome is the same. A man we loved will never appear before us again in the flesh. "Oh Michael," I hold him against me, reach for the baby from my mother, "I'm afraid he is gone. Gone like Babu."

His tears come at first as little sniffles, then open up into giant gaping sobs. Andrew wakes, disturbed, and adds his own cries. I question my mother with my eyes. Have I done the right thing? Have I lied in a way that will protect my son? She nods at me, gently reaches out to hold Michael. I loosen my embrace and he lurches into his grandmother's arms. "I want my Daddy, I want my Daddy," he repeats over and over as she strokes his hair.

Andrew flails his arms back and forth as if he is beating me. I lift my shirt. He angrily latches on my breast and soon quiets. I lean back and feel the pressure easing. The words have been said, the milk is flowing, the tears are running down my cheeks.

The next few days pass in a blur. Ted returns to San Diego and tells his wife, Janet, we will be moving in with them. My father takes charge of reviewing all of our documents, talking to the bank, the landlord, the insurance companies. My mother takes charge of the children, who do not return to school and daycare. She takes them out to the park, the library, the ice cream store when the FBI officials come to the house every day. They ask again and again the same questions: who did Rashid associate with, where did he go, who called him? My father guards the door, my mother guards the telephone. At the center of this flurry of activity, I participate only as a source of information, intelligence, milk. I want to stop something, to exert some influence that will reverse these events, return me to my previous life. But I am mute, as in a dream when you are threatened or attacked, but incapable of letting out a scream that might save you.

The people around me reveal surprising facts in this process. My father finds Rashid had purchased an expensive life insurance policy, just after he returned from Pakistan, that covered almost every conceivable event. The FBI shows me phone records displaying calls Rashid had made and received with a young Palestinian man who had begun frequenting the mosque in Artesia—the man who was also in the truck when it blew up. Rashid's company sends letters detailing a series of small discrepancies in the inventories of their tools; electrical connections, small quantities of explosives, even a radioactive source that had gone missing for a couple of days and then mysteriously reappeared.

Every night after the children sleep, my parents sit with me. They attempt to construct a story, a new iteration each day as we learn more.

I feel as if I am developing a relationship with a different man, a man who only speaks to me from the past and through others. I want to hate him. But I see in every bit of information a meticulous devotion to his family, both his Pakistani family and us. Every time he spoke with the Palestinian, he then texted me asking about us, or the children, expressing his love, asking me if he could pick up something I needed on his way home.

Tonight my father seizes on this point, speculating. "The Palestinian," my father says, as he might have chosen *the butler* from a cast of characters in the murder detective board game we played when I was a child, "he no doubt felt some sympathy with Rashid. Both their fathers had been killed by powerful militaries. The Homeland Security analysts couch this as a political action, inspired by a fanatical Islam. But Rashid reached out to his family after each call…this was much more personal."

I think about their fathers, Rashid's I knew, Ali's I imagine. I watch my own father, here on my couch, loving me.

"We should ask about the Palestinian's phone records," my mother says, "see if he also texted his family after their conversations." She writes this down on the everpresent yellow legal pad that records our evolving to do list: provide a death certificate for the insurance company, provide the FBI hair samples from the boys to confirm Rashid's DNA in the wreckage so I can receive a death certificate, take new passport photos of the boys so I can request a legal name change, revise my resume to eliminate any international work. The list grows more complex than I can comprehend.

Nowhere on the list, however, is any funeral. Without a body, of course, there is no need to call a mortician, decide on cremation or burial, choose a casket or call about plots. Muslims would have made sure to bury the body in a simple wooden box and say the ritual prayers as soon as possible after his death. But we are not Muslims, my parents are not equipped to orchestrate such a cere-mony—I tell myself—we have very practical reasons preventing us from observing the usual death rituals.

But there is not even any mention of a memorial. The writing on the pad shows my parents straining to be helpful, even-handed. In my father's hurried, almost self-important block letters, I see a proud man, careful about his actions. In my mother's classic flow-ing cursive, I see a desire to return to a pleasant order. But I know between those lines, they are so deeply disappointed in Rashid, and perhaps even in me for my choices, that I cannot possibly ask them to produce or cooperate with some ceremony that would eulogize the man I loved.

So I am left; a sentence without a period, an envelope with an open flap, a door swinging without a latch, a departure without a goodbye.

"Kathryn," my father says, "I think we've done about all we can from here. We also have to get back to our own lives, check our mail, the house, the garden."

I pull in my lower lip, bite hard.

He reaches out for my hand. "Everything is in motion with the insurance, with your move. Ted and Janet will be here next week to help you bring the children down. The movers are scheduled to come the same day. Janet has enrolled Michael in the same school as his cousins and arranged a spot for Andrew in a very good day care."

"We know it won't be easy for you, Kathy." My mother sets her hands on her knees, very properly. "You're a strong woman, you've shown that you can handle anything, anyone. This will be no different, but you'll have to grieve, there's no shortcut, and that's not something we can do for you."

I have a moment to make it different, ask them to help me say goodbye with some ritual. I look into my lap. "Do you think... could you maybe...?"

My mother rushes into my pause. "We can come back down as soon as you need us. And we will call you as soon as we land, and as often as you need. We will always be here for you." I can see her saying all the right things. "We just need to check back in on our responsibilities at home, it's been three weeks."

I understand. This is a nightmare for them too, and they need to escape. My mother glances at my father. He tilts his head ever so slightly in approval. Age has eroded the firm line of his jaw, a few whiskers remain just below his lip, eluding the razor in his now less-steady hand.

"We're planning to leave the day after tomorrow." A reediness creeps into my father's voice. "Will that be all right for you?"

I will have failed my parents, denied them the ease they deserve at this point in their lives, I will have failed to honor my husband in his death with a memorial service, and I will have failed to provide for my sons the one man they will need most in their lives. A trilogy of little tragedies, one for each generation I touch, tattooed across my heart.

"Of course." I sigh. "Of course."

———

In the morning, I take charge. I prepare the coffee. I set the yellow legal pad at my place on the table. I make a round through the rooms, gathering up the things they have forgotten to pack. My parents seem relieved, my mother hugs me and praises my new persona as if it were the prodigal son. I can see the tension ebbing from their faces, I see my father focus intently on Michael, alternately pulling and tickling his ears. Michael laughs with delight. My mother holds Andrew on her lap, his little feet kneading her middle as she traces the features of his face with her fingers.

The window has closed, I can ask them for no more. They have given me all they are capable of. I maintain my charade for a full day, occasionally believing my own performance, before shepherding everyone into the car. And before I can stop them, I am waving them off at the airport.

On the way home I make a point of seeking out an unfamiliar grocery store. I don't want to be recognized as I purchase eggs and milk and apple juice. Michael chatters up and down the aisles, asking me when Grandma and Grandpa will be back, how far is San Diego, what will his new teacher's name be. I don't take off my sunglasses, he can't see as I squeeze my eyes shut, suppressing both tears and uncertainty.

We pull into the parking garage, I ignore the reporter who tries to flag me down, and take the elevator up. As I slide the key into the lock, I notice a triangle of white paper sticking out from under the door. I usher children and groceries inside before I pick up the paper—an envelope that has been slid under the door.

In a simple, almost childish script, six words written on the envelope cause my heart to skip a beat. *To the family of Rashid Siddique.* I turn the envelope over repeatedly, seeking out some additional information, some evidence of the sender. Nothing. I sit at the table and take a deep breath before slowly tearing open one corner. I slide my finger in and tear the crease along the short side of the envelope. I feel several sheets of paper, softened, worn. I tip the envelope. A sheaf of hundred dollar bills spills out into my hand.

I peer inside the envelope looking for a note, an explanation. Nothing but emptiness remains inside the paper. I carefully set the envelope on the table, thinking I shouldn't alter it, shouldn't contaminate it with too many of my own fingerprints—a trick I must believe from some long ago observed crime show. I count out the bills, stare at them. A mistake? The envelope so clearly states that the money is intended for me and the boys, although neglecting to mention us by name. A bribe? Nothing indicates the sender wants anything in return. A debt returned? Rashid often lent his countrymen money when they were returning to Pakistan for a wedding and would need extra cash. A payment? For a martyr's wife.

I push my chair back, take a step away from the bills, repulsed.

"Mommy! You promised me juice when we got back. Can I have some apple juice?"

When Michael notices the bills on the table, he reaches out for them. Instinctively, I slap his hand. "No!" I command. "Don't touch that."

Until now, I have made a point of never hitting my child, prided myself on my even-tempered parenting. His tears come reflexively. I have hurt him, crossed some seemingly inviolable line. I collapse to kneel next to him, immediately gather him in my arms. "Oh beta, oh Michael," I correct myself, "I'm so sorry. I just don't want you to touch that money. It isn't ours. Someone made a mistake leaving it here."

"Really?" he whimpers. "So much money? When did they leave it?"

I wipe his tears away with my thumb. He tries to pull away from me, but I hold tightly, will not let him slip away from me. "I don't know. But we have to make sure we don't touch the money, so we can return it just as we found it."

"But *you* already touched it."

He's right. I find a paper towel, gingerly use it to pick up the bills as if they are a wild animal that might bite. With my other hand I hold the envelope open again—this I have already touched when turning it over and over—and slide the money, this filthy blood money back from where it came.

Michael watches.

"Let me get you some apple juice. Do you want a snack as well?"

Still sullen, Michael nods.

"Yogurt? Crackers? Dried fruit?"

"Crackers."

I retrieve cups and bowls, juice and crackers. I open the wrong cupboards, accidentally pour the juice in the bowl before Michael giggles and I pour it into the cup. As I put everything on the table, I realize I have prepared two sets of snacks. I shrug and sit next to Michael wishing my own mother were still here to make me a cup of coffee.

My parents. Should I tell them about the money? I glance at the clock in the kitchen, they might still be on the plane. And what could they do? I have no other information, they would just worry. Who else might I tell? Ted? Homeland Security? A friend? Each time I think about explaining this money, I imagine my interlocutor's reaction, a mix of pity and accusation. An assumption that I am somehow complicit, have withheld some piece of intelligence, one more twist in the story.

I will tell no one.

The crackers are gone, a few crumbs are scattered around Michael's bowl. He looks at me expectantly. "Now what?"

There is no job, no school, no planned interview, no immediate deadline, only the looming to do list, the yellow legal pad outlining the assignment to reinvent my life, our lives.

"Can we watch a video?" He waits, expecting my standard disapproval. "*Sesame Street*? Just a short one?"

"Yes. Yes. Let's watch *Sesame Street*."

"Yes, let's!" Michael leaps out of his chair and chooses an episode from the bookcase. I gather Andrew who fusses on his blanket. I load the shiny silver disc into the player.

We all sit on the couch together, two boys and their mother, our whole family. A hole in our family. And the television rewards us with cheerful singing, animals and humans, grouches and big birds. I listen, desperately, to a song I know by heart. "Sunny day, everything's A-OK…"

Chapter 2

I see the envelope in Rashid's hand. He holds it out, baiting me as an owner would tempt a dog with a bone. Rashid in his coveralls seems to have just come off a job. Why does he smile like that, looking from the words on the envelope to me and back again? "The family of Rashid Siddique. That's you Kathryn. This is for you," he seems to speak directly into my mind, without moving his lips.

I look again at Rashid, but his face transforms, framed with a white turban and long beard, the very image of a terrorist, seething with the hatred of radical Islamists determined to destroy our way of life—as the politicians tell us. I step back, looking past the man who holds the envelope, this stranger who was once Rashid. I hear an explosion and the air fills with shards of bright red cloth embroidered with gold thread that falls to the ground, dissolving into puddles of blood. Three men run past me to tackle the man who offers me the money. I can see their black jackets bearing the homeland security department insignia. I am shoved to the ground, kicked in my back, someone is wrenching my hands behind me, shouting at me, slamming metal cuffs around my wrists.

I jerk away, force my eyes open. There are no men, no cuffs, no man with an envelope. But my heart races. I leave the bed, go to the kitchen to pour myself a glass of water, hoping to wash away the nightmare. I open the refrigerator and nearly jump with fear. The envelope confronts me from the top shelf. I must have set it there in my haste the day before. I will have to find a place for it, a hiding place. I crave something, but cannot determine what. I open cupboards and drawers, rummage through the refrigerator. Finally I settle on a bottle. The stopper squeaks as I uncork it. I pour a small quantity of Scotch into a glass, taking my time to replace the stopper, to put away the bottle before sitting at the table to drink. It looks like liquid gold, but sears my throat. I close my eyes, inhale the peaty smell. I drink all of it, feel a pleasant disembodiment. I drift back to the counter, wash the glass, dry it, and put it away so I will not be reminded in the morning.

———————

My keys rattle in my purse as I open the glass and chrome door to the bank. I shepherd Michael through and then Andrew in the stroller. I am glad to be standing after the long drive to San Diego. I rationalized that a bank in our new city makes more sense than our local bank in Los Angeles. I have tried to obscure my identity with my hair tucked away under a baseball cap. Andrew smiles at a slowly spinning sign, an advertisement, enticing working class people to dream of new homes and businesses, a reality but for the miracle of a bank loan. Michael pulls on my hand, "Does this bank give lollipops like our old bank?"

I approach the teller window. The envelope in my purse feels like a lead weight.

"Welcome," the teller says with practiced cheerfulness, "how can I help you today?"

"I'd like to add a safety deposit box to my account, my son's account actually."

"Certainly. I'll call a banker to assist you."

A young Latino man, in suit and tie, walks me through the contract, the sizes (I will only be needing the smallest size), the access hours (I nod impatiently, I don't plan to visit this money again) and the price (an automatic deduction from my son's modest savings account will be fine).

He points to a small notice posted to the cubicle wall behind him. "I have to confirm you have read this." He recites the warning. "In cooperation with the Department of Homeland Security, and in an effort to reduce terrorism, we report all transactions larger than $10,000."

I let out a disgusted snort. As if such flimsy precautions could have prevented what happened.

"Of course it's not meant for people like you," he says apologetically.

I laugh, darkly. He smiles, uncertain. On any other day I would notice he is handsome, but today I see him as some kind of clown.

He pinches the baby's cheek, offers Michael a lollipop, and escorts us all past a reinforced steel door into the bank's vault. His spiel about the safety and privacy of the service blurs in my head as I grow increasingly anxious to rid myself of this money. The man can see I am not paying attention. He finally opens a door into a small room with one seat and a small built-in countertop. He retrieves a steel box from a wall of similar boxes, reminiscent of a columbarium to hold the ashes of the dead. With the box on the counter and the keys in my hand, I watch the man deferentially excuse himself. I send Michael in, try to follow with the stroller. The room cannot accommodate all of us. Flustered, I pick up Andrew, leave the stroller outside and squeeze us all inside. I sit down and open the box, briefly examine its emptiness, its potential to shield me from the imposition of the martyr's wife identity.

"Mommy, what will you put in there?" Michael asks. "Can I see how the key works?"

"No. It's not a toy, nothing in here, see?" I hold it up, turn it upside down, demonstrating its emptiness. Andrew starts to whimper.

I shove my hand into my purse, grab the envelope and place it in the box as if it might singe my fingers. I peer in, the words are face down, so I am not forced to read them again.

"What is it?" Michael asks.

I hadn't planned for this. Hadn't decided what story I would tell, I had stupidly envisioned this as a private action.

"A letter," I improvise.

"From who?"

"Someone," I evade. "It's not important to you."

I reach with my left hand to close the box and notice the glint reflecting off the small band of diamonds on my finger. I remember the gold band I have been carrying in my wallet. The FBI had let me keep it in what they believed was a gesture of good will, a bribe for my cooperation.

I place Andrew on the floor, hand my car keys to Michael, "Can you rattle these in front of your brother, play with him?"

Michael obliges me, twisting the lollipop between his pursed lips.

I have a minute, maximum, of simulated solitude. I retrieve the ring from my wallet, place it on the counter. Then I slide the band off my own hand and place it on top of the gold band. *Is it heaven?* I wonder. *Do you share it with your father? With Shoukart? With the thousands, the millions who have died for someone's ideals, some nation's greed, some political necessity, some long-forgotten blood feud?*

I lift both of the rings to my lips, kiss them, whisper a silent blessing. I drop them into the box, wishing I had some appropriate eulogy for the man who was my husband, for the marriage we used to have, for our murdered future.

The children are asleep in the bed when I open my eyes, I hadn't meant to fall asleep myself when I lay down to put them to bed. I glance at the clock—I have already missed an hour of undisturbed time in which I can pack, separating the essentials we will take with us from what will go into storage. I open the closet. Rashid's clothes remain, unpacked. Jeans and shirts, one good suit, a few kurtas. Maybe I can call someone else to deal with them, someone who will simply see them as clothes. I see them as they were when he animated them; dancing at our wedding in the kurta, calmly confident in the suit at a company party, musky and sweaty in the casual shirt painting the bedroom walls.

I slide my hand between two linen button-down shirts. The

hangers jangle against each other. I step in and I am surrounded by his shirts and pants. I inhale the fragrance of his life, persisting in these fibers. I lift my arms so they encircle a generous quantity of garments. How many shirts will it take to occupy the same volume as his chest, his waist, his shoulders? Who was he really—the man who wore these? I squeeze the clothes harder, lean into them until the wooden clothes rod creaks. Gone. How will I ever know? And I am still here. Responsible for the family, for making the money, for dealing with these fucking clothes. I step out, pull on a sleeve until I hear a seam rip. And the sound, my act of destruction, of harm, causes a rent somewhere inside me. I lean back and then slam my palms into the plaid of the first shirt. Like a catapult, the weight of my body plows into the all of these costumes that camouflaged. Like a succession of paper dolls each one collapses into the next, until they are all shoved up against the wall, immobilized, routed. I bang my fists against cotton, wool, silk with gold threads. "God damn you, you bastard. God damn you!"

From the other room comes a crash, the sound of glass shattering and a heavy thud. Somewhere outside an engine revs and tires squeal. I rush out of the bedroom. Cold air billows in from a gaping hole in the living room window. Shards of glass litter the floor. On the edge of the Persian carpet, a brick has landed. I shiver, turning the brick over with my toe. One side bears a message, in black ink. *Fuck you.*

A few cars move through the intersection as the light turns green. One photographer persists in his news gathering vigil—did he throw this brick out of frustration? Maybe a teenaged thug just randomly threw the brick. Or maybe a survivor of the bombing, or a relative, an uncle, a cousin of one of the people killed, looking for a way to express their anger? I remember the window in the bedroom and run to that glass, imagining with terror another brick landing on the bed, the sharp edges of broken glass cutting my children's perfect skin. I unlatch the bedroom window and swing it out on its hinge, so any broken glass would fall down instead of in. I pull the curtains shut and pile up three boxes in front of them.

In an adrenaline frenzy I gather a pile of diapers, a toothbrush, a few clothes and bundle it all into a bag. When I slide shoes onto Michael's feet, he grumbles sleepily.

"Michael," my urgent whisper sounds like a hiss. "Get up. We have to go. Can you get up? You need to help me and walk to the car."

He opens his eyes, his eyebrows wrinkle in confusion. "What? Why?"

"Just come. We are going to get in the car, and go to Uncle Ted's." He does not move. "Now!" I shout.

He whimpers and then cries. I am already setting Andrew in the stroller.

"I want my daddy…I want my daddy…" Michael cries from the bed.

"Stop it!" I place my hand over his mouth to silence him. "He is gone. Gone!" His eyes grow wide with surprise, with fear. I know I am just making this worse. I will ask his forgiveness later. I pull him up, drag him into the other room.

Andrew starts to kick his legs in the stroller. I don't have time for this. I grab my keys and purse. The door locks behind us, and we are running down the hall, down the elevator, into the parking garage. I check the back seat, the trunk before I open the doors.

Only when we are on the freeway, when we pass the lights at regular intervals and the hum of the engine grows constant can I speak in soothing tones to the boys. "Everything will be fine. There was a problem at our home. A window broke, but we'll feel better at Uncle Ted's. Please stop crying, I didn't mean to shout, we just needed to leave quickly."

"Does Uncle Ted know we're coming?" Michael asks.

"He is expecting us, we are just coming a little early."

"Will we go back home tomorrow?"

I consider the question. "Uncle Ted's guest house will be home." I look in the rear view mirror. The freeway lights briefly illuminate his face.

"So we won't go back to our home in Los Angeles?" A note of panic sours his question.

"I don't know. Maybe."

"But Mom," his distress now obvious, "what about my Legos, my Spiderman toothbrush?"

"Oh Michael, don't worry about that, we'll make sure to get those things." If only all our problems were so simple.

"Promise?"

I reach back and stroke his hand. "I promise. Now sleep, we still have a long drive."

He is silent for a moment. "Mom?"

"Yes, love?"

"I miss Daddy."

I want to tell him I do, too. To tell him about the impossible void I feel, the enormous hole I must fill in our lives. But maybe it was all false, maybe the man we loved was just a façade, an apparition. I look in the rear view mirror again, watch as the lights pass. One. Two. Three times.

"Tomorrow I'll get you a Spiderman toothbrush."

He nods, closes his eyes.

———

"Excuse me, Mrs. Capen…"

"Ms. Capen," I correct the principal at Michael's new school.

"Ms. Capen then, the name on the application doesn't match the name on your son's birth certificate."

"That was his father's last name, his father is…" I hesitate, "he is no longer with us."

I see the principal, sitting smugly behind his desk, glance at Andrew in the sling over my shoulder, and then at my naked ring finger.

"Michael Capen is my son's name," I assert. "I've made the change on his passport, on both their passports," I nod at Andrew as well. "We're still waiting for them to arrive."

I pull a copy of my passport application out of my purse, see my mother's neat letters in each of the boxes. I remember how she had simply filled in the names and the information as if she were applying for a new credit card. Her handwriting shows none of my turmoil over the implications of the request.

The principal places the copy squarely next to the school registration form, I see his eyes move from one paper to the other. He glances at Michael, who makes an effort to look well behaved. The man glances back at me, frowning momentarily before accepting my documents as valid. "Ask my secretary to make a copy of the passport application," he holds it out to me as if it smells bad, "and welcome to Hoover Elementary, Michael. I will introduce you to Miss Lopez. She will be your teacher."

The principal stands and guides Michael by the shoulder, out of the room. He holds the door open for me to follow him, but otherwise he does not acknowledge me. Does he know? Did he recognize the last name from the birth certificate, or is his disdain for a woman he assumes has failed in her marriage?

Michael turns to look at me and Andrew as the principal tries to hurry him out into the hallway. My instinct to rush to my child, to take him into my protection and retreat to some safe place overwhelms me. But where? What place is safe? The danger in our lives originated in our own home, with our love for a man.

I kiss my hand and blow it in his direction. He mimes catching the kiss and slapping it to his cheek. And then he and the principal turn a corner and disappear down another hallway.

———

Janet meets me at her front door with a cup of coffee and a business card. "My salon. I made an appointment for you. My stylist is great, she'll give you a cut and a new color."

"What for? I think I really need to go back to LA to finish the packing."

"No way. Ted doesn't want you going back there after the brick accident. I have taken care of everything, called the movers. Don't worry. Your new life is starting, you should have a new look too."

I think maybe she is afraid the neighbors will recognize me from the news photos. "But the baby," I start to protest, holding him tighter to me in his sling.

"Andrew can stay with me. Just feed him before you go and he'll be fine. Really," she says with forced politeness, "it's my treat. I insist."

The stylist pumps on the foot lever, raising me in the chair, with a flourish covering me with the waterproof cape. I feel small and helpless.

"So Janet said you're moving to San Diego from LA? You'll love it here. We've got everything you'd want that LA has, the beach, the weather, the fashion, but without the traffic or the smog. You came for a job?"

"No." I am not in the mood to chat.

"Oh, so something else?"

"I came for a new start," I say repeating Janet's explanation. And I close my eyes to shut her out. I guess I doze off until she calls my name.

"Kathryn, Kathryn, do you want to see? It turned out really well."

I open my eyes. My long hair has been reduced to a chin length bob, a bright platinum blonde strip dramatically framing the left side of my face. I think of Cruella deVille. Dark lines below my eyes undermine the lightness of my new hairstyle. I resist the urge to cry.

"Do you love it? You won't have to do anything in the morning, except add a little comb in conditioner, especially since your hair is already so straight. If you wanna make another appointment, we also do facials here."

I can't even muster a smile before I nod and say thank you.

When I pick up Michael, he does not hug me. He looks at me and takes a step back. "What happened to you?"

"What do you mean?"

"What happened to your hair?" I have assiduously avoided

looking in mirrors since I left the salon. I am not yet ready to confront this new woman.

"Auntie Janet arranged for me to have a haircut. Do you like it?"

I see his upper lip disappear inside his lower lip, prelude to a cry. "I just want everything to be like it was."

If Michael cries, I won't be able to hold myself together. "Kiss baby Andrew, he missed you today," I chirp. "Kiss?" I nearly plead. He kisses the baby perfunctorily, keeping his eyes on me. I thank God for Andrew's giggles as he reaches out for Michael.

Chapter 3

Janet stands, almost triumphantly as the movers busily wheel their handtrucks down the gravel path, depositing stacks of cardboard boxes next to the little backhouse. I recognize my own handwriting on several: *clothes, toys, Michael's, baby's*. On other boxes I can see the hurried handwriting of the men who have handled my belongings: *kitchen, television, papers*, written in a block script reminiscent of the graffiti lettering I recognize from freeway ramps.

I watch the three men drop boxes in my temporary retreat—the guest house Janet has arranged for us—and return to fetch more. Janet follows them back around the front house, directing their actions.

I look at the stacks, step inside again, surveying the limited space.

I step back outside, waiting for the next load of boxes. A diesel engine ignites, crescendos and lumbers away into the distance. Confused, I walk around the front of the house in time to see the back door of the moving truck heading down the lane. *Trusty Movers*, the door boasts in bold cursive lettering, *Helping You On Your Way*.

I turn around and hurry to the front door, thinking to tell Janet they have left with some of my things still inside.

"They brought all of your things," she asserts. "I watched them pack up the truck."

"But what about my furniture? What about the mirrors? The artwork?"

"You mean the things from…Pakistan?" The nasal *a* of her American accent makes the country sound childish to my ears.

"Yes!"

"Well, those were…his things. I arranged for the Goodwill to pick them up."

"What?!" I curl my fingers into an angry fist. "*I* bought most of those things."

"With him," she says derisively. "You would have had to store them anyway, there's no place for them in the backhouse. And they certainly would've made for a different, how can I say, aesthetic."

I am dumbfounded. I search for the words to express my anger at her.

"You won't need them. It'll be better for you not to have those reminders of your past. I thought about it, Kathryn. I really think it'll be easier for you to make a clean break."

I look around, my mind racing about how I can get my things back before they become anonymous curiosities in a musty second-hand shop. I notice a piece of pink paper on the counter, the Trusty Movers bill. Two thousand dollars, written in the same hurried graffiti-like script, circled at the bottom.

I look up at Janet, realizing how much she has paid to give away my things.

She misreads my anger as fear, her expression softens. "Don't worry about the money, they charged by the mile for the truck. You can pay us back when you have everything settled, and when you're able."

I repress the urge to shout at her. I turn and leave through the front door.

"You're welcome," Janet calls, the rise in the last syllable requiring a *thank you*—a response I refuse to provide.

I let the door slam shut.

———————

I lay on the bed, staring at the ceiling. Michael plays with Andrew, wiggling soft toys in front of him and recounting nursery rhymes. How wise Michael is, understanding not to come to me now.

I am still, paralyzed even. But my mind races. How can I escape, regain some control, reassert some power in my own life? I consider every possibility, even the most outlandish. Return to Los Angeles? Repair the window and continue as if nothing had happened? Move to my parents? They have a guest room, I could search for an affordable studio near their prestigious neighborhood. Reach out to Rashid's mother in Lahore? I have refused to think of her, but surely the family would welcome me—the mother of their male grandchildren. Return to Dubai? Look for a job, any expat position would include a housing package and salary. Stay in a motel here in San Diego? I could find a more permanent place later. Contact my college boyfriend? He never married, has a beautiful house in Carmel. Apply for graduate school? My father's university offers subsidized student housing. Buy an RV? Park wherever I like.

But any move would require cash, funds I can't yet access. The bastards at the life insurance company still require more documentation from me to process my claim. Their adjusters' usual reluctance must be compounded by their distaste for my circumstances. I consider the envelope sitting in the darkness of my safety deposit box. Perhaps I could even sell the rings. Then I remember my wedding gold. A Pakistani bride's insurance, Sabeen had called it. I will sell that filthy metal and start over.

I hear movement in the garden, the crunch of gravel under several feet. Ted's daughter, Amanda asks, "So was he really a terrorist? Why'd she marry him?"

"I never want to hear that kind of crap out of your mouth again," Ted admonishes.

Silence.

"You hear me?"

Amanda mumbles a response to her father.

A knock on our door. I remain motionless, staring at the ceiling. Again the knock.

"Kathryn?" Ted calls.

Michael approaches me, gingerly leaning against the edge of the bed. "Mommy? Uncle Ted is here."

I wish we had already left. I should have just kept driving when I picked up Michael from school.

"Kathryn, please open the door. I'd like to talk to you."

Michael tugs on my hand. "I can open the door, Mommy, do you want me to?"

I close my eyes and nod my head with a tiny motion.

My son, now the man of the house, opens the door. "Hello, Uncle Ted. Sorry, she's not feeling well."

"We brought you some pizza," Valerie, the younger one, says. At ten, she must know something is wrong, her perky pre-teen cadence sounds coached. "Here, let me set it on the table and get you some."

Michael stands aside, allows her passage. Amanda approaches Andrew, makes artificially happy cooing noises.

Ted sits on the edge of the bed. I cannot greet him, cannot move.

"Um, I understand there's some issue about the moving process and your stuff."

I close my eyes. I don't want to dwell on this topic, have to keep my thoughts moving forward. After a long pause, I force myself to speak. "Don't worry, we'll be gone soon."

"That's not the point. You're welcome to stay here as long as you want. I mean, *look,* we've made a place for you, Janet has bought everything you would need, dishes, food, everything."

I stare at the ceiling. I can't bear to see him.

"Really, I know this sucks for you." He lowers his voice to nearly a whisper. "I can only imagine…your husband turns out to be someone else, but he's dead before you understand that. You're stuck with everyone's judgment for marrying the enemy. You've got to raise his kids, protect them from this shitty aftermath. And then, just as a kicker, you get a four-letter brick through your window."

His chronicle of my life sends me into a miasma of self pity.

"I know you think Janet was harsh, but you probably owe her a shitload of thanks."

"For giving away my things?"

"She managed your whole fucking flight from Los Angeles, it's no small thing."

I roll my eyes.

"The least you could do is show a little gratitude." He is angry. "It's not exactly a cakewalk for us either. And I didn't sign up to play peacemaker between my wife and my sister."

Through the noxious mists of my mind I understand that Ted is not my ally. I feel my self shrinking inside my skin, whatever energy animated me, whatever sense of self-worth or responsibility once fueled me, shrivels, dries, retreats, leaving a hard little ball in my stomach. I close my eyes and take shallow breaths, allowing in only the bare minimum of oxygen my lungs require.

"All right, if you're going to play mute, at least get some good sleep. We'll deal with this tomorrow." I feel the bed spring back from his weight as he stands.

"Girls, go ahead and finish your dinner with the boys. I'll leave the back door open for you."

I wish they would leave immediately. Their immature voices grate on my ears as they pretend to enjoy my children. Michael says evenly, "You don't have to stay, I can put away the dishes. It's OK. Thanks for the pizza."

I keep my eyes shut, trying to protect myself from the humiliation of their forced hospitality. And they are gone.

I exhale, the tension in my eyelids abates, and I allow a bland comfortless sleep to dull my consciousness.

Then the baby is crying. Michael is talking, trying to get my attention. But an invisible lead weight above me presses, paralyzes.

A baby's angry cries grow louder and I hear Michael grunting with effort. I feel a plucking at my blouse. "Please Mommy," he pleads, "feed him, he's hungry."

The words mean nothing to me, they cannot penetrate the murky distance to my desiccated interior.

Like a spider, I understand some movement at the extremity of my web. Something sacred made profane. A baby's body is clumsily

116

shoved over me, and a little hand haltingly positions my breast. I perceive heat, pressure.

Michael cries. The baby is quiet. I feel nothing.

———————

I go through the motions for days, I'm not sure how many. My limbs perform everyday tasks like washing and dressing and feeding. I observe myself without judgment, I have become incapable of higher-level thinking. I prepare the same dinner for Michael night after night. I feed Andrew formula. I speak only as necessary. I neither laugh nor shout at the children. I do not try to retrieve my belongings, or even think of them again. I watch myself in the mirror as I comb the short hair of a woman, a person I can no longer name, a woman I no longer know.

Tonight I sit at the table, another day's ration of pasta and tomato sauce before us. Michael places a piece of paper on the table, the outline of a tree photocopied on its surface.

"I need to fill in my family's names here. My parents, grandparents, aunts and uncles."

He looks at me and then at two lines at the center of the image. "I know your name, I can fill in Kathryn Capen." He slides his finger across that line to the blank next to it. "What about this line? What should I write?"

I understand the line is intended for Michael's male parent. I cannot conjure the name. I see only a daunting void, a line that leads to painful questions of who and why. I consider the line no further, just lift another forkful of pasta—penne tonight, we had linguine last night.

Michael understands I will not help him, cannot help him. He looks again at the paper, crumples it up in his hands. I hear him say under his breath, "I wish I were dead too."

The words reach me, hurtling through the fog of my mind. And I see him, see this tiny man, alive before me. In my sabbatical of self pity he has suffered through abandonment, not just once, but twice. He appears before me, as if out of thin air, his brown hair shaggy, his nails dirty, his clothes mismatched. He is so beautiful. I have neglected this living boy as I wallowed in my self defense against the dead.

"Let me help you." My voice sounds like a croak after so much silence. He pulls the paper away. "Michael, let's see it. We can work it out together."

His little hand releases the ball of paper. I smooth it out and he looks at me, his need so obvious.

"Go and get me a pencil, we can write in the words."

He dutifully opens one of the kitchen drawers and finds a pencil. How did he know it was there? He hands it to me, waits, watches me attentively.

"Let's do the easy ones first. Here is you. Write your name, can you write your name?"

Slowly, the letters take shape, his childish handwriting deliberate, careful not to cross below the line.

"Good. And now your brother, here, next to you."

"How do you spell his name?"

I say the letters one at a time, waiting for him to transcribe each one. We continue in this fashion through my side of the tree, listing my parents, Ted, Janet, and their girls. As the weight of people on my side of the tree threatens to topple the whole thing we arrive at the empty line that could lead to others that would balance the tree, the whole cast of paternal aunties and uncles, cousins and grandparents that would connect Michael with the other side of the world.

His hand hovers above the line. He fidgets in his seat, bites on the corner of his lip.

"Write, 'father'," I say. "f-a-t-h-e-r." He looks at me and I nod my head. When he finishes, I hold my hand out for the pencil and in my own hand I write in parenthesis *deceased*.

"What does it say, Mommy?"

"It says your father's dead. If anyone asks, you tell them he died in an accident."

His eyes are trained on me, waiting for me to say more. "You don't need to explain anything else."

He exhales, relieved. He pushes his way onto my lap. "Thank you for helping me. I was scared you'd be mad."

"Oh Michael, you should never be scared of me. I'll always be here for you. I won't ever leave you." I hold him tightly, gripping him to me, my hands moving almost frantically from his shoulders to feet, his head to chest, ensuring he is still whole.

I carry him to Andrew's play pen, lift the baby and hold them both to me, feel their breath on my skin. We are all alive.

———

In the morning, I wake early, before the children. I walk to the door and open it. Morning shadows stretch long. The crisp air carries the scent of flowers Janet has so carefully planted. A humming bird dives to a shrub near the house, feeds from the blooms.

I have a plan today. After I drop Michael at school, I will go to the mall. I will buy the boys new shoes, new clothes. I will take Michael for a hair cut. I will find a park and take them to play.

I inhale deeply and return to wake the boys. I see our living space; a pile of dirty clothes at the foot of the bed, a stack of unopened mail on the counter, fruit flies hovering above unwashed dishes in the sink. It's too much. How can I possibly handle it all?

And then I see the boys. Andrew sucks on his teddy bear's paw and whimpers. Michael holds tight to an object, red and blue plastic protruding from the end of his fist. I kiss him to wake him. "What's this?" I pull his fingers back, recognizing the Spiderman toothbrush. Defensively he pulls it back from me.

"It's mine," he says. "He protects me at night."

"You hold him every night?"

He clutches the toothbrush to his chest and nods.

How long have I been gone? How much have I missed? Will I ever be able to fully return? I have so much work to do, maybe too much work. I see Andrew smile at me before the bear paw is back in his mouth. Just take a little bit at a time, I tell myself. Today just the new shoes and the laundry. Tomorrow I can look at the mail and call about Michael's haircut.

———————

I emerge from the elevator into the mall's giant gleaming concourse. Upbeat pop music pumps through speakers. Giant potted palm trees tower over me in the light that shines down from skylights four stories above.

No one notices me. The shoppers, mostly women in groups of two or three, or pushing strollers like me, all appear perfectly at ease here, carrying giant paper bags emblazoned with store brands. I long for their contentment. I marvel at how they seem so perfectly adapted. None of them are crying, none appear grey with grief. One woman smiles at her companion, a dazzling smile of bright red lips.

Maybe that's it, bright red lipstick. I turn the stroller and walk deliberately to the department store cosmetics counter.

"Can I help you find something?" the salesgirl asks.

"Lipstick," I say quickly before I change my mind. "I need some bright red lipstick."

"Sure. Every woman should have some bright red lipstick now and then." She comes to the front of the counter and pulls out a wide drawer to reveal lipsticks in a rainbow of pinks and reds, oranges and browns. She looks at my face more carefully, her eyes glancing up to my hair, taking in the streak of white blonde hair. "I think you need something with a bit of cool tones, more to the maroon than the orange shades."

I simply wait until she finds the right color. As she dabs a bit on the back of my hand, soliciting my approval, she notices Andrew in his stroller.

"Oh what a cute baby! He's yours?"

"Yes."

"Wow, his color is just so different from yours. What's his father?"

What's his father? Does she mean is he animal, vegetable, or mineral?

Does she mean is he a butcher, a baker, or a candlestick maker?

"He's dead."

I watch her blanch, she flusters to recover. "I'm sorry, I didn't mean to…"

I smile, feeling a bit like Cruella deVille myself. "Just the lipstick please."

She busies herself with the purchase, thanking me with excessive formality.

I immediately apply the color to my lips, observing myself in the countertop mirror. I see my brittle expression, my haircut and bright blonde streak, red lips like a target in the middle of my face. I force myself to smile. I frown and pull the corners of my mouth down. Comedy, tragedy. I smile again.

I look different. I can be different. I will assume another identity—one I choose. I kneel down and kiss Andrew, leaving the imprint of my lips on his cheek. He kicks his feet and smiles. Once I have bought new shoes for the boys I will go to the jeweler to sell my gold.

Michael smiles out from the stylist's chair, pumped up to its maximum height. His eyes are so clear beneath the neatly trimmed bangs.

"You look so handsome, little man," the stylist coos as she pulls off the drape, revealing a bright green shirt, one I just bought today. He reaches up and touches his hair, darker than mine, but not black. No one can tell he's half-Pakistani. Maybe Turkish, Greek, Italian even. I will say Greek if anyone asks me. Something apolitical, non-threatening.

"Should we have some dinner to celebrate your new haircut, maybe some pizza?" I ask.

"Really?" he is almost incredulous, "could we even have pepperoni pizza?"

"Whatever you want."

We will eat pepperoni without even a moment of hesitation,

without a care for whether the meat may be pork, in some way *haraam*, forbidden by some long-dead prophet. Our family is mine now. I will make the decisions, I will care only about my culture, my set of rights and wrongs. "We can even have it with Coke," I pronounce it deliberately, almost defiantly, seeing my bright red lips form a nearly perfect *o* shape in the mirror. How American I will be, consuming our national drink, my beautiful sons dressed in matching Levis and little Ralph Lauren shirts. No one will suspect anything of me. We will be indistinguishable from the people in magazines, on billboards, in malls; people who are safe and happy and whole.

I run water in the sink until it turns warm so I can wash the dishes. The ritual of scrubbing and rinsing plates and utensils comforts me. I have performed this task in so many different places, always feeling a satisfying sense of accomplishment to see the sink empty, to see the dishes stacked for drying. Only in Pakistan was I not expected to wash dishes, as the bhai, the housemaid, did them quietly, a faded tribal tattoo on her forearm bobbing in and out of the water as she worked. I close my eyes, allow the memory to fill my vision, before I remember the event that has changed everything. Perhaps the bhai also perpetuates this culture of revenge. Perhaps she raised her little son to seek vengeance for wrongs committed against his family. And a door in my mind slams shut, pushing away the image of her hands at the dishes. I am exiled from my memories. Those once happy places are no longer safe for me. I must remain here in the present.

As I place the last dish on a towel on the counter, I hear footsteps in the garden coming toward my door. My brother calls my name from just outside.

I open the door, pleased at the distraction. "Come in, come in, the boys are sleeping." I move aside and gesture for him to join me at the table. He looks around, taking in the whole scene before he turns back to me and sits down.

"Something different in here?" he asks.

"I'm different." An awkward silence settles. "And, uh, I guess I cleaned up a bit, it had gotten pretty bad in here."

"Yeah, Janet was getting a little worried."

I get up from the table, suddenly self conscious about having a guest, and open a cupboard for glasses. "Can I get you something to drink? Wine? Water?"

"No, I'm good. Just doing mail delivery." He places a stack of envelopes on the table, bearing yellow forwarding stickers from the post office. "You know Janet set up the forwarding request, but it doesn't last forever, you should let all these folks know about your new address."

"Yes, you're right, I'll look in to that." I take a wine bottle out of a cupboard, suddenly craving company, conversation. "Can you stay and have a glass of wine with me?"

"Well, now. That's a switch. Guess you're back in the land of the living?"

I pull out the cork and let the red wine splash into the glass. "I guess one can only retreat for so long."

Ted tips his glass toward me before taking a drink. "It was getting a little bit old. I wondered if I was going to have to come in here and smack some sense into you."

I flinch, drink my wine so I can change the subject.

"What do you think about a car, Ted? I'm thinking I should trade in my car for another."

"What's wrong with your car?"

"Nothing. I just want something different. It doesn't have to be new."

He raises an eyebrow.

"And I think I want an American car."

"Why?" He rotates the glass in his hand. "Your Toyota will probably last forever."

"Yes," I shrug. Does it look like a nervous shrug? "I just think, well, I was thinking, everything else from my old life is gone almost, so why am I holding on to this car?"

He nods his head in thoughtful agreement. "And an American car will make you more American?"

"I *am* an American and so are my kids," my shoulder twitches defensively. "We can drive around in an American car."

"Suit yourself, drive American, go Yankees." He takes another drink.

"And can I ask you a favor?"

"*A* favor?"

"Another favor," I say quickly, looking into my empty glass. "If I were a man, I wouldn't ask, but you know how car salesmen are about dealing with women, especially a woman with children."

"You want me to play husband?"

My back stiffens. I grip my glass with both hands. "I don't need a husband, even a pretend one. I'd just appreciate another opinion on a car, and the fact that you're a man might be helpful. If it's too much to ask, nevermind."

"Down girl. It's no problem. I can help you with the car, just tell me when." He gulps down the rest of his wine, and stands quickly. "Glad to see you starting to move on. Do you all want to come for dinner this weekend?"

I soften my posture, suddenly so grateful for an invitation. "Yes, we'd like that. What can I bring?'

He is at the door already, his hand on the knob. "Nothin', just wear the same lipstick, Janet will get a kick out of that."

I smile. I am starting. The new identity is emerging. I can do this.

I pour another glass of wine and pull the stack of letters toward me. I sift through them. A couple of credit card bills, a regular insurance statement, some junk mail, and an odd-looking envelope—no forwarding sticker and the return address of my old apartment building in Los Angeles. The address, typed directly on the envelope says: Kathryn Siddique, c/o Ted Capen, followed by Ted's address. I hold the envelope before me, try to stare it down, as if it is some kind of challenge. I gulp my wine, and push the other letters out of the way. I study the postmark, Los Angeles, dated yesterday. I carefully tear at the corner of the flap, anxious at the thickness of the contents. The tear reveals another envelope inside, which I slide out and turn over. I recognize words I have seen before. *For the Family of Rashid Siddique.*

God damn it. How did this get here? I feel the flimsiness of my efforts, the residue of lipstick at the edges of my lips. I want to throw this envelope out, to call Ted back and demand he take it away, to complain to the post office about this intrusion into my place of exile. My hands shake as they tear open the inner envelope. Hundred dollar bills, the bewildering, infuriating symbols of value that someone is forcing into my life. I count them out, exactly the same amount as before.

I want to scream. I want to escape. I stand up and open the front door, step out into the chilly night air, look at the sky, clench my fists. I feel no relief. I turn around and storm to the bathroom, wash my face with very hot and then with very cold water. The mask is gone, the same grey woman of days past looks out at me. But in my chest the depression of the previous weeks gives way to defiance. Fuck it. I will fight it. I will never be the martyr's wife.

I return to the kitchen, pull out an unopened bottle of Scotch. I pour myself a hefty quantity and throw it back in two gulps. I stand over the sink, waiting for the alcohol to perform its task, to dull my perception. And when I start to feel the distance, the disassociation, I slide the money to the inner and outer envelopes, before shoving it into the darkest recess of my purse, until I can deliver it to the darkness of the safety deposit box, from where it cannot harm me.

I prepare for sleep, lying beneath the covers, eyes wide open, limbs stock straight. The weight of my body burdens me. I cannot tolerate the unease, the encroachment of this money. I throw off the covers and head to the bathroom, desperate for something to do. An impulse to purge overwhelms me, so I strip off my clothes. The mirror reflects my body. How long since I have noticed it? I spread a towel on the tiled floor and lay down on it, closing my eyes, bringing my hands to my skin, feeling my belly. I move my hands down my thighs, feel the muscles tighten as I lift my hips off the floor. I feel my own touch in my long-dormant sex. The contact rustles a sensation, a flow of warmth as my body reacts. My actions are thoughtless, devoid of emotion. I simply long for the energy, the nerves firing in once familiar ways. My fingers press inside my body, registering heat, moisture, pressure. I ride my hips up and down, without a partner. I press against myself, without tenderness, with only a need to reach a limit. And the orgasm arrives, radiating through my pelvis, a wave passing through my consciousness. I hold, hoping to grasp it, to make it last, to dwell in the heat. I laugh. I have asserted some authority, some independence within my tiny geography. I do not need a man. But the pleasure passes, like a handful of steam.

———————

The same young banker opens the bank vault door for me. Today, his tie catches my attention, an abstract dragon impaled on a knight's sword. He notices my look. "We've all got dragons to slay. But mostly I just use lollipops." He smiles and pulls a handful of candies out of his pocket.

I wave my hand to refuse them, step past him, lugging Andrew, asleep, in his car seat. The man leaves and I bolt the door, then lean my head against it, wanting to cry. I remember last night's dream, the nightmare. I heard an explosion, saw fragments of red cloth in the air. A man had come to me, wearing a white turban, like the terrorists we see on television. I could not see his face, but knew he was Rashid. He pushed me to the ground, kicked me in the back. I tried to scream but could make no sound.

It was only a dream, I tell myself, even as my lungs tighten with the memory.

Enough. I should finish this task quickly. I fumble with the keys. Will the FBI know about this? Try to subpoena this box? I reach for the envelope in my bag and drop it inside. I slam the cover closed, trying to prevent even the fragrance of the contents from escaping.

———————

As Andrew and I round the corner of Ted's house, I am startled by two men in coveralls checking the gas meter on the side of the backhouse.

"Hello?" I call out, to alert them to my presence.

Only one looks up, "Hello ma'am, just checking your meter." The other man quickly gathers his tools.

I nod, but do not move toward the door, I feel safer in the open air of the garden. The first man jots something in a little notebook and they make their way out of the yard, past the gas meter on Ted's house, without another word.

———————

"More steak?" Janet offers me the platter, three sizable fillets remaining.

I help myself to another piece. I see Ted smirk as I begin slicing. I feel so hungry, ravenous.

Janet refills our wine glasses with an expensive wine. The girls chatter away about a reality fashion show.

"Seems like you, my little sister, have discovered a taste for some expensive things, huh?"

"What do you mean, Ted?"

"Well, you know that all the shopping you've been doing doesn't come free, right? Soon enough, the credit card companies come knocking."

"Sure. I'll deal with that later. For now I need to give my kids what they need." I bring a forkful of potatoes to Michael's mouth, urging him to eat more.

"Right…but I expect pretty quick you're going to look around and figure out that you need a job. We aren't made of money, you know. That backhouse isn't paying its own mortgage."

I look up, fork mid-air, feel my stomach drop in fear. I try to read his expression through his well-trimmed goatee.

"I'll get the dessert," Janet says, leaving for the kitchen.

"Ted, is it time for me to leave? Are you asking us to leave?"

"Look, there's no rush. I'm just saying this isn't a permanent situation, hiding out with us. You're going to have to get a job, get your own place, make your own life."

He stresses the word *own*, as if I had somehow been living his life, her life, their life.

"Is this about the money, Ted? As soon as the insurance settlement comes I can pay you for the movers and the utilities. We can even work out some kind of back rent."

"No, Kathryn," he catches Janet's eye before she sets down a chocolate cake. "It's not about the money…" he pauses, brings his hands to rest on his lap.

"Is that why you called out the meter readers today, to see how much electricity I'm using?"

"What?" He looks at me with a combination of confusion and disgust. "Nobody called any meter readers. We don't even have a meter on the back house, there's only one meter, one utility bill."

I set my wine glass down, thinking back to the afternoon, trying to recall the name of the agency on the van or the men's coveralls.

Ted continues. "I have a buddy, a guy at the *San Diego Sentinel*, sports section editor. He says they're always looking for good writers and editors. I told him about you."

"Ted, I specialize…I have specialized in foreign policy, I don't know anything about sports," I say derisively.

"Oh, I know you specialize in all things foreign. Tell me, how's that working out for you?"

My cheeks flush. I have no retort.

He leans his elbows on the table, his tan forearms exposed. "I don't think your old journal is going to be calling for your services right about now. So maybe you should think about a little reinvention of your brainiac self."

I push my fork to the edge of my plate, look down, feeling the same diminution as when our father would lecture me at the dinner table, pontificating on some topic ostensibly for my own good.

"Use your imagination, sports is more than just football and locker room reporting."

Michael whispers in my ear, "Can I be excused?" I nod, he and his cousins head for the TV.

"Look, why don't you just meet my buddy for lunch. It never hurts to meet some new people."

I pause a moment too long, unintentionally allow Ted a final volley.

"It's not like anyone else wants to talk to you."

"Ted!" Janet admonishes from the kitchen.

"I meant professionally."

I feel sick. Why did I eat so much?

"I'll tell him to expect your call."

I step out of the back house, careful not to wake the sleeping children with the creaking door hinge. I hear crickets, let my eyes adjust to the moonlight. I scan the garden before making my way to the side of the house where I had seen the men earlier today. I walk past the lupines and sage, the toyons and native grasses that Janet has cultivated. In this idyllic setting, my suspicion strikes me as paranoia. What made-for-TV movie do I think I am part of? I stand in the place where I saw the men, notice the gas pipe coming up out of the ground and entering the wall at waist level. The shutoff valve is turned perpendicular to the pipes, as it should be so the gas will flow to the stove and the heater. At the top of the pipe, at the junction with the house I see a little metal box enclosure. Not a meter, not a joint in the pipe, not anything that looks functional. I reach for it, feel for a latch, a hinge, some opening. Nothing. I look at the unusual octagonal screws that hold it in place. No regular screwdriver would open them. I look down at the ground, notice what looks in the moonlight like paint flakes on the gravel, as if the wall had just been screwed today.

I shiver. Gravel crunches as I step back and look again at the metal box.

I return to the house, relieved the boys have not moved in their sleep. I stand in front of the stove, approximating the position of the gas line. I climb up onto the counter to peer behind the stove. What do I expect to see? A tiny camera? A little microphone? I wouldn't even know what they would look like, if in fact someone had bugged the kitchen. I run my hand down the wall in the little gap between the stove and the drywall. I feel only dust. In the quiet of the house a voice begins in my head, *person of interest* the voice repeats over and over. I am a person of interest, surveillance is required. From the edge of the cupboard my hand frightens out a spider, his long thread-like legs carrying him to safety behind the refrigerator.

The house must be bugged, the FBI would not have spent so much time questioning me only to let me go freely. I imagine that all of my actions are being observed, I start to feel self conscious. What happens if they know I am aware of their surveillance? What are they expecting to see me do? How long have the cameras been here?

I slide off the counter and stand in front of the stove as if an actor on a stage. I smooth my hair with my fingers, brush the dust off my pants. I clear my throat and address the stove. "If you are observing me, let me just tell you directly. I know nothing I haven't already told you. I did not know of any plot before the..." I hesitate, I have tried not to speak of the incident—the reporters have dubbed it *the double freeway bombing*—since I arrived in San Diego. "I didn't know of anything before the bombing. I've not had any contact from anyone of interest since the event." I think of the cash-filled envelopes. Did they see me open the second one a few days ago? Do my eyes blink in a telltale expression of deceit? No, my statement is true. I have not contact with anyone. I have only had contact, unwanted contact, with someone's money.

"So stop watching me. I have nothing you want. I'm just trying to start a new life, to raise my boys. Leave me alone!" In the silence that follows, the stove does not respond, my imagined audience does not react. How absurd I must seem, addressing an appliance. So I start to dance, I sing a song from *Sesame Street*. I tap dance with an imaginary muppet. Is some intelligence agent laughing somewhere? Would he call his colleagues to watch? Pronounce me emotionally unbalanced? As I come to the end of the song's lyrics I turn around, stick my backside to the stove and slap it with a satisfying crack. "And fuck you!" I say with a bitter smile over my shoulder.

As I stand, Michael startles me. He is perched on the edge of the bed, a bewildered expression on his face.

"Michael," I exclaim, as much embarrassed as surprised. "I thought you were asleep."

"What're you doing? Who are you talking to Mommy?"

"Um," I stall, "I was just playing."

The corners of his eyes turn up with interest. "Playing?" He slides off the bed, and reaches out for my hand. "Can I play, too?"

I start to refuse, beginning to retrieve my stock excuses about how late it is, how much sleep he needs. But I see the wonder in his eyes that I might play again.

"Yes. Yes! Come and play with me." I lead him to the circle of light in the kitchen. "Same song again?"

He nods enthusiastically and we begin singing together, shuffling our feet and tapping our toes. When the song ends, Michael suggests another, one I don't know as well. We sing until my remembered lyrics run out. When his run out a few lines later, I jump back in, making up the words, singing about Michael, lines about a little boy who is strong and fantastic, shmantastic, absolutely grantastic. He giggles at first and then laughs, one lungful and then another, waves of giant, trilling laughter. The sound is so delightful, so magnetic that it draws out more songs. *Row, row, row your goat, quickly all in green, merrily, merrily, merrily, merrily, life is just whipped cream.* He doubles over, holding his stomach, rolling on the floor.

"Stop! Stop!" he cries gulping for air, "I can't breathe…more… sing another one."

And I sing. I sit down on the floor and gather him in my lap, singing an imaginary world for us of animals eating with chopsticks, boys floating to the moon with toy tops, mothers who cook nothing but saltwater taffy. Let them listen to me, let them watch. My only crime is loving this child, lavishly, helplessly, as if my life depended upon it.

Chapter 4

Giant Chinese lions guard the restaurant gates. I approach, the keys to my certified pre-owned Ford economy car jingling from my fingers. I pause to check my appearance in the glass doors. I had blow dried my hair, applied my red lipstick and pulled on a pair of so-called premium jeans that Janet chose for me. I am a persuasive simulation of a normal American woman. I should be able to convince Ted's friend that I have a newfound passion for sports.

Oscar Ramirez spots me quickly, waves me over from his seat in an oversize booth, two menus on the table. He stands to greet me with a cheerful handshake, "So nice to meet you, welcome to San Diego."

"Thanks, I appreciate you taking the time to meet with me."

We exchange pleasantries, ask a few innocuous questions, establishing our provenance, delicately gathering information, like dogs sniffing circles around each other.

By the time the waitress comes I have decided that his immigrant background vouches for a certain open mindedness and his polished English vocabulary belies a considerable intelligence.

I order spicy pork with fried rice. He smiles, nods, requests the house special, *rich man's curry and rice.*

"So I'll get to the point," Oscar says, "I can hire freelancers and if they work out, I can usually bring them on for a full-time position.

Ted says you can write anything, and I saw from your resume that you have impeccable journalism credentials."

"That's very kind of you. I've made my living as a writer. I'm sure you also saw from my resume that I haven't done sports writing before. But I'm a quick study," I try to sound eager.

He fiddles with the chopsticks in their paper wrapper. "I'm sure. We don't have too many Stanford graduates writing for the sports section, or too many women really. It would be great if we could draw more female readers to the section. Maybe with some non-traditional story angles."

I have thought about this, actually considered some of the things that might make this job a legitimate pursuit for me. "That's an interesting idea, maybe a series on female Olympians in the middle of the Olympic cycle, or looking at the rise of more female-oriented sports like tennis and volleyball."

He tilts his head and raises an eyebrow in polite consideration. "We were actually thinking more along the lines of stories about the Williams sisters' clothes designers, or interviews with the wives of some of the high-profile players on the big teams." He proceeds to rattle off men's names, presumably those who can demand enormous salaries. I nod politely, trying to bluff that I recognize any of the names as my stomach turns at his chauvinistic ideas.

The waitress comes, splashing tiny puddles of frigid water on the table as she places enormous water glasses in front of us.

"Sure," I concede, "whatever you assign I can cover." I reach for the bright red plastic straw, draw hard with my inhale.

"That was my attitude when I first came to the *Sentinel*. Whatever they asked of me. I figured that over time I'd work my way up so I could choose my own stories." He leans in, hinting at the confidence he is about to reveal, "I thought I was so much smarter than my editors, thought they were dumbing the paper down. 'The people aren't just dogs,' I told them, 'they know how to read, they want to learn things.'" He sits back, draws imaginary graph lines on the table, "But they have market research, demographic studies, all kinds of data about what newspaper readers want and what kind of readership our best advertisers require."

I listen, surprised by his frankness.

"I realize now the sports section is just a part of the business. If the paper makes money, I make money." He looks me in the eye. "My family's from Juarez, I'm sure you've seen the news about Juarez? The drug cartels are waging a war there over territory, over the border and access to the American market. People are dying for making the wrong alliances, stepping into other peoples' revenge killings. I've got two kids, one at UC San Diego and another here in high school. I'll do whatever it takes to keep those kids here instead of in Juarez."

I let out a low sound of affirmation. With these few words he has distilled our common purpose. I will write whatever pablum will help me protect and provide for my children.

The waitress brings our food on plates the size of serving platters.

I look up at Oscar, slightly embarrassed at the abundance.

"When can you start?" he asks.

"Today."

———

An elderly woman unlocks the door of apartment number 31. "It is not very big," she says, "but there's a view." She opens the door allowing me to enter first. I step into the kitchen; worn linoleum floor and slightly shabby appliances. "You'll want to see the living room and the balcony." She steps past me, pulling back floor length blinds to reveal a sliding glass door and a view of the ocean beyond the freeway. I can see how the sun will drop to the horizon and into the sea. The glass door squeaks on its rollers and I step out. The neighbors' balconies are filled with surfboards, beach cruiser bicycles, volleyball nets.

"There's a pedestrian bridge," the landlady explains. "You can see it just to the north, a block from our parking garage so you cross over the freeway to the beach."

"I have two little boys," I say, still staring at the horizon.

"The railings have been redone in the last couple of years. They're up to code, so a child can't slip through. Just as long as you have no pets, kids are fine."

"I want it. Can I leave a deposit, Mrs…?"

"Call me Elaine. Don't you want to see the bedroom first?" She chuckles. "Everyone falls in love with the view, as if they'll just spend all day looking at the ocean."

I follow her into the bedroom.

"Great, should I sign a rental agreement?"

She opens the door to show me the bathroom. "You can fill out the application and I'll run a credit check."

"Um, is that really necessary? What if I just give you an extra month's deposit, could you skip the credit check?" I try to sound nonchalant, thinking of the names that would appear on my credit report. The pile of crisp 100 dollar bills in my purse—the exchange for my wedding gold—should eliminate such questions.

She turns and scrutinizes my face. "You have a job?"

"Sportswriter at the *San Diego Sentinel*." I proffer my brand new business card.

"I guess an extra month's rent would do. Cash."

I smile. "Perfect."

Michael runs along the beach with his cousin Valerie, her elder sister Amanda carries Andrew on her back. Ted and I walk along without talking, allowing the sound of the waves to substitute for conversation. The crispness of the air fills my lungs and I feel alive.

Michael runs back to us, and holds both of our hands. "Do, 1-2-3. Pleeeeease. 1-2-3 me."

"OK, hold on," Ted grins. He and I call out 1-2-3, swinging Michael into the air on the third stride.

Michael squeals, and cries out, "Again!" We repeat the acrobatics a few times, and I feel for a moment like a picture book family. The deep fractures in my life obscured, erased even, by the sound and motion of Michael's body.

"All right, I think that is about all my back can take," Ted concedes.

"Just one more!"

"All right, one more," Ted smiles at me.

Michael rises into the air with our support and then lands safely back on the earth, intact, beautiful, happy. Ted gives him a playful smack on his backside and Michael breaks into a run toward his cousins to beg their launching services.

"So Janet's totally relieved," Ted says to me, as we watch Michael.

"Why?"

"She thought you might crash with us forever, and turn into one of those freaky broken widows who never recover."

I am careful to modulate our path between the soft dry sand that swallows up our footsteps and the wet sand that makes a sucking sound around our shoes and threatens our feet with the tail ends of the waves. "Your friend Oscar said he'd like to bring me on as staff."

"You're way more skilled than they need. How's the salary?"

"I'll get by."

Ted leans down and picks up a discarded clam shell, turns it over in his hand. "*Tivela stultorum*, Pismo clam." He dusts off the sand, examines the tightly closed seam between the shells. "Hardly find these clams anymore, thanks to the pollution and the refineries." He tosses it gently into the water. "Hey, what's happening with the insurance settlement?"

I misstep too far to my right and my foot sinks into the wet sand leaving a border of brown grains on my shoe. "Nothing."

"What do you mean nothing? What the fuck are they waiting for?"

"A body. No body, no cause of death. No cause of death, no final report from the FBI. No report, no claim." I reach down and pick up a stone to throw into the water. "Honestly Ted, I don't think that money will ever come, and that's probably fine. I don't want it now. He's gone, no longer part of my life and I don't want anything that ties me to him."

"Well how about those kids? Seems like they still tie you to him."

I stop walking. "Those kids are *mine*."

Ted stops, turns back to face me.

"They don't have his name, they don't need his money, they don't need to know anything about him." My voice has grown loud, loud enough that even the few sunset surfers might hear me as they ride in.

Ted's characteristic bemused expression transforms into something that borders on sympathy, or at least a reservation of judgment.

"Andrew won't even have any memories of him." My voice grows quiet again. "Anyway, at this point, you're more like a father to them than he is."

He turns to look at the children and then back toward me, avoiding my eyes, "So, let's turn back and go to your place and eat. Janet's waiting for us."

Chapter 5

Oscar leads me through the newsroom past a row of cluttered cubicles toward a glass walled office at the far end of the room. He pauses next to an empty cubicle, "Hopefully you'll be sitting here. We just need to convince Ed that you can crank out copy on deadline—he doesn't know anything about sports."

I smile my bright red lipsticked smile, "Haven't missed a deadline yet." I have brought copies of my resume and my little collection of sports articles I have written for the *Sentinel* as a freelancer.

Just before we reach the glass door bearing Ed Harley's name, Oscar turns to me. "Oh before I forget, here's your mail—the marketers and PR people are always quick to pick up a new reporter's name in the paper." He hands me a few postcards—advertising upcoming sports events—and a single white envelope.

Oscar opens the door and I stop, still outside the threshold. I recognize the envelope, no return address.

I look at Oscar and wonder what he knows. What has Ted told him about my past? What does he think of this envelope? Has he reported this piece of mail to anyone? Does the mailroom maintain a mail log?

Oscar looks at me curiously, "You look scared. Don't worry, Ed's great." Oscar gestures me into the room.

A balding, white-haired man turns away from his computer screen and stands to greet me, extending a hand over stacks of paper on his desk. "Ed Harvey. You must be Kathryn. Heard a lot about you."

"You have?" What has he heard? What does he know? I shove the envelope into my purse.

Ed offers his hand again, and I compel myself to respond. He chuckles, "Don't worry, it's all good. Oscar says you add a level of sophistication to sports writing that would make even me want to read it." He comes around the front of his desk to remove a pile of newspapers from one of the two chairs for guests. "Sorry, I'm a bit behind in my reading. Have a seat."

I sit stiffly, setting my purse under the chair, hoping that the leather bag will protect me from the envelope. Ed asks me questions about my experience, my interest in the paper, my availability for the job. I feel like I am in a witness box. Although the questions are friendly, I am careful not to reveal too much, I try to speak only about the present.

The phone rings and Ed picks up the handset and barks a few terse sentences into the mouthpiece. With the interview suspended I start thinking about my next move if I should fail today. I will be back at the beginning. I will comb the job listings, make cold calls, I will have to tell Ted and face his disappointment. I close my eyes and brace myself for the effort.

Ed hangs up the phone. "What the hell does 'above the fold' mean to the web designers," he mumbles to himself. He looks back at me as if he just remembered I was there. "Oh, yes. So let's finish this."

I start to thank him for his time, posturing myself for a quick exit.

"So then you'll start on Monday? Oscar, talk to HR so we can get Kathryn's contract in the next day or two."

"Perfect," Oscar says. "I'll call them now."

Stunned, I take a few shallow breaths. "Monday? Sure. Yes. Great." I force out a little smile. "I'll call the daycare to arrange for full time."

"Good, see you then." Ed turns back to his computer.

As Oscar and I step toward the door, Ed looks up. "Kathryn, one more thing."

I freeze. Oscar looks at me and nods reassuringly as he closes the door on his way out.

"Sit down again."

I do as I am told.

"Let me speak to you frankly, to put your mind at ease."

The muscles of my thighs involuntarily tighten.

"I'm aware of what's happened to you this year. I know you were married to Rashid Siddique. Of course I know about the bombing."

My intercostals turn to stone. I can barely breathe.

"I run a newspaper, I can't hire someone without doing some basic investigative reporting." He folds his hands in front of him, a gesture of sincerity. "I can only imagine how difficult this has been for you and your family."

I clutch my purse tighter. Don't cry now, he's already hired me.

"You were not responsible, it's obvious from the reporting that you weren't involved, that his actions were a shock to you as well. This is America, and we're only responsible for our own actions, we're individuals. You have the right to rebuild your life. And I'll be lucky to have you on my staff with your skills."

I blink and nod, trying to project the thanks I cannot speak.

"We don't need to discuss it again. I just wanted you to feel comfortable here and know that I'll consider your work without prejudice."

He stands; conversation over. I reach out my hand again across his stacks of papers and he responds quickly. I feel the warmth of his flesh in mine, and I reach out my other hand. I see a flicker of affection in his eyes and he joins his second hand. We stand there in a kind of four-handed embrace. For the first time since the bombing I feel a calmness, a thawing in a stranger's presence. The crags around his mouth and the wrinkles that crackle out from the corners of his eyes deepen as he smiles. Despite his balding head and his belly protruding against the buttons of his shirt, I think he is the loveliest man I have ever seen.

Chapter 6

I set Andrew at one edge of the carpet and I take up my place next to Michael at the other edge. Andrew lifts a bare foot and plops it down in front of himself. His other foot follows. I see his weight fall too far forward and his eyes grow wide with anxiety, but he recovers and repeats the process, quickly, hurtling himself across the length of the carpet and into our arms. Michael and I cheer and kiss Andrew on his cheeks. My baby is breathless with excitement.

"I am so proud of you, little brother," Michael says reaching for Andrew's hand, practically towering over him. "Walk to the balcony, so we can see the ocean." Andrew eagerly toddles along holding his brother's hand for stability. I follow them quietly.

"Now you can grow up to be a big boy," Michael—unaware I am listening—speaks in a voiced tinged with his idea of paternal gravitas. "After you get good at walking, you'll be able to run, and then ride a bicycle." Andrew holds onto the spindles of the balcony railing and looks up at his brother. "After I could run my father said he'd teach me to ride a bicycle. But he died in an accident. But it doesn't matter that I don't know how to ride a bicycle, because I'm going to learn how to surf." He kneels down so he shares his brother's perspective, as I have done with Michael thousands of times. "Can you see the waves? Surfers ride the waves, like dolphins. I'm going to learn to do that, Mommy says it's the best sport because there are no teams, no fights."

Andrew sways on his feet, leans his backside out and back and finally lowers himself to sit on the balcony. "Mie Mie," he smiles with his version of his brother's name and he points at the ocean giggling.

"Don't be sad that we don't have a daddy," Michael rests a hand on Andrew's shoulder. "We don't need one, we don't even need to talk about him. Mommy takes care of everything for us. And I'm getting bigger so I can help too."

Andrew plucks his toes and sings random notes to himself. "Daddy was from Pakistan, but tell everyone he was Greek. Greekland is better, no one likes Pakistan."

I take a few steps back so I can walk to the sliding glass door as if I had just arrived there. "Come in now, it's getting windy."

Michael helps Andrew to his feet and steps back, encouraging his little brother to walk to him. I look over my shoulder, instinctively looking for their father to share my pleasure at this milestone. Of course, I am alone, only ghosts could hover behind my shoulder. Never mind. I walk to the phone and call out in my most sing-song voice, "Let's call Grandma and Uncle Ted and tell them Andrew's walking!"

I greet my nieces who are watching television cartoons. Janet calls out a greeting from the back yard. We step outside. Ted rummages in the garage as Janet makes a bee line for Andrew. She squats down before him, flattening the precise crease in her pedal pushers, "Andrew! Show me your walking."

I smile and let go of his hand. Janet and I must look like mirror images of delight. Andrew rushes to her and she embraces him, still not the full-bodied hug I would give him, but genuine.

Ted emerges from the garage, a red bicycle with tassels dangling from the handlebars held aloft as he wades out between neatly stacked and labeled boxes. Do they ever use the things in those boxes? I wonder with a tinge of jealousy about their intact history.

"Come on little man," Ted booms with a smile. "Time you learned how to ride a bicycle."

Michael looks at me for permission first, and when I smile he runs to Ted, who has set the bike on its kickstand in the driveway.

Andrew pulls on Janet's hand, trying to lead her back into the kitchen. I look back at Ted who holds the bike and positions Michael's feet on the pedals. For a delicious moment I stand alone in the garden, absolved of demands. Safe. Welcome. I have learned to take these moments, recognize these fleeting spaces, the interstitial seconds, when I need not project anything for anyone else's benefit. I am simply a woman living, breathing, feeling the air on my skin, hearing the sounds of the world moving around me, a simple presence with neither future nor past, neither regret nor hope.

And then Amanda's voice calls out from the living room, "Mom! Dad! Come quick. You should see this." A curious tone in her voice—a deadly urgency—transposes to a happy note. "Hurry!" I rush in. Andrew has led Janet to the drawer where he knows she keeps cookies. Janet sweeps Andrew into her arms, still holding a cookie, closing the drawer with her foot before joining her daughters in front of the television.

The cartoon program has been replaced by the somber face of President Obama, the backdrop precise, dignified, serious. "The ten-year search for Osama bin Laden is over." The man who has terrorized us has been hunted down and killed. "He was killed in a precise surgical strike in his compound in Pakistan." I think of the compound, the cluster of rooms where I lived for brief periods as part of a Pakistani family. I understand that even a patriarch like Osama—a man who had perfected hatred and terror mongering— would have been surrounded by women and children.

Ted lets out a cheer, as if he were at a football game. "About friggin' time we got that bastard."

"It's been a long war." Janet sighs. "Hopefully this means we've turned a corner." Andrew squirms in Janet's arms until she returns him to the floor.

The ticker along the bottom of the television screen repeats Obama's statements almost as quickly as he makes them, interspersed with tallies of the deaths Osama's side has inflicted. 2,977 killed in the September 11, 2001 attacks. 1,864 soldiers in Afghanistan. 52 in the London subway attacks. 202 in the Bali bombing. 3 in the double freeway bombing in Los Angeles. My blood runs cold. Did they all read that luminous statistic on the screen? I hear the awkward silence in the room. Are they are all avoiding my gaze? Are they holding me responsible for that last number? Perhaps they didn't see it. Perhaps this is just my imagination. As Obama completes his address the broadcasters display a selection of file footage; Osama in his videotaped addresses, Osama standing outside at a training camp in Afghanistan years earlier, the iconic image of Osama the wanted man. Suddenly a little hand strikes his face. Andrew has swaggered to the television screen and continues to hit at the oversize face on the wide flat-screen television.

"That's right Andrew. Give him what he deserves." Ted eggs on my little boy.

The image changes and Osama's face is replaced by Obama's. Andrew continues to bang at the screen. I know I should retrieve him, know he is behaving badly, but I dare not step in front of them. I don't want this family, this whole, healthy, normal family to notice that I am here.

Janet hurries over to Andrew, "All right baby, not him." She grabs his arm mid-strike. "Don't hit him, he's one of the good guys." She places her hands on his shoulder and he pivots in place. He takes a few steps toward me before tripping and banging his head on the corner of the coffee table. He lets out a little cry then unleashes a terrible scream. Janet reaches to lift him, but I rush to him, gather him to me. I am his mother. I will be the one to comfort him, to wash away the blood, to examine the cut, not her.

I retreat to the bathroom, so I can escape their eyes, the eyes of Ted's family, the violent eyes on the television screen. I hold Andrew's head to my shoulder, trying to muffle his shrill cries. I clutch a washcloth at his brow. After a moment his sounds diminish to whimpers. I pull away the perfectly white terrycloth, see the little blot of blood. I rinse out the cloth, wash the spot as I stroke his head. "Don't worry, you'll be fine." The superficial cut will heal quickly, but I welcome it as a pretense for us to leave. I open the door to start making my way out.

"So what'll happen now?" Amanda asks from the sofa. "Does this mean the wars will end?"

"Do you think my friend Jeremy's cousin will come back from Iraq?" Valerie picks up the train of thought.

"I don't know girls, bin Laden wasn't running the wars. But even if the troops don't come home, the end of Osama bin Laden is a very good thing. We should be very happy about this."

My stomach tightens like a fist before a punch. I want to tell the girls, *Of course the wars won't end, Iraq is about oil and regional occupation, not terrorism—the media has blurred the issues, the politicians are delighted for us to confuse the meanings of these two military campaigns.* Arguments and rationales that I had carefully edited when I was at the journal, balanced opinions I had exhorted reporters to articulate tumble through my head. I want to recite them, lay out my logic, convince them of the historical folly of trying to tame Afghanistan, of trying to impose a democracy on a foreign culture, of thinking the rule of law could outshine centuries of clan-based loyalties.

But I do not speak. It doesn't matter if I am right.

Michael tugs quietly at Ted, who is now sitting next to the girls on the couch, glued to the continuing coverage. "Uncle Ted? Can we go back to the bike?"

I take a step toward Michael, perhaps a bit too forcefully. "We're going home now, Michael. Andrew needs to take a nap. And this has nothing to do with you."

"But Mom, what about the bicycle? Uncle Ted's teaching me to ride." The weight of the disappointment pulls his shoulders down.

"No. Ted is watching the television," I say, perhaps too crisply. I kneel down beside my boy, hoping to soften the blow. "Perhaps we can take the bike with us. *I* will teach you to ride."

"Promise?"

"Promise."

I walk from my cubicle to the water cooler and go through the motions of taking a drink. From here I can see into Ed's office. He is not on the phone. He doesn't yet appear stressed about the afternoon deadline. I knock on his door and he motions for me to enter.

"What can I do for you?"

His chairs are stacked with newspapers so there is no place to sit.

"May I?" I gesture to the obstructed chair seat.

"Oh excuse me." He pushes his chair out so he can get to the stack.

"I've got it." As I lift a dozen newspapers to set them aside, I see the above-the-fold photo of today's paper. A crowd of people celebrate bin Laden's death; waving American flags, arms outstretched, mouths open mid-cheer, illuminated by the streetlights that surround the construction site at ground zero.

I sit down and point to the paper. "Actually, this is what I want to talk about."

"You're wondering why we chose to lead with a photograph of New York? We thought about going with a photo from San Diego, but the celebrations were more subdued here. We thought that New York was more emblematic of the end of that chapter."

"But that's the problem, I don't think it *will* be an end. People the world over who have followed Osama bin Laden will feel obliged to avenge his death. I feel less safe this morning than I did yesterday morning." I look down at my naked fingers, the absence of rings marking my isolation. "I know how seriously Pakistanis and Muslims take their revenge."

He is quiet for a moment. "I see your point. So what do you think would be a better option? You think we shouldn't have killed him?"

"Why not capture him, put him on trial? Don't we follow the rule of law?"

He purses his lips, thinking. "Let's play that out. Say the SEALS break into the compound under cover of night, and imagine that by some good stroke, they're able to get Osama bin Laden out of his home alive, never minding the inevitable firefight his guards will put up." He puts his wrists out in front of himself, as if they are cuffed together. "And we bring him back to American soil in a military plane. The Pakistanis will *love* this—we make a big show of how they were protecting our most wanted enemy as we set him up on trial here. And which court of law should we use? A regular civilian court? A court martial? Like we have handled with the detainees at Guantanamo Bay?" He places one hand over his heart and the other over an imaginary Bible. "And suppose we get old Osama to take the oath of truth over our trusty Bible, what truth do you think he's going to spew? His truth about the return of the caliphate? His truth about the coming victory of Islam over the infidels?"

"Well, that would be pretty incriminating, right? And don't we enshrine freedom of speech? Doesn't he have the right to speak on the witness stand?"

"Are you really worried about bin Laden's first amendment right?" Ed leans in. "And let's continue with this. Suppose we do somehow manage the Herculean security feat of keeping bin Laden alive to stand trial, and preventing some wacko extremist from blowing up the courthouse, or the prison, or the vehicle that transports him between the two, and we manage to get a conviction, and assuming he hasn't died from kidney failure by then, what's his sentence? The American people couldn't possibly accept anything short of a death sentence." He brings his hands together on the desk. "One way or another, we had to kill Osama."

My nostrils flare with inhalation. "We had to take our revenge."

"Yes. And I have to say after what he did, he deserved what he got, and I think the President did it pretty well."

I am silent. I gaze down at the images of patriots, people intoxicated with the glory of our country's revenge. On other days I have seen images of other people, men with dark beards wearing pale kurta pajamas similarly imbibing on the wine of revenge. Different countries. Different perpetrators. Common emotion.

"What're you worried about, Kathryn? Are you concerned that your connection to the bombing somehow singles you out for an attack? Seems to me it would be just the opposite."

"No, I guess it's not that I worry about my physical safety. But I worry about what this says about us. What does this mean for us as a nation? Who are we if this is how we treat our enemies?" I press my lips together, feel the lipstick between them. "When I married

Rashid I went to great pains to describe Muslims as peace-loving people. I was open minded about his culture to a fault. I explained away their tendency toward violence as an artifact of the British empire and Partition. I was so naive. I looked the devil in the eye and remarked about how rich were the colors of his irises."

I look Ed in the eye, feel a force rising in my chest.

"I hate their system of justice." I clench my jaws together, feel the pressure behind my eyes. I fight back my tears, I did not come to Ed's office to cry. "I hate the way it rips apart families, not just mine, countless families across the region. I hate the way it elevates death over the living, glorifies the suffering of others as the thrill of revenge. I want nothing to do with it. I have reengineered my life, I have amputated my memories so that my sons and I will not have to live with the ugliness of revenge. And now..." a tear bursts onto my cheek despite my efforts, "and now I feel like I see the same ugliness in my own country, these people who are supposedly my people." I let my hand rest over the newspaper photo in my lap. "I just want to believe in a place where people settle their disputes in a civilized way, where you know that if you behave according to the rules, you won't have to fear."

He gives me an avuncular smile and moves to me. With a little heave he lifts the double pile of newspapers and sets them on the floor. Sitting next to me, he exhales a sigh. "Kathryn, you should be proud of yourself. After all you've been through, you still hold on to an idealism. I've been in the news business a long time. We've printed every kind of barbarism, and crooked political deal, every corrupt self-interested banking scheme and bombing the world can dish up," he thumps his hand on the stack of newspapers. "I have achieved a nearly perfect cynicism about the world. I hate all systems almost equally, I maintain dismally low expectations of any politician, businessman, military leader. I'm almost never disappointed."

"So then why do you bother with any of it?"

"I figure, the only thing I can depend on, the only actions I can control in this world are my own. I no longer care if the paper is elevating the debate, or illuminating the conversations of our subscribers. I know my job is to send out ink on paper everyday that gets peoples' attention, so we can sell those peoples' attention to dish soap manufacturers and car dealers." He picks up a newspaper and lets it flop back onto the pile. "But what matters to me is the people in my newsroom. Do they take pride in their work? Do I create a place where they can feel respected, where they can do their work without interference, where they can learn from each other? If my reporters go home and can't use me as an excuse to beat their wives, or drink an entire six pack, if they can take their paycheck and go out for dinner on the weekends, I figure I've done my job well enough." He runs a hand over his thinning hair. "Saving the world, and perfecting systems…that's not my job." He looks at me, reaches out to take the paper from me. "It's not your job either. Your job is to take the best care of your boys that you can. Bring me some good stories so you can keep a roof over their head, and then show them love even though they live in this world where you can see hatred and violence everywhere you choose to look."

"But what about the rule of law? Doesn't that mean anything to us as a country? Doesn't it mean anything to you?"

"Certainly nice if you can get it. God bless the ACLU and the human rights watchers. If they continue to do their work, and you continue to believe in the law, you're probably on the right track."

I squeeze my hands until my knuckles turn white.

"Kathryn, don't think so much. We can only carry little bits of the world on our shoulders, not the whole thing. Take care of your bit."

"Take care of my bit." I nod, release my hands.

Chapter 7

Five years after the bombing

"Mom, my cape!" Andrew shrieks as we return to the apartment, his Superman Halloween costume caught in the door.

Michael rushes back, holds Andrew's chest so he doesn't move, and carefully opens the door. "OK Andrew? Superman can still fly."

I pour myself a glass of wine as the boys unload their bags of trick-or-treat candy on the kitchen table.

"Mom, I want to eat everything!" Andrew lays his face down on the pile of candy, as if to hug it.

"How much can we have?" Michael's fingers have already clutched a couple of candy bars.

"You can eat as much as you want, but remember," I point to a yellowed piece of paper on the refrigerator, a set of rules I wrote out shortly after bin Laden's killing.

"Which one?" Andrew pushes his candies around.

"Capen Code number four," I touch the paper, "you must 'Understand that your choices will have consequences.' So eat as much as you want, but if you eat too many, you'll probably feel sick."

"Awesome! As much as we want!" Andrew tears open candy after candy, stuffing his mouth.

Michael—ever the older and wiser—reminds his brother,

"Andrew, you're a lot smaller than me, you're only five, so don't try to eat as much as me."

I strike a match and light several candles on an altar, the flames illuminating photographs of a handful of people. I have set out flowers, chocolates, good coffee, even a tin of caviar I keep only for this purpose.

"Mom, why do you put out food for photographs every Halloween?" Michael asks between bites.

"*Dia de los muertos*, the day of the dead," I blow out the match, adjust a picture frame with a photo of my grandparents on their wedding day, stoic expressions and starched clothes. "This is how Oscar taught us to honor people that've come and gone."

The first Halloween I had worked at the *Sentinel*, Oscar had told me he populated his altar not only with his loved ones who had died, but with newspaper photographs of people in Juarez who had been killed by the drug cartels; people who might have been schoolmates, people who could have been his neighbors, even people with whom he had no connection. *Maybe it's pointless*, he had told me, *but I believe the souls of dead victims want to be remembered, want to have a little of the life that someone stole from them. Thank God my girls don't have to live in the danger, but I still live with the death of that place.*

I dust off three pictures of people I never met, pictures I photocopied from the *Sentinel's* archives more than a year after the paper had included them in coverage of the bombing; a 36-year old man on his way to the office, a 52-year old man on his way to a Santa Monica garden he maintained, and a 19-year old girl on her way to morning classes at UCLA.

"So who are all the people?" Michael stands next to me and points to each photo in turn.

I tell him the names of my grandparents and his great aunts, a childhood friend who died in a boating accident.

"And what about these people?" Michael points to the newspaper portraits.

"Those are people I want to respect."

"What people?" Andrew joins us, flapping his cape up and down.

"These people," Michael points again. "Why do you want to respect them?"

"Just because." I step back to the kitchen. Each year I avoid this question. I am willing to acknowledge I have some connection to them, to ask forgiveness of their souls, but not to speak of it with the children.

"'Just because' why?"

Michael has never asked why there is no picture of his father on the altar. Maybe I should start adding other victims, other people I don't know so these three pictures aren't so obvious.

"Because I said so. Now stop asking questions."

Andrew flaps his cape again. "Can I eat the chocolate for the dead people?"

"No!"

"They can't eat it," he says indignantly.

"No more questions. Eat your own chocolate."

Chapter 8

Ten years after the bombing

The security guard at the bank—they seem to get younger each year—leads me back to the safe deposit box viewing room. I repeat my routine, it only takes me a minute or two; usually I don't even bother to sit down.

I pull the envelope from my purse, double check to make sure there is nothing inside the layers of paper besides the 25 one hundred dollar bills—there never is, but this has become habit—and slide it in the box next to the previous envelope. Even after all these years, the nightmare still haunts me whenever the envelopes arrive. The next day, I feel angry and bewildered as if the Rashid who kicks me in my subconscious were real.

The box is nearly full. Out of some morbid sense of accomplishment, I take out the envelopes and count them. Forty. Like clockwork, an envelope has arrived every three months, four times a year for the last decade. Ten years since I became the martyr's wife, ten years of rejecting someone else's reality, repressing the past, asserting an identity of my choosing. One hundred thousand dollars in this box that I have rejected, money I have taken out of circulation, power I have kept in suspended animation. How long will the envelopes continue to come? Who sends them? I can barely imagine the fidelity, the dedication of the organization, the sender.

At the bottom of the box, almost forgotten, rest two rings. The symbols of my marriage, inert, intact. Leave, I tell myself. Walk out. Replace the envelopes and lock the box. Don't disturb these memories. But something propels me to take the rings. So easily the small band slides onto my ring finger. So naturally does the man's band slide right next to it, the engraved words encircling my finger. I remember the Rashid of the nightmares. Sometimes he appears alive, sometimes dead. In the nightmare I always scream. I scream for his safety, I scream in anger, I scream out of fear. He never responds with words. "God damn it!" I say out loud. I shake the larger ring back into the box with a hollow jangling sound. I look at the smaller ring still on my finger. What if I walked out of here wearing this ring? What would change? Even without it, I haven't acted like a single woman, available to another man. Have I been faithful to a memory? What the fuck am I waiting for?

I pull the ring off and throw it back into the box. Those rings can have each other.

———————

"So Ed tells me you cover sports. How did you first get interested in sports?" Ed's friend, Johannes, lifts his water glass.

"I'm a journalist and I needed a job. Nothing more to it." Despite my evening dress and high heels, I respond as if he is an interrogator, not a date.

"Fair enough," Johannes smiles. "And do you enjoy it? Ed says you've got a remarkable perspective on sports. How did he describe it? That you see it as a 'cultural phenomena,' not just a bunch of scores."

"Ed. What would I do without Ed?" At the mention of his name I feel at ease. When I asked him if he could suggest a dinner companion he had seemed relieved, told me he wondered how long I was going to play a nun in red lipstick.

"I used to think sports were just a stupid distraction from all the things that really matter," I reply to Johannes. "I mean, war can be overshadowed by the Superbowl. Millions of people will spend less time thinking about who they'll put in Congress than they think about who'll win the NBA playoffs."

"You're right."

"So I came to realize that sports distract so well, because they tap into some of our most basic instincts."

"How so?" He leans in, interested. He really is a handsome man. Ed had only described him as a divorced doctor in his fifties.

"I think all sports are a substitute for war, our most basic competition. Some sports are like hand-to-hand combat, others are like a battlefield, and some are just to display physical prowess, like how men have competed to lead the tribe and win the favor of the most desirable female."

"Really? Hand-to-hand combat?"

"Think of boxing and wrestling, of course, but also golf—I mean it's about swinging a club."

Johannes nods, amused. "Battlefield?"

"Anything where teams vie for territory, American and European football, basketball, rugby, hockey."

"And so the other sports, swimming, track and field, skating…"

"All about demonstrating physical prowess, the prerequisite for both leadership and the attentions of women."

The waiter brings the wine Johannes had ordered. We pause in our conversation as he skillfully slices the metal casing, twists the cork screw and removes it from the bottle in a single flowing motion.

"I think he'd win the gold if cork pulling were an Olympic event," Johannes winks at the waiter and approves the first pour of the wine.

"Oh, and the Olympics," I continue, "are an incredibly efficient substitute for a global war. Every four years nations demonstrate their power for very little cost, either in blood or treasure."

"Hmm," Johannes seems impressed with my analysis, he raises his glass in a toast. "Well, here's to more sports and less warfare."

"I'll certainly toast to that."

"And especially the kinds of sports that win the affections of a woman!"

———————

Johannes sits next to me in the concert hall, the entire string section vibrates, the musicians send their bows back and forth with amazing speed, then break into a melody I think I recognize from the opening of a news program I watched years ago. A musical interpretation of Mercury, god of flight. The musicians on the stage bring us through the solar system, one planet, one melodic theme at a time. The effect is magical. As we approach Jupiter—the bringer of jollity—the tones expand into a rich resonant strolling arc. I weep at the beauty. I reach for Johannes' hand as the strings join with the horns. "Thank you," I mouth without sound. I don't know if he understands me or not, but he places his other hand over mine.

Before we reach Neptune I want to have a man again. I do not need a man, I have proven that to myself over and over in the last decade. But now I want Johannes, the way I sometimes want a chocolate cake or a beautiful pair of shoes, as a luxury, a delicious experience.

After the concert we sit on the couch in my home.

"I've seen patients heal more quickly after surgery when they have music in their hospital rooms." He touches his fingers to his heart, traces the path of his aorta, "It's as if music can act like a lifeblood."

"I can imagine that. It's been so long since I've heard live music. The Jupiter melody…" My hands make arcs in the air as if drawing the music. Johannes reaches for my hands mid-flight, and kisses them.

I stop talking and smile. He caresses my fingers, running his own into the spaces between them. I shift my hips on the sofa allowing my legs to separate slightly beneath my skirt. He proceeds, raising my fingers to his mouth, one, then two of my fingers disappear into the warmth of his tongue, his lips, his beard bristling against my palm. I close my eyes and lean back. His hand is at my knee, reaching inside. A surgeon's hands, I think, delicate and precise.

He pulls me down onto the carpet, I feel the wool fibers against

156

my back, I feel the weight of him over my hips. The intensity of his movements increases.

"Wait, not yet." I press my hands against his hips to slow his movements. He looks at me with a confused expression. I roll him on to his back and sit astride him. "It's been a long time, I don't want it to end yet."

He laughs and relaxes, allowing me to lead. And I take my time with our bodies, feeling skin, feeling muscles and bone, hair and lips. I allow him to breach my self-reliance, I accept the pleasure of a man.

In the silence that follows we drift into a sleepy oblivion.

At some point later, I wake. I sit up and look around the room. The darkness of the night still promises hours of sleep. I walk to the kitchen to pour myself a glass of water. Even this simple act of walking through the room, feeling the air on my naked body provides a new sense of freedom. I drink the entire glass and fill it again for Johannes. I return to him, whisper into his ear, "Come, let's sleep on the bed."

He opens his eyes, focusing on my face to remember where he is and who I am. He sits up on his elbow and accepts the water from me. He looks to his sex, now flaccid, and checks his watch. "I should leave now."

"No," I say with conviction. "Sleep, you can leave in the morning."

"All right," he smiles, "I appreciate the hospitality." And he follows me to the bed. We slide between the sheets, I wrap my legs around his and tilt my pelvis into his body. He puts his arm around me, runs his hand down the length of my back.

"I don't know if I have it in me for more tonight. Turn over."

I do as he says and he begins to massage my back. His hands are strong but with soft skin, the hands of a man whose work is indoors. I must drift off to sleep, images of the distant planets spin in my mind

Then I feel a leg strike my back. I sit bolt upright in bed. "Goddamit! Why do you always do that?" I accuse.

"Do what?" Johannes asks, startled, half-asleep.

157

"You kicked me!"

"No…no, we were just laying together, maybe I was turning over."

"Oh…Johannes," I say, disoriented, "it's not you."

"Its OK," he strokes my shoulder, coaxes me to lie back down. "You're all right. We all have bad dreams sometimes."

And I lie down, wide awake in the arms of a different man.

I turn the key in the mailbox lock. I nearly throw away the whole pile of mail, political flyers for the upcoming mayoral election, and newsprint ads for the local grocery store. But then I notice an extra envelope, better quality paper than the usual bill or solicitation. Addressed to the *Beneficiaries of Rashid Siddique*, the envelope bears the name of an insurance company. I am so glad I have never allowed the boys to fetch the mail, have never given them a key. What would I have to explain if they had found this envelope before me?

I turn my back to the building, where the boys are already upstairs, and open the envelope. As ten years have passed without correspondence as to the status of my claim, the company has determined to resolve the claim by paying a quarter of the policy's death benefit. Several pages describe the process by which I can appeal their decision, with proper evidence of the policy holders' death.

The settlement check, even though it represents tens of thousands of dollars, seems cheap and flimsy at this point, as useless as the two-for-one cantaloupe coupons in my other hand. I laugh, scoff, at this unexpected reminder.

"Mom," Andrew shouts from our doorway, "what's for dinner?"

I use the newsprint to wrap up the check and the envelope and shove it into my purse. Maybe I should ask Ed what to do with it. Or maybe I'll just shred it at the office.

"Mom?!"

"Omelets," I call back.

Chapter 9

Twenty years after the bombing

I stand at the kitchen counter, rushing to sort the mail with one hand, while I pour my afternoon coffee with the other. I will respond to the fundraising packet from Loyola Law School after Michael's graduation tomorrow. The symphony subscriber's magazine can go on the stack of reading material next to the couch. The envelope with the quarterly payments for the family of Rashid Siddique will have to go to the bank. I resent the timing, the necessary trip to the safe deposit box, the inevitable bad dreams when I have so much to do to prepare for Michael's law school graduation party.

I place the money in my purse, next to a printout of directions to the hospital where my father is dying. My mother discouraged Ted and me from coming earlier this week. As Father had already outlived the doctor's expectations given the cancer, my mother expected he would hold on for news of his grandson's graduation.

"Mom! Open up," Andrew bangs on the door. I open it to see him struggling under several restaurant catering trays. I clear a space on the table, where he sets them with a groan. "Are we really going to need all this food? Who's coming?" He takes off his UC San Diego baseball cap and combs back his sweaty dark hair.

"Hello," I say, demanding a proper greeting.

"Hi, Mom," he says dutifully. "So who's coming?

"I've invited our usual people, Ted and his family, Oscar, Ed. Mostly, Michael invited a lot of new friends from law school, and some of the people he'll be working with at the ACLU."

Andrew rolls his eyes as he opens the fridge and pulls out a bottle of juice. "So a whole room full of lawyers."

"Is Hema coming?" I ask.

He sets the bottle down. "Why do you always have to use that tone when you talk about my girlfriend?"

"What tone?" I turn to open cupboards so I don't have to mask my discomfort from him.

"You know, the tone that tells me how much you dislike her. Is it because she's Egyptian? Muslim? You're prejudice against Arabs, aren't you?" He moves closer, so when I turn around he stands in front of me, challenging me.

"It's not Arabs," I say, feeling my stomach tighten. "Hema's a beautiful girl, I'm glad she doesn't wear a headscarf, so you can see how beautiful she is."

"But?"

I step around him, pull paper plates and napkins from a grocery bag on the floor. "It's just more complicated to be with someone from a different culture. It can cause you a lot of problems."

"What the fuck, Mom…"

I spin on my heel to face him, "Don't you dare swear at me."

"Sorry," he says too quickly, "but really. I mean *you* married a *Greek* guy," he emphasizes the words sarcastically.

This is the first time Andrew has mentioned my husband, his father to me, taking a sideways strike at our family taboo.

"And this Johannes guy you try to keep away from us, what is he? Dutch? Danish? Isn't that another culture?"

"Johannes came to this country as a child." I stumble, reach for the counter to support myself. "That has nothing to do with this. Is Hema coming or not?"

"No," he says defiantly, "I didn't want her to have to drive over here to take this kind of crap from you."

I sigh. "Can you just help me get ready for this party? I have enough on my mind without you..." I let the sentence hang, unfinished. I look around to assess my preparations. "Can you go and get a couple bags of ice?"

"Like it isn't already chilly enough around here." He steps out and slams the door behind him. I wonder where the sweet child who used to sit on my lap has gone.

Chapter 10

I sit between Andrew, Ted, and Johannes. Before and behind us rows and rows of people have come to witness the milestone of graduation. Ted beams like a proud father. I think maybe I shouldn't have invited Johannes after all, Andrew didn't speak to him even once at the party last night.

I squeeze Ted's hand, "Thank you."

"For what?"

"For all your help raising Michael. He wouldn't have been here if not for you."

He shrugs, "I just fed you dinner once in a while. You're the one who fed his obsession with rules. And now you're the one forking over for the tuition." He laughs.

Johannes taps my shoulder, pointing to the embossed commencement program. "Did you know Michael's speaking? Looks like he's giving the Statement of Class."

"What?" I hold my own program at arm's length. "I wish I hadn't forgotten my reading glasses."

"Looks like we'll find out soon enough," Johannes points to the elevated dais in front of the graduating class. The dean—authoritative in his black robe, complete with a velvet lined hood draped over his shoulders—walks to the podium.

"Welcome. Welcome to all of you who have spent the last three years learning the law with us, welcome to all of you who have supported these students through their academic journey." He goes on, offering a few words about the pride we should feel in these graduates, the honorable tradition of the law, the drive toward excellence that the school embodies. I wonder if he gives the same speech every year. "And now, I will let you hear from the class itself, from its representative. This young man," he intones, "has been an exemplary student, responsible, intelligent, compassionate." I like to think he is describing Michael, but it could be another student. "But what distinguishes him, what radiates from his mind is an indelible belief in the power of the law to allow individuals and communities to solve their differences, to resolve their wrongs not for the benefit of the richest and most powerful, but for the youngest and most vulnerable. It is my honor to introduce Michael S. Capen."

My mind stumbles over the S as my son stands and strides confidently to the podium. He has no middle name. Why would he add an arbitrary letter to his name?

He grasps the podium with both hands, looks out over the audience as if to ensure our collective attention. "Justice," he pauses, "is a fundamental human requirement. Without a sense of justice, individuals and societies will engage in almost anything to achieve it. Deceit, wars, murders, mass killings," he inhales, "terrorist acts." His roving eyes seem to focus on me with these words. "All have been justified as attempts to achieve justice. Such seemingly barbaric actions are often successful, providing for the aggressor some satisfaction, some salve to a psyche wounded by injustice. The fundamental flaw with such systems of justice lies in the emotional toll they inflict on the families of both the wronged and the avenged." He stops, looks down at his notes and then challenges the audience. "Imagine the children of a man in a tribal society, orphaned when he is killed over a land dispute. Not only are they deprived of their father, but they are then raised with the purpose to balance their sense of injustice, to make things right according to their own sense of fairness—an eye for an eye. Their future is stolen from them, their actions are predetermined by an archaic system of justice."

I feel adrenaline shoot through my body in response to these hypothetical orphaned children. From where did he imagine such a story?

"Worse still, in our globalized world where we brush up against and even welcome into our country millions of people who have been acculturated into such revenge-based justice systems, their systems and ours can clash in the most explosive ways. Of course the dark day of September 11, 2001 still haunts our national consciousness."

I feel tremendously exposed, as if my son were revealing secrets I have long sequestered—for his own protection—here in the blazing public sun. I reach for my purse and slide to the front of my seat, looking for the easiest way to flee. I don't want to be here, trapped among the folding chairs and fancy spring dresses.

Ted places a hand on my knee. "You need to stay. *He* needs you to stay."

I slowly slide back into my seat, but keep my purse on my lap. Johannes' raised-eyebrow glance to me goes unanswered.

"Thankfully," Michael continues, "my mother taught me from an early age a set of rules, our own family code, designed to govern our lives in a rational, dependable, peaceable way. As children my brother and I learned that if you want something, you must ask nicely for it. If you are asked nicely for something, and feel you cannot give it, you must at least share it for a time."

I see them, as children fighting over toys and treats, hear my relentless repetition of this rule.

"Knowing we could rely on a set of rules, parameters for our conduct, with fixed and predictable consequences should we violate them, instilled in me a desire to learn and use the rules of our legal system.

"Our obligation," he sweeps his arm over the podium, including in the gesture the rows of his fellow students before him, "our mission, as a group of students privileged to study perhaps the most evolved and sophisticated system of justice, is to act as a beacon to the world, to illuminate the ways in which a non-violent, legal method of solving disputes and meting out justice is superior to systems founded on a primitive hunger for revenge which employ tools of violence and intimidation."

He pauses, allowing his words to settle. "May you meet with success."

The audience responds with warm applause. Tears spring onto my cheeks. I hope Ted and Johannes will misunderstand my emotion as pride. My son's eloquent words, however, have filled me with dread.

I stand up, awkwardly step over Ted's feet.

"Mom, where are you going?" Andrew asks, reaching out for my hand.

"I have to go to the bathroom," I lie. I must reach Michael before the others when he comes off the stage. I must protect Andrew from whatever Michael knows. I move to the edge of the stage, hovering there through the keynote address of some fabulously wealthy lawyer-turned-entrepreneur, through all of the students' names, called out in monotonously alphabetical order. My mind blurs so that I don't even see Michael as he receives his diploma.

And finally the ceremony concludes, the newly ordained students—now doctors of justice—move en masse to the edge of an expansive lawn to greet their families in a frenzy of squeals and shoulder thumping.

I find Michael, among a clutch of students, accepting their congratulations. He sees me and opens his arms, embracing me now as a man, not just my child. I can barely raise my arms to reciprocate.

"Michael, the S, why the S in your name?"

He inhales, the smile evaporating from his face. "It's short for Siddique."

The blood drains from my face.

"I wanted it as a reminder of the debt I owe."

I feel as though I am falling, an elevator suddenly dropping, dangerously free from its tethering cable.

"How?" I try to form a question, "what do you know?"

"Mom, I've known for years. It wasn't difficult, the research, putting the story together, to realize we are the family of Rashid Siddique."

I feel my expression tremble. "Why…"

He reaches for my hand, "It's all right, Mom. You were trying to protect me." He wraps his arms around me again, I feel his black graduation robe against my cheek. "I appreciate all you did. But you don't have to protect me anymore."

I sob, find myself in unfamiliar territory. My son now shielding me.

"Here you are," Johannes emerges from the swirl of people around us. "I wondered where you had disappeared to," he does not touch me, respectfully observes something private between my son and me. Ted and Andrew join us, congratulating Michael, hugging him.

"Hey, good speech," Andrew puts his arm over his brother's shoulder, now exactly the same height as his own.

"Did you know he was going to speak, Andrew?" I ask.

"No," Michael quickly responds. "He doesn't know. He didn't know."

I am grateful for Michael's answer to my implied question.

"I knew," Ted volunteers, "We talked about it lots." He looks at me directly, so I understand his larger meaning. "He didn't tell you about the speech, because of Dad's...hospitalization." He reaches out for Michael's hand, looks at me, "you've got one hell of a kid." His usually cavalier tone quavers with emotion.

"Perhaps we should all toast to Michael before we have to get you and Ted off to the airport," Johannes suggests to me politely.

"Yeah," Ted recovers, "Let's get ours now, you know free champagne never lasts long."

My mother looks tired. Without her delicate makeup, the lines in her face seem to stand out like a map of the emotions she has so carefully regulated over the decades. She holds my father's hand. His body looks so thin, as if the hospital bed held not the steady, capable man of the world who was my father, but his shadow, or perhaps his shell—hollow evidence of his life.

"I'm so glad you're here. He's been waiting for you," our mother says to us.

I kiss my father's cheek, hear a slow shallow breath emerging from his mouth.

I hug my mother, feeling strangely like the parent in this situation. "How is he?"

"You know, your father's always been very determined. The doctors say he's lost almost all his lung capacity. He said he'd take antibiotics for the pneumonia, but made me promise I wouldn't let them intubate him for oxygen."

She leans down and whispers in his ear. "Robert, the children are here." He doesn't respond. "Kathryn and Ted flew up from San Diego to see you. Do you want to open your eyes and see them?"

His eyelids flutter and I see his hand move slightly in my mother's. His watery eyes reveal a surprising clarity, a lucidity starkly contrasting his body, which is so obviously shutting down. He looks from my face to Ted's, the tiny muscles around his eyes flexing to express a smile, an expression too taxing for his mouth. From deep in his throat, comes a reedy sound. I bend down as the sound comes again, a word, words. The air passes through his voice box and reaches my ear. "Michael...graduated..."

"Yes, Dad." I squeeze his hand. "He graduated today. He gave the speech for his class. We were all very proud."

His eyes shine from some mysterious source. Ted leans down next to me and the sounds come again. "I'm proud...of..." he inhales, "you...all."

"We love you, Dad," Ted looks at him and then looks up at the wall, tears at the corners of his eyes.

"You've been a wonderful father." I stroke his hand, "I'm grateful for all..." I can't finish the sentence as my throat constricts.

He blinks, I imagine in acknowledgment, then closes his eyes. We are all silent for a moment, waiting for my father to breathe again. When we hear the inhale finally come, I turn to my mother. "Do you want to take a break, maybe get a cup of coffee?"

She runs her hand over her silver hair. "Maybe I'll just go to the bathroom." She leans down and kisses my father's forehead. "I'll be right back, Kathryn and Ted are here with you."

Ted and I do not look at each other. The slight tension in my father's hand dissipates, and minutes seem to pass since we last heard him inhale. Suddenly his eyes open, still clear. The inhale comes and his lips part, his lower lip sliding under his upper teeth. His faint exhale pushes against his lip, vibrating until we hear the first letter, and then a series of tiny changes take place in his mouth. His tongue and lips sculpt a word from his breath. "Forgive." His eyes roll, taking in the whole room. I wait for the rest of the thought, the subject and the object. His eyes find mine and lock for a moment.

"Yes, Dad? I'm listening." His eyelids cover his eyes, like a curtain closing. The rest of his thought hangs, incomplete between us.

My mother returns to the bedside. She looks so out of place here. Her ever-feminine blouse, her classic gold jewelry—a world apart from the plastic and chrome hospital bed, the sockets in the wall for electricity, computers, fluids, oxygen.

I relinquish my father's hand to my mother. I touch his feet, a little protrusion under the sheets at the end of the bed.

My mother kisses his forehead, his cheeks, his eyes. She whispers in his ear. I feel both an intruder on this intimacy and a privileged witness to the end of a lifetime of love and respect. I hear my mother's words. "You can go now, Robert. No need to hold on for us."

We all sit quietly, the air between us charged with expectation. I silently wish him Godspeed in whatever journey or transformation this end brings. I notice my own shallow breathing, the coldness in my body except for the place where I can feel my father. Then, despite the absence of an inhale, my father exhales, a rattle echoes up from deep in his lungs and for a moment I feel some movement in his feet before they are still.

————————

My handkerchief absorbs another wave of tears, red lipstick smeared across the corner of the cloth.

"Robert Capen was the kind of man many of us wish we could be," the minister says in his resonant voice. "Accomplished in the larger world, yet always devoted to the private world of his family. He was a man with a sharp understanding of what divides people, but an abiding faith in what connects us." He goes on, describing my father, with stories of their interactions, inferences about his early life. The minister's words conjure images of my father I haven't considered for years. I look at Michael, did I give him enough opportunity to know his grandfather? Why didn't we go to visit more often? Now we have one more absence in our lives.

"Once when I asked him about his experience as a young man, living in the Middle East, surrounded by customs and faiths that are so foreign to us," the minister continues, "people so seemingly different from our Presbyterian congregation, he told me, 'We all live beneath the same heaven'."

I catch my breath as I remember when my father had repeated his quintessential phrase to me, see again when he said it to Rashid's sister-in-law to translate to Rashid's father just before our wedding. I used to believe him. But since everything changed I have built walls, divided us from them, tried to keep them carefully separate in the columns of the newspaper.

Will my father really join them in the same heaven? What would he say to the spirit of Rashid's father? To Rashid? I think of the man who was my husband, the man who held me while I birthed my sons, the man who used to gather us all in his powerful arms. I see our wedding in Pakistan, the swirling colors. I remember the bride I was. She is gone too. I sob openly.

Ted follows the minister, taking his place at the pulpit. He takes several moments to compose himself, carefully avoiding the coffin, or the eyes of the mourners in the pews. "The older I get, the more I realize a father's job is never done. No matter how old a kid becomes, his dad is always older, more experienced, and if a kid is lucky, his father is always wiser." He gasps with his inhale, continuing on quickly so as not to weep. "I was such a lucky kid. Even to his last day, my dad showed me how to think of others, how to express care. Some of his last words were about his grandchildren."

I close my eyes and hold my breath trying to suppress my grief. I tremble with the force of my losses. Even the opportunity to grieve for my husband as my mother now does, in the open, with her loved ones around her, was lost so long ago.

Andrew surprises me by reaching his arm across my shoulders, and I rest my head against his strong shoulder, feeling a childlike need for comfort. My mother reaches across Michael's lap from the other side to pat my hand. I raise my head to look at her. Her stoic smile seems neither forced nor fearful. She leans in and whispers to me, "We are lucky to have so many memories of such a wonderful man."

She has so many memories. She has a full married lifetime of memories with my father. I have only a pearl, a brief densely beautiful period from a different lifetime, the luster of happy memories forbidden beneath strata of little lies, omissions, denial.

Ted returns to sit between my mother and Janet. The organist presses out the first line of a hymn I remember from childhood. The congregation stands, and I feel myself girded by my sons, the fruit of a union I have never told them about. I reach my hands into theirs and I tell one and then the other, "Your father loved you. He loved you the way my father loved his children. He would have been proud of you."

They squeeze my hands in acknowledgment. They stand mutely, listening as others sing a hymn they never learned.

Chapter II

The waves push up on the sand, I am careful to walk just inland of their apex and watch the water retreat. Now that I have raised my sons, buried my father, I struggle with a ragged sense of incompleteness. How does the ocean never tire of its waves? From what endless source of energy does it draw? What does it hope to achieve? I walk past a tangled clump of seaweed, marooned on the sand. I note with some satisfaction that not a single piece of plastic has come ashore with it. Ted's institute achieved some measure of success from its massive pollution prevention campaign on this stretch of beach. Ted must feel more fulfilled, must not experience this hollowness I feel.

Am I just hungry? I walk as far as the next lifeguard tower and turn around. Or should I go shopping? Out to the library? I stop and watch two surfers paddle past the waves. Three young men wait in the calm waters beyond, alert for the next big wave that will challenge them, and if they are lucky, take them into shore with a satisfying thrill.

I miss the times Andrew and I used to sit and talk, watching Michael surf. I squat down and run my fingers through the sand. Don't hold to those memories. Doesn't the future always generate itself? Don't more experiences, more pleasures always come?

I continue home, climbing the stairs of the pedestrian bridge that crosses the freeway, almost wishing I were rushing somewhere with purpose like the countless cars beneath me.

I approach the building; a car pulls out of the parking garage, a child shouts from one of the balconies above, a man with a turban approaches the bank of mailboxes next to the stairwell. I am surprised to see the maroon turban, the full beard of a South Asian man, as my neighbors are exclusively white and Latino. I approach the stairwell and notice he doesn't have a mailbox key. He is not retrieving his own mail, but holding an envelope in his hand, seeking out a mailbox.

I slow down, waiting to see which box he chooses. He seems to hesitate in front of each one.

I pause before I get to the stairs. "Can I help you?" I ask, wondering what business this stranger has being here.

He turns, surprised, looks me in the eye and quickly looks to the ground. "Excuse me," he says. "I am only looking for a certain mailbox."

"I can see that. Which one?"

His beard is streaked with grey, and a few errant eyebrows have turned white above the eyes that I see for just a moment. I have avoided South Asians for two decades now, but I remember something of their hospitality.

"I know almost everyone in the building," I say more generously, "I can probably help you find the mailbox."

"In fact," he pauses, "I am looking for Kathryn…Capen."

"*I'm* Kathryn," I say, startled. He stands still, curiously unhurried. I look at his cheap shoes, his hands deeply soiled like a mechanic's. I look past him, quickly scanning the driveway for his car, or some other person, some sign of danger. "Who are you?"

He does not answer. I see the envelope in his hand, a few words on the front, no stamp in the corner.

"Is it you?" I say quietly, almost a whisper. "Are you the one who brings these envelopes to me?" The hollowness of the morning fills; the future generating itself with shocking speed.

He shakes his head, the bulk of the turban seems to make the gesture more emphatic. "This is the first time I have come in person." He stands there in front of me, a tall man, shoulders rolling forward so he looks almost contrite as he holds out the envelope. I can read clearly, *To the Family of Rashid Siddique.*

I take a step back, prepare to flee. He reaches out, offering the envelope. Then he looks up and I see his eyes again. I know them. His paralyzing gaze sets my heart racing. I can think only of the most irrational question. "Are you Rashid Siddique?"

The man closes his eyes draws a deep inhalation and looks at me again. "I used to be."

Part Three

The Book of Rashid

Chapter I

Lahore, Pakistan.
Months before the bombing

"I told him not to go," my mother speaks to no one in particular. "I told him the frontier areas are too dangerous for a moderate modern man like him."

I sit in the middle of the train berth, between my mother and a young man from Karachi. His five relatives occupy the rest of the berth with their loud banter and piles of pre-packaged snacks.

"He smiled and patted my hand and told me life is dangerous," she continues. "'Even in our home' he said, 'we keep men with rifles stationed at the perimeter of our lands, bring extra guards for our weddings. I shouldn't let danger keep us from our ties of loyalty.' You know," she looks at my hands, "he felt he owed Shoukart his presence at his son's wedding. After Shoukart's father had provided refuge for your father and his brother during those mad days of Partition, he has felt bound to their family."

Her Punjabi sounds so formal, absolutely devoid of the English loan words and Urdu slang that pollutes the Punjabi I grew up speaking. She looks out the window, seeing something beyond the Lahore train station outside the window, past the mass of people on the platform.

"Mummyji," I say, calling her back into the train, back to the present, "you did the right thing. You tried to warn him."

She looks at me directly and I see the milky whites of her eyes, the graying edges of her irises focused with a steely intensity. "The people in the tribal areas have always been difficult to control. The British tried and failed to tame them, the Pakistanis have known enough not to try to occupy their valleys. Don't the Americans know their war in Pakistan is pointless? Every person they kill just creates more enemies, more people hungry for revenge."

I close my eyes. I used to love train rides, I remember befriending berth mates every time we traveled to Karachi for my father's business, or to the mountains for a holiday. But this train ride will bring us only to the scene of a crime, not to a carnival or a market.

I look out the window as we wait to leave the Lahore station which the British built more than a century ago. Men dressed in kurta pajamas carry satchels and balance boxes on their shoulders, tightly coiled Sikh turbans occasionally bob through the crowd, a few women with brightly colored headscarves drag children almost invisible among the legs of their elders. Amidst the swirl, a man stands still, like an island, in his military uniform, rifle slung over his shoulder, he watches for any unusual motion, any suspicious packages. A group of three tribesmen, their turbans wrapped like birds' nests atop their short hair, the end of the cloth tailing over their shoulders alongside their long beards, garner the soldier's attention. Even from a distance I can sense the energy between them as they pass, the soldier unyielding, slightly narrowing his eyes as he scans their bodies for evidence of malintent.

The unspoken tension—not just the rush to find a seat, to adhere to the schedule, to pay the ticket taker the petty bribes he is due—but the uncertainty of the crowd, the potential for a backpack to blow up, for a scuffle to escalate into a riot, all of the simmering energy only accentuates my fatigue. I close my eyes and try to focus on the smells, the grilled meats and potato cutlets of the platform vendors, the diesel, my mother's familiar rose fragrance.

I never left, I lie to myself. I have always been here with my mother, my family, my clan. I never abandoned them for the clean surfaces and right angles of the West. London, Dubai, America, these places are all just dreams. This is where I belong. As the train engine heaves to pull us out of the station, I hear the call to prayer projected through some distant speaker, distorted at maximum volume over the din of the platform.

After some hours, the train pulls in to Shahdara station and passengers depart and arrive in the shuffle to and from the branch lines that reach out to the east and west. We do not speak over the activity. As the train slowly pulls away again to the north a chai wallah makes his way down the aisle. He stops to dispense sweet milky tea into little paper cups from a spigot in the stainless steel drum he carries slung against his torso. My mother pulls two coins from her purse and presses them into my hand, just as she did when I was a child. I hail the chai wallah and hold up two fingers.

"For the lady," he passes me a cup, respectfully looking at me rather than her. "And for you, sir." He hands me the second, his arm motions displaying an efficiency born of years of repeated effort. He will likely move up and down these aisles, slowly wearing down the car's wooden floors until he is too old to carry the drum, or until he can pass it onto a younger relative who will provide him a small daily commission for the privilege of the profession.

I can see my mother's shoulders relax with the habit of the tea. She begins to talk of the family businesses; the lack of rain and how Riaz worries about the cost of diesel for our tractors, Majid's dealings with both Chinese and Korean manufacturers for our family's trading business. She falls into these conversations as though I had never been away. She asks me my opinion on small questions about the price of commodities, and the trustworthiness of certain of our neighbors in comparison to others. She never refers to my wife or my children, she does not ask about my life in America. And I follow her lead, answering her questions, acting as if her topics fill my life like they do hers.

After we stop in Gurjanwala the railway porters serve dinner; little steel trays with *naan* bread, a portion of *daal*, and sterilized water in a flimsy plastic bag. We eat quickly. Our trays are empty when the porters return to collect them, and then lay out the stiff white sheets and pillows on the berths. By Wazirabad station, most of the passengers have settled into their berths, their shoes stowed under their luggage to deter petty thieves. I help my mother onto the top berth and settle into the middle berth, listening to the congested breathing of the young man from Karachi beneath me.

The rhythm of the train, the syncopated clatter of wheels against rails, the creaking of the car couplings transports me not only toward my brothers and their angry grief, but back to my traditions, away from the adoptive life, the hybrid culture I have carved out of the larger outside world.

I can imagine how this story plays out. I have seen enough Lollywood films, I have seen our clan-based culture projected onto makeshift screens of white sheets strung across fields in our village. The family will not rest until they achieve justice, fortified by the crowd of villagers who gather around the offended hero. But in these simulations of our tradition, the antagonist always has a face, a recognizably malevolent expression, usually with a scar around his eye or across his cheek. The antagonist in my reality does not bleed, does not scowl or speak, he did not look my father in the eye before pulling a trigger, before thrusting a knife. My father must have appeared as nothing more than a small circle seen from above, a shadow of electrons moving across a distant screen in some military operations room.

I wake just as we arrive in Rawalpindi, the sun breaking over the horizon. I can see men on the sidewalk with prayer rugs tucked under their arms answering the first call of the day. I remember my father's comments about such men, 'In heaven, Allah will reward their discipline for sure. But here on earth, I enjoy the reward of a bit of extra sleep.'

My mother is awake already, her grey hair combed, her headscarf gracefully draped over her head. She looks down at the cell phone in her hand, typing out a text message. "Your brothers will meet us with a driver in Peshawar," she reports from the phone. "I have let them know the train is behind schedule. Pakistani Railways saves petrol by running the trains slower," she clucks her tongue with disgust. "Your brothers will have one of Shoukart's relatives drive us to their village in the Khyber Agency. And I checked in with Jagdeep, he will keep watch on the rest of the servants and workers." I haven't thought about Jagdeep in years. *Our Singh* we used to call him. My father had trusted him since they were in school together. Jagdeep wore his turban proudly, upholding the Sikh reputation for honesty and hard work with unfailing sincerity.

"The body," I ask, "where is he buried?"

"I suppose next to Shoukart and his family. With only one day to get the body in the ground, we aren't able to choose." She tucks the phone into her purse. "But I need to know where it is. I don't know when I'll be able to make this journey again." She closes her eyes and pulls her lips shut tight. I can see she wants to cry.

I stand there, next to her upper berth, her grown child, and rest my head on her knee. She places her hand on my head and we both weep silently.

———————

After the tedious final leg of the train journey to Peshawar I am relieved to step out onto the platform. My brothers are waiting with the Pashtun driver who stands pulling at his beard. We greet each other with handshakes and hands on shoulders. The driver takes our bags and says he is sorry for our loss.

"How was the train ride?" Majid asks.

"We're here aren't we?" my mother responds.

"Well, be prepared for the rest of the way." Majid smiles ruefully. "The roads aren't like Lahore, and the car's nothing like my Mercedes."

I squeeze into the middle of the backseat—even as an adult, I still have the status of the youngest.

After an hour or so, Peshawar's brick buildings give way to the Afghan refugees' makeshift villages. The mud, plywood, and metal constructions rise up from the side of the road like dusty extensions of the earth itself. At a non-descript fork in the road, the driver points to a sign, slightly bigger than a man, amidst the jumble of border-style commerce, *Entering Khyber Agency, Keep Left.* Just next to it, practically on top of a *halal* butcher's stand with three dangling goat shanks another sign warns, *No Foreigners May Enter Beyond This Point.* We haven't discussed this yet. I have tucked my American passport in a hidden pocket in my bag; opting to carry my Pakistani passport with me, even though it has expired. A Pashtun with a weathered face and pie-shaped woolen hat doesn't bother to raise the rifle slung over his shoulder. He peers into the backseat through the open window.

The driver speaks in Pashto. Although I understand only some of his words, his intent is clear. "They are Lahoris, but their man was killed by a drone this week in Dargalabad. They came for mourning." I wait for the driver to turn around and request our identification.

But the Pashtun briefly touches his hand to his heart in a gesture of sympathy. "Then in grief they are my brothers." He steps back to let us pass. "American bastards," he says loud enough for all of us to hear. Although he raises his fist in solidarity with us, I can't help but feel his words condemning me.

The narrow, potholed road and the din of the car engine prevent us from discussing anything on the way to Dargalabad. We pass through treeless terrain before climbing up the mountain and down into the valley through a series of switchbacks. I feel as though I am not actually present, just observing. I grew up only a day's journey from here, but I've never seen this world. My stomach turns with each rotation of the steering wheel. I am in my own country, but in a foreign land. I am a foreigner approaching the village of a man who was like my brother, the place where my father was killed, but this is not my place. I feel lightheaded. I close my eyes and my body seems to disappear. The breath moving in and out of my lungs is only the flimsy tether of fate pulling me along to a place I cannot resist.

The car stops. A disorderly flow of humanity and livestock pass in front of us. "This is the main road in Dargalabad," the driver says. "We are near." We slowly advance into the moving mass. At the intersection a traffic sign commands travelers, *Yield* in English, Urdu, and Pashto. A vandal has amended the sign, writing in a defiant English script, *NEVER*.

The driver navigates past small blocky buildings, houses surrounded by high walls, and the occasional tree. Abruptly he pulls up at an unmarked wall, indistinct from any of the others we have passed. An old man opens the wooden door in the wall, quickly moving to embrace my brothers and me. I assume he is Shoukart's grandfather. He beats his chest and speaks in a torrent of Pashto sprinkled with Urdu. He offers his condolences, welcomes us to his home as family, as honored guests. "Your father's death," he cries, "pains me even more than my grandson's death, he was our guest."

I stand mute, uncertain how to react. My brothers seem to understand this ritual better. They touch their hearts in gratitude for his hospitality, they reciprocate condolences for his loss. Riaz places a calm hand on the old man's shoulder and suggests we go inside. The old man steps aside and looks to the ground as my mother passes inside, "*Um Riaz*, mother of Riaz," he says respectfully, "Please be in your own home here."

I follow as we pass through the walled courtyard, a carefully tended apricot tree spreads its delicate branches in a small circle of shade where several chickens scratch in the still moist ground where the tree has been watered. At the threshold of the home's inner rooms, we step out of our shoes. I place the black sandals I had borrowed from my brother's closet in Lahore next to two other similar, but worn, pairs. Outside the door, the earth has been beaten smooth. Inside, the floor is covered in thick felt carpets. A small, deep red carpet, covered in a tribal design of orderly guls, marks the center of the room. A young girl steps silently from behind a curtain which divides the room, and sets down a large brass tray with tea and bread.

Instinctively the men sit down in a circle. Several of Shoukart's male relatives gather around his grandfather. My mother ducks inside the curtain and I hear the voices of the women consoling her, welcoming her. She returns and sits next to me as the young girl pours tea for all of us, hot liquid steaming up from the spout stained by years of use.

After several minutes of formalities over the tea, the distribution of bread and apricot preserves, we finally turn to the matter at hand.

"I had just gone down the road," the old man says, his voice reedy with age, "I wanted to replace the string of electric festival lights we had in the courtyard, because they weren't working properly. I went on my bicycle, it should've only taken a short time." He took a sip of his tea. "Your father was with my grandson. We'd recently come back from the mosque, the marriage contract signed, the mullah had given his blessing. We had everything ready for the celebration. The girl's relatives were here with us, the food was all ready." He pauses, looks at the teacup resting on his palm. "I didn't hear the drone. We never hear the drones."

"Have there been drones before?" I ask. Perhaps I should not have interrupted.

"Of course," he looks up at me. "The young men with good eyes and lenses see them a lot, at least once a week. Like hawks, so high I cannot see them. Sometimes they just go back to the Afghan side. Sometimes…"

We all look down at our teacups.

"The Americans think that anyone with a turban or a beard is Taliban," one of the younger men practically spits out his words. "So even if we come together for a wedding party in a courtyard, we are a gathering of the Taliban."

"There are no Taliban in our village," the old man speaks again. "But if today they came asking for fighters, I would join them before I even finish this tea. As sure as your father is in the ground, I am now an enemy of America."

The sweetness from my tea dissolves in his vitriol. As I sit here and share his grief, his hospitality, and his love for my father, do

I also share his hatred? I hate the drone, I hate the men who sat behind some screen and engineered my father's death, I hate the generals and policy makers who treat foreign lives as trivial. But is that my America? Is that the America of my wife and children? Of me?

He continues, "Have you thought how you will avenge his death? We also have many lives to avenge, but he was the head of your family. This kind of offense cannot remain unanswered."

My brothers turn to look at my mother. "Not only have we been deprived of our man, but since he died far from his home, we were deprived of the funeral," she says, counting the offenses as she would tally up the mustard harvest. "All of our relations, all of the people who are close to our families and our farms have not had a chance to pay their respects."

"You are correct," the old man shakes his head, "and *masha'allah*, God willed it, there should be hundreds of people who must come for a man like him."

"The problem, of course," Riaz begins, "is that the killers are not here. We cannot satisfy our grief in Pakistan."

"Yes," nods the old man. "If that were possible, I myself would seek revenge to uphold your family's honor. I expect we'll have to cross over the border and look for a target in Afghanistan. We have relations on the other side…"

Majid looks briefly at me before interrupting the old man. "We do have a different advantage." The old man raises an eyebrow, curious. "Rashid. He has an American passport, he has no difficulty entering America."

My brother is careful not to call me an American. The old man and my mother both nod. "Because of his work, he has experience with explosives, he has high level security clearance."

I start to correct him, to explain that my hazardous materials commercial driver's license isn't the kind of security clearance they imagine. But my mother joins my brothers in extolling my qualifications as an avenger. "My youngest son is also very clever, and can easily mingle with Westerners, he will not arouse suspicion."

I want to protest, I want to tell them there is no way we can fight the U.S. military. With a rush of adrenaline I want to leave the room, to run away from the future they are planning for me. I uncross my legs to stand but my mother sets a hand on my forearm. The strength of her grip compels me to recross my legs, to sit down, listen, obey.

The young girl steps around the curtain with a large copper bowl of curry. She pauses to catch the eye of the old man. He nods at her, beckons her with his hand. "Let us eat. Decisions are always easier on a full stomach."

"Mummyji, I have a family, children," I whisper to her. "This is not a simple matter in America."

She squeezes harder. "We all have children. It's *because* we have children that we must not allow others to come into our lands and destroy our families."

The girl offers me a large oval shaped naan, then ladles a portion of curry into the center of the bread, leaving three hefty chunks of goat meat befitting my status as an honored guest.

The old man breaks his bread and dips it into the curry, raising it to signal for us to eat before he will. "The women of my brother's house make a beautiful curry. I wish I could host you in my own house, but it is rubble now."

"Uncle, you will take my youngest brother to see it?" Riaz asks.

"And he needs to see where our father is buried," Majid echoes.

The old man nods somberly.

The conversation pauses as we concentrate on our meal. A child cries in the other room. A woman tries to comfort him.

"Virji," I whisper to Riaz, "we need to talk about how we will seek revenge. This isn't something I can do in America. I have obligations to my family."

My eldest brother wipes his mustache with the back of his hand. "Rashid, we all have obligations to the family," he says sternly. "Majid and I stayed here and married the girls our parents chose for us. Our wives have cared for our parents. We've handled the farm and the trading business. Daddyji indulged you." He looks to Majid for confirmation. "He gave you the opportunity to go abroad. He did not object when you chose an American woman. But you cannot avoid your responsibility now."

"I'm not avoiding my responsibility." I say sullenly. I lower my voice so the others cannot hear. "I've always sent money home. I was the one who sponsored Daddyji to go to *Hajj*." I cannot offer any defense about my wife. No matter how she has tried to understand and accept our culture, she will never be one of us. The food is warm in my belly, but my heart burns with the understanding that she is of their tribe, she was born in the same nationality as the cowards who killed my father. I clench my fists. The gold of my wedding ring presses into my flesh. I hide my hand in the pocket of my kurta, as if this could obscure my alliance by marriage with America.

The old man and his relations sit back and rub their palms together, pressing any grease from the meal into their dry calloused hands.

Riaz looks up to see that everyone will listen to his words. "Rashid, if you are truly our mother's son, you will understand what you must do for the family."

This line, this taunt to action I have seen dozens of times in films. How much more serious it sounds coming from my brother's mouth. Does my face redden with this challenge? Instead of the dramatic music which would heighten the moment in a film, I hear only the clink of teacups being washed behind the curtain. The men around the room sharpen their focus on me. They will all hold me to this moment, to know if I am a man, to look for proof that I deserve my family's name. I choose to respond in the most honorable way I can. I say nothing.

"We will go now?" the old man asks. We all push ourselves up to standing. I step into the courtyard. I feel the cool air dissipate some of the smoldering heat in my body. At the far end, near a small opening in the wall that leads to a gutter, flies have gathered around a puddle of blood. Our hosts must have slaughtered the goat for our meal earlier in the day, the cries of the animal were already silent before we arrived.

My mother steps out over the threshold.

"You will want to stay here?" the old man asks.

"No." She is firm. "I will see as well. I've already come this far."

We sit in the car. The squeak of the car door hinge sounds like the first few notes of a song I remember. As we drive through the village, and past farms green with mustard and melons, the memory of the melodic line of a dance tune from my time in Dubai echoes through my head. My mind seizes it, works to remember the lyrics.

Eventually we arrive at an abandoned lot. Piles of trash and debris have been separated into their constituent parts. A mangy dog licks a stained brick.

We all step out of the car, an acrid, smoke-scented breeze confronts us. I hold out my hand to help my mother to her feet. The old man walks into the lot, narrates the space with his hands. "This is where my house was. You can see the outline of the courtyard here."

My eyes start to notice the patterns in the disorder. What I had taken for rubbish are the remnants of the house. The walls toppled into piles of bricks. What must have been a bookshelf, reduced to piles of fluttering papers. The stain on the bricks—I realize with horror—must be the blood of the wedding party. The guests. My father.

"This is where everyone was gathered, outside." The old man's face glistens with tears. One of his relatives, a nephew, I assume, rests a comforting hand on his back. "The lights I had gone to replace were going to hang from the wall to this tree." He points to a stump. He continues to tell the story, his words coming faster, his tone increasingly shrill.

I separate from my mother, walk among the piles, stepping over a brick, a piece of burnt and melted plastic. I lift up a broken wooden beam with my toe. A swarm of flies swirls out from under the beam with the metallic smell of blood. I see a tangled clump of hair, black with strands of silver grey, matted into the ground, a small piece of flesh still attached.

My stomach churns. I turn around, looking for a place where I can retreat. I see fragments of red cloth with gold embroidery—the bride's dress—a tiny boy's shoe next to a twisted shard of metal. I see the memories of things that were only recently intact. I double over and wretch, trying not to draw attention to myself. The remnants of my goat curry will decay here in this place of death.

I hear a vibration in the sky and I look around trying to identify the source. From behind our heads we see a dark shape in the sky, like a giant metal hawk. As the shadow of an aircraft sweeps across the jagged edges of the ground around us, my mother reaches down and grabs a broken brick. She throws it into the sky and screams. She curses the machine with a string of profanities—sister fuckers, dogs, sons of bitches—the likes of which I have never heard from her. She reaches again and again for bricks, rocks, sticks, anything she can throw into the sky. Her headscarf falls back, exposing her silver hair. Her voice loses its power as her projectiles fall back to the earth just a few feet in front of her.

My brothers and I, stunned, do not move. We feel her rage, understand her need to act. But we cannot recognize our proud strong mother in these childish gestures. Only when she collapses to the ground, spent and shrieking, do we all rush to support her.

The old man, suddenly agitated, frantically herds us back into the car. "Sometimes a drone will follow a plane. We won't be able to see it, but we should take cover, they don't like it when people make rash motions or fall to the ground."

Back in the car, we move quickly, the nephew, slightly older than me, is driving erratically, peering his head out the driver's side window, trying to spot any danger from above. My heart is beating so loud I think I can hear it over the engine. I place my arms over my mother's head, as if I could protect her.

Once we turn on to a bigger road, and join a steady flow of cars crawling along, the nephew seems to relax. The old man turns around, "Please forgive me for frightening you. We can never be too careful. And I should never forgive myself if your mother were harmed while she was my guest."

"Thank you for your care, brother," my mother says, lowering my arms without looking at me. "I can only imagine how you suffer with this kind of fear." Composed again, she raises her hands to include the whole dangerous sky. "I am a woman, all I can do is throw stones." She sets her hand above mine, making a fist. "But my son can accomplish much more."

"*Insha'allah*, God willing," the old man says, "insha'allah."

———

The gravesite is unremarkable; a patch of disturbed earth, small piles of stones above the mounds that cover the bodies. We do not speak as we get out of the car. My brothers have been here before, they were here to lower the plain wooden box into the ground. Later I will ask them about the condition of my father's body.

My mother walks unsteadily toward the mound that the old man indicates is her husband's grave. I follow, hold her arm and shoulders to support her.

"Husband," she says quietly. "You were a good man. You raised your sons well. And your daughters. We will carry your name with pride, uphold your honor." She steps toward the grave and squats down, running her right hand in the dirt. I can hear her whispering, but cannot make out her words. I watch her hand moving gently over the ground, as if she were caressing him through the soil. She looks down and then up into the sky, perhaps she is trying to locate his spirit, to know where she should send her words.

I remember when my grandfather died. The old man had a heart attack during Ramadan. My father had spent the whole day after Babu's death holed up in the little booth in the phone store down the lane, his voice growing hoarse as he called our relations. Never once did he break his fast or ask for water. I was a teenager, my voice just starting to change. We buried Babu at the far end of the mustard fields, at the top of a little rise. My father said even in death, we should understand that Babu would watch over the farm. The whole village came, as did all our relations who were within a day's train ride. My mother had arranged for the washing of the body and all of the food and drink we would need prepared for the hundreds of mourners to break their fast after the sun set. We found comfort in the sheer mass of people who supported our family in our grief. Of course I felt the sadness, but even as we repeated the solemn burial ritual, I couldn't help noticing a girl across from me. She stood out in my mind as she was my age, with beautiful cheekbones, a lustrous sliver of her hair left uncovered before her headscarf. As the breeze blew, the thin cotton of her kameeze blew against her skin so I could discern the outline of her firm breasts, and I wondered about the rest of her body.

I close my eyes as my mind returns to the sight of my father's grave. Stones crunch underfoot as my brothers and Shoukart's relatives move gently around me. A car passes along the road, a lone bird cries out in the distance. What do I say to my dead father? How do I thank him for his care, his guidance, his wisdom to send me abroad? How do I repay the pleasures I have enjoyed, the expanse of the West that I have known because of his decisions? I simply say, "Peace be upon him," the same words I have repeated after the name of the Prophet.

Riaz steps close to me, so that I can feel the heat of his body. I long for the crowd of mourners that should hold us up, that should remind me of the continuity of our community, despite the interruption of death. I reach out for Riaz, grateful for his masculine arms encircling me.

———————

"I have called some people who can help us," says a young man I hadn't noticed earlier. He is slim, his beard carefully trimmed, his eyes reflecting a clear intelligence.

Shoukart's grandfather leans back on a bolster inside his brother's house. "Help us in what way?" he groans with an ache in his bones.

I accept a cup of tea from the young girl who had served us earlier, feel the adrenaline of the afternoon dissipating, leaving a hard anger. "Help us to take our next steps," the young man replies crisply.

Three men appear at the door, simple wool shawls draped around their shoulders. Shoukart's grandfather begins to rise. The men gesture for him to stay where he is. Speaking in Pashto, they lean over, grasp his hands in greeting. They make their way around the room, greeting other relatives, the young man, my brothers, me.

"They are my brother's neighbors," the old man explains, "they have come to share condolences with you."

They sit, drink tea, the hardened and stained soles of their feet poking out from under the billows of their pants.

The young man continues, "I have called Abu Omar because he knows how to plan things, he knows people."

Majid sits on the floor, hunched over his tea cup. "I don't know how much planning we need. I think if we could bomb the ring road in Los Angeles, we would make our point."

"There is no ring road in Los Angeles," I say quietly, "it's a network of freeways."

"So pick one," Majid shoots back.

"It's not that simple," I tell Majid.

Another group of men arrive, repeat the same ritual as the first group of neighbors.

Shoukart's grandfather rubs his shoulder. "They say that Abu Omar is the lion of Afghanistan, he knows how to strike at the Americans. He will chase them out of the country…or kill them."

The young man nods. "He has had very good training, he has friends abroad, he can make things happen."

A few of the strangers continue the conversation in Pashto. I follow some of their words, they mention the Americans in Afghanistan, the CIA in Peshawar.

Again, a few more men step inside the room. I move closer to my brother and a guest who had arrived earlier moves closer to me to make space. A water pipe appears and the smells of sweet tobacco smoke and sweating men fill the room. One of the neighbors, or relatives—I can't really keep straight who is who—points at me. The others begin talking more quickly. I lean over to Majid, "Do you understand what they're saying?"

"They're talking about what you can do in America, what Abu Omar can do to help arrange things for you." He pauses, "I've told them how smart and capable you are."

Majid's compliment catches me off guard. My middle brother has spent a lifetime demonstrating all the ways in which he has surpassed me.

A few men push themselves up off the carpet and make space for new guests. Now familiar with the ritual, I greet them, thank them for coming, nod at their curses for the Americans, their calls for justice.

The young man continues in English, "If we took action in Los Angeles, we would be staking out new territory, no one has touched the American west coast yet."

"But innocents would be killed," I shudder thinking about my wife and children.

"Innocents!" the young man roars, "Tell me brother, wasn't your father innocent? Shoukart? The bride? Do you think for a moment the *kafirs*, the infidels flying the drones wonder about the innocence of our women, our children, our fathers?" He opens his arms to include the other men in the room who nod in somber agreement. "Do they wonder about our innocence when the drones come and drop bombs on the people who gather to bury those they have already killed in an earlier drone attack?"

An indignant murmur ripples through the room.

"Because we are men with beards, because we are Muslim, because we believe in the honor of our families, we are all guilty in their eyes. Even you," his eyes narrow as he points at me, "even you, brother, with your American passport and liberal ways, are an enemy the Americans would kill if they could."

An older man, stoic and quiet stares at me from just a few feet away. I stare back, clench my fist to hold back tears, to hold back my anger. Finally he speaks, almost a whisper. "It's good you have come back to your country, to sit among your brothers. We'll help you accomplish a great thing. The Americans need a reminder, a prick in their side. You can help to protect us."

I wrinkle my eyebrows in question.

The man passes me the hose of the water pipe. I take a long draw, wait for the feeling, the lightness in my head.

"Look at us," he continues, "we are men in a poor country, every day we fear what will drop out of the sky. Look at you, you live in America, you are rich, accomplished, intelligent." He moves closer to me, sets his hand on my shoulder. "We need men like you to carry our message, the memories of our dead, of your father."

My brothers nod. I look around the room, recognize shadows of my father in the faces of the men who have come. I see the intelligence of my father's eyes above the beard on the young man's face, see my father's long sharp nose in a man with a deep scar across his cheek, see the roundness of my father's lips in a wizened old man who scratches his beard with mangled stumps where his first two fingers should have been.

"We understand your suffering," speaks the old man, squeezing my shoulder. "All of us have lost someone, or have been forced from our homes. I have seen my own children bleed because of the Americans." He looks up, turns to the others, "Yes?" Around the room, I see men nod, tears sparkling in the eyes of a few. He looks back at me. "Your father would help us if he could. He would ask you do to the same…" My mother peers out from the kitchen curtain, nods forcefully at me. "…if they hadn't blown him to bits."

The image of burned flesh rises again in my mind. I press the heels of my hands to my eyes, try to block the vision. And I cannot hold back any more, tears come. My lungs gasp for breath. I have lost my father. This single death has blown my world apart, ripped away my future. I open my eyes to see every man in the room touching the shoulder of the man in front of him, all hands reaching out in a web to this man who has set his hand upon my shoulder. He draws his forefinger across his forehead, then across mine. "It is written."

I nod. It has been written.

After all the men leave, save the young man with the neat beard, my brothers and I stand with him at the door. I want only to collapse right there and sleep. I suddenly remember his first words of the day. "You said Abu Omar would come, he could help us. When will he come?"

The corners of the young man's mouth turn ever so slightly, "He was already here."

I feel disoriented. "Who? Which man? Why didn't you introduce him?"

"You will know all in due time."

I wish for another draw on the water pipe, for the patience I feel with the smoke in my lungs. "And brother, I didn't properly hear your name."

Again the corners of his mouth turn up. He nods deferentially. "I am Omar."

He embraces me and turns, walking away without another word.

I stand silent under the stars, trying to think back on which of the men I saw today could be his father, Abu Omar.

Chapter 2

Los Angeles, California.
Months before the bombing

A sterile white corridor opens into the cavernous receiving hall of the international terminal in Los Angeles. Asian women with designer handbags rush past me, high heels clicking on the floor, to get to the front of the U.S. citizen line. I slow my pace. I am in no rush to return to this country.

When I reach the front of the line, I consider telling the immigration official I would like to renounce my passport, make my way back to the plane and return to Pakistan. But he has a set of prepared questions, an interrogation of friendly chit chat.

"How was your journey?"

I don't respond.

He looks at my American passport, looks at my face to confirm I am the same man in the photo. He has no idea how different I am now from the man in the photo, how my journey has changed me.

"Did you visit family in Pakistan?"

I resist the urge to reach across the counter and throttle him.

"Funeral," I say curtly as he swipes my passport through the magnetic reader.

"I'm sorry to hear that," he says looking at the screen. He turns and hands me back my passport. "Well, welcome home."

The first time I saw this place, Kathryn and I had queued in separate immigration lines, my green Pakistani passport fortified with a U.S. fiancé visa. I had spoken eagerly with the immigration official, even pointed out Kathryn in the other line as he asked me about my reason for coming. I felt Pakistan impossibly far away. I knew that with an American wife and American children in my future, America would become my home.

I proceed to the baggage carousel, feeling the overwhelming bigness, the formal sturdiness in such contrast to the shoddy haphazard feel of the Pakistani frontier. Two young women take up position in front of me to watch for their luggage. One turns to face her companion and I see the tops of her breasts, practically bursting out of a tiny tank top. I feel the instinctive surge in my loins. I move away, I don't want the distraction.

I scan the room, the baggage carousels, the piles of luggage carts. I notice a DEA official with a sniffer dog, alert, stern. Groups of people laden with luggage queue before the customs inspectors, the final bureaucratic hurdle before stepping into the vastness of America.

Today I realize that I didn't absorb America, I merely stepped into it. I wore an American identity as I might wear a sport coat over a t-shirt and jeans. Being with my mother, feeling the absence of my father in the company of my brothers, Shoukart's family and neighbors, reaffirmed my identity. Rashid the American has faded, like a suntan after returning from a beach holiday; revealing, restoring Rashid of the Siddique clan, of Lahore, of Pakistan, of the *umma*.

And I am back in America. My brothers were right, I have no difficulty entering America, I can mix easily with Westerners, no one suspects me. Nor should they, I remind myself. I have done nothing wrong. I have only promised my mother that I would carry out what was written.

I step into a taxi. Perhaps I should not even return to Kathryn and the boys. Perhaps everything would be easier for them if I just disappeared. But I hesitate, and when the round-faced Armenian driver turns around and asks a second time for my destination, I can only remember my home address.

The wide open freeways at this early morning hour deliver me too quickly to my building. I remember Majid's comment, which freeway should I pick? I still haven't thought of what I will say to Kathryn. How can I explain anything of what I experienced in Pakistan, in the frontier? I stand on the sidewalk as the taxi pulls away, trying to remember if I have ever told her stories of other families that might have prepared her. I reach back to images of our wedding, but my mind can't hold them in focus. I am exhausted, I need to sleep.

I step inside our home and shut the door quietly, ensuring I hear the click of the bolt before taking off my shoes, and walking silently across the red Persian carpet to the bedroom. I breathe in a lungful, the smell of coffee, laundry detergent, and breast milk triggering a wave of recent memories. Part of my being returns to this place, even as I try to resist it, to retain the essence of Pakistan in my consciousness.

In the bedroom Kathryn occupies the middle of the bed. Michael and baby Andrew on either side. The baby is awake, playing quietly, moving his arms and legs. I go to him, touch his cheek. My father would have done the same, he always loved a baby. Caring for babies was women's work, but loving babies was an extension of his responsibility as the patriarch, his investment in his legacy. I wish my father could have met this baby. Andrew starts to fidget with hunger. I pacify him for a minute with my finger before he fusses in earnest. From her deep slumber, Kathryn reaches for the baby, pulling aside her nightshirt to reveal her breast for him. I recognize this universal gesture of comfort, and in this interaction, my wife transcends nationality, culture, tradition. She is a woman, I am a man, and this is our child. I stroke her other breast, reach out to touch our other child, and wish I could inhabit this world with them forever. I close my eyes and allow sleep to overwhelm me.

————————

I spend the next few days evading Kathryn's questions. She asks me about my mother and the funeral and our rituals. I answer with generalities, which, thankfully, she accepts. I can see from the way she makes me tea, from the extra effort she takes to boil the dried black leaves with ginger and cardamom that she will be patient with me. She thinks that with enough care, I will eventually open up and explain everything to her. Instead, I retreat to a place where people understand without the need for explanations.

In the early morning light I can see the mosque is small, not really a mosque, but a converted storefront. The windows have been covered with heavy white curtains, so we may pray in private. I leave my shoes just inside the door, next to a handful of others. I feel awkward with my old prayer rug rolled up under my arm, the polyester fringes brushing against my ribs. I have not once bothered to pray since I came to America. I wonder for a moment if the others will judge me for my lapsed practice of the faith. But on another rug on the floor, I recognize the same image of a dome and minaret on a pale green background—the kind of rug available in any grocery store in the Persian Gulf. I roll out mine an acceptable distance away and wait. In a moment a man walks to the front of the mosque, and leads those of us who have gathered, through the familiar ritual of prayer. I have always touched my head lightly to the ground, my symbolic submission to God. In Dubai very devout men showed off a persistent bruise on their forehead as proof of their ardent belief.

I sit, my feet tucked under me, lift my hands in supplication, touch my head to the floor in the direction of Mecca, look over each shoulder. My muscles remember every movement. These simple actions arouse images of my father, who must have taught me how to pray before I could even remember learning.

When we finish, we all stand, roll up our rugs and return to our shoes. Most men leave quickly, the metal frame of the glass door clanging behind them. But a few linger. An old man sits with his back against the wall, lost in thought. A young man stands near the door waiting for a middle aged man to finish with his shoes and then they walk out together. I feel an emptiness. I know no one here. I tie my shoes and walk back to my car.

I sit outside the public library for nearly an hour waiting for the doors to open. I'm not yet ready to go home. I want to find something, something that connects me to Pakistan, something that documents what happened to my father—something that might help me understand what has been written for me.

At the appointed hour, the library opens and I enter after a small tribe of homeless people who have gathered clutching their battered bags. I have never been to this library. I consult the map on the check out desk finding the half dozen computer carrels along the far wall. A clipboard with a waiting list for users sits on one end. I sign my name as George Smith—no one needs to know I have been here—and proceed to the last open terminal, taking my spot next to the regulars.

The familiar search engine appears, its bright simple logo promising all kinds of cheerful results. I type in *drone attack* and click on the image finder. I want to see if the reporting matches my memory of what a drone attack looks like. I wait the few seconds until the screen fills. But amidst all the photos, there is not a drop of blood, not a single destroyed building. I scan row after row of photos of drones, glamour shots of military hardware in cloudless skies. Some of the pilotless planes, like moles of the air, appear almost cartoonish. Biting my lower lip, I click on one. *Drone Attack—3-D* slides across the screen, advertising the lifelike simulation available for players who *crave the thrill of the real thing.*

I slam my fist into the keyboard, eliciting startled looks from the people next to me. The computer misreads my action as a command to begin and the game launches into a demo clip; providing a bird's eye view of a drone, zeroing in on a target, dropping its bomb, and moments later a small puff of white smoke erupting in the far corner of the screen. Digital particles aggregate into letters, *Mission Accomplished!* the game proclaims. From somewhere beyond the frame I hear my mother screaming, hear the thud of thrown stones falling to the ground.

I think to leave, to get up and drive away from this place, but even if I drive and drive I will still be in this country. No, there is no where to flee. I type into the keyboard, invoke the cheerful search engine again. Look for the words, I tell myself, maybe the words are more sincere. I scan through results, mostly articles that briefly mention individual drone attacks. Then I see the words *systematic drone attacks*. I click through. A website, the Bureau of Investigative Journalists, displays articles, comments, even maps of drone attacks. The Bureau, a group of fringe British journalists have compiled local reports and plotted out each attack in the last five years. A red dot on the publicly available global satellite imaging program symbolizes each attack. I zoom in on the Khyber Agency area of the frontier territories to see if the journalists have plotted the attack that killed my father. As my mouse hovers over each dot, a text box pops up with the date, location, a single sentence about the circumstances, and statistics about the numbers of adults and children killed.

There are only a few red dots in the Khyber Agency. I have never looked on a map at where Shoukart's family lived, so I do not recognize anything on these maps. I read all the red dots, and come to one that describes the situation as, "Attack of village wedding, justified as gathering of Taliban because several male wedding guests fired AK-47s. Total Deaths: 15 Children killed: 2."

I pause, read the information several more times. For the first time since I have returned from Pakistan, I see that my father's death has registered as significant to someone else. I see in the number 15 evidence that something happened, something that has caused my family so much grief, something that will change the trajectory of my life.

Shoukart's father had never mentioned the weapons. Perhaps this was some supposed evidence conjured up by the US military.

Though, the description is hardly implausible. I saw lots of guns and rifles when we passed checkpoints and drove past family compounds. The AK-47 has been familiar to me for as long as I can remember. My father even asked our Sikh, Jagdeep, to distribute several to his most trusted guards whenever we had a function—a wedding or festival, or even the movie screenings on our compound. *Those of us who enjoy much,* my father used to tell me, *in a world where most have little, cannot depend on the law or the government to protect us. We only continue to enjoy through our generosity and our guns.*

The librarian touches the shoulder of the man two seats to my left. "Five more minutes, please and then you need to allow the next person on the waiting list to use the computer." The man grumbles.

I place my hand over my heart, expressing my gratitude to these distant British journalists. They have documented my tragedy, however briefly, however facelessly, but in a way that strikes me as compassionate, a digital shout of righteous indignation.

I zoom back out of the satellite image, until the whole frontier region appears on the screen. The biggest cluster of red dots appears in Northern Waziristan. I read below the image that the intensity of attacks significantly increased in 2007, with 147 reported attacks throughout the frontier territories in one year. The website reports the drones appear to be launched from a remote compound in Baluchistan, a part of Pakistan historically known for its close ties with Iran and the Persian Gulf. The compound, the journalists report, is owned by one of the United Arab Emirates' royal families, as a retreat primarily used for falcon hunting. I am not surprised. I can only imagine the negotiations between high level U.S. officials, and the sheiks in their elegant robes, perhaps in a private room in one of the luxurious hotels in Dubai or Abu Dhabi. The Americans use a falcon hunting retreat for another kind of hunting.

I search the site for the Bureau's address, a place where I might contribute to their work. I can see the librarian approaching my shoulder, letting me know my time is up. Hastily I use a little yellow pencil to scribble their address on a piece of scrap paper and slide it into my seat pocket as I stand up, remembering to close the browser before I step away.

Still I am not ready to go home, not ready to leave this place. I make my way to the far corner of the library, where stacks of colorful children's books surround low tables with small chairs. I sit down, reach for one of the board books stacked into a basket at the center of the table, thinking I should look like I have a reason for being here. On each page brightly colored images of a hungry caterpillar eat through a series of fruits. The author cares only about the caterpillar, not about the fruits he ruins. After tunneling his way through the middle, most of the fruit is still left, but will be left to rot. Who will care for the rotten fruit? These American children, raised on such tales of excess. My American children, will they be as greedy, as arrogant, and self-centered as this insatiable caterpillar?

I close the book before I reach the end. The stories of my childhood were different. My mother told me of Hari Singh the vengeful warrior of Afghanistan who would come to get me in the night if I didn't go to sleep. My nanny sang songs of Jeonya Maurd who stole from the rich and gave to the poor. I loved to see the traveling troupe of performers who would come every year to sing songs of revenge, I remember yearning for the glory the hero enjoyed as he rightfully slayed the murderer who had attacked his sister. I grew up with a call to action, with a craving for justice, not just a craving for consumption.

In my car, I drive slowly down the street past the low wide buildings of the local suburban commercial establishments. From the radio a melodic line practically carries the smell of stale smoke and alcohol, the perfume of our favorite disco in Dubai. The singer's words about the curve of a woman's body, her skin as a landscape, a wonderland, bring back feelings I felt about Kathryn. I miss those days, the sex, whenever, wherever we could. I haven't had sex since before I left for Pakistan. I feel myself stiffen in the car, try to ignore it, turn off the radio.

I notice an Indian restaurant and make a U-turn. I wish it were a Pakistani restaurant, but I can tell Punjabis own this place, so at least the food will be familiar. I crave lamb shish kebab, the heavy powerful food I remember from Eid, from the holiday celebrating the end of our month of fasting. My father used to follow every piece of meat he ate with a slice of onion. He said it helped with digestion.

Inside, I order lamb. The waiter, a stoic *sardarji*, doesn't make conversation with me. But the décor of the restaurant broadcasts his beliefs. In an alcove toward the back of the restaurant sits a shrine, a small wooden canopy protects an image of Guru Nanak, the founder of Sikhism. Next to the Santa Claus like image of the guru are the symbolic weapons of the religion, the various swords and blades that the Sikhs used to fight against the Hindus and Muslims who found their religion subversive. He is probably one of the militant Sikhs, dreaming of a separate Sikh state, a member of the kind of groups Pakistan supported as destabilizing forces in India.

I wish I had a set of prayer beads that I could lay on the table, some symbol of my Muslim identity. This impulse from deep in my past surprises me, Americans don't make a point of broadcasting their religious identity. In Pakistan and India, we learned our religions practically before we learned our names. The lamb arrives in an aromatic swell. I nod and thank the sardarji, at least he will understand that I am not a Hindu.

I eat quickly, trying to satisfy a surprisingly deep hunger. With the pleasure in this food comes a nostalgia, a craving for the past that grows stronger the more my stomach fills. Any past; my childhood in Pakistan, my studies in London, my wild days with Kathryn in Dubai, even the past of last month would be a brighter place than this valley of foreboding. I brush the crumbs from the crispy naan off my lap, leave a big bill on the table—and return wordlessly to my car.

At home, Kathryn sits on the couch, her eyes red, tears clouding her face.

"What happened?" I ask, fearing news of another death in the family.

"You tell *me* what happened. You didn't answer your phone. You just leave me again without saying where you're going, without telling me when you'll be back. Where have you been? How long am I supposed to handle all of this alone?"

I have been gone for hours. I didn't think to tell her where I was, didn't think to call her to let her know when I would be home. In fact, I didn't think of her at all, except to feel that I wanted her.

"I was at the mosque," I say simply. I sit next to her, I want to be close enough to feel her warmth.

"The mosque? What for?"

"I miss my father. I'm trying to sort out some things in my head. I don't expect you to understand."

"Of course, how can I understand anything when you won't even talk to me, won't even touch me."

I can see the shape of her breasts through her shirt. I draw her to me, feel her release her tension with a stream of tears and angry words. I can understand I have hurt her.

"I'm sorry," I tell her. I will not argue with her, I need her to open to me.

"You are?" she says, drawing back so I can see her eyes. The blue is as startling today as when I first met her. I have nothing more to say, cannot restrain my hunger. I want only the uncomplicated fact of her body around mine. I reach for her breasts.

She holds up her hands to stop me. "Rashid, the children."

I leave her to close the door on the bedroom where they are napping and I return to her. She yields. I remove her clothes. I press into her darkness, into the space where I am safe, where I am most alive. I want her to become the world, I want her to crowd out everything else, all my other thoughts. I kiss her skin, run my tongue over the contours of her shoulders, slide my fingertips over the depression between her collar bones.

She arches her lower back then tilts her pelvis up to meet mine. She reaches for my back in big handfuls, pulling me to her every time I raise my hips. I close my eyes and pretend. I imagine I hear the call to prayer, plan that tonight we will head to the disco, picking up shwarma sandwiches along the way. I see her white skin against mine, as if she were illuminated against my shadow. And easily she engineers my movements to take her pleasure. I recognize with satisfaction the quickening of her breath, the small wordless sounds, a whimpering exhale. And I turn her over, raise her hips to reach me and I see the line of her spine descending away from me, the curves of her waist beneath my hands. The image crowds out all other thoughts. The motion crowds out all other sensations. I push and I pull and demand what I need. And she gives.

For a blinding moment the world ceases to exist. I feel only the pleasure of completion. I close my eyes and collapse, covering her body with mine, feeling the reflection of my breath against her neck. And then it is enough. I push my hands into the floor and leave her body, leave the room, and go to wash myself.

Chapter 3

Preparing to leave for a rig, I repeat my tasks in the workshop as if I had never left. My muscles seem to remember the feel of the tools, the rhythm of the jobs. After the funeral, and these subsequent days of idleness, I am glad for the work, the illusion of purpose. I pack a three-foot steel canister with small explosive charges. I methodically count them out…sixty-five…seventy…seventy-five. We will be perforating the cement in a section of a newly prepared oil well at a depth where we have confirmed the presence of oil. The perforations will allow the oil to seep into the well, the rocks will hemorrhage their fluids to be pumped to the surface. The small charges, half-moon metal spheres the size of marble shooters are designed to start oil production. They will only create pressure, poking holes painlessly, through rock. The smooth, harmless look-ing objects are not designed for destruction, they are not like the pyrotechnics or the ammonium nitrate bombs or any other kind of explosive I had to study to receive my blaster's permit when I came to California. I have never actually seen dynamite explode above ground. Perhaps the drone operator who killed my father hadn't seen real explosions either. How could I find him? Would he be the responsible one? Or was he just carrying out a job, taking the orders of the government as I take the orders of the oil companies? Maybe there are hundreds, thousands of people who are responsible for the campaign of drone attacks in Pakistan.

A heavy metal door bangs, breaking my train of thought, and my superior—a Norwegian man recently transferred from our base in Nigeria—bears down on my work table. "Come on, we need to get these tools out in the next fifteen minutes or we'll miss the ferry. I don't want to have to pay for any lost time."

I look up and catch the eye of my Lebanese colleague. As our Norwegian engineer moves to inspect the truck we will take to the rig, my colleague approaches me, whispers, "*Nazel*, asshole, he only thinks about his job bonus. You should fuck him up, mispack the tool. When it fails and he has to repeat the job you can see him cry about lost time."

I know his expletive well, used it daily when I was in the Gulf. But I don't respond, I am not interested in the petty divisions and allegiances my Lebanese colleague fosters within our base. I finish packing the charges and load the tools on the truck. I am just doing my job. I don't want to draw any attention to myself.

The ferry pulls away from the shore delivering me again into the familiar culture of the rig. The Norwegian supervisor makes small talk with me, comparing his current posting with his experiences in Nigeria, Sakhalin, Bakersfield. The company moves its employees every three years, developing a community of workers and their families loyal to company over country.

We arrive before the sun is overhead. I go through the motions of the job. We trigger the charges as planned, the tool performs without error. The engineer is able to tell the company man that the well is producing, we perforated at the correct depth. I wonder sometimes about these places my tools travel. Do borders exist in those places? Does it make any difference in the darkness of the geology tens of thousands of feet below us which company, or country, or culture penetrates from the sunlit surface to extract the remains of what was living millions of years ago? Do the ghosts of the dinosaurs care what we do with their decomposed bodies?

The sound of the motor that drives the winch blocks out all other noises, and thousands of feet of cable coil on a giant spool, retrieving our tool from the depths—the explosive charges spent. I know how to drive the winch now, taking care not to go too fast. When I was training in the Gulf, I saw a guy drive the winch too fast, when the tool got stuck on the way up the well, he didn't realize it. The gears pulled on the cable until it snapped, the spool spun too fast and the frayed end of the cable flew out of the well, severing the winch driver's arms. It occurs to me now that perhaps the ghosts of the dinosaurs took their revenge with that cable—punishment for stealing, Saudi-style. In the Gulf, the Arabs sometimes claimed jobs went bad or accidents happened because of *djinns*, the spirits that dwell on the earth with us, making mischief and interfering in the lives of humans. If only I could call on a djinn to avenge my father for me, to take from me the anxiety of making a plan, to protect my wife and children from the blowback of whatever I determine I must do.

As if on cue, my phone vibrates in my pocket. Once the tool is back up on the rig floor, I pause in my work, unlocking the phone to see the message. When I was in the Gulf, Kathryn sent me messages everyday, carefully composed missives, sometimes humorous, sometimes erotic, often bordering on poetry. Since the arrival of the children, those kinds of messages have almost completely disappeared. This one is from my brother Majid, asking me to call.

I secure my tools, complete the paperwork recording the number of charges we have used on the job, and head to the doghouse so I can rest and call my brother.

I lie down on the bed and dial a long series of numbers and wait. "Majid…yes, it's Rashid….Fine. And you?"

He speaks to me in Urdu, asking about what I am doing, how I am planning. "Well, I'd like to talk about that," I say in English before slipping into Urdu. "I think I can't follow through with… with…with what we had discussed with those people. My life is here now. Kathryn. The boys. My job. Everything is fine for me."

I pull the zipper on my coveralls up and down, again and again as I listen to him. "No, not nothing. I *will* do something, something better. We know some people here who can bring revenge through the courts."

I hold the phone away from my ear because Majid is shouting now.

"It's not the same here. There are better ways. You have to trust that I know what I'm doing."

I move the zipper faster. Listen.

I disconnect the phone without saying goodbye.

I dial Kathryn's number. "Hey, what's up…so I was thinking, when I get home, I want to talk some more about the lawyer you mentioned at the Civic Union…yeah, the Civil Liberties Union, whatever the name is. Let's see what they can do…OK, I'll let you finish that…I love you too."

I close my eyes. Maybe if we are smart about this, maybe if we use America's own tactics against herself, maybe we can bring the whole band of people ordering these drone attacks to justice. I think of the old man in Shoukart's brother's house. Maybe he was right, maybe men in a poor country do need a man like me to help protect them. I scratch my forehead. But maybe he didn't really know how my future is written.

I must doze off because when my phone rings again, I open my eyes disoriented, confused about why I am sleeping in a cell-like metal room. I answer the phone, my heart racing. "Who?...Majid… fuck, you scared me…Yes, I know today is Tuesday…Really? Already almost forty days? Yes, of course I can go for that."

I hang up. So simple, next week I will go to the mosque to mark the forty days since my father's death. I will observe my culture's traditions and use this country's legal traditions for my advantage.

I touch my forehead to the floor, the green color of my prayer rug momentarily filling my field of vision. The chanting of the *imam*, the men murmuring prayers around me, gives me comfort. I think of my father, hope his spirit has settled wherever it has gone. I feel my own spirit settling after the roller coaster of these forty days as well. Kathryn and I sat together when I returned from the job. We took notes about what I had seen of the attack in Pakistan, I showed her the website with the map filled with the red dots of past drone attacks. She has scheduled an appointment with the ACLU lawyer. The process is starting. I continue with the prayers, hold my hands out to receive, I will call Majid when I leave the mosque, tell him I have completed the prayers as he requested. Everything will be fine.

I roll up my rug and step out with the other men as we return to our shoes.

"*Salaam*, brother," a young man to my right greets me brightly. "You are new to the mosque? I haven't seen you here before."

I shake his outstretched hand. "Yes, I am relatively new to the mosque."

"And new to the country?"

"No," I say quietly.

"How long have you been here?"

"A long time, maybe too long."

He responds with a little snort of understanding. "I am Ali, from Palestine."

"Rashid, from Lahore, Pakistan. And how long have you been here?"

He runs a hand over his beard, "Since before my father was killed. I mean about two years. Now I am measuring everything as either before or after his death."

I am stunned at his answer. "I'm sorry for your loss. How was he killed?"

"Israelis," he says as if the word itself were a mode of killing.

I incline my head, waiting for more explanation.

"Somebody from our neighborhood planned a bus bombing. Killed a couple of Israeli people on the bus. They traced the bomber's family back to our neighborhood. So they shelled us one night, killed a dozen people sleeping in their flats," I can see his face flushing with anger, "even some kids."

"You weren't there?"

He shakes his head. "I was here, at university."

I wait for more.

"I was studying at Long Beach State, I had a scholarship through an organization of American Jewish people trying to improve Israeli-Palestinian relations."

I raise my eyebrows at the irony.

"I quit." He notices I have yet to put my shoes on. "Do you want tea? We can talk more outside."

"Is there somewhere nearby?"

"An American restaurant a couple of blocks away is twenty-four hours. The food is not good, but they serve Lipton tea." I can picture the tea label clearly, the symbol of quality that seemed to appear in every restaurant in Dubai.

"Sure. Should I drive?"

"*La, la,* no, no," he says slipping for a moment into Arabic as he shakes his head. "Let's walk, I will have to come back here for catching my bus."

He reaches down for his shoes, a pair of expensive tennis shoes, now shabby with wear.

Outside the sidewalks are empty, cars queue up at the stoplights waiting for permission to approach the droning freeway. We pass three blocks of small businesses, shops, car dealers not yet open for the day's business.

"What were you studying?"

"Civil engineering. I was thinking to work to build infrastructure, roads, bridges, aqueducts." He points down to the sidewalk and motions out to the street, "America has beautiful infrastructure, and still people only complain about the traffic on the freeway. They've never spent three hours trying to pass a checkpoint."

At the restaurant we seat ourselves on the orange vinyl upholstery of a corner booth. A waitress comes to the table, "G'morning, what can I get you?" She stares at her order pad.

"Tea, please. Two teas," Ali orders.

She looks up, "No food?"

"And two eggs," I tell her, "scrambled with tomato and onion." She scribbles on her pad. I look to Ali, who seems unexpectedly quiet. "I'm paying. Tell her what you'd like."

"The same as my brother, please."

"And do you have cilantro for the eggs?" I ask.

The waitress raises an eyebrow and shakes her head.

"Mint for the tea?" Ali asks.

She shakes her head again. "We got parsley if you want."

Ali shakes his head. "Only the eggs then." She walks away and he turns to me. "Can't put parsley in my tea," he says derisively. "Do you know how many attacks the Palestinians have endured?" He launches into what sounds like a prepared monologue, indignantly enumerating deaths and dates faster than I can process them. He repeats the word *Palestinian* in almost every sentence, until they seem to populate the whole world.

When he pauses for a breath, I interrupt. "It is not only the Palestinians."

"Of course not!" He says in agreement, "All Muslim lands are under attack."

"America's at war with Afghanistan," I say, "but Pakistan is supposedly a U.S. ally."

Ali shakes his head sympathetically. "But the drones don't stay on the Afghan side of the border."

"No." I tighten my fists until my knuckles turn white.

"And they kill our people...your father." He looks at me with an expression of naked compassion.

I look up stunned. "How did you know?"

"It is written...all over your face." He takes a moment. "Masha'al-lah, God willed it. We are brothers in this way."

The waitress comes, setting down coffee cups on saucers, teabags still in their packets, a flimsy metal cream pitcher. Relieved at the distraction, I pour cream until the cup overflows. Ali grabs a bundle of sugar packets pouring the contents of one after another into his tea. As he stirs I reach for the sugar, finding only a single packet left among the saccharine.

"Was your father Taliban?"

"Ali!" I take offense. "Look at me. Do I look like my father might be Taliban?"

"Al Qaeda?"

I shoot him an angry look, won't justify his question with an answer.

"Don't look like that. You'd be surprised what Al Qaeda look like. Doctors, engineers, people who have money and influence, people tired of fighting local conflicts and who want to make a bigger impact." He holds the cup Arabic style—at the rim rather than with the handle—and slurps. He glances up to gauge my reaction.

I sip my tea. Not sweet enough—the kind of tea that would have caused my father to scold the maid for being so stingy toward him.

"My father was just an innocent person also," Ali continues, "PLO, intafadas, Fatah, none of these things he ever paid attention to." He takes another sip and the hard edge of his prior monologue crumbles. "He always said he just wanted to raise children and olives. He used to say the Israelis want to raise children and olives too. Even, he admired the drip irrigation they invented and their crop breeding programs. He thought when there was peace, the Israelis would teach us to grow olives as good as they did." He folds a used sugar packet in half over and over again, unable to make it small enough to disappear. "Look at me, he allowed me to come to America on Jewish American money!"

I think of my own father proudly sending me off to the West to study. Perhaps our fathers would have felt comfortable with each other, would have shared a cup of tea as Ali and I are now.

"He didn't even hate America." Ali unfolds the sugar packet, flattens the white paper against the Formica tabletop. "But now *I* do. How can a country like America, a powerful country, support a government that kills innocent people as my father, as yours?"

I clasp my hands together. I have not allowed myself to think that I hate this country, only that I owe my mother to take revenge against it. But how can I deny Ali's question?

"The good thing about America," Ali says, the hard edge creeping back in, "is that once you are inside her borders, you can do almost anything. There is money here, and powerful systems, you can get on the freeway and drive all the way across the country without a single checkpoint. Now that I'm here, I'll use what America offers, let her know that she can't just kill innocent people around the world. What will you do?"

The waitress arrives with two servings of eggs. "Eat your eggs, Ali," I say as I would to my little son when I run out of answers to his questions.

Ali smiles, seizes his fork and scoops up the eggs in great hungry portions.

In the evening I call Majid, to let him know I have made the prayers he requested for our father.

"Good," he says. "And did you meet Ali?"

His question leaves me speechless as I try to trace the connections that might link Ali and my brother.

"Ali," Majid repeats, "the Palestinian?"

"Yes," I say slowly, "how...?"

"Abu Omar has many friends around the world. I hear Ali is very interesting, you will want to get to know him better."

"Why?"

"It's always good to have a brother near us. Riaz and I are far from you. Please, think of Ali like one of us."

The idea surprises, then comforts me. I have never associated anything in America with my brothers, have always felt isolated—though independent—in this other country. But a brother, a man who understands something more of my culture, the structure of my family, this could reconnect me to the community I felt in Shoukart's grandfather's home.

"Sure," I say quietly, "I'm sure I'll see him around."

Ali comes to the mosque every morning. If I have arrived first, he always places his rug next to mine. The other men in the mosque will nod their heads, greet me politely, but Ali always talks to me, puts his arm around my shoulders, offering a warmth that satisfies a deep hunger.

On Saturday morning Ali is already sitting inside the mosque when I arrive with Michael.

My son silently turns his head back and forth to take in the surroundings. Everything will be unfamiliar to him; the Arabic calligraphy, the lacy latticework designs painted around the perimeter of the ceiling, the old men with orange henna camouflaging the white of their beards. We move to sit next to Ali. I instruct Michael to sit and I move his hands to rest properly in his lap. I told him in the car not to talk and to follow all of my movements.

As the imam leads us in the prayer, the familiar Arabic words settle into well-worn routes through my memories. I don't remember how old I was when my father first took me to the masjid in our village, but it would not have been an unfamiliar place. I heard the call to prayer every day, the radio and the television always broadcast the Friday afternoon sermons—thankfully after the *Star Trek* episodes we watched religiously—the Koran with its elaborate calligraphy on the cover always rested on a carved wooden book rest in a nook in our hall. The masjid and the prayers were only a natural concentration of the Islam that permeated our everyday lives, the religion and culture that gave rise to our nation partitioned from India, separated from the Hindus with their pantheon of gods who looked down on us as if we were second-class citizens. But here in America, I have distanced myself so much from my culture that I have not even given my son the most basic introduction to Islam. My father would not mind Michael's ignorance of the Prophet, the Pillars, and the guidance of the *Hadiths*, but perhaps he judges me for ignoring the food, the art, the sense of history and hospitality that made us Muslims as much as any doctrine.

In unison, the men around us bow down and we touch our heads to the ground, the sound of our collective prayers muffled by our closeness to the earth. I feel my son follow, a beat behind. My chest fills—almost painfully—as I shepherd him into this community. Anywhere in the world he will be welcomed in a mosque as part of the umma, part of the global community of Muslims. When my father made the Hajj, fulfilled his obligation to travel to Mecca once in his life, he returned not with a renewed sense of religiosity, but awed at the spectrum of the faithful, people of every color and culture, almost every language who endured the trip to participate in a massive display of common beliefs.

Michael understands nothing of the implications of his actions. His only motivation is to win my approval. So when we stand and turn to leave through the back door, I pat him on the head, tell him he has done well.

Ali is ahead of us, following a man dressed in a perfectly tailored dark suit, their shoulders touching repeatedly as they walk to their shoes. I cannot hear their words, Ali is unusually quiet, almost deferential to the man, whose thick, wavy black hair, softens to salt and pepper grey in his neatly trimmed beard. The man does not look back at me or anyone else. He slides his feet into a pair of immaculate leather wingtips. He moves to leave, pausing only to kiss Ali's cheeks with four alternating kisses. I have intentionally unlearned this kind of physical intimacy, broken the habit I had of holding my male friends' hands, resting our arms on each others' shoulders when we walked to our classes, habits too easily mistaken for homosexuality in this culture.

Ali approaches us as I kneel down to help Michael into his shoes, pulling the Velcro straps closed. "Brother, introduce me to your son," he says.

"This is Michael, my eldest son. Andrew is the baby."

"Michael, like the arc angel." Ali squeezes my son's shoulder in greeting. "That makes you Abu Michael," he says to me. The Arab custom of referring to a man as *father of his eldest son* feels contrived with my son's American sounding name.

Another man, perhaps an Egyptian, approaches us, his new leather jacket pulled tight around his barrel-shaped belly. "Glad to see you bring your son."

"The child is lucky enough to still have a father," Ali's retort is surprisingly bitter.

"We all lose our fathers," the man says in return. "Mine is gone too," he says as if picking up on an earlier conversation.

"But you lost yours to old age. We have lost ours to the infidels," Ali shoots back indignantly.

"You don't need to call them infidels," the man says, "they were Israelis. You Palestinians need to learn to stop stirring the pot. When you kick a giant, he'll always kick you back." He turns to me, "Was your father also killed by the Israelis?"

"No," I say quietly, "the Americans."

"How? You are Afghan?"

"No, Pakistani. My father was killed in a drone attack near the Afghan border."

"I'm sorry," he says, his Arabic accent caressing the r's. "Very unfortunate. For me, I love this country, she has given us much opportunity."

"And in return, you have become stingy with your fellow Arabs."

I am uneasy at Ali's rudeness.

"Ali," he says as if reprimanding a child, "be a man, take care of yourself. Once you have a family you'll see the world is more than just politics and Islam."

"And maybe you'll see that America is the enemy, but she is blinding you with money and profit."

The Egyptian releases a string of words in Arabic which I understand only in tone. Ali responds in kind, animating his words by rubbing his fingers together to indicate money. Perhaps Ali asked the man for money in the past.

The older man places his left hand on my shoulder, shakes my hand with his right. "I have argued enough with this young man on other days. I only want to say you are welcome, and of course your son is most welcome." He turns to Michael, "You're very handsome with your fair skin. Do you take after your mother? Where is she from?"

Michael, pleased to be included in the adult conversation, rushes with his response. "She's American," he says smiling.

Ali turns away.

"Very good, young man," the Egyptian smiles, almost gloating. "You see Americans are modern tolerant people." He pats Michael on the head and leaves.

———

"Salaam aleikum *habibi*," Ali greets me affectionately through the phone.

"Hi, Ali," I respond, intentionally avoiding the basic Arabic that I know well.

"My cousin is planning to get married next week. They're spending a fortune on the wedding hall, they're planning to have two live bands, one to play Arabic music, one to play rock 'n roll. Can you imagine! What do they need rock 'n roll for, can't we even get married in our own tradition, without bowing down to Western style?"

"Ali," I cut him off, before he can launch into a full-blown tirade about the evils of cultural hegemony. "What about your friend? I'm calling about your text," I hold myself to American-style directness on the phone.

"Yes," he says, "my friend. We need a photo of you, a passport-style photo. But listen, you cannot go to just any passport photographer. We have our own photographer. He's in Glendale, a Syrian guy. You just go and tell him your name is Ibrahim. He'll take your photo and keep it there, and then my friend's contact will go and pick it up. You don't take it with you."

"Wait, who is your friend? What does he do? You said in your text you have a friend who could help me."

"He's the uncle of a man who comes to the mosque."

I remember the man in the wingtips.

"The uncle can help with passports, visas, these things."

In Pakistan I always knew somebody who could forge certificates from colleges, technical schools, universities. These were the currency many of my impatient or poorly connected classmates used to apply for jobs abroad, the credentials they gave to labor agents. My father disapproved of the forgeries, not on principle, but because he had seen misfortune or even disaster follow everyone he knew of who used them; the job would be lost, the man would be injured, his wife would miscarry while he was abroad. In one case, we even heard of a young man who was stabbed and killed in a London pub after he went abroad with fake certificates about his education. But Ali's connection is not trading in shortcuts to jobs.

"What for?" I ask. "I already have a passport, two in fact, if you count the expired Pakistani one."

"He helps the organization move people around."

I don't know which organization. I am afraid to ask.

"Blacklists can cause problems sometimes."

"But Ali, I don't need to travel anywhere."

"I knew of a man who planned an action on a bus in Israel. He sent his ID and his father's dagger with another man who actually carried the explosives onto the bus. The neighbors identified the dagger on the dead man to the intelligence people. Those fuckers left the planner's family alone, because they thought he was already dead. But actually he fled to Morocco."

"So?"

"So when the investigation died down, he called his wife and children to him in Morocco where they were reunited and lived together."

I am silent trying to understand how this story relates to me.

"We both need to make a point to this country," Ali speaks as if he were explaining something to a child. "You have a wife and children. I don't."

"I'm not ready for this. I'm still thinking about what I need to do. I don't need a passport."

"Not yet." Ali pauses for effect. "But you don't know what is written for you. And when you do understand, you won't want to be waiting for this detail."

I absorb his words. He seems to know more than I do. What could be the harm in taking a photo? "What will it cost?"

"If you wanted to buy a passport this good, from a good country like Canada, the black market could charge you maybe six, eight thousand dollars. But this is my friend, he's interested in your situation, he'll provide it to you, no cost."

Labor agents in Pakistan also promised people fabulous opportunities for no charge up front. But I knew laborers in Dubai who had not seen their families for three years because they were paying off their labor agents for ostensibly free visas rather than buying tickets home. I switch the phone to my other ear.

"Then what's my obligation? What's his interest?"

"His interest is the same as yours. He believes that this bitch of a country can't go around the world killing our people without any consequence."

I bristle at his words. "I don't know. Not now."

"The Syrian is at Yerevan Travel in Glendale."

I laugh. "Yerevan, the capital of Armenia? The Syrian's geography isn't very good."

"No one notices him in the Armenian community, you know the Armenians run everything in Glendale. Anyway, the shop is on San Fernando three blocks west of Brand Boulevard."

"I'm going to sleep, Ali. I don't want to talk about this."

"*Damam*, fine." His tone softens, and his voice fills with warmth. "Whatever is written will happen. Sleep well, my brother."

I walk in the store telling myself I will buy milk and bread and coffee, and maybe call Kathryn to see what else she needs. I don't get more than a few steps down the center aisle before I stop, close my eyes, and breathe deeply of the smells of dried thyme, walnut, and pomegranate. By blocking out the view of all the looping Armenian script on the labels, my olfactory memory tells me I am at the Lebanese grocery in my old neighborhood in Dubai. A long ago habit compels me to look for small bitter green olives and hard salty haloumi cheese for frying with tomatoes and onions, and then go next door—as if I was still in Dubai—to the Afghan baker where I will leave my coins on his counter and hold out my newspaper to receive the hot flat circle of bread he will retrieve from the intense heat of his clay *tandoor*.

I must look strange in my paralysis of memory. The Armenian butcher behind the counter asks me if I need help. I shake my head and the force of my current reality causes me to stumble. I reach out for the shelf to steady myself, stare at a jar of pistachios packed in honey.

I will buy my things and go home. This is just a side trip into Glendale, I just wanted some imported foods, I tell myself. I make my way around the store, quickly placing items in my red plastic basket. I buy Palestinian olive oil, imaging that the Armenians must be sympathetic to the Palestinians in their struggle for their own state. I pay for everything with cash, rather than my bank card—no need to leave a record that I was here, I tell myself.

In the parking lot, I will myself to walk to my car. I am going home, I assert in my mind. But my feet will not obey, they carry me into the storefront three doors down. A small bell clangs as the door of Yerevan Travel closes behind me. It is written.

I lay in bed with my sons. I murmur lines from the Koran about a father's love. I hope that on some level these lines will lodge in their memories, that should they suffer in the future, these verses will remind them of the intensity of my love.

I can hear Kathryn in the other room, finishing with the dishes, packing the children's things for the next day. I will not think about the way we argued on another night about revenge, about the things I could only say to her with alcohol again in my system. She is a strong woman, responsible. If only she were Pakistani, she would understand my situation. But if she were Pakistani, we might not be here, I might not be the one chosen by my family as most qualified to assuage our grief. But it was written that I should marry her. It was written that I should suffer this way.

Chapter 4

And the days pass by quickly. Almost too quickly. Ali becomes a fixture in my life, a secret relationship, a hidden flirtation with death. I feel as if I am having an affair, taking Ali's phone calls when I am out of the house, sending him texts when Kathryn is out of the room. My father told me when I was a teenager that Islam allows a man to take up to four wives, but only if he treats them all exactly fairly. He cannot favor one over the other, either with love or with property. *And of course,* my father would say, with a twinkle in his eye, *it is impossible not to favor one woman over another.*

So I have established a kind of tally in my head, an accounting system to record my expenditures of love. Every phone call with Ali I follow with a phone call to Kathryn, a conversation about our plans with the ACLU, which I now realize will be fruitless.

From the rig floor I can see a cargo ship in the distance, on its way to the port. The sky is still overcast, the usual morning gloominess of the Pacific has not yet burned off. The ferry will arrive in a half an hour to bring us back to shore. I call Kathryn at her office, explain that there was a problem, I won't be home for another day or so.

"All right," she says. I can hear the resigned disappointment in her voice. "When you come back, can you look at the sink disposal? The motor has stopped working again."

"Of course."

I hang up and wait for the ferry, checking my watch. Within three hours I should be at Ali's place. He has directed me to drive to the train station, take the Metro line north and then transfer to a bus line that will take me to within a few blocks of his neighborhood. I am eager to be there, haven't felt this kind of anticipation since I was a teenager arranging for a clandestine meeting with a girl.

Ali opens the door of his little run-down back house only as far as the chain lock will allow. He closes it and I hear the chain rattling. The little structure is a converted garage, the paint peeling to reveal tired grey wood, the weeds gone to seed in the cracks of the concrete foundation.

I step inside when the door opens, and just as quickly he shuts it again. "Welcome," he spreads his arms, "you are welcome. I'm making us some tea."

The place is nearly empty, as if he hadn't actually moved in, but were camping for a few days.

"Have a seat."

I sit at a little kitchen table on one of four mismatched chairs. Ali pushes aside a stack of Arabic language newspapers. "There is an imam in Iraq," he points to a photo of a cleric in a neatly tied circular turban, "he is calling on the Cubans to demand that the Americans abandon Guantanamo Bay. He has even invited a Cuban delegation to come to Iraq to discuss it."

"The Cubans can never do it, they don't have the political clout or the military might to back it up."

"Of course not," he turns off the gas on the stove and takes the steaming kettle to the counter, "but he is highlighting for the world to see that America is not playing by the rules, that she will occupy and control whatever place she wants. And her purpose is usually evil." He brings the teacups to the table. "Sugar?"

I nod. "How long have you lived here in this place?" I don't want Ali to launch into one of his lectures. I am here because Ali claimed to have some information about a time and location that he couldn't discuss over the phone.

"A couple of months," he answers, "the place belongs to the

cousin of a friend from the mosque. He's not charging me rent, and I get free wireless internet from the main house."

He sits next to me and pulls a brand new looking laptop from the bottom of the stack of newspapers.

"Nice computer," I say, suspicious of how he came by it.

"Yeah, this is also from my friend. He loaded software that allows you to use a proxy alias, so no one can track your movements on the internet. You know the U.S. government closely monitors who visits the *jihadi* websites. When there's a lot of traffic, they raise the color of the threat level."

I raise a skeptical eyebrow.

"The government loves it when Americans are afraid, let's them kill more of us Muslims."

The screen comes to life without delay and helpfully displays the most commonly viewed pages. Amidst the Arabic language sites with green banners and Saudi flags, up pops a porn site with images of blonde women performing oral sex. I laugh, almost involuntarily.

Ali is embarrassed. "American women are whores!" He tries to turn the computer screen away from me. "I was showing a friend how wrong this culture is. Can you imagine a Muslim man allowing his sister or daughter to dishonor him like this?" He clicks on another screen, obscuring the naked women behind it.

"Not all American women are like that, Ali." In Dubai, I remember my buddies and I joked that American women were not whores. They didn't fuck for money, they fucked for fun. One of my Indian Punjabi friends always tried to pick up American or British girls in the discos. If he was unsuccessful, he would try for a white skinned prostitute—Latvian, or Bulgarian, or even a fair-skinned Chechen. Occasionally he would be short enough on cash to leave a club controlled by the Russian prostitution rings for one frequented by the less expensive Chinese prostitutes. Once I met Kathryn I no longer listened to the banter about the relative costs of sex by nationality.

"I'm sure your wife is an exception," Ali avoids my gaze, brings his teacup to his lips. "But insha'allah, I will know women in a pure state."

I turn to look at Ali. His brown untrimmed beard conceals a few pimples, his dingy button-down shirt smells of his sweat. His appearance is not one that would attract a woman. When I was a teenager, I knew boys like this, driven by their hormones to visit the brothels for relief from small dark Bengali women.

"Ali, you've never had a woman?"

Ali straightens his shoulders, but still will not look at me. "I am pure, Brother. Allah has other plans for me, and in heaven I will be rewarded for my discipline."

This gives me pause. I look around the grimy room and through the space between the outdated curtains to the neglected yard. Perhaps Ali does not see the ugliness of these things. Maybe in his mind he carries around the sumptuous gardens, the beautiful women, the endless delights of heaven. I will not try to convince him otherwise. Who am I to tell him the world is beautiful, women are generous, children are a miracle? I myself sometimes doubt these things, am engulfed with rage at the ignorance of those who are not like me. Ali enjoys the luxury of a singular purpose. Without a wife and children, without the rights and privileges of a citizen, or even status as a legal alien, without money or prospects, he is unfettered by the attachments that drive my own thinking in endless circles, forcing me to contrive justifications for my every action.

Ali navigates through his proxy alias to an Arabic language website, drilling down to a list of bulleted items. Although I have read the Arabic script of the Urdu language since childhood, I do not understand the text before me.

"Successes, brother. These are the dates and locations of all of the actions our people have taken around the world. Here are the events which show the infidels they are on the wrong path. We're drawing attention to our message. So many countries want to be like America, following her like a herd of stupid sheep." He clicks on a link to a curated map of the world. Small green dots appear over London, Milan, Nairobi, Kabul, Mumbai, Bali, Washington D.C., New York. Unlike the cluster of red dots marking the drone attacks in the frontier territories of Pakistan, these individual green points span the globe, reminding me of one of Michael's coloring books, requiring him to connect the dots to create an image. Ali points on the screen to an area far from any dots. Southern California.

"Here is where we must act."

"We?"

"Yes. You and me. Together we can act. I am ready to martyr myself, to accept my fate. You still want to live for that woman and those children. But you have many things I need."

I do not speak, my lips drawn tightly against my words.

"You have hazardous materials clearance, a blaster's permit, a commercial driving license. You understand tools and careful planning. And," he pauses, "you're American."

"I'm Pakistani," I retort.

"Yes, habibi. I mean you have an American passport."

He rises to the stove bringing the kettle to refill our teacups. I hate tea brewed from a used teabag. I use extra sugar to mask the weak bitterness.

"Los Angeles is known for her freeways," Ali says sitting down again. "Imagine if we could stop the traffic on the freeways. Think about bombs on the 405, the 110, the 10, the 101, the 5. With just five bombs, detonated at the same time, we could bring the city to a standstill. In Bangladesh, our people detonated two dozen bombs within a few hours."

I remember the news of these attacks, attributed to Al Qaeda. I had talked to my father on the phone that day. He thought it just as likely they were planted by Pakistani elements still bitter over the way Bengalis had massacred Urdu speakers when East Pakistan declared its independence from West Pakistan in 1973. *The desire for revenge may go dormant in a man's heart*, my father had said, *but it never dies.*

I look at Ali and then around the room. "Are there others who are planning with you?"

He shakes his head.

"Then the freeways are too complicated. You need too much coordination." I'm relieved at the improbability of his idea. "You might as well target an airplane." I am careful not to say *we*. I am not involved yet, I tell myself. I am only having a theoretical conversation with this young man.

"Impossible. Some of our people are still fascinated with plane bombings—of course they were so successful in the Twin Tower attacks. But the security is too complicated now." He turns again to the computer, pulling up a spreadsheet, also in Arabic. "Here's the list of targets and the impact over the last twenty years. Discos, hotels, office buildings, airplanes, cars, trains, subways, buildings. Really, habibi, no one has tried a freeway."

"Why not target a government building, try to reach some of the people responsible for what's happening in our countries?"

"Tell me, brother," Ali asks with mock gentleness, "did the drone that killed your father think to target only those people responsible for attacks against America?"

I look down at my hands, see again the flies alighting from burned flesh and singed hair. "What about the factory that produces the drones?"

Ali raises an eyebrow. "Perhaps." He turns back to his computer, types *predator drone manufacturer*.

The search engine returns images of huge low buildings southeast of Los Angeles, surrounded by wide open space.

"Too isolated," I quickly assess, "you wouldn't get past the front gate. But why the freeways? What message do you send by bombing a freeway?"

"Brother, do you really mean to be so blind? The freeways are about oil. Without oil, America shuts down. And without control of the Islamic lands, the oil supply shuts down."

Oil; the dross of ancient dinosaurs, the object of my offshore efforts, the treasure that fuels the military occupations of the western economies. I can't refute his logic. I sip my tea, my stomach growls. "But you could only be on one freeway at a time."

"Two."

I look at Ali. His eyes look right through me. He does not flinch. I feel trapped, as if fate had triangulated me into this location. My adoptive country, my mother, and my friend—all preventing me from making my own decisions.

He turns again to the computer. "On the 405 flyover from the 10. You get two freeways with one location."

Only one bomber. I look down at my hands around the teacup, feel as though I have cheated my fate for another minute. Though I see in the reflection of the overhead light on the surface of my tea, the explosion Ali imagines. Even if the charges were placed to direct the force down, any flames or fumes would always travel up. "Not from above. You'd have to be on the 10 under the flyover. You probably wouldn't actually be able to damage the flyover. But you could stop traffic." I look at the computer screen. "And the highway patrol and emergency vehicles would probably respond on both freeways."

Ali thumps the table energetically. "Yes. Excellent! This is why I want you here. You understand technical things, logistics."

Conditioned by years of planning jobs, working with engineers, developing backups against failure, troubleshooting malfunctions, I can't but help review the parameters of the situation in my mind as if my manager had assigned it to me. I remember the types of bombs outlined in the study guide for the blaster's permit. I see the volume of the car, the overhead clearance beneath the flyover. I estimate velocity, trajectory, force.

"What kind of explosives do you use in your work?" Ali asks.

"They're not right. They only work under high-pressure conditions."

He presses me with his questions about radioactive materials, shrapnel, how to obtain C4 plastic explosives. And I continue to answer, the value of my professional knowledge starting to dawn on me.

"What do you know about detonators?" Ali asks me.

"A lot. At least about the detonators I use on my jobs." My stomach growls again. "I need to eat something, Ali. Do you have anything here, or should we go out?"

"Forgive me, Rashid! I've lost my manners since you came to my house." He hurries around the tiny kitchen, retrieving a large pot from the refrigerator, igniting the gas burner with a cigarette lighter. "The woman who owns this house made me a big pot of chicken and rice this week. Sometimes she cooks for me. She told me she won't be able to face my mother in heaven if she doesn't feed me here on earth."

The smell of the food reminds me of so many Arabic restaurants in Dubai. The pot appears filled with the huge quantity that Arabic women instinctively prepare, ever ready for the arrival of unexpected guests. But no other food appears. No waiter or mother or sister arrives with olives and platters of fresh vegetables, no bowls of hummus with olive oil, no tabbouleh, or fatoosh salad sprinkled with bright sour sumac powder. Ali's unadorned food marks him as an orphan, an Arabic man without a female relation.

"Ali, where is your mother?"

"Al-hamda'allah," he says looking heavenward, "at least my eldest brother is there with her and my sisters in Palestine so she's not alone. He says everything is fine, I shouldn't worry about her." He stirs the pot on the stove. "But my sisters tell me she's not the same since my father was killed. She's not going out to call on family or neighbors. She only takes bread and tea and prays." Ali scoops a big portion of rice onto a plate, reaches back into the pot and pulls out a chicken leg, the meat still on the bone. "She's been praying that I should succeed in taking revenge." He brings the plate to the table and places it in front of me. "And her prayers are working." He places a hand on my shoulder. "Abu Omar has brought me to you."

The sun is just rising when I step out of Ali's house and walk over the cracked concrete driveway on the way to the bus stop. Despite my body's exhaustion, my mind buzzes with the ideas Ali has planted. He offered a way, a way to serve my mother without completely sacrificing my wife and children. Is this my fate being revealed? Or is this the madness of a young radical? Do I need only have faith in the process? Or am I abdicating reason?

230

I wait for the bus across the street from where I arrived last night. I transfer to the train and finally arrive at my car. Following habit, I take the entrance to the 405 north, merging into the stream of cars moving surprisingly quickly as the morning rush hour approaches. Kathryn will be surprised when I arrive home in the morning. Even when jobs run past our expected schedule, I don't usually return until after noon, because of the ferry schedule. I turn on my blinker, check my rearview mirror to change lanes to transfer to the 5 north. Directly behind me a Ford SUV moves dangerously close to my back bumper, piloted by a huge white man in a baseball cap tapping away at his mobile phone. I feel a surge of adrenaline and swerve into the lane on the other side, narrowly avoiding his front bumper. I swear and honk my horn. He passes, glancing disinterestedly at my compact car. His bumper stickers urge me to Buy American! and to Support Our Troops.

I have missed my exit, so I continue on the 405 north, Ali's words about freeways echoing in my head. As I approach the 10 freeway, the traffic slows to a crawl. I do not take the eastbound exit toward home, but inch my way along the flyover, to take the westbound exit. I follow the curving ramp until I am oriented 90 degrees away from my previous route. I drive under the 10, rolling down my window, allowing the sound and smell of thousands of impatient cars to enter. I stick my head out and look up. The traffic is moving slowly, but not slowly enough that I can get a very good look at the structure of the freeway above me. I stay in the right lane, following the curve of the exit ramp back down to the southbound 405, quickly exiting onto the eastbound 10, only to follow another exit ramp back to the northbound 405, where I had been a few minutes earlier. I repeat these maneuvers in the thickening traffic, wishing for the first time in my life, for our collective movements to slow. Of all the days I have sat on the 405, packed like a parking lot, I have never really seen the physical infrastructure, the traffic flowing, the number and spacing of the lanes, as I do now.

On another approach from the 405 north to the 10 west, I pause at the bottom of the entrance ramp. I resist moving the car for a few seconds, until the lane ahead of me clears for about a hundred feet. The car behind me stops, honks. I sit taller in my seat, so I can see further behind me. Very quickly eight, ten, twelve cars line up behind me and start to honk. I can almost smell their irritation, I feel the same perverse delight I felt as a teenager when I would stand still in the doorway of my school, just ahead of a group of girls I wanted to tease, forcing them to notice me before they entered the school. This simple action, this absence of action, really, affords me an unexpected power, the thrill of exerting my will upon others. Eventually, I put my foot on the gas pedal, driving at a modest speed while I watch a line of cars overtake me for the space in the lane ahead of me. A few drivers take the time to roll down their windows, raise their middle fingers and tell me to fuck off. If only I could have enjoyed such a provocative response from my pretty classmates in their green and white school uniforms, chunnis tossed modestly across their shoulders.

When I arrive home, the rooms are still, silent. Kathryn has left for her office. The remains of Michael's breakfast are in a bowl in the sink, a few Cheerios litter the floor beneath Andrew's high chair.

I check all of the rooms to make sure I am truly alone. I take refuge in the bathroom. I feel better in the small room. When I was a child, my brothers used to make me enter empty rooms in our home before them. They expected me to clear the room of any djinns, the mischievous, sometimes malevolent spirits the bhai was always trying to appease. When I protested they would promise me crumbly *ladoos* or milk cake, or even a rich piece of cashew *barfi*.

I pull back the shower curtain and swing my arms into the space in the corners, making sure to chase out any unseen visitors, closing the bathroom door behind them. I strip myself of the clothes I have been wearing for the last 24 hours and submit myself to a scalding shower. The hot water runs down my body in rivulets, pulling the black hair that covers my chest and my limbs flat against my skin. My dick begins to stiffen at the thought of the plan Ali outlined in the last grey hours of the night; my dreams of action riding along the flow of testosterone in my veins. But I resist the urge to handle myself. I scrub away the residue of Ali, the freeway, my illicit night away from my family before Kathryn might smell the strange perfume.

I confront my image in the mirror. Naked, brown-skinned, dark-haired, circumcised, I can see that I am a Pakistani Muslim. But my haircut, my clean-shaven face, my well-fed frame mark me as an American. As a young man I never indulged in looking at myself in the mirror. Such immodesty would have seemed haraam. I knew I was handsome though, by the way girls would glance at me outside of my college. Kathryn told me on our wedding day, she thought I was the most handsome man she had ever seen. Last night Ali told me that I will have no difficulty crossing borders because I am so clean-cut and when I smile my teeth are so white.

―――――――――

I smile at Michael sitting at the low circular table in front of a pile of brightly colored blocks. He has set them in neat rows and is now building a narrow tower. He looks up, sees me, and hesitates before running into my arms. Michael smells of laundry detergent and store-bought cookies. I look past his shoulder to the well-equipped classroom. Shelves full of books, bucket after bucket of neatly stacked toys, a brightly colored carpet where the children gather for story time. Already, the neatness of his handwriting stands out among the dozens of recent writing assignments taped to the wall.

I am proud of the education, the opportunities he will enjoy here in America. In Lahore, even in the well-maintained neighborhood where my father dropped us for school, we passed clouds of flies and the occasional long tailed rat before we reached the towering wooden doors of the arched brick school.

Michael dutifully puts away his blocks and retrieves his school-bag from the cubby bearing his name. We walk down the hall and Michael points out some of his artwork posted outside his classroom. The children had cut out circles in a rainbow of construction paper colors and arranged them on black paper, mimicking the style of

Kandinsky. When I ask him about his day, he reports on his lunch and recess.

"And when I was on the playground, I fell down when we were playing kickball."

"How come?"

"Another kid stuck his foot out and tripped me."

"So what did you do about it?"

"Nothing. I got up. There was no blood, but my pants got kind of dirty."

I worry about his American softness. How will he defend himself? How will he ever make his way in the world when his teachers tell him to worry about other peoples' feelings before his own needs? Kathryn has made me promise not to encourage him to fight. Maybe I could teach him to fly kites the way I did—with crushed glass dust glued to the strings so we could sever the lines that controlled the flights of other boys' paper kites.

"Daddy, can I watch a video when we get home?"

"What video?" I ask.

"Maybe a movie, you know, the one with the lions?"

I reach for his hand and nod.

After we return home, as we sit together on the couch, Michael curled up against me, beautiful cartoon lions parade back and forth on the television screen before us. Michael has seen this movie a dozen times already, but sits mesmerized, occasionally commenting on the characters or their actions. The lion cub's scheming uncle engineers a situation to kill the cub's father in a stampede of wildebeests. When the uncle forces the cub out of the pride, Michael looks at me with concern.

"Don't worry, Daddy. The little lion is lost for a while, but he grows up and grows strong so he can go back and take over. He makes sure the bad lion that killed his father dies in the end."

"Why?"

"Because the uncle is very bad, see what he did?" he points to the television. "A good lion can't let the bad lion get away with killing his father." Michael readjusts himself on the couch and doesn't speak again. I sit next to my son, feeling the heat of his little body until the bad lion falls to a pack of hungry hyenas and the remaining good characters break into song.

I think of the freeway and Ali and our plan. Michael understands already, I tell myself. He will understand what I am doing. I am trying to be a good lion.

———————————

Something jars me awake. I look to my right and see the digital clock. In the green glow of 3:45am I can make out Kathryn's profile, the outline of the children between us. Did I hear a noise? Did Michael kick me in his sleep? What woke me? I reach for my forehead, feel sweat above my brow. I remember my dream now, I heard an explosion, but I don't know where it was, in the frontier village, on the freeway, in the oil well. I look at the clock again. 3:46am. Two hours and fourteen minutes until Kathryn's alarm will go off. But how much time do I have after that? What will my fate allow? How many more times will I love Kathryn, hold the baby, talk with Michael? I can still pretend nothing will change.

I step into the bathroom, splash water on my face, and take a drink of water. I hear the explosion again in my head, after the initial thunder of the detonation, I hear the heaving of metal, the twinkling of glass, the roaring of fire. The explosion was on the freeway. The dream must have been a sign, a foretelling of my fate. Somehow I need to prepare Kathryn without telling her anything. When the government comes to interrogate her, she must not know anything. But she must understand enough to wait for me, to bring the children when I have reached a safe place.

I return to the bed, shift the children so I can lay next to Kathryn. The clock glows 3:52am. I ache with the six minutes I have been away from her. I stroke my wife's forehead, the blonde border of her hair. I trace every contour of her face with my eyes: her eyebrows which animate her expression; her eyelashes—she has often remarked that our boys inherited long beautiful eyelashes while she possessed only short light-colored lashes; her creamy smooth cheeks; her lips, thin and pink, all the words of anger and frustration they have uttered over the years have evaporated, I think only of how she has kissed me with these lips, the way they move when she sings lullabies to the boys. I look until I can close my eyes and still see her image in my mind's eye.

I practice a series of words in my head, ways I might explain, forewarn. I try out different combinations of context and conjecture, approach the future from a dozen different angles. I even inhale, preparing to wake Kathryn, to speak. But the words will not come. So my hands take over. I reach my arm around her and press my palm to the curve of her breast, drawing her closer to me. In her sleep she recognizes my body next to hers and presses her hips back against me. I feel no desire for sex, only the desire that this intimacy, this present, her presence should last forever. 4:36am. And then without forethought, two words arrive, and my tongue delivers them with perfect clarity. "Forgive me."

"For what?" she whispers.

"For everything."

Chapter 5

"Did you see the news?" The anger of Ali's voice slices through my phone.

"No. I'm on a job. What happened?"

"Three more drone attacks this week."

I exhale, the power of my grief rising in my throat. "Where?"

"Two in Pakistan, one in Palestine."

I move behind a steel container on the rig floor so I can speak out of my colleagues' line of sight. "Deaths?"

"The defense department commented on the Pakistani attacks. They are saying three militants near the Khyber Pass and five Afghan Islamic insurgents were taking refuge on the Pakistani side of the border."

I note that Ali has told me about the Pakistani attacks first. His usual Palestine-centric worldview momentarily shifted.

"But they're not talking about Palestine. The Israelis are beating their chests with pride, because they hit one of our bravest Hamas leaders. Killed in his bed. Sister-fuckers. The Israelis think they are so clever, but the drone was American." He continues in a familiar screed about America's complicity in everything the Israelis do. His words crescendo to an uncharacteristic silence.

I wait. I know Ali will fill the void in a moment.

"Now is the time for us to act." His tone is completely devoid of his previous near hysteria. "My friend has received your new documents. Canadian Sikh. So now we need to make some arrangements on our end."

"When?"

"No more waiting. As soon as you come back from your job. We can store materials at my house until we arrange for the U-Haul trailer."

"I…I don't know if I'm ready, Ali."

"God will make you ready Rashid. Call me as soon as you are back."

I close the phone, pace back and forth, banging my hand against a steel railing. Years ago, when my father had made arrangements for me to study in London, I had sat close to him in our courtyard. Even though we were the same height, even though I could have physically overpowered him, I sat next to him like a child, trying not to allow any fear to creep into my voice. *Daddyji*, I had said, *I don't know if I'm ready*. He had smiled. *You're a man now. God has made you ready, beta.*

I retrieve my wallet from the bag in my rig locker and pull out a phone card. I calculate the time difference and figure that my brother will be sleeping. I dial the long string of numbers to reach him. I hear the distinct rings of an international phone call through the speaker. The rings stop and I hear a shuffling before a voice speaks into the line. "Hahllo?"

"Majid?"

"Han ji, yes."

"It's your brother."

"Rashid? How are you?"

"Majid, I need you to do me a favor."

"Yes, what?"

"I need money. I want you to bring ten thousand dollars to the *hawala* we use in Lahore. Not the village one near the farm."

"What for?"

"I just need it. Maybe not all at once, but make sure, it's there with him. And depending on how things go, I may need more. I'll let you know the hawala that will receive it on this end."

"You need a transfer? I can send it through my Citibank account."

"No. Just do what I say. Use the money I have in my bank there. If something happens, tell the hawala to send money to my wife and sons, every three months. Make sure the money is there."

"Of course, I understand."

One week. I return to shore and Ali tells me that we have one week to prepare, plane tickets have been purchased in my new name. Scores of details fill my world. I don't even have time to go to the mosque. Every morning I check the traffic reports, trying to understand when the freeway interchange is busiest. I use the library computer to find U-Haul rental locations. Surprisingly, Ali calls less frequently.

When I arrive at his backhouse this morning, his behavior vacillates between extreme anxiety and serenity. I notice that his refrigerator contains only a shriveled lemon and a few packets of ketchup.

"I am ready," Ali tells me as I heat the water for tea. "My father came to me last night in a dream. He said he has prepared a place for me."

I am not surprised. I have been thinking of my own father often, just before I sleep, almost hoping he will come to me in my dreams. "What did he look like?"

Ali smiles and closes his eyes, recalling the image of the man in his dreams. "He looks as he did in the photo on his wedding day. Young and handsome and happy."

"Ali, have you warned your mother or your family?"

"No. Insha'allah, they'll be surprised. My mother will be proud that my jihad is successful."

Guilt strikes me. My mother will also be proud that her husband's death will be avenged. But Ali's mother will also lose her son in the process.

"Are you sure this is the way you want to do it? Perhaps we can plan some other way, so you don't need to be in the car. Perhaps I can pick you up before we detonate."

Ali cocks his head, looks at me curiously. "Why would I want to stay? To live in this horrible place?" he gestures to the room. "So I can continue to grieve my father and watch the kafirs continue to kill Muslims?" He places his hand on his heart. "I have only one regret, I didn't make the Hajj. But Allah will forgive me. He knows I wasn't able."

I stir my tea out of habit. Ali no longer has sugar to add.

"What's the name of your town, where your mother is?"

"Nablus. We are the Nassan clan of Nablus." Ali sips his tea, winces as he burns his tongue. "We have had olive groves there for generations. My great grandfather was able to protect them during the 1947 war." He looks up at me, his usual anger returning to his eyes. "You know the British supported the Zionists. They supported drawing lines in Palestine. The British drew lines all over the world, leaving people to kill their neighbors on the other sides of the lines." He holds his hands in a circle on the table, outlining the globe. "We should plan something to hit Britain too." He draws his fingers together, then floats them out, miming an explosion where London would be in his imaginary globe.

"Others will take care of that," I say. "We have our plan."

"Yes. Yes we have our plan." He sits up in his chair. He starts to pick at his thumbnail with the opposite hand, abandoning the imaginary globe. "Brother, don't call me unless it's absolutely necessary. The closer we get, the more we have to worry about surveillance. The government can listen to our calls, read our emails. It's best we talk in person." He practically jumps out of his chair, turns off the light and pulls back the shade to look out the window. "Did you hear someone outside?"

I strain my ears, but hear only the dull roar of the freeway a few blocks away. "No. Probably just a cat. Sit down, I want to make sure we have everything in order."

Ali returns to his chair, but does not turn on the light. Eventually my eyes adjust to the pale light of the streetlamp leaking into the darkness and I can see enough to write down a list in a notebook

I have brought along. Ali quietly fidgets in his chair. Somehow the news of the latest drone attacks has flipped a switch in my mind. I bear a responsibility not only to my mother, but to the Pakistanis, the Muslims I don't know, the umma—our collective community persecuted by the drones of the West. I list the materials we will need, the expected times we will accomplish each detail, everything must be planned precisely.

"You forgot the Koran," Ali says when he looks over my writing.

I look again at the paper as I would a packing list for a client job. I write down *Koran*, then look up, waiting for more.

"The words of the Prophet, peace be upon him, should be with me."

"It will burn up."

"Let's get a fireproof box, so when they investigate the remains they'll know we are Muslims."

I add *fireproof box* to my list.

Ali gets up and disappears into the bathroom.

I flip the page on my pad to reveal an unblemished sheet. I start writing, not a list, but a letter. I don't address it, as I am not sure who might read it. 'I am acting out of love. I loved my father, I love my mother, I love my homeland. I am not alone, all over the world sons are loving their parents, seeking to honor their wishes or their memories. Your drones do not understand the love we feel. They are inhuman. They do not fear Allah. We are responding in the language the drones will understand. We will destroy a little piece of what you love. You will feel the same kind of pain.'

Unaccustomed to writing such words, the effort exhausts me. I realize Ali has not returned to the table. I look around the room, walk to the back of the house and find him asleep on the little cot in the bedroom, the Koran next to him on the bed, his hand clutching the cover as Michael would clutch a stuffed animal.

I let him sleep, leave him to his dreams.

Chapter 6

"What were you doing on the West Side?" I bark into the phone.

"I went to meet one of our contributors at the Federal Building," Kathryn raises her voice defensively. "He was trying to locate some government documents and I thought I might be able to help."

"Why didn't you tell me? You have to tell me these things!"

"Rashid!" she raises her voice in irritation. "I'm a grown woman, I have a job, why should I have to tell you everything?"

I pause, try to temper my tone. "Where is the Federal Building?"

"In Westwood, right off the 405 just north of the 10."

I feel my stomach turn. I take a deep breath, change my tone so I will not anger her. "Were the children with you?"

"Of course not." She is exasperated. "I went during school hours."

"Please promise me something. I am very serious. Please just promise me."

"What?"

"Please promise me you will let me know where you are going... on the freeways. Anyplace not on your usual trips to work or to get the boys."

"What for?"

I know I am straining her patience. She bristles sometimes at what seem like simple requests. In Dubai I had asked her not to go out on the sidewalk in a tank top. She argued fiercely, told me not to try to control her, she was not a Pakistani woman. On the sidewalk she felt the leers of the Eastern men. When a Pakistani laborer asked her how much she charged, as if she were a common prostitute, she came home and changed her clothes, satisfied she had done it for her own reasons.

I take a breath, considering my reasons. "I lost my father when he traveled away from his usual route. I just want to make sure you're safe." I can sense her hesitating on the other end of the telephone, surprised I have mentioned my father.

"All right. I'll try."

"It's just because I love you."

"I know," she says. "I know."

I hang up.

I sit in my car outside an agricultural supply store. I can't help but notice my hypocrisy. I am far from my usual routes. I haven't told Kathryn a word about this trip. What if Kathryn is on the freeway during the time Ali has planned to act? I must make sure I know where she is. I must tell Ali we have to start very early in the morning.

I can't bring myself to enter the store yet. So I turn on the radio. "You can have it all," the advertiser promises brightly, "great beer taste and fewer calories." If only my desires were so simple, satisfied with a mediocre light beer.

I change the radio station. "…as stocks closed lower. In other news, a State Department spokesman told reporters today the American presence in Afghanistan is bringing stability to the region. President Mohammed Karzai's government is moving towards democracy. He warned, though, that Osama bin Laden is still at large, and the intelligence services are tracking other Al-Qaeda operatives such as Al-Zawahri and a man known as Abu Omar."

I shouldn't think too much about this. I need to go inside and purchase nitrogen fertilizer. I change the station again. The high end of my radio dial—which plays popular rock and roll from a station in Los Angeles—plays country Western music here just east of Bakersfield, two hours north and a world away from the city. I listen to a sad song about a U.S. soldier returned from the war in Afghanistan, fighting for God and country, only to return to a wife who had left him for another. "But our love for you is true," the refrain repeats, "we give our thanks for what you do." My stomach turns acidic. I step out of the car and slam the door, as if the singer might feel the force of my anger.

The store is an unremarkable single-story structure filled with tools and supplies for the vast farms of the central valley. Irrigation tubing, spare parts for tractors and fruit conveyors, pesticides, and, of course, fertilizers. I examine the aisles. I know the substance I seek will come in big white bags. I have seen these bags in the online videos, ANFO tutorials. Ammonium nitrate fuel oil. At the far end of the warehouse, a padlock secures an area enclosed behind wire fencing. Piles of 50-pound white plastic bags are piled neatly inside. I do not approach them. I busy myself examining irrigation connections, joints for delivering water to individual fruit and nut trees.

I move closer to the far end of the store and notice a few men in turbans. Their long beards and thin cotton kurta pajamas mark them as Punjabi Sikhs. I am surprised to see them here, appearing familiar with the piles of tractor tires and soybean seeds. I can understand their banter in Punjabi, can tell from the way they hold lightly onto the vowels at the ends of their words, that they are *jatts*; farmers, likely from Indian Punjab, the other half of my British-divided Punjab. They make their way through the pile of tires, arguing amongst themselves about the relative merits of each. When they have selected four, they stride up to the counter, set their purchases down in front of the counter and one fishes his wallet out from the pocket hidden in the side seam of his kurta. He pats his hand on his round belly, telling his companions he is hungry.

The door clangs. A Mexican man, dressed in blue jeans, a faded red t-shirt, and a dirty baseball cap steps in and allows his eyes a moment to adjust to the interior lighting. He walks to the counter and pulls a folded paper out of his pocket. The man behind the counter, who also looks to be Mexican, chats briefly with him in Spanish. The clerk eventually comes from behind the counter and starts to load up a battered metal trolley with goods. First a box of large O rings, some Teflon tape, and a faucet handle. Then he moves toward the back of the store. I meander down another aisle so I can continue to observe. The shop owner pulls on his key ring and pops the padlock opening the door to position the trolley for loading. He pulls a clipboard down from the inside of the fencing and reaches out to the customer. Knowingly, the customer reaches into his back pocket and pulls out his wallet, its outline visibly worn into the denim. He withdraws his identification, which the shop owner slides under the metal clamp on the board, and then copies down the information on the paper. He is following the federal requirements I have read about, the list should include the names and details of each customer buying nitrogen fertilizer.

I continue moving round the end of one aisle into the next, so as not to attract attention to myself. The shop owner asks "*Quanto?*" and the customer replies "*Dos.*" I hear the small white grains of chemicals crunch against each other as two bags of nitrogen fertilizer land on the trolley. This substance, which will spur green plants to grow bigger, will accomplish another purpose for me. Once I have altered it, the transformed material will respond to a small charge, growing almost instantly into a fireball. I have seen the blasts online. From a screen in the Hollywood public library I was bewildered to find the FBI had posted a video of their own experiment detonating a bomb similar to that used in the Times Square Bombing. Cameras placed at four different angles recorded the force, played back in slow motion, ripping one car apart, leaving only a smoking black frame, and flipping over each of four surrounding cars. The FBI even opened the video with a helpful graphic explaining the bomb included 250 pounds of ammonium nitrate and a remote controlled trigger.

My phone rings. I step outside into the parking lot to answer.

"Rashid?" Kathryn says. "Should I plan to make dinner for all of us? Will you be home? The boys have been missing you."

"I don't think so, the job is still going on," I lie.

The top of my head grows warm in the midday sun. I look up

at the blue sky framed by the powerlines running along the road. An airplane flies overhead, leaving a tiny silver vapor trail. No one fears the sky here in America. No one checks frantically for what the planes might drop from the sky.

"So you won't be home today?" she sounds a little disappointed.

I imagine us around the table, a little cluster of relationships, love, biology. I ache for this, the simplicity of it.

"No. Not today. I think tomorrow."

"All right," she sighs. "Keep me posted."

"Sure."

I sit back in my car, avoid walking back in, I don't want to attract too much attention to myself. The radio plays another song, "Through all the years, the babies and the tears, I just couldn't imagine lovin' this life without you…"

My palms are clammy as I call Ali.

"What is it?" he asks curtly.

"Can't do it."

"Can't do what?"

"Any of it." I drum my fingers nervously on the steering wheel. "The store requires identification, they record all the purchases. I can't get what you need." I long for the easy excuses of my child-hood, *I can't do it…it's too hard,* I had told my father when he pushed me to finish my math lessons in eighth standard. *Of course it's hard,* he had told me, *that's why the teacher sends you home to practice, so it'll get easier.* He never let me give up. He always nodded in satisfaction when I delivered top marks at the end of the term—he expected, indeed, he accepted nothing less.

"You will find a way, brother. Your intelligence will guide you."

"No, it's more than that." I close my eyes, set my jaw, "I'm pulling out, Ali."

"No, it's too late for that." I can hear him smiling.

"Sorry." I hang up the phone, set the car in reverse and jerk out of the parking space. A certain lightness buoys the car. That's it. He has no authority. I can step out of his world, shut my eyes on his vision, sit around the table with Kathryn and the boys like nothing has happened. Suddenly ravenous, I pull into a fast food restaurant, order a hamburger, fries, hot and spicy sauce. I crush the wrapper when I have finished. My phone vibrates with a message.

I don't recognize the sender's number. *No turning back. The lion has spoken.* The phone vibrates again, this time the message contains an image. I see myself sitting, my hands to my heart, surrounded by a group of men, their arms networked to me, an older man at my side—the man who told me my fate was written. I feel dizzy, look around to see if anyone in the restaurant has seen my phone. I hold on to the tabletop to steady myself, look at the photo again. Given the perspective, I imagine Omar took the photo. I didn't notice at the time. He took a photo of me, touched by his father, Abu Omar, the lion of Afghanistan.

I walk out of the restaurant, not bothering to clear my trash, my feet leaden. In the safety of my car, I call Ali. "Did you send me messages?"

"Messages? No. Our friend who helped with your document said he would provide you some encouragement."

"What the fuck are you doing, Ali?"

"Allah's will, brother. Do your shopping."

My heart thumps in my chest, thinking about how I could explain that photograph if it landed in the hands of law enforcement. "And then?"

"Think of your father, habibi," his voice suddenly tender, "think of how he was celebrating in a courtyard, holding a child in his arms, he was wishing well to the groom, showing his kinship to the family that had protected him during Partition."

I am silent, feel almost naked—he describes the scene as if he had been there.

"The food had been prepared, the bride was inside, a string of lights flickered from the branches of an apricot tree to the court-yard wall."

I bite my lip.

"And then with a single blast your father was gone." Ali pauses, waiting. The silence is excruciating.

I try to breathe, but my lungs are tight, as when I used to race with my brothers down our lane, always trying unsuccessfully to match their speeds.

"If I do your shopping, then I want out. I'm done."

"Yes, habibi," his voice sounds relaxed, "then you will have completed your obligation."

"And you will leave me alone?"

"Praise be to Allah, we are never alone, but then I won't ask any more from you."

————————

The freeway rolls out smoothly before my tires. How easily I return to the store, the path laid clear, even as my phone rests on my thigh, suddenly capable of endangering me.

Perhaps I should tell Ali's friend I am doing my part, before he does anything with the photo. I dial the message sender's number, whatever his name is. I hear the rings as I see the almond orchards reach from the edge of the freeway seemingly to the horizon. "Congratulations!" a cheerful American voice calls out from the phone, "you have qualified to win a $500 gift certificate toward your next cruise." I hang up, try the number again, hear the same message. Somehow he sent the messages on a telemarketer's number. I shudder at this simple sleight of hand, wondering what other deceptions I may encounter.

Back in the parking lot I wait, hoping some idea will come to me.

Eventually two Punjabis leave the store pushing a 55-gallon drum of chemicals to the flatbed of a big late model American pickup truck.

"*Sat sri akal*," I call out to them their customary Sikh greeting, stepping out of my car. They turn to look at me, responding back in kind.

I speak to them in Punjabi, trying to affect their village-style accent. I ask them if there is another agricultural supply store nearby. They look me up and down, my clean jeans and casual button down shirt mark me neither as a farmer, nor as one of them. After a moment, however, the elder of the two explains that north along the county road about five miles is another store, run by a *gora*, a white man, but the prices are more expensive. The other man then tells me his friend's cousin also runs a store a ways further on toward Fresno. The first man frowns, telling me it is too far. I thank them and get into my car, speeding away empty handed.

I return to the freeway, stop at a fast food restaurant just next to the entrance ramp. In the parking lot, I open my trunk and reach into the bottom of my rig bag. I pull out an old pair of kurta pajamas. Sometimes, when the jobs are long, I wear them to sleep in. I head inside the restaurant, stepping into the bathroom to change my clothes. Quickly, I wash my hands and look in the mirror. I wet my hair and use my fingers to comb it into a center part, trying to look the part of a recently arrived immigrant. I step out with my Western clothes tucked under my arm and hastily order a soda. The passing of the day presses against me. I rush back to the car clutching my waxed paper cup and stuffing all of my cash into the hidden pocket in the seam of my kurta.

Before Fresno, I turn off the freeway and pull into a gas station, asking directions to the store the Punjabi farmers had mentioned. I follow the gas station attendant's directions away from the freeway. I pass a modest Sikh temple, and a restaurant serving both Indian briyani and burritos. I think of the Punjabi Sikhs I knew from my childhood. They all called themselves jatts, they all emphasized their background as farmers, even if they had moved off their lands and made their living in transport or trading. Here in America, this community has not assimilated, they simply continue with their traditions on unfamiliar soil.

I come to the store, turn off the paved road into a graveled parking lot.

Inside, I walk up and down the aisles, collecting O rings, Teflon tape, and a faucet handle. I take my purchases to the counter. The Punjabi Sikh behind the counter moves his big frame slowly, as he examines each item, ringing up what seem to be arbitrary prices on an old cash register, the numbers on the keys almost completely obscured with dirt from soiled fingers. As he totals my bill, I glance around the store, reassuring myself that he also maintains a supply of ammonium nitrate fertilizer for sale. As I count out the bills to pay for my sale, I notice the relatively pale color of my hands, my clean fingernails. Although my palms have developed protective calluses from years of handling the tools of my job, I have kept my hands meticulously clean. My colleagues in Dubai used to tease me, claiming I was successful in picking up girls because they could never tell from my hands I was an oil worker.

I bundle my purchases in my arms and leave the store. In the parking lot, I unload them into my trunk, then reach down and scoop up handfuls of gravel, kneading them with my hands as my mother would knead dough for roti. Then I step to the edge of the parking lot, pressing my fingertips into the soil, taking care to dig deeply, until I can feel the earth wedge beneath my nails, so that I might look like I belong here, among this community of foreign farmers.

I stand, rub my dirty hands along the sides of my kurta, then halfheartedly brush it off so that I may share in the dull grime of the local look. Now I wait. My heart begins to beat faster as I think of what I am about to do. But I remain still. I think of my mother, I remember how she had perfected the art of standing stock still when directing our workers. Her motionlessness only heightened their sense of urgency as they respectfully hurried to carry out her instructions.

The cars pass periodically on the road, mostly pickups and occasionally transport trucks carrying crates of produce. Finally, a late model Ford truck pulls into the parking lot. A Sikh man gets down and slams the door behind him. He looks at me and nods.

"Sardarji?" I call out to him with the respectful title I learned to use as a boy with all turbaned men.

"Han ji?" he replies, stepping toward me.

"I need some help."

He crosses his arms over the top of his belly and waits for me to explain.

"I need to buy something," I say in Punjabi, careful not to pepper in English, as immigrants do after they have lived too long in the West. I describe that I have come to purchase supplies as my employer has directed me. He is a very difficult man, the eldest paternal uncle of my new wife. I want to be sure that he is happy with my work. I stutter with some of my words, shift my weight from foot to foot, exhibiting a genuine nervousness with this deceitful story.

The man grows impatient. "What do you need help with?"

"I've purchased everything he wants," I gesture to the plumbing parts in my trunk, "except one thing. I'm supposed to come back with two bags of fertilizer."

"So? You can buy it here. What's the problem?"

I kick the ground, avoid his eyes to signal my deference to his position. "I don't have the proper identification. My visa status is…is not…well you know…" I wobble my head a bit, "it's not all proper and legal yet."

"I see." He says, recrossing his arms. "And he doesn't know?"

"His niece was born here," I try to explain, pulling up some horror story I heard from Indian rig mates years ago. "He said as long as I could arrange my immigration, he would arrange the marriage." I pause, then look at him directly. "Please virji," I call him brother, appealing to his larger sense of kinship.

"You just need two bags?"

I wobble my head again. "Han ji," I confirm. "I have the money here." I reach into my pocket and pull out two twenties and a ten dollar bill.

He opens his hand, his palm darkened by his familiarity with the soil, and accepts my money. "I remember how difficult it is when you're new in this country. Meet me at the next intersection down the road and I'll transfer it to your car. I know the owner here, he won't be happy if he sees me buying for you."

I return to sit in the driver's seat, my heart racing. Slowly, I pull out of the parking lot, glancing in the rearview mirror every few seconds. I pull over just before the intersection. I alternate my view between the road I have just passed and the traffic sign in front of me. The bright red octagon commands me to stop. I think about pulling back onto the road and driving away. I should return to

Kathryn and abandon this plan. I close my eyes and the image in my phone returns to me—Abu Omar with his hand on my shoulder. Perhaps I am not the one actually driving this car. I look again into the mirror and see the man's pickup truck speeding toward me. My brother Majid would love these long straight roads, he would open up the throttle on his car and drive as fast a possible in his beloved car. If I do not take action, if I do not honor the family, I imagine the disdain and disappointment he will show me. At the last minute the car pulls off the road and stops behind me. The moment to avoid this transaction has passed. I should have driven off before he arrived. He does not get out of his car. He honks. I pull the latch to my trunk and step out of my car.

My car climbs the freeway through the mountains faster than the big rigs carrying goods to the grocery stores and strip malls of Southern California, but not fast enough that the highway patrol would have any reason to stop me. I recall Ali's comments about American infrastructure, not a single checkpoint, not a single bribe to pay, just the wide open freeway. As long as I don't give law enforcement cause, they have no reason, and more importantly, they have no right to search my car.

I altered my story slightly at each different supply store. The success of my ruse surprised even me. I feel an unexpected excitement about the full complement of plastic bags in my trunk, as if their latent power were propelling me up the mountain. I take the last sip of an energy drink and drop the empty can next to two others at the foot of the passenger seat. Within a few miles, I need to empty my bladder. I pull over at the next opportunity, onto one of the few roads along the 5 freeway not equipped with franchise gas stations or restaurants. I stop along the shoulder and get out of the car. Outside, I brace myself against the cold night air. I step around the idling engine and relieve myself in the ditch. I look down to make sure that I do not make my billowy clothes wet and then I look up.

The stars shine with a brilliance I had not noticed from the car. I lean against the passenger door and force my lungs to expand with the cold air. I hear the cars speeding along the freeway behind me, but the mountain before me is silent, as if in homage to the stars in the heavens. As a child, when we visited a hill station on holiday, my father and I had stood out on the verandah and looked up at the sky. He explained that each point of light in the sky was really another sun, but so far away it appeared tiny. *Does Allah live in one of those stars?* I had asked him. He had smiled and pulled me closer. *Allah lives in every star, beta, and in all the places in between.*

I shiver under my thin cotton clothes. I retrieve my jeans and shirt, quickly strip out of my Pakistani costume. I glance up, pausing for a moment to hold my right hand against the flesh that covers my heart, thanking the memory of my father for that memory of the stars. From straight overhead I see a streak of light. Faster than the blink of an eye it falls in front of me. A shooting star. Spurred by the cold, I shove my hands through my sleeves and pull up my jeans, not bothering to fasten the buttons before I return to the driver's seat. Protected from the wind and the cold, I button my shirt, wondering about the meaning of the shooting star. A sign? An omen? I glance at the dashboard, noticing the compass pointing south. The shooting star was oriented to the right. I know it burned up in the atmosphere, the bit of rock hurtling to the earth was consumed in a bit of brilliance, but if it had survived to fall to earth, I imagine, where might it have landed? Beyond the range of mountains before me, on the west side of the city, perhaps where the 10 and the 405 freeways meet.

Ali steps out of the door before I have even turned off the car.

"What took you so long?" In his agitation, he nearly trips over the edge of the concrete at the driveway. "I thought maybe something had happened to you." The neighborhood is quiet. Darkness fills the big house where Ali's hosts live. "It's like fucking midnight."

"So?" I am in no mood to chat with Ali. My hand trembles as I open the trunk, revealing a beach blanket spread across the width of the car.

Ali places a hand on top, feeling the mass beneath the blanket. "Enough?" he asks.

"Enough," I confirm. We had discussed using twice the amount the FBI used in their videotaped field experiment.

"Al-hamda'allah," Ali holds his palms up and gives thanks.

"Get me a couple of towels so that we can cover these up as we carry them in."

"I only have one towel," Ali says.

"Do you have a fucking bed sheet?"

He shakes his head. "A blanket?" he offers.

"Fine."

The floor creaks as I step into Ali's little backhouse. The place is littered with disposable aluminum cooking pans. I look around and wrinkle my eyebrows in question.

"You said we would need roasting pans," he responds defensively.

"Yes, I said buy a half a dozen."

"I went to a warehouse store. The smallest package was twenty four." He starts to stack them up as I go to the darkened bedroom for the blanket. "In America, you have no choice but to buy too much."

I flip on the switch, but the room remains dark. "Ali, the light doesn't work?"

"The bulb burnt out. I have a flashlight."

"It's easy to change the bulb."

"I know. But what is the point? I won't be here to use it." His words seem to slur together.

I fumble around in the bedroom until I feel the blanket under my hands. I pull it off the bed and head back outside. After I have carried in the third bag and stacked it near the stove, I notice Ali with irritation. "Can you help instead of standing there like an asshole?"

He just sits down at the table. I step back out, expressing my disgust in the darkness. When I finish ferrying the bags into the house, I look pointedly at Ali. "What the hell is wrong with you?"

"Nothing." He slumps back in the chair. "I took a muscle relaxant."

"What for?" I pour myself a glass of water from the tap.

"Jihadis, you know, before they act, sometimes they take them." He inhales slowly, "to cut the tension."

"But you can't do this now. You'll need days to put this all together." I need that interval, that time to figure out how to clear myself from this.

"I know." His hands rest clumsily in his lap. "I just wanted to know what to expect. Anyway, I already got the other stuff." He motions with his eyes toward a plastic shopping bag behind the front door. I look inside, see wires, plastic connections, electrical tape, and an outdated cell phone.

"Took me hours," he sounds like his mouth is full of cotton. "Had to change three buses to get to the right hardware store."

"What for? There's a hardware store right down the street," I snort.

"That's one of those franchise stores. Too many security cameras." He reaches into his back pocket. "And I needed to go and get this," he pulls out a folded piece of paper and hands it to me.

One side is covered with a hand-drawn engineering design, with labels in English and Arabic.

"Can you make it? It's our signature detonator."

"I can see what it is, Ali, I'm an engineer."

He gives me a leering smile. "I know, that's why I was so happy to meet you."

"No. I'm done. I'm not your tool." I move toward the door.

"We're all tools of Allah, brother. Don't resist it." He slams his fist dully on the table, then closes his eyes and slumps back in the chair, like a puppet released of its strings.

He looks ugly. His hair unwashed, and several weeks past due for a trim. I think for a moment that I hate him. That I want to beat him up for his childish sermonizing and tiresome opinions. I take a step back toward him. It would not be a fair fight. He is hardly more than a boy, and in this state, couldn't even return a punch.

He cracks open one eye, smiles. "We need each other, Rashid. I can't do this without you, you can't do this without me."

"I don't need anything from you." I turn and walk back into the night.

The early sun begins to chase away the darkness on my street. After two nights at home, the way seems clearer. I will talk with Kathryn's father. I will tell him I have some information. He will know who to contact, what to do. This is his country.

I ride the elevator down to the parking garage. In the car, I look in the rear view mirror, catch the reflection of my eyes as I back out of my space. If only I could wash away some of the things these eyes have seen. Robert Capen, he will help. I'll call him this afternoon.

Pulling out of the garage, I slam on the brakes as a man nearly jumps in front of my car. Ali. He raps on the window glass on the passenger side. I unlock the doors.

"What the fuck, Ali? Get in," I hiss. I don't want anyone to see him here with me. He jerks back into the seat as I peel out of the driveway.

"Nice building, Rashid."

"What do you want?" I rack my brain, but can't remember when I might have given him my address.

"I need a detonator." He says matter-of-factly.

"That's not my problem."

"I think you don't understand this situation."

"No, Ali," I slam my brakes at a stoplight, "I think you don't understand. I'm done. I did what you asked. I'm sympathetic to what you're trying to do, but I won't give up my wife and children." I look at him, feel unsteady even as I will my voice to sound forceful. "I'll take you to your bus stop. And then…and then Ali, I don't want to see you again."

We drive in an eerie silence. My mind racing through my options. I need to call my father-in-law today. How to explain this to him? He can do something. Will I be arrested?

I pull up to a bus shelter. Ali looks at me, with something that looks like kindness. "I'll see you soon brother, our fathers need your help, it's not complicated." He slams the door and I leave him.

———————

The ferry will leave for the offshore rig in an hour, and the tools still haven't been packed properly. I try to keep my mind on the checklist, hurrying so I will have time to make a phone call. My stomach rumbles, but the thought of food makes me nauseous.

At the vibration of my phone in the pocket of my coveralls I lose control of the tool in my hand, it clangs to the floor. "Fuck," I mutter to myself, ashamed of my own weakness.

The phone again shows me an unfamiliar number. I open the message, another image sends fire through my veins. The little screen shows an office window, seen from outside. Through the glass I can see the outline of a woman holding her own breast in one hand, a little bottle in the other. Another vibration. Another message. *She is a devoted mother, making your son's milk. Keep them safe.*

I flee to the bathroom, fumbling over Kathryn's office number three times before I get through.

"Kathryn, where are you?...are you pumping?...why the fuck do you keep the blinds open?"

Kathryn replies defensively. But in my head I hear my father's words: *We don't show our women, when other men see their flesh, they can't help but lust. So we protect our women, keep them safe.*

"Close the fucking blinds...and please, just be careful..." Of what? What could I say that she would understand? "I love you." I cut the call before she can respond.

I dial another number. "You take a step closer to my wife and I'll kill you with my bare hands."

"Habibi," Ali says smugly, "no need to sound like a Hollywood film hero."

"She has nothing to do with this."

"Yes, your American wife must be innocent." He pauses, "So you will make it for me?"

I exhale, bang my hand against the bathroom lock.

"Come to my place, now. Bring your tools."

"You promise me she won't be harmed."

"I promise…on my father's soul."

"I'll be there in an hour."

I drop the phone in my pocket, turn and double over, retching into the toilet.

Chapter 7

Ali looks disheveled, tired. I don't speak except to ask him for water. I work at his kitchen table, devising a simple plastic explosive trigger than he can set himself. Every few minutes he comes to me, touches my shoulder, recites verses from the Koran, praising me as a good Muslim. I try not to think about anything but the mechanics of what I am doing. After several hours I explain the trigger to him. He presses me to configure the signature detonator his paper describes in both English and Arabic—as a back up.

"I won't go with you," I say.

"I know," he says softly. "But you will leave this country." He places a piece of paper on the table next to me, an airline itinerary for flying to Dubai via Vancouver. "It will be better for you, for your sons, if they cannot find you in America."

The flight departs tomorrow. Ali places a Canadian passport on top of the paper. The photo inside is me, the name belongs to another, matches the name on the airline itinerary.

Ali pulls out his phone. "Look at the camera, Rashid." I look up, surprised. He snaps a photo of me sitting with my tools, the detonators I have assembled. He presses a few buttons.

I reach up to grab the phone. He slaps my hand back. "I have already sent it. My Egyptian friend will be sure it goes to the proper authorities if you cause any trouble." He pauses, waiting for me to understand his seriousness. "Now, you will travel with this passport as far as Dubai."

"No, I can't go tomorrow." What will I tell Kathryn? I need to see the boys again.

"When the time is right Sheikh Omar will be able to help you in Pakistan."

"Sheikh Omar?"

"You've met him. Everyone in the CIA would like to get as close to him as you have been."

"Abu Omar's son," I whisper to myself.

Ali recites an address in Pakistan's southern port town of Karachi, makes me repeat it a half dozen times until he is sure I won't forget. He refuses to write it down.

The sun has set and Ali pulls back the curtain. No street light shines in. "The darkness will cover us as we load the truck."

I look up, distraught. I haven't thought about loading the truck.

Ali shakes his head. "Don't even think about complaining, you've come this far. I still need your help with this."

I only want to sleep. I close my eyes and pray for this whole scene to disappear.

"Now!" Ali roars, suddenly livid.

I look up, astonished.

"Please, habibi," he softens.

I stand, follow him to the truck, listen to his explanations for how we will pack the canisters, with shrapnel—nails, ball bearings, nuts and bolts—above the explosives. I do as he tells me, he has planned more carefully than I believed possible. I don't speak, only think of how I can warn Kathryn, get word to her father.

Near dawn Ali closes the back doors of the truck. He opens the driver's side door, shows me a small metal safe on the front seat. "Fireproof," he says proudly. He opens the door, places a Koran inside. He holds out his hand, "Your ID, Rashid Siddique. You won't want to be that man after tomorrow."

"But if you have my ID, it will look like I was in the van with you."

"Exactly, brother. If they think you have blown up with me,

they won't go looking for you." He talks to me simply, my mind must reach across the chasm between our thinking to understand him. "I'm giving you a chance. A chance to go safely. A chance to go someplace. You can call your wife and children to you later, insha'allah."

"No. No." I can only shake my head.

"Brother, you can't resist your fate. Come."

He takes my arm and we walk inside the house. He closes the door, locks a padlock from the inside.

———

Ali drives me to the airport departure level. All of my identification, my phone, even my wedding ring, sits inside the fireproof safe between us. A small suitcase with clothes Ali has provided; a wool coat, a change of shirt, some socks, rests at my feet. He has filled my wallet with enough cash to see me through a few weeks. I stare at my image in the Canadian passport, trying to memorize the spelling of this other man's name.

Ali's clothes are immaculate, a white button down shirt—perfectly ironed—and a pair of black dress pants. He has trimmed his beard and washed his hair. I feel a strange intimacy with him, as if I have been with him the night before his wedding. He is nervous and excited.

The freeway delivers us to the airport dangerously fast, inexorably in one direction. And here we are. Ali pulls up to the curb.

"Please, just wait a day, Ali. Just one day."

He doesn't want to stay too long at the curb. "Fly away, brother. May the blessings of Allah be upon you."

I don't move. He starts to look irritated.

"All right. Sure. I'll give you 24 hours. What does one day mean when I'm bound for heaven?"

I nod. "And blessings upon you too." I step out, turn back. "There will be no shame if you change your mind."

But he is already looking over his shoulder to pull into the next lane. I recite the license plate number.

I proceed to a computer kiosk for my boarding pass. Once I am safely past security I will find a phone, alert the authorities, call Kathryn. Or when I arrive in Vancouver, once I am safely out of this country. I have 24 hours, don't I?

I stand in the security line, my shirt sags with perspiration. A businessman stands in front of me, grumbling about the inefficiency of the TSA. Two teenaged girls chatter meaninglessly behind me. I see a Sikh man in a turban reach the conveyor belt, remove his shoes, belt, jacket, steel bangle. I have no turban, no bangle, how can I pass as a Sikh man?

My hand trembles as I show my boarding pass and passport to a woman in a blue shirt with a black badge. She shines her light on the passport, looks me in the eye. I blink. The girls behind me snap their gum. She looks again at the passport, scowls. Her latex glove-covered hand scribbles with a pen on my boarding pass. She nods and I move through.

I follow the business man, who is already setting his shoes in a plastic tray. "I sure do feel protected from the terrorists with this extra security," he says in disgust. He pulls out his belt, holds both ends the same way I had once seen my father loop his belt before he struck me for disrespecting my mother. I freeze, feel myself a teenager again, wonder if he will whip me for my behavior. Then the man throws his belt in the tray and the girls shove their own trays onto the conveyor belt. And I am through.

I walk quickly to the gate, avoid looking anyone in the eye. The plane is on time. I have time, I can call. I just need a phone. When did the pay phones all disappear from the airports? I hear a woman announce the boarding for my flight.

I glance around, notice a mounted television screen. A live helicopter shot shows a plume of smoke, flames rising toward the sky. Scrolling across the bottom of the screen ...*car explosion on the 10 freeway at the 405, unconfirmed reports of several fatalities.*

"Oh my God," a woman near me covers her mouth

I close my eyes, bow my head. He didn't wait. He knew he

wouldn't wait. He did this. He couldn't have done it without me. I can only move in one direction. I join the queue to board.

Chapter 8

The air hostess pantomimes the safety procedures, points to the emergency exits with practiced boredom. My foot shakes, almost uncontrollably. I remind myself the foot is not mine. I am no longer Rashid Siddique. The foot belongs to Srabjeet Dhillon, Pakistani-born Canadian citizen. This flight will return me to my "home" in Vancouver and then I will take a connecting flight to Dubai.

We taxi down the runway and I force myself not to look out the windows. This is not my city, not my country, no longer my home. I reach for the in-flight magazine, flip through the pages without seeing any of the images. The plane accelerates and lifts off the ground, I feel the invisible tether that holds us to the earth strain and then snap against the force of movement. For a moment I am weightless, homeless, disconnected from both the head and tail of my family. I must think only about myself during this trip, I must be alert to any commotion, any security alert, or unusual announcements from the pilot. If someone comes to me to ask questions, I must have my answers, my story ready. I close my eyes, I will stay alert with my ears. The woman next to me chats to her husband about who will pick them up from the airport and then about the grocery shopping they will need to do. I resent the triviality of their lives, then envy their connection to each other, to the person who will deliver them from the airport. I wonder about Kathryn and the children. Exhaustion overtakes me and I drift into a black sleep.

———————

I hear a question, once, then repeated, twice, three times. "Sir," the woman is starting to sound agitated. I open my eyes, scrambling to remember how I will answer questions, which pieces of false information I will provide. "Sir, do you want anything to drink?"

I exhale, letting my shoulders drop. "Water, please." She hands me a plastic cup and I pour the water into my mouth, feeling only a void where my body should be. Trapped between the other passengers, I fear the flight crew. Can they tell what I have done? What in fact did I do? I took revenge. I honored my family, I tell myself. Maybe Ali pulled me through what was written for me, to take a stand against an aggressive and inhumane military. Innocent blood shed for innocent blood.

Paralyzed with anxiety, I do not leave my seat during the flight. So once the plane lands and I walk the jetway unmolested, I dart into the nearest restroom. I relieve the pressure in my bladder, only to understand my vulnerability as soon as I leave the stall. I pull the wool coat out of my bag, pull up the collar against a phantom cold and join the flow of people on the concourse. Without speaking to anyone, I check in for my flight to Dubai at the electronic kiosk. Without baggage to check, I proceed directly to the security line. I resist the urge to seek out a television screen, to stand before it and wait for the ticker line at the bottom of the screen to tell me about what I have set in motion.

I look at the floor as I pass through the metal detector. I wish to be invisible against their eyes. So many ways they have to look into my physical presence. But this will give them no clue of who I really am, the history of my family and my actions. I must shield the contents of my heart and my mind, protect my memories so they will not betray me.

I brace myself for the pressure of a guard's arm, for the sternness of an alerted voice. But only the usual irritated flurry of the airport surrounds me. Within minutes I am on another airplane, strapped into a seat. The plane ascends into the sky and as if my heart felt only the decreasing pressure of the atmosphere outside, it expands, almost to bursting. I am filled with a giddy lightness. I have done what was written for me. Somehow I have accomplished my mother's wish and have escaped not only the country, but the continent of those who murdered my father. I look at my hands, press them into fists and open them again to expose my palms. They are copies of my father's hands. When I was a child, I wondered at how big his hands were, the flat nails and calluses, always clean, despite his work. I touch each of my fingers in turn. Perhaps my father was working through them. Perhaps he recognized them as his own and took control of them. I interlace these fingers, his or mine, I can't be sure, and rest them in my lap, closing my eyes to pray for my father's soul. May it rest now.

When the meal comes, the man in the next seat passes me the little plastic tray, making an opening for conversation. He asks if I have been to Dubai before. I begin to answer yes, but then catch myself. Has Srabjeet been to Dubai before?

"I flew through on my way to Canada."

"I have not been before," he says, a faint roll on his *r* hints at an Arabic accent. "I flew from Beirut directly to Montreal when I emigrated."

I nod my head, hoping to end the exchange, but he continues. "I will be teaching Islamic history in Dubai. Well, not exactly in Dubai, but nearby, at the American University of Shaharjah."

"Sharjah?" I ask, correcting him.

"Yes. I meant Sharjah. How do you know it?"

I shouldn't have said anything. I shrug my shoulders, allowing for the possibility that the name is common knowledge.

"Well, I understand it's a very good university. I'll be teaching about Islamic history, you know, the time when we dominated the world because of the power of our collective intellect, our grasp of mathematics and astronomy, poetry and geography. We could, of course, return to that golden age. But we are continually disgraced by a small group of radicals. You know, people with narrow minds, bent only on showing the West they have devised clever ways to surprise and kill people, like those crazy people in Los Angeles." He takes a bite of his food. "You are a fellow Muslim, yes?"

I shake my head. No. My stomach turns at this small act of renunciation, this denial of my identity. I push my food away. "Good luck with your teaching." I say to close the conversation. I push my seat back and shut my eyes against his opinions.

On the screen of my mind I see an endless series of images. The helicopter's view of cars on the freeway, the aluminum trays in Ali's kitchen, Michael explaining the lions in the movie, Ali bowing down in the mosque, my mother throwing stones at the sky. I am not one of those radicals. My reasons are my own. My father was killed. And before that our family was nearly decimated in the Partition of India, and before that the Hindus treated Muslims as worse than the Untouchables. And still the West fights wars in our lands as if they were entitled to our resources—the oil, the water, the territory—then they leave our people in poverty. Only the very smartest, the very richest leave to join the West…as I did. Stop thinking, I tell myself. Do not recriminate yourself for obeying your mother, for trying to protect your wife and sons, for following your fate. None of this would have been possible if I had not come to America, if I had not met Kathryn. Perhaps this was all part of my fate, which only now I recognize.

Chapter 9

Dubai, United Arab Emirates.
One month after the bombing

The Afghan baker reaches into the shimmering heat of the clay tandoor with his long metal tongs, skillfully flicking his wrist to slide the bread from the side of the oven onto the sheaf of newspaper I have set upon the counter. I leave my coins in payment, hear him murmur, "Al-hamda'allah," and I step out into the humid heat of the sidewalk. From the shop next door, I purchase a portion of chicken *karai*, which a skinny Pakistani man ladles into a plastic bag. I walk across the street—clogged with the ubiquitous green and yellow Toyota taxis that ferry people up and down the whizzing freeways of Dubai—and enter a run-down three-story building.

I have spent the last month here—just one of a hundred Pakistani laborers and taxi drivers—ducking under the lines of laundry strung across the halls, listening to the constant drone of televisions, hearing the grunts of men relieving their sexual desires with no access to women. The landlord had offered me a room to share; three cots, a window air conditioning unit, and a bathroom. I paid him in cash for all three spaces, and politely declined his offer to find me two other Pakistanis to share the rent.

I pour my meat and gravy into a plastic bowl, sit down on the floor and set it out on the corner of the newspaper next to my bread. I give thanks before tearing off a piece of bread which I use to scoop up a mouthful of gravy.

Although I may be free to come and go, although I could choose to eat in the five-star hotels along Sheikh Zayed Road, I have established a kind of self-imprisonment. I go out only once a day to purchase food, which I eat at noon and at sunset. I sleep. I wake and perform a set of simple calisthenics to maintain my strength, and I wait for the days to pass. My implicit guilt paralyzes me. No longer can I claim any innocence, the authorities would crucify me if I tried to return. So I cultivate a flicker of pride. I made something happen, I stabbed the giant, exploited America's weakness.

I spend long hours looking at the image in my passport, obliterating the memories of the man who walked into Yerevan Travel to have his image recorded, conjuring up an alternate history, set in Vancouver, connected to a man named Srabjeet. I memorize all the details of the passport, develop stories to explain the few stamps on the stiff pages. I will my hair and beard to grow faster.

At night I see the cockroaches come out from their hiding places, scurrying across the patches of light that penetrate from the hallway. I wrap my arms around myself, trying to simulate the warmth of another's body. Only in these moments, when I have paid for the day in discipline and isolation, do I open up the corner of my mind that holds my wife and children. I allow myself to review their faces, the shapes of their bodies, the sounds of their voices. I pray for them, remembering them only in happiness, in laughter, in wonder, and in sleep. I remind them, and myself, and my father, that I have arranged for their care, I am doing what we all need, I will protect them—and eventually I will reunite with them.

The chipped mirror above the bathroom sink shows me the

time has come. My beard is long enough, covering my face. Eventually it will grow longer, occasionally touching my chest, and I will look as if I have always been a Sikh. I clench my teeth around the end of a length of cloth, start pulling it around the back of my head, and over my brow. The cloth is clean, but soft with wear. I didn't want a brand new turban, so after purchasing six yards of cotton at the shop next to the tailor, I made an exchange. In the middle of the night, I moved silently in the hallway scanning the laundry. In the saltwater humidity of the Gulf, the clothes take two, sometimes three days to dry. On the floor above mine, I found what I needed, the single length of cloth, almost six yards long—slightly faded in strips where it had been exposed to the sun. The owner had looped it over the line four times so it would not touch the floor. I took the cloth, and replaced it with the new length. Now, with a single bare bulb above me, I attempt to coil another man's turban around my head. I draw on long-ignored memories of Jagdeep, the Sikh guard who oversaw our farm. I wrap and then unravel the cloth several times before I am satisfied with the look. "Srabjeet Singh. I am Srabjeet Singh," I tell the mirror. "I am returning to Pakistan for a cousin's wedding."

I leave the bathroom, carrying the few toiletries I have purchased here, packing them into my bag. I have no goodbyes to make. I simply walk out the door and lock it behind me. I pass the building manager's room and slide the key underneath the door.

At the airport check in, the attendant asks my destination. My voice cracks on the word *Karachi*, as if my vocal chords had become rusty without use. The men in line behind me, all of them laborers, drag along their parcels; cardboard boxes, cheap plastic cargo bags, all taped and labeled with their names. They are bundling goods they have bought here with the little surplus from their salaries, bringing them to frustrated wives and fatherless children to compensate for their long absences in the Gulf. I share their sense of apprehension, excitement, but for other reasons.

They jostle each other in line, displaying the Asian dislike for queuing. But when they reach the front, they stand obediently, like emasculated sheep, until the attendant behind the counter calls them. This is why they are poor, not one of them acts like a real man. They have followed the promises of a labor agent to this desert city, like rats following a piper, but not one of them could have done what I have done. This is what I learned in America, how to take action. America, I think, what a mixed bag of seeds you sow.

Srabjeet Singh carries himself proudly, but I try to imagine this man, myself, as invisible. I want to draw no more attention to myself than this flock of sheep-like men.

Once again, I brace myself, prepare my stories for the authorities who may seize me. And once again I find myself safely strapped in to a seat. The local airline, famed for its beautiful air hostesses, staffs the flight to Karachi with well-groomed men who will not face harassment from the repressed laborers. Years ago I took a flight to Pakistan with my own beautiful woman, my white American woman. I had tried to protect her from the lustful stares of the other passengers. I glared at several men, daring them to dishonor me again with their eyes. They always looked away in shame.

When the plane loses altitude I see the southern coast of Pakistan come into view. The great sprawl of Karachi spreads out—a cancer of humans, concrete, steel upon the earth. I must have some old friends from university who have returned to elite jobs in the financial and construction industries. But I cannot call on them. I am not even here, I remind myself, and my old friends do not know Srabjeet Singh. In this city of more than twenty million, not a single person awaits me, no family will embrace me, no employer will help me settle in to a new life. But somewhere in this labyrinth, I will find the man who can provide me with yet another passport. I can hear Ali's voice in my head repeating his address.

I disembark, passing through the throngs of women, children, and old people who have come to receive the laborers.

In the taxi, I ask the driver to take me to a hotel, something simple and not too expensive. I have succeeded, I have returned to my homeland, I have accomplished my family's revenge, I am undiscovered and unharmed. But none of this is sweet. I only want sleep. I close my eyes and let the driver deliver me.

———————

I shiver beneath the covers. The fever seized me just hours after I checked in to the hotel. I unwrap the turban and fold it to cover my neck and chest. When I was a child and fell ill with a fever, my mother would sit by my bed, sing me songs, pray, urge me to sip hot milk with honey and turmeric. I wish to call her to me now. I have done what she asked, but now I am suffering alone, with no one to sit at my bedside. A shapeless anger rises in my chest.

In the morning, I walk down to the hotel lobby—nothing more than a little closet by the entrance—and ask the attendant to send someone to fetch medicine for me from a pharmacy.

The man looks at me, I recognize him as a Punjabi. "You are very sick?" he asks disdainfully, "have you vomited?" I can imagine his thoughts, his fear of catching my illness, his disgust at the thought of sending a worker to clean up after a sick man.

"No. Not very sick. I am only asking for fever reducer." I reach into my pocket for an additional bill, "and please, also ask the tea shop next door to send up hot milk."

"Fever reducer and hot milk," he looks out the door.

"With turmeric and sugar."

He walks to the door, sets his hand on the frame and shouts out onto the street. Only the street noise—cars and rickshaws, horns and hawkers—seems to answer him. But soon a teenage boy, a dark-skinned Bengali runs up and listens to the man's instructions. He pockets one of the bills I gave the man and quickly disappears.

"I will bring it to your room when the boy returns," he says to me. His voice seems to soften and he pulls on his beard. "We Sikhs need to take care of each other."

Without responding, I return to my room. I lie down on the bed, cover my face with my hands and weep. I hear my own sobbing, like the sounds of a child. The unfairness of my suffering pains me more than the fever. How long must I endure this isolation before I can return to my family? I cannot see my mother in Lahore—the Pakistani authorities would be observing her. I cannot reach out to Kathryn and the boys as the U.S. authorities would be monitoring all her communications.

I hear a knock at the door. I drag myself to answer it only after the third set of knocks. The man offers me a small paper bag and a glass of hot milk.

"No turmeric," he says. "And they charged me a deposit on the glass." He stands in the doorway, waiting. "The boy expects his tip."

I reach into my pocket and pull out another bill, not bothering to even look at it. I realize after handing it to the man that I have given him far too much.

"Sardarji," he says, "I will come to check if you need anything later."

I return to the bed, open the paper bag and pull out the plastic bottle. Without a spoon, I just drink the sweet syrup directly from the bottle. I sip the milk, relieved it is sweetened. I pick up the paper bag to drop it on the floor, noticing it has been fashioned out of an old newspaper. Out of date newspapers contain a world of goods in Pakistan; street snacks, little bits of hardware, ladies bangles all come wrapped in these words and pictures. In America the system collects old newspapers, ships them to a factory where they are destroyed, purged of their previous identity, bleached and repulped into new paper before Americans would dream of using it to make a paper bag. In Pakistan, the paper retains its identity. A photo of the Pakistani president is bisected by a fold in the paper, the words of the article below it, cut off mid-column at the seam of the bag.

I lay back pulling the bed sheet and turban over my chest again. I open the bag, pulling apart the glued seam so I can hold the page open. Across the top of the page the bottom of a headline remains: "…Pakistani National Responsible for U.S. Bombing." I scan the page for my name, find it buried in the third paragraph. I look up to ensure that the door is locked, the blinds on the window are closed. Did the boy know who I was when he brought me this bag? Was it some kind of a sign, a warning?

I read the sentences one at a time. "U.S. officials have concluded the car bombing executed in the American city of Los Angeles, on a key expressway, was planned and carried out by a U.S. citizen and a Palestinian. The explosion killed three drivers in nearby cars and caused damage to the flyover. The incident has caused the U.S. government to pressure Pakistan to share more intelligence related to Pakistani nationals around the world, and so-called Muslim extremists.

"In a report, the Department of Homeland Security has concluded that Ali Muhammed Nassan of Israeli-occupied Palestine, and Rashid Hamid Siddique, originally from Lahore, worked as an isolated terrorist cell, using a homemade crude bomb typical of Al-Qaeda. The report concludes that both men were killed in the bombing.

"An Al-Qaeda spokesman in Kabul has not claimed responsibility for the attack, but issued a statement reminding the U.S. that the practice of bombing, invading, and occupying Muslim lands, especially along the Pak-Afghan border will continue to face resistance.

"The father of Rashid Siddique…"

I run my finger along the bottom of the page. The scissors of some laborer, probably some illiterate woman doing piece work in the slums of Orangi has cut off this news about my father. Even here, he is taken from me. For weeks I have intentionally avoided the news, assiduously turned my head from the reaction of the newscasters, the speculation, the investigation. But I cannot escape the story, my story. Five deaths. Three victims and two bombers. I am dead to America.

I slide the paper bag under my pillow and close my eyes. I hear the words of the story in my mind spoken in an ominous voice. I know the fever powers this distorted thinking. As a child my mother told me not to listen to those voices, which were, of course, the work of *Sheitan*, Satan. But I cannot resist the voice, which speaks of my weakness, my vain pride. Rather than acting like a man and accepting my own death to avenge my father, I have run like a coward. No one wants a coward. No self-respecting woman can love a coward. I try to recall something that I can use to crowd out the voices, a verse, a line of poetry, anything that I could repeat to myself. After the first few words, my memory fails in my delirium.

Images come.

...I see the van again. Ali opens the window to wish me Salaam. He has put car seats on the passenger side. Michael and Andrew are strapped inside, smiling, excited for something new. I try to run after the van as Ali drives away, but my legs move as though wading through mud...

...Kathryn calls me to the table, she tells me she has made Pakistani food. I sip a glass of water, it smells of her perfume but tastes of saltwater. She sets the plate down before me, chunks of meat with hair and skin still attached. I turn to look at her, her smile opens into a gaping laugh roaring with the sound of an explosion...

...My mother walks toward me through a field yellow with mustard blooms. She sings a song I remember from my childhood. I see a man behind her, but cannot make out his identity. When she comes before me, she does not stop, does not greet me. She passes right through me, like vapor. But the man behind her, his hair and skin bleached completely white, walks into me with such force that I fall to the ground. He laughs and I recognize the voice of my father. "Death comes to us all, yet we act surprised each time...."

———————

Out on the street I follow the smell of food, swirls of smoke from grilling meat. I have taken only milk in the last three days. The fever has left me depleted, empty. I salivate with anticipation as I barter with the shish kebab vendor. He speaks with a heavy Pashtun accent. From his frayed shirt I assume he is a refugee. We make the exchange and I bite into a bit of seared goat flesh.

But I taste nothing, experience no pleasure. When I have eaten enough that my stomach ceases to complain, the remaining food in my hands becomes a burden, further evidence of the death I have caused. I walk down the street looking for somewhere to relieve myself of this food. In the shadows of a small doorway a man, bent and distorted, crouches on a bit of plastic sheeting. I reach down until my hand comes within the range of his downturned eyes. He does not look up, draws his hands together to receive the offering. The ends of his arms appear like paws, deprived of their fingers by accident or disease. He seizes the meat, and begins to eat, one animal to another.

I continue to walk, accomplishing block after block without purpose. The mass of people dizzies me. I walk out of the Sikh neighborhood where the taxi driver had first dropped me. I pass through an area of nouveau riche gated houses with guards peeking out from behind the walls. I pass a mosque where men at prayer sport the beards and austere posture of the Saudi *Wahabis* who have impressed them with new mosques and money for *madrasas*. I pass through a Chinese neighborhood, rows of trading houses boasting red signs with both Chinese and Urdu in faded gold at the front, the squalor of Chinese living rooms at the back. I see the towers of the financial district, the international style bred into clumsy second-rate forms that somehow only highlight our self-conscious-ness as the bastard child of India. I pass the Gol Masjid, its graceful breast-shaped dome shoved above a rigid masculine block, as if it had been severed from a woman's body. I consider going to pray, thinking the familiar ritual may comfort me. But I am a Sikh now, have exiled myself from my community, the umma, even in my home country. I walk toward the ocean, a great expanse of unre-markable beach greets the water. Young men and women, some in scandalous unmarried pairs dodge pot-bellied policemen perched atop a straining motorcycle. I walk east toward the cliffs.

I can hear my father's voice telling me Karachi is one of the wonders of the world, a great city comparable to Cairo or Istan-bul. I try to envision the city through his eyes. But as I climb the littered path to a lookout point, I can only despise Karachi for the cold selfish hospitality of its sweaty streets. At the lookout I can see out across the ocean, fishing boats and cargo ships, vessels of all manner, plying the waters.

I take a step toward the ocean. I wish for the oblivion of the endless water. I take another step. I hear the waves washing over the rocks. I inhale, thinking I should have just sat in the car next to Ali. I shouldn't be here living, breathing in this painful numbness. I lean into the air, imagining the descent to the rocks and waves below. I could end this feeling. What more does this life require of me?

My foot slips. I feel the force of gravity pulling me down. Adrenaline surges through my body. But the earth stops me. The hardness of the ground will not let me fall. I am on my hands and knees, nearly prostrate before the glow of the day dimming in the west.

I bring my hands to my face to weep. But no sounds come. My emotions have grown impotent.

Chapter 10

I wake. The hotel room appears just as it did the day before. My legs ache from the previous day's walking. With something approaching disappointment, I confirm I am still living. I am not yet meant to be freed of this body.

There will be no point to further avoid the next obvious step. I must find the man whose address Ali made me memorize. I will come to know my next incarnation. I rise from the bed, watch myself go through the motions of washing and dressing myself, a stranger in the mirror. I pack my few things, check out at the front desk, resisting the proprietor's attempt to make small talk, paying him an extra tip for caring for me during my fever.

I hail a taxi. Inside, the driver only nods when I tell him the address. From the rearview mirror hangs a small embroidered banner. I puzzle through the letters of stylized calligraphy reserved for Koranic verses. *Submit to no man. Submit only to Allah.*

I repeat the words in my head, thinking they should provide me some insight, remind me of some profound belief. But I hear only their hollow echo.

After several minutes the taxi driver stops, turns to me. "Is this the place?"

I look around, trying to makes sense of the row of narrow store-fronts, the faces of the men walking along the edges of the narrow lane. I repeat his question. "Is this the place?" I have no idea.

"This is the place," he confirms impatiently.

I pay the fare, step out. Sewing machines whir in a tailor's shop, small boys drone through memorized Koranic verses in a madrasa. I look for numbers on any of the doorways to indicate which one is the man's location. I enter a halal butcher shop.

The man behind the counter looks suspiciously at my turban. Flies land on the skinned goat carcass hanging from a hook behind him.

I ask about the address. Without a word he points across the street to a small door, marked only by a crescent moon. I follow the butcher's silent direction. When no one answers my knock, I turn the knob and proceed up a set of creaking wooden stairs ending in another closed door. I knock again.

I don't know what to expect. A residence? An office? A secret hiding place? Anxiously, I turn to go, but I have no other destination, no other purpose.

"Who are you?" a deep baritone voice calls out in Urdu from two steps above me. I turn back to face a big Pathan man.

"I am here to see Sheikh Omar."

The Pathan looks at me for a long time. I do not drop my eyes. I am fearless, not out of bravery, but because I no longer feel sentimental about my safety. Finally he steps aside, so I can pass through the doorway.

Inside, the man motions for me to sit in one of two small rough-hewn chairs next to a brass tray on a stand. He walks through a side door into another room.

I set my bag down on a pale green carpet, sit, and wait. The man returns, opening the door just enough that I can see his eye. "Do you have an appointment?"

"No."

The door closes. In America, waiting rooms are always furnished with a stack of magazines; outdated news and women's fashions to distract until a doctor or a dentist is ready. Here, I see only the leaves of a mango tree in a courtyard beyond a window.

The door opens again and the man hands me a cup of hot tea,

holding one for himself. "Sheikh Omar is not here."

"Should I come back at a different time?"

"No. He may be here later, or he may send a message." The man sips his tea. His lips curl back delicately and he very gracefully replaces the cup on the saucer with his massive hands.

"Does he live here, or is this his office?"

The man shakes his head only once. "Who are you?" he asks, still standing.

"I am Srabjeet Dhillon. I have a friend who suggested I come here to see the Sheikh."

"What friend?"

"I will discuss that with the Sheikh."

Beneath his beard, the corner of his mouth turns up in a smile. He leaves the room abruptly.

I wait. An hour passes and then another. I doze off. My back begins to ache from the sitting. I wander around the room, look out the window, but cannot see past the leaves of the mango tree. I turn back and notice a hole in the wall just above the door frame. I reach up and try to push my finger inside—feel a piece of smooth glass. I cannot be sure, but imagine the hole is some kind of eye, a lens, a window, something peering at me. I knock on the wall around the hole, hearing something solid, then a hollowness next to it. I follow the line of the door frame to the floor and then along the floor to another hole in the wall where a single cord emerges and connects to an electrical socket.

I stand back, put my hand to my heart and address the eye. "I would like to see Sheikh Omar. His name was given to me by an Egyptian friend of Ali Nassan of Nablus." I pause, unsure what to expect. Nothing happens. "Today I am Srabjeet Dhillon. I have not always carried this name." I pause again, crafting my words carefully, unsure who might be hearing them. "I hope to carry a different name in the future."

After a long minute, I turn in the direction I figure is east, I try to line up toward Mecca before I raise my palms and kneel down in prayer. I know I have not washed my hands first as I should, I know I appear as a Sikh man, but I perform the ritual, recite the words with a familiarity, a sincerity only a Muslim could possess.

Finished, I continue to sit on my legs and turn to look out at the leaves of the mango tree. As a child one of my cousins persuaded me that the mango tree on our lane hid a djinn. He tried to throw rocks at the djinn to force the spirit out. When I told my father, he explained that we must never throw rocks once the fruits had started to form. *A bad djinn would never live*, my father said, *in the presence of such sweet fruits.*

The side door opens. The Pathan sets a bowl of gravy with meat and a piece of naan on the brass tray.

"Once you have eaten, we will go."

"Go where?"

"To the Sheikh."

He leaves. I eat quickly. As soon as I have swallowed the last bit of bread, the man returns, this time with a companion; a young man, Arab perhaps, though dressed in a simple Pakistani kurta pajama. Neither speak as they lead me through the side door into a long hallway and then down another set of stairs. At the bottom the back of a dingy white van has backed up to the doorway. The Pathan leads, the Arab pushes me on when I pause. I remember the goats before Eid, corralled into the slaughter house, incapable of turning around to save themselves. I find myself bundled into the back of this windowless van, sandwiched between these two men, sitting on a wooden bench.

I wonder if I should feel afraid. "Where are we going?"

The Pathan answers, "To the Sheikh." He coughs in the darkness. "You don't need to know where the Sheikh is."

The van lurches to a stop and I slide into the Pathan. Then the engine revs and we jump forward so I press against the Arab. I close my eyes as the van turns back and forth, seeming to drive in circles. The air in the van grows hot and stale, the men's odor thick and pungent. I close my eyes, focus on my breath to prevent vomiting. And when I think that I will no longer be able to hold on, the van stops, the engine is cut, and the back door opens with a blinding flash. The men at my sides shield their eyes and nearly drag me out by my arms. As my eyes adjust to the light I see we have pulled into a walled courtyard, completely enclosed by a steel fence. I follow the Pathan up another set of stairs and into a hallway which leads to a restroom.

"Clean yourself before you meet him. It's nearly time for prayers, do your ablutions."

I step into a simple restroom; new and clean, a Western-style toilet, a porcelain pedestal sink with a bar of soap, and a small green towel. I am glad for this moment. I wash my hands and face, my forearms up to the elbows as the man had instructed. I look at the image in the mirror, the image of a Sikh man with my face, and wonder who I will be in the future.

I open the door. The men are gone, but I follow the sound of their voices into a large room. Immediately, a different man reaches for my arm, drawing me in, pressing his shoulder to mine, encircling me in a generous but awkward embrace.

"Salaam. Salaam aleikum." He says in a gentle voice. "Let us pray first, then we will talk." I recognize the man's voice.

I leave my shoes by the doorway next to the others, and he leads me to a prayer rug set out for me.

We move through the *salat*, the prayer, in unison, dropping to our knees, touching our heads to the ground in submission, seeking Allah's blessings, looking over our shoulders to the south and the north. Camaraderie, comfort, passes over me, and I believe for a moment that we are all brothers, as I felt that day in Shoukart's relatives' house, all connected in the beautiful tyranny of a common set of beliefs.

I wait for my host to rise from his prayer rug. He motions for me to follow him into another room, lined with cushions bordering a fine Pakistani wool rug. Small tables are set with tea and dried fruits. Windows of lacy Islamic latticework look out onto a courtyard of a few palm trees. I sit down on a cushion, no one joins us.

"I have been waiting for you," he says in Urdu, lifting up the back of his neatly starched kurta to avoid wrinkling it as he sits back in the cushions.

"You have?"

"Yes. You have become quite a remarkable man since I met you in Dargalabad." He runs his fingers over his neatly groomed beard that sits below his incongruously naked upper lip. "A man with admirable strength."

"They call you Sheikh Omar?"

The corners of his eyes turn up in a smile, "Please, just call me brother." He opens his arms. "And what would you like me to call you," he pauses, "Rashid?"

The sound of my name evokes a painful nostalgia. I wish to embrace him as if he were an old friend, as if we have some common history. I wish to flee, to pass through the geometric spaces in the windows like a spirit into the past.

"Of course I remember your name. We have mutual friends who have helped you change it. But I've eagerly followed the news of your success."

When I do not speak, he pours us cups of tea.

"We are living at a time of a great shift, we are poised to regain something important that we have lost. The umma is reminding the kafir all around the world that only Allah is all powerful. They cannot control the world with corporations and the greed of the few." I have been so long without conversation that his articulate words flow through my mind like rain washing through a dry streambed. "They cannot continue to subjugate entire countries by force and through their great mountains of debt." He sips his tea, and in this pause, I find myself longing for the sound of his delicate Urdu. "In Islam we know that it is wrong to charge rent for money. Those who have surpluses should not profit from those who want. This is usury. We are making great strides in Islamic finance, sharing with those-who-have-not the assets that we buy. We will develop the poor, through inclusion, not through exploitation."

"How?"

"You know the sovereign wealth funds. Islamic states are increasingly controlling their own wealth. The days when America and Britain could control us, could extract our resources and keep us poor are ending. You and I, we have learned from their universities," he smiles ironically at our common Western education, "and we are starting to beat them with their own knowledge."

He takes a few almonds from a bowl on the table, handling them thoughtfully. "Imagine, the Sheikhs of Abu Dhabi, the Sultan of Brunei. They own big chunks of Western banks. Eventually all of the arrogant financial institutions that think they run the world will have Islamic financing departments, and once their societies collapse under the weight of their own excess, Islamic countries will be their sources of capital." He tosses an almond into his mouth and chews.

"You think the return of the caliphate will come about through financial means?" I ask, incredulous.

"Not exclusively. We have a multi-pronged approach." He touches each of his fingers in turn. "We are building mosques and madrasas in South Asia, Southeast Asia, the Philippines. We have educational outreach in the U.S., especially in the prisons where the Americans keep their dark-skinned people. We have online news and media analysis in Arabic and Urdu, we offer scholarships so the faithful can make the Hajj." He looks for a moment out the window and speaks again in a lowered voice, "and of course we offer training and tools for direct action."

"Direct action," I repeat quietly.

"Actions to attract the attention of many around the world, as you have done." He holds up his palms, "Masha'allah, you have acted to establish the strength of our movement in a new territory."

The music of his voice fades. I respond flatly, "I acted only to avenge my father, to protect my wife and children, not for any movement."

His eyes narrow for a moment. We are both silent, as I struggle to protect what little I have left, the memory of my intention. His beard is flecked with grey, though his close cropped hair is still black. We may be about the same age, but his skin retains a strange youthfulness, his teeth straight and white. His eyes roam over me, I can feel them on my turban, my shoulders, my feet on his carpet, and back to my face, as if observing secrets I may not know I am exposing.

"That may be true. Fortunately it doesn't matter. The media

have already decided who you are and why you acted." He smiles. "Sometimes we cannot see Allah's designs in their great glory, but when we willingly submit, all will be made clear."

I reach for my tea, suppressing my anger.

He shifts in his seat, tucking his feet under himself. "And let us look toward the future. How can I help you, my brother?"

I swallow, understanding that I need this man, even if I dislike him. "I was told you're able to assist with documentation. That you could help me establish a new identity here in Pakistan."

"I'm able to arrange for some helpful things." He straightens his kurta over his knees. "But first tell me something about what you plan to do here. Where will you settle? How will you earn money? What are your skills?"

"I'm from Lahore."

"I know that," his tone condescending, "but of course you can't go there."

"Maybe I'll stay in Karachi, it's a big city. Perhaps I'll work as a mechanic, I have technical skills."

"Fine. You'll be a new *mujahir*, a new refugee joining this city created by a previous generation of refugees from Partition."

"Your family came over with Partition?" I ask.

"Hmm," he affirms. "We lived in Delhi. Even though my grandfather was educated, even though he maintained a successful small business, his Hindu neighbors always treated him as less. A policeman beat him one day with a baton when he tried to drink from the same fountain as a Hindu. Imagine their stupidity, their worship of superstition, their ignorance leading them to see God as a zoo of animals rather than the one true God." He draws his finger across his forehead. "But of course, my fate was written differently than my grandfather's. I have this house here. Now I drink the finest filtered water."

"How?"

"My grandfather was a good Muslim. When he arrived here he prayed at a mosque with others from Delhi. A man at the masjid recognized my grandfather, noticed his faithfulness, his dutiful prayers. He asked my grandfather to assist him, working with Jinna's administration, establishing the bureaucracy of our new country. My father served him, made connections. Everything was in flux, so he moved quickly in the bureaucracy, received a good posting in Islamabad when they moved the capital north. In time, my grandfather arranged a useful position for my father, useful enough to send me to London for my formal education."

"And you? You are also a government servant?"

"No. International finance. I have served a number of the Western investment banks in their Islamic financing endeavors." His eyes twinkle as he watches my eyebrows arch in confusion, disbelief. "We all help in our own ways. I have certain unique skills that are useful to the organization."

My head spins, I try to resist the force of his words, the gravity pulling me to a dark center I do not wish to see. I close my eyes, turn away. I look again out the window, see the courtyard beyond with a small reflecting pool, among palm trees planted in the cardinal directions. I try to imagine the courtyard is in Morocco, try to imagine that Kathryn and the boys will meet me here, will embrace me beneath these swaying palms, tears on our cheeks, full of sorrow and longing, but we will be together, she will understand my intentions, she will accept the sacrifices required of us.

"I will be in Karachi only temporarily," I say. "Only until I will be able to travel again. Likely I'll head to North Africa."

"Yes, good," the Sheikh nods his head. "You will be able to connect with others who will help you in Libya. Of course we also have friends in Egypt, but the American presence can be problematic."

"All I need is the passport," I reply curtly. "I have made my jihad already, successfully—as you know," I attempt to leverage my only advantage using words he will understand. "I need to be able to travel on a passport without notice." I think of my father who sent me off to London proudly so many years ago, who told everyone around him in the airport, *That is my son, he's going to London to study at university.* I turn to look at the Sheikh directly, "If the authorities should discover me, I would tell them a very different story than your interpretation."

He looks at me, blinks and looks out the window himself. What does he see out there? Does a woman ever meet him there? Do children gather round his legs begging for his affection?

"Why did you marry?" he asks gently.

"For love," I answer.

"Why did you go to America?" he pronounces the name of this giant country in three crisp syllables, as if truncating her appeal, belittling her importance.

"For love," I answer truthfully.

"And why," he pauses, "did you inflict a wound upon her, your new country?"

"For love," I nearly choke, unable to protect my heart from the sting of his question.

"And why did you return to Pakistan?"

"For love." A great rushing of heat presses against my ribs from a strangled internal source.

"Brother, I can see you suffer." He lifts his hands to my temples. The Sheik's slightest touch crumbling the dam I have erected against the truth. "You are like a boat bandied about on an ocean, tossed between the love of a woman and the love of your parents. Remember, Allah requires that we submit to no man—or woman—submit yourself to Allah, and you will see the straight path clearly...I understand more than you may think." He lowers his voice as if to speak in confidence, "I have been in the West, I know the temptation of their faithless women, the ways they seek to entrap us. I have strayed off the path, and found a hell in that place, in the arms of a woman. Al-hamda'allah, I had an experience that returned me to my faith."

I remember the nightclub in Dubai, the way Kathryn softened to me on the dance floor, the way she came to the hotel room, even before I understood her nationality. Perhaps the Sheikh knew a woman like this. But he did not know this woman. "She is the mother of my sons," I say, not so much to him, but to myself, marveling at the time and distance I have crossed in my life with her.

"Yes, well we can help you build a new life, with a more suitable woman. You can again live the life of a good Muslim."

"What I need," I say with a quiet ferocity, "is a new passport."

"Have no illusions, Rashid, you will not be able to return to her. All men need a woman, and eventually when you realize you must find another, you'll not make the same mistake of looking outside your community."

"Fuck you," I say in English and stand to leave.

My host recoils for a moment in shock, then laughs. "You've spent too much time in America. Sit down. Let us talk about your passport. You'll be a proper Pakistani again."

Chapter II

I hear the *azzan*, even before the sun rises. A dream still hangs in my head, so clearly I felt them around me, Kathryn and the boys. They slept with me in Pakistan, in my father's house in Lahore. But I knew I could not leave that dream bed, that outside the door men were waiting for me. Interpol, ISI, Al Qaeda—I didn't know who, but they all wanted me and I knew none would let me rest.

Awake, I can feel the tropical, humid heat of the day already seeping in through the window, but a chill lingers around me. I ache to feel warmth, skin, softness next to me. After a long absence, my morning erection has returned. I observe this as some kind of affirmation of life, a shift from the process of flight. But I cannot think of satisfying this need. I step into the bathroom. I give a wry smile to the man in the mirror, "Srabjeet, I think I'll say goodbye to you today." I wash my face with cold water, slap my cheeks, and tug at my beard. My erection retreats, ignored.

I step into my clothes, though today I do not tie the turban around my head. I step into a no-man's land of namelessness. I will float in this place between passports, between identities and lives. I step out of the room, today a different room, a different hotel, a different neighborhood, and I follow the few men on the street with prayer rugs rolled under their arms. A little masjid, tucked behind a faded brick building, already accepts a handful of old men, still clearing their eyes of sleep. I leave my shoes with the others; cracked sandals, dusty flip flops, a pair of Punjabi juttis already worn and soft.

In the dawning light, I can see the colors of tinsel garlands hanging from the ceiling. The breeze sends them fluttering. I raise my hands, bow at the waist, feel the old men on both sides of me. They move in unison with a certain grace, though with none of the Sheik's Islamist precision. As I recite the prayers, I attempt to let them fill me, to push out all other thoughts. Let me focus on this ritual, let me perhaps wrest from it a measure of peace. With each line, though, some piece of my past remains attached.

Oh Allah, is greater. Glory be to you the most high. I remember a man in London who insisted that I join him for the first prayer, urging me to spend my mornings with God, not with a hangover from the disco. Was he Kuwaiti or Qatari? I only remember the way his Arabic words settled in the back of his throat, in the authentic accent the Pakistani scholars attempt to imitate.

O Show us the straight way, the way of those whom you have blessed, who have not deserved your anger, nor gone astray. I remember my Babu, my father's father, had held me in his strong arms and said *Beta, whatever path you follow, try to do right, take care of your brothers around you, for most others in the world will try to do wrong.*

Oh Allah, forgive me and have mercy on me. Touching my forehead and then my nose into the floor I remember the smell of the mosque in Dubai, the carpet still new, the wall paint still fresh. Curiously, in the Gulf, in that place closer to the birthplace of Islam, on the same bit of land as Mecca and the *Kabba*, I spent the least time in the mosque, preferring the dance floor with almost religious regularity. I disdained the small Pakistani men working for my company who lost their dicks in the billows of their clothes, while I pressed through my jeans against the willing hips of women from a dozen different countries. I touch my head and nose again to the floor, I remember the sound of my mother's voice over the phone telling me she had selected a few girls from good families that I could meet when I returned for Eid holidays. How had I managed to refuse her wishes, drunk on my own youthful confidence? Should

I have allowed her to choose my wife then? Should I have refused her later decision that I would be the one to act for the family?

Peace be upon you and the mercy of Allah. I stand and bow again, my back parallel to the floor. My knees ache, my lower back creaks with the effort. How do these old men move so easily?

Chapter 12

"You are back," the Sheikh says with a hint of amusement. "The passport isn't ready. Do you need money?"

"No. I've come for another reason."

He points for me to sit in a chair across from his desk, he has received me in an office rather than the sitting room where he saw me before. He glances repeatedly at the screen of his laptop computer. "Yes, tell me quickly, I am monitoring something in Europe."

"I want to see my mother, my siblings. Can you send them a message and arrange for a safe place for us to meet?"

"Here in Pakistan?"

"Yes. My mother is old, she shouldn't be traveling abroad."

Behind him on the wall hangs a giant photograph of Mecca, a sea of pilgrims swirling around the Kabba, the central axis of the Muslim world captured within a gold picture frame. "Can she come to Karachi? Do you have other relations here?"

"Yes, I think she can come," I perch uncomfortably on the hard plastic chair beneath me. "We have no family here."

He looks back at the screen, distracted. Next to him, the Koran sits open in a carved wooden bookholder, atop a shelf of scholarly Islamic books in English and Urdu. "I cannot address your request right now," he says.

I gather my thoughts to protest, to try to explain how he is in some way obligated to arrange this.

"Just leave me their names and contact information. I will leave word for you with the same Pathan who brought you here." He hands me a pen and a notebook opened to a clean page. I write down my mother's name and address and numbers. The pen, I notice, bears the name and logo of an upscale hotel in Dubai, one I knew for its flashy bar tucked discreetly on the third floor, away from the rich Emirati families who mingled in the lobby. I look up to ask him when I should expect an answer, but he dismisses me, holding up his hand to prevent me from speaking again.

In a tiny cubicle in a cyber café sandwiched between a tailor and a shoe store, I type in Kathryn's name. For months I have avoided this portal to global culture, have sought to disappear into the backwater eddies of people and tradition that swirl far away from the international current in this city. But I must confirm her address, want to be sure the payments I am sending are reaching her. I ignore the references to her in news articles with headlines about the bombing, the Pakistani terrorist, the Palestinian Pakistani Islamist cell. I type in the name of her international policy journal. I click through, but don't find her name with the editorial staff.

I want to reach through the screen to find her. I imagine our home in Los Angeles now empty. I tap the Sheikh's pen between my fingers. She had told me the bar in that Dubai hotel was too Western, the night we went together the dance floor was packed with blonde Lufthansa air hostesses and awkward young British businessmen. That night she was not yet Kathryn Siddique, but Kathryn Capen. I type her maiden name.

My screen offers a couple of links to articles about sports; tennis fashion, beach volleyball styles. I scroll down and recognize some of her articles from her days at the Chamber of Commerce. I click through to the tennis fashion, wondering who might share

Kathryn's name. Last week, a woman named Kathryn Capen wrote a brief about how tennis unitards and form fitting miniskirts are now being designed from high tech materials. I click through to the publication's home page, the *San Diego Sentinel*, and then to the masthead. The name appears again with a photo of a woman in a short haircut with an artificial looking blonde stripe and bright red lipstick. After a few seconds I recognize this unfamiliar image as the face of my wife.

My limbs tingle. I touch the screen and then my lips. Perhaps she feels she has gone underground also. Her costume is so American, just as mine is so Pakistani. Our lives have pivoted 180 degrees. When she came to Lahore with me, those many years ago, she so carefully mimicked my sisters in their chunnis and bangles, their juttis and hennaed hands, while I strutted next to her in my jeans and t-shirt, showed off my expensive tennis shoes and Swiss watch. Were we just pretending? Were we playing our parts like actors on a stage, shedding these contrived appearances when the effort proved too difficult, too dangerous? No. She must know this is only temporary. Like me, she will return to herself when we come together again. I write down the mailing address of the *San Diego Sentinel* with the pen from Dubai.

I cross the street and step into a tea shop, taking a chair in the rear, my back to the rest of the world. The waiter, hardly older than a boy, comes and stands mutely next to my chair, waiting to be commanded.

"Bring me chai and *namkeen*."

He retreats without a word.

Why do we teach our children to be so passive in this country? I think of my own sons; Michael jumping and talking and laughing, Andrew happy in his baby play. Never will they have to work like this boy. American children go to school. American children must grow up before they are allowed to take a job. American children grow into American men, the kind of men who then go out into the world and kill the kind of men this Pakistani boy may become. No. Not my children.

The waiter comes with my chai and salty cracker snacks. Not my children. I stir the tea. Me. I bring the cup to my lips. I became the kind of man who killed people. I sip the liquid. The Americans must know their actions are not without consequence. I pick up a little crunchy square of namkeen. We all know that if you harm someone, the revenge of their family will be visited upon you. The snack crumbles between my teeth. Why don't the Americans ever learn that? I lick the salt from my fingers. How many bombs must explode in the buildings, on the buses, the trains of the West before they stop attacking us?

The azzan interrupts my thoughts. I drink the rest of my tea quickly, without enjoyment. Too much thinking. Too much waiting—for the passport, the visit with my family, the chance to leave this country. I will rot with all this waiting.

I leave my money with the boy and step out quickly. Passing through the door I nearly knock over a policeman on his way in. He reaches out, grabbing my arm to steady himself. He looks me directly in the eye, pausing for a moment as if he recognizes me. I pull away from his hand, dart out into the brightness of the street. I take my steps almost at a run. I think I hear him call out behind me but I don't look back, turning into the next alley, then around a corner into a narrow lane which opens out onto another street.

I duck into another tea shop and hear all the customers laugh. Confused, I think they are laughing at me. But all eyes are focused on a television screen, where actors shout their lines from a flimsy stage set and the broadcast station's logo occupies the lower quarter of the screen. A teenaged boy approaches me, "Chai? Samosa? Biscuit?" he chirps energetically.

"Uh…samosa."

He pulls out a chair for me to sit at a table already occupied by two other men, almost every other chair is taken. Then he turns on his heel toward the kitchen. On the screen, the low quality production continues. A woman and then a man run across the stage and duck behind a curtain, followed by a stout man wearing a policeman's uniform two sizes too small. Two other actors, sitting on a sofa center stage, shout at the policeman. "Why have you run into our house?" they demand. He demands in return, "You saw that man and that woman? They are not married! I saw them holding hands in the park, making lewd expressions with their eyes, and they are not married!" One of the men on the sofa stands to confront the officer, "So what? She has done nothing wrong, you cannot arrest them for that." The policeman shakes his head and grins, "No, I am just hoping she does it right!" He thrusts his hips forward suggestively and makes a move to search out the girl elsewhere on the stage, the audience erupts in laughter as the other actors restrain him.

All around me in the tea shop people laugh. I glance at the door, but the real policeman has not followed me here.

On the screen, the first man emerges from behind the curtain. "What kind of policeman are you? Such moral corruption! I should go get a mullah to teach you something." The policeman shouts back, "No, the mullahs only offer us young boys," stamping his foot in disgust. Again the audiences at the stage and in the shop roar. Then one of the actors breaks character and points out into the audience, "We have a bunch of mullahs here, they call themselves censors, but they watch the dancing girls very carefully!" Even the policeman on the stage can't resist the spontaneous joke. I find myself laughing with him.

The teenage boy returns with my samosa and tamarind chutney. "What is this program?" I ask him.

"This?" He points at the screen. "It's called *Our Brother*. We show it everyday. In fact, people come so much just to watch this that we changed the name of our shop to Our Brother Hotel." He pronounces the last word in the local accent, throwing away the last syllable. Kathryn used to puzzle over the fact that *restaurant* did not exist in the Pakistani vocabulary, every establishment that served food became a hotel, regardless of whether or not it also offered rooms for travelers.

I ask for a sweet *lassi,* yogurt drink, to go with my samosa, aching to capture the mirth around me. I glance at the door again, angle my body so other customers will obscure me from the sidewalk. The jokes continue, simultaneously appealing to the universal base aspects of our humanity, while critiquing the absurdities of our culture. I laugh. I laugh with the men around me. I laugh to myself. I laugh nearly non-stop until another dancing girl appears. I sip the lassi again, taste the sweetness, the treat I begged from my father every time he brought my brothers and me to the hotel on the main road beyond our lane. *Sweet and sour,* he used to muse, *just like life. Better to have them together than separately.*

The program ends and the customers begin to leave their chairs, empty teacups littering the tables. "When will the show be broadcast again?" I ask the young waiter.

"Tomorrow, same time. These people can barely live without it."

The man sits at his desk, runs his hand along a dark computer monitor. "The machine is not working today," he says. From the dust coating the screen, I suspect the machine has not been working for months. He straightens the implements of business: pencils and pens, a stapler, paperclips, an inkpad, an ancient adding machine with a roll of white paper, yellowed at the edges. "But the telephone is in perfect working order." He proudly caresses the handset of a phone, its rotary dial protected by a plastic doily.

"I have a standing transfer order that I set up through a hawala in Lahore," I tell him, "and I need to change the location where it should be sent. And I also need to collect a sum here."

"So you are needing two transactions, yes?"

I nod.

"So first tell me from where the money is coming."

I give him the name of the hawala agent in Lahore. When I was in school, my father had called on the agent every month to transfer money to London. Like clockwork, I would visit the Pakistani grocer in Brighton two days later to collect the money from the back room. I knew some of my fellow students preferred to have their money transferred through their parents' Western bank accounts, but my father always distrusted them. *No one of us has met any of those bankers,* he would say wagging his finger, *it is much better to shake the hand of the man responsible for getting the money wherever it is going. If it doesn't arrive it is not just a matter of his salary, but of his honor.*

The man opens up a ledger book with a thick cardboard cover. He looks over a list of names written in careful Urdu script. He finds the name of the Lahore agent and nods his head. "And who will receive the funds?"

I pass him the piece of paper where I have written in English Kathryn's name and the address at the *San Diego Sentinel.* He peers at the paper, adjusting his glasses, then scratches the edge of his bushy black mustache. "Amrika?" he asks. "So where do you want..." he pauses, reading the paper again, "Kat-he-rin Cay-pun and San Deego to collect the funds?"

"No, I want my agent in Los Angeles to take the transfers he receives from Lahore and mail them to this name at this address."

The man scowls. "But there is no way to guarantee the money will arrive to these people. The recipients will have to go in person."

I take the paper back and write down the name of the agent in Los Angeles. "I know you can't guarantee it," I hand the paper to him again, "I trust the agent there, he only needs to put the cash in an envelope with this address and send it."

The man sticks out his lower lip and shakes his head in disapproval. "Not possible."

"*Saheb,*" I resort to extra politeness, "I appreciate your concern. I only need you to convey this address to my agent in Los Angeles. He has already delivered the funds twice to different locations. He understands the transfer, this is just a change of address."

He looks up the name of the Los Angeles agent in his book, turns through several pages before pointing a finger at a name written in Urdu, next to the words New York, written in English. "I don't know of your agent, in Amrika, I only have contact in New York." He looks up and then closes his book. "I can't do it, can't be sure."

"I can give you the agent's telephone number, you can call him."

The man crosses his arms across his plump belly. "No. How will I know who he is? You'll need to find another hawala."

I had not anticipated any kind of refusal. With a sinking feeling I realize I have connected myself with Kathryn, he could easily alert the authorities about my request. I quickly reach out for the paper I showed him and conceal it within my pocket. "Can you tell me again the name of the recipient?"

He shakes his head gravely. "I cannot remember the names of any of my transfers, never."

I stand up to leave, ask him if he can refer me to another agent.

He describes a DVD shop about a mile away. "But remember," he warns me, "do not trust the postal system to deliver cash. A man you can trust, even a family, a clan, you can trust. But an organization, a government or a business, never, always you will find them corrupt."

At the back of the DVD store, I face no resistance. The hawala agent, a young man who swaggers with a contrived sophistication in his tiny office, composes a telephone text message, his fingers flying over the tiny plastic keys, and sends it to a Los Angeles number. Within ten minutes he receives a reply that satisfies him about the feasibility of changing my standing transfer instructions. Kathryn will now receive the payments through the mail at the *San Diego Sentinel*.

The sound of a film-y love song seeps through the grey-colored wall from the front of the store. A young man croons a dozen variations of *why*? Why did she allow him to fall in love with her? Why did she not resist her parents' wishes that she marry another? Why does she still look at him from beneath the red of her wedding veil? Why does he still love her? Why wasn't he born into the right family to have been a suitable boy? The theme of the suffering that arranged marriage brings to the dream of romantic marriage burns like an eternal flame in South Asia, flickering in almost every film, every song, every tale we learned in school. Somehow, I knew this story did not apply to me. I was not destined to suffer with a woman not of my choosing. I would not be so passive, allowing my parents to choose my wife.

The agent picks up a different mobile phone and makes a call to Lahore. He speaks quickly a few simple words and a string of numbers, before putting the phone in his pocket. "No problem," he says with an oily smile. "Come back in two days, I will have your money for you."

I nod in appreciation and leave the little office. I will have enough to see me through a couple more weeks. Rows of DVDs and CDs are crammed on the shelves. Cheaply reproduced images of musicians and actors stare out at me. I cannot bear the syrupy images of the love stories, the weddings.

Another image catches me. A man, seen from behind, walks down a dusty village street, an elongated stringed instrument resting on his shoulder. The starkness of the image, the sense of longing, the presence of the instrument as his only companion, speak to me. Without thinking, I purchase the disc and leave the store, only to realize I have no way to listen to the recording. I walk back toward my shabby hostel room and read of the musician, Hamyouk Hussain. The liner notes explain he had grown up in a family of *rubab* players, on a Kabul street full of musicians. But his music had to wait. "Music requires an atmosphere of quiet," the notes quote him, "and that quiet disappeared with the war." So the family moved to Pakistan, he reunited with his instrument in Peshawar, playing with musicians both local and exiled from Afghanistan. Even before I hear the music, I feel an affinity for it, for the rebirth of his love on a foreign soil, for a successful transplanting of life. Such miracles are possible.

Chapter 13

I step out of the taxi, retreat into the shadows of a doorway, mindful that no one see me. I wear a crocheted skullcap over my closely cropped hair, I am now Ismail Khan, according to the nebulously procured passport in my pocket. I look around to see who might be observing me. I know that Sheikh Omar has arranged the meeting with my mother, an opportunity I hesitantly trust, but I wonder if anyone has followed my mother. Bubbles waft across the street from a man hawking cheap plastic toys and bubble guns. I wonder for a moment, perhaps the toy wallah really serves the intelligence service, perhaps he observes the comings and goings at this hotel. Perhaps when he leaves the cart of balloons and plastic cricket bats he reports to men in khaki uniforms, feeding them details about the appearance of men who come in cars to this place, men who walk cautiously through the door, men like me. The small iridescent orbs fall on my face, painlessly bursting into a bit of soapy residue. The toy wallah looks up. If he is an informant, I want to know his face.

Then I lift my shoulders and walk into the hotel. I do not check in with the front desk, I do not take the lift, opting for the stairs. I walk the five flights and step quietly down the hall. Before I can raise my hand to knock, the door to room 505 opens and Sheikh Omar's Pathan pulls me into the room. He steps past me to look both ways down the hall before closing the door and sliding the lock into place.

"Is she here?" I ask, disoriented. I hadn't expected to see him.

The Pathan just nods and points. I step into the room and see my mother sitting on the edge of the bed, her head erect, her shoulders square. Something tells me to turn and leave, to run from this woman who has directed my life out of my control. But my weakness wills me to run *to* her, to crawl into her lap so she will comfort me, so she will stroke me and sing to me as I remember from my childhood. She looks up at me, her eyes clear, her face proud. She nods at me, raises her hand, waiting for me to bow down and touch her feet, seeking her blessing. How many times have I respected her in this way? How many times have her fingers grazed my hair, reassuring me of her approval? I begin to reach down, but the inhale catches in my lungs, the man I have become pulls me back up and I can only stand before her, Ismail Khan, a stranger.

Almost imperceptibly, she flinches. She watches me as I sit down in a chair, not touching her, not speaking.

"Al-hamda'allah," she says. "You have accomplished our revenge." She doesn't know that I would have chosen not to, that I only acted to protect Kathryn and the boys from Abu Omar's network. Her head is still, but I hear the rings around her now frail fingers rattle as she trembles. "Do you need anything?" she asks as if she were asking me if I wanted another roti, or a bit of lemon pickle.

I practically growl at the absurdity of her question. What don't I need? I need a home, I need my wife, my children. I need safety and protection, privacy to rebuild a life. I need comfort and love. I need to forget. And I need to remember.

She looks at me, her chunni falls to her shoulder revealing her hair now thinned, with only a few streaks of grey amidst a ghostly white. "Do not think this is easy for us either. I will not tell you how the government men came and questioned us, the ways they laid their hands on your brothers, trying to extract information. The Americans pull the strings of their puppets in our government, and the government men come to yank our strings." She clasps her hands together, as she used to do when one of the laborers would challenge her, or when a man would come from the market and explain to her that a quantity of our rice harvest had somehow disappeared. "But we have called on our relations, we've made contact with your mamaji's cousin by marriage. He has influence with the security services. Now we are protected, but of course, many had to be included in the *bakshish* we provided in return."

"Did you give them our land?" I say, knowing that government officials seize on the misfortune of others to enrich themselves.

"No," she shakes her head. "I refused to give them even an inch of our farms. Your brothers arranged for cash, to be delivered over time." She pulls the chunni back over her head. "I will ask you again, do you need anything?"

"I don't need anything for myself. I only need Majid to be sure the funds are available for my sons. I've paid whatever I owed to you and my father, now I must pay the debt I owe my sons."

"You have my word."

I sit still, silent.

"Beta," my mother calls to the Pathan, "I need to be alone with my son."

The man looks at both of us before lowering his head and stepping outside the door. I half expect that she will cuff me on the ear as she did when she felt I had disrespected her as a child.

"Despite our sufferings," she begins, "I will be able to leave this life contented. I will be with my loved ones again in heaven, you've made this possible. I'm proud of you, you have maintained our culture, honored our traditions even though you left our lands. In the West they believe in their lawyers and judges, as if their tedious arguments in the courtroom could compensate a victim's family for their loss. They act as if humans are robots, as if all of our actions could be explained with laws and in books." She thumps her hand over her breast. "They don't understand that we all carry the law around in our hearts, that the love and suffering we experience must be balanced by love and suffering. This is the natural order of things."

She stands and walks stiffly to me. "You killed. The Americans killed for hate but you killed for love." She takes one of my hands in hers, turns my palm up and runs her fingers along the deep crease in the center of my hand. "You have your father's hands. But not your father's fate."

The warmth of her skin in my palms shoots through me like lightning. When was the last time someone I loved touched me? Hungrily, I grasp her hands in mine, I press her palms against my eyes, blocking out the light. I will myself to be strong, not to cry. Shame and hope, anger and relief, hubris and grief swirl into a knot—like the legendary knot only Sikander's sword could detangle—until my insides are still, constricted with the enormity of what I have done.

Carefully, gently, she retrieves one of her hands from my grip and places it atop my head. In this gesture she offers me whatever blessing she can bestow, whatever goodness she still contains, her legacy of strength and honor are now mine. I look at her feet, understand the paths they have walked, the journey that has brought her here to this secret meeting. I know this will be the last time I see her.

Chapter 14

The lane appears as though lined by caves. Dark green awnings, grimy at the edges, flap lazily over a row of mechanics shops. Each one seems to belch black dust and exhaust. Piles of cast off car parts litter their perimeters, an advancing front of material encroaching on the thoroughfare, occasionally beaten back by a pulverizing truck wheel, or an irritated rickshaw driver. I search the shops, trying to discern the most successful one. As I stand at the end of the lane, beneath a maze of tattered power lines, slumping my shoulders so as not to draw attention to myself, a shiny black late-model Mercedes pull into one of the shops—luxury swallowed into darkness. Almost immediately, the car pulls out and drives back the way it came. Perhaps the car whisked the shop's owner in to collect the day's profits, perhaps the car came to demand tribute in return for protection from the underworld kings, perhaps the men in the backseat simply wanted repairs. Regardless, I find the Mercedes auspicious.

Before I can hesitate, I walk across the street into the same shop, finding two men sitting atop broken engine blocks sipping tea out of chipped cups. Oblivious to me—a man without a car—they sit in silence.

"Salaam aleikum," I say gingerly, so as not to startle them. They look up, but do not respond. "I wondered if you need a mechanic.

I see you work on high-end cars and I have a lot of experience with modern engines."

They look up at me suspiciously, skeptically, I assume because of my clean hands, the absence of grease on my clothes or body. The younger of the two says flatly, "You have to talk to the boss man. He owns this place, he just left."

"When will he be back?"

The man shrugs his shoulders.

"Tomorrow?"

"Maybe."

"All right, I'll come back tomorrow."

Before returning to the hotel where I have spent the last few days, I step into an internet shop. I direct the mouse—soiled, likely from the hands of an endless string of frustrated men searching for porn sites—to guide me to mechanics' blogs and technical sites about late-model Mercedes. My mind seizes on the engineering drawings, delights in the outlines of the precise fittings, the indications of the electrical flows. Ever since I peered over my father's shoulder at the technical specifications he held for one of our irrigation pumps, I have been unable to resist diagrams. I craved the ideal worlds they seemed to describe, the linear assemblies, the rational joining of form and function. These black and white, two-dimensional images hinted at orderly manufacturing plants, organized systems that seemed a world away from our farms—jumbles of humans and tools, animals and plants.

The internet offers mechanics' discussions seeking help to solve their problems with Mercedes. What causes the high-pitched hum when the engine is idling? How to reconnect the electrical system that powers the dashboard display? Troubleshooting. In Dubai, I often answered middle of the night calls from anxious engineers whose tools were stuck, or lost in the well. I could usually pinpoint the error, even over the phone. I had poured over the manuals for each tool, read the diagrams and descriptions a soon as they appeared from regional headquarters in three ring binders, before my colleagues could mar the white pages with their spilt tea and dirty hands.

Soon, I understand how Mercedes electrical systems frequently cause glitches, how to hear whether the problem is in the cylinders or the timing belt, when it is easier to order a replacement part, or fine tune a fix on the spot.

I pay for my internet time, surprised to realize three hours have passed. Not once did I think of Kathryn or the boys, or my mother, or the sound of Ali's voice telling me he would wait another day. I feel a smooth lightness in my thinking. I can contemplate a purpose, an objective beyond my own survival.

My cheap new CD player whirs to life and the headphones bring sound to my ears, muting the noise of the teashop. The first few notes, delicately plucked from the rubab transmit a haunting melody, a rhythm infused with nostalgia, with longing. I close my eyes, blocking out the people around me, their movements, the dull tans and grays of their clothes. This music, Persian-tinted, conjures colors in my mind's eye; the emerald stone set in the player's gold ring, the delicate orange of a plate of apricots, bright red pomegranates set against a dusty landscape. I listen. The *tabla* joins the rubab and they seem to walk together, the rhythm sometimes rushed, sometimes tedious, but always companionable. I am transported, momentarily transformed. The waiter brings my tea and biscuits. I consume them in the tea shop, but I enjoy them in the company of the rubab player, believing we could be friends, stoking the little flame of a relationship with this music. The player spins the CD to the end of the last track and then comes to a stop with a little sigh, as if even the plastic shares my disappointment.

I remove the headphones, allowing the chatter of the shop to reach me again. I look up in time to see the opening banner of *My Brother* parade across the television screen. I order another cup of tea, a flutter of pleasure rippling through my caffeinated heartbeat. I shift to a more comfortable position in my chair, incrementally accepting the habits of my new life. My life with Kathryn and the boys shifts an equal increment toward the realm of memory and myth.

———————

I return to the mechanics shop the next morning.

"You stupid sister fucker," the older man shouts, "I told you to hold the wrench still. A donkey has more sense. I should kick your fucking ass back to that stinking brothel your mother came from, I don't care if you are the boss man's son."

I hear the sound of flesh hitting flesh. I don't know which of them has launched the blow. But the impact achieves a silence, one breath, and then another. "Now hold the wrench still," the older man says in an even tone. And metal clangs against metal.

I step into the darkness of the shop. "Salaam aleikum," I call out to announce myself. The two men look up, their hands still in the bowels of the car engine. I step over to look at their work.

"Aleikum es salaam," they mumble and return to their efforts. They are trying to reach the steering column from the top of the engine, reaching past a maze of parts in the process.

"You'll have an easier time of it if you raise the car and reach from the bottom," I offer.

They look at me with disdain, but I can see the older man hesitates to apply any pressure to his tool. "You worked on Mercedes before?" he asks me gruffly.

"A lot," I lie. "From below, you can easily recalibrate the direction of the steering column if it's pulling." I glance at the tires, "If you've already determined that the car isn't pulling to one side because the wheels aren't aligned."

The younger man suddenly looks up at the older man. "We didn't check the wheel alignment."

"*Bain chod!*" the older man spits out at the younger one, "I told you to do that first!" Deliberately, he pulls his hands out of the engine and wipes them on a filthy rag. "What's your name?"

"Ismail Khan," I reach out my clean hand to shake his dirty hand. He hesitates, my gesture too formal, a touch too Western perhaps.

"And your name?" I ask to bridge the physical distance.

"Azim." He offers no family name. "Get the blocks out," he tells the younger man. "He is Zakir," he says pointing.

I help Zakir get the blocks in place. Azim puts the car in neutral and we push it up the little ramps to the blocks. Azim lays on his back on a wheeled platform and slides under the car. He lets out an expression of satisfaction and then barks out orders for tools. Zakir scurries to hand Azim each one in order. In a few minutes Azim reappears, a grin on his face, dominant over Zakir, even in this subservient position.

"The boss man will be back this afternoon to drop off another car. He'll be pleased when he checks on this one."

"How many cars does he have?"

"Maybe a dozen, he keeps buying, sometimes he sells. Whenever he feels like one brings him bad luck, or if someone gets shot in the back seat, he changes it."

Zakir flashes a nervous look at Azim, startled at the older man's revelation.

I don't respond. What is it to me who the boss man is? Who am I to judge, to jump to conclusions about what happens in the backs of his cars?

With a groan, Azim lifts himself to standing. "Do you know why the engines sometimes sing in idle?"

I pause for a moment, wondering if perhaps he is hinting at some kind of car metaphysics. Then he makes a high-pitched humming noise. I smile. "Of course," I tell him, "of course I know what makes that sound."

———————

With my first earnings from the shop carefully folded into the pocket of my kurta, I step again into the music store. I scan the shelves for Hamyouk Hussain, half expecting he will appear and greet me with a familiar smile. I choose a disc which seems to be his first, so I can hear his early memories, understand the progression of his expression. I will allow myself this small pleasure, I rational-ize, promising to save the rest of the salary for my future house in Morocco. I shudder at the years I would have to work at this rate to save enough to reunite with my wife and children in Morocco. But life changes, I remind myself. I will not always be a personal mechanic for a rich man of dubious reputation.

Chapter 15

Azim and Zakir are beaming. They have brought me roasted goat and briyani, daal, pickle, even kaju barfi—the dense cashew sweets that remind me of the color of Kathryn's skin. Since I moved my few possessions into the tiny living space at the back of the shop, they have been relieved of the nightly security detail they used to perform. They can't understand why I am not married, why I am not trying to find a wife, but they don't really care, since my solitary lifestyle allows them to return to their wives and children each night—even enjoying the full Eid holiday for the first time in years.

I eat the cold remains of their holiday feast. I tried my best to ignore the festival atmosphere, the gathering of goats everywhere in the city, the rivers of blood that ran in the gutters as families slaughtered the animals for the required sacrifice. I contrived elaborate justifications for why I couldn't leave the shop—thieves, rivals, mafia, djinns. I would protect against all of these. I could not have left the shop, could not have gone out to reflect on the story of Eid, the relief of Ibrahim who, centuries ago, was spared the agony of sacrificing his own son on an altar by the divine appearance of a goat who could be slaughtered in the boy's stead. How could I contemplate the good fortune, the faith, the fearlessness of a man ready to kill his own son when my own sons are living, but beyond my grasp? In Morocco, I will observe the holiday again, I will allow

Michael to hold the knife himself, I will place my hand over his as he slices the goat's neck, as we somberly give thanks for the look of fearful resignation in the goat's eye and repeat an ancient ritual. But until then, I need not spill more blood.

A car pulls in as I sop up the last of the gravy with the bread—a dark green Mercedes, C class, several years old—not the best of the boss' collection. The window rolls down, chilled air spills out. "You are good with cars, yes?" the driver says.

I nod.

"Even the complicated parts, the meters and dials?"

"Usually."

He cocks his head, indicates for me to sit next to him in the passenger seat. I hesitate. "Let's go," he says, "the boss told me to fetch you."

"I'll need to gather some tools."

"Fine. Do it quickly."

I fill a bucket, assembling tools for unknown problems. From the passenger seat I can see Azim and Zakir gaping at me, silently staring at the car as we speed down the lane. I close my eyes and listen to the sounds of the engine, the acceleration and deceleration, the driver's hands on the steering wheel. The leather smells of my memories of sitting in my brother Majid's car, showing off for girls in our village.

As we turn off the Karachi 1 Ring Road, the driver tells me to bend down, to tuck my head between my knees.

"What for?" I ask, bewildered.

"You either have to drop your head down, or I will have to pull over and tie up your hands and blindfold you."

My heart races, I feel like I have been duped, like I am the goat, walking to my own slaughter, perhaps sparing someone else's son. "Are you kidnapping me?" I choke out.

The driver laughs, genuinely. "No brother, it's for your own protection. If the boss knows you know the way to his house, or if somebody else knows you know the way to his house, it could be dangerous for you." He reaches out with his hand and pushes my shoulder down, "so it's better if no one sees you on the way to his house."

So I tuck my head between my knees, breathing in the smell of my clothes—sweat and salty metallic vapors. I hope he is sincere, I hope he is not leading me to some location where ISI goons will interrogate me and torture me before throwing me to the Americans. I remember my father warning me not to turn my back on a man who was not bound by ties of clan. I start to lift my head. As the car turns the driver roughly shoves my head back down. "Bain chod! I'm telling you, this is for your own good."

The car slows. The driver briefly exchanges a few familiar words with someone, perhaps a guard. The driver explains I have been as good as blind the whole way here. We are moving again, then stop. I brace myself, waiting for rough hands on my shoulders, waiting for shoves and taunts. My mind races through the lies I will tell, the identities I will claim or deny, the justifications and alibis I will explain. But as the air conditioning sighs to a stop and stillness settles into the car, the driver laughs and slaps me on the shoulder. "Enough now. Get up, we're here."

I uncoil myself without releasing my tension. I step out into a carport attached to a big house. Beyond the car I can see a court-yard—covered in concrete and glazed tiles—a fountain spouting water into the air through a gold nozzle, a covered gazebo. The sun beats down, only four spindly palm trees to diffuse the heat. I don't see another person, but hear the hum of giant air conditioning units.

The driver waves me around with his hand, points to a beautiful silver Mercedes. A door from the main house opens into the carport and a man steps delicately toward me. My mind tumbles and my muscles contract to flee as I recognize the well-trimmed beard—Sheikh Omar.

With a restrained smile, he offers me his hand in greeting. "So it *is* you." He takes a step closer to me when I don't reach for his hand. "I heard stories about this excellent mechanic, a man who seemed to work miracles on the kinds of cars that leave most of our mechanics scratching like village dogs. I wondered if it might be someone with more sophisticated training, perhaps someone who had been abroad."

I force myself to accept Sheikh Omar's hand.

"You need not be afraid of me, brother...Ismail," he drops his head in deference to this contrived identity. "If you are as good as your reputation, I may have a much better situation to offer you."

I wipe my hand off on my kurta. "What do you mean?"

A little peep chirps repeatedly from his pocket. "I must take this call," he explains. "We'll talk more after you have a chance to work on my car." And without another word, he steps back into the house.

The driver crosses his arms across his chest, looks at me more closely. "So you already know Sheikh Omar," he marvels. "Then why would you live in that filthy shop, like a cockroach afraid of the light?"

I don't answer, my legs threaten to give way. I lean against the car.

"Well, whatever your reasons, you shouldn't disappoint the Sheikh. He's always a man of his word, so if he can get you something better, he will."

I look around, half expecting other men will appear and grab me. A fly passes in front of my face, an irritating intrusion, a reminder of rot and decay in the artifice of clean concrete. The driver continues, "Aren't you going to look at the car? I hear the speedometer is broken."

I retrieve my tools, careful not to turn my back to the driver, still not trusting this situation.

Inside the silver car I immediately ascertain the cause of the malfunctioning speedometer; a hole just the size of my little finger has punctured the dashboard casing, cracks splintering out from the center of impact like a spider's web. I stick my little finger into the hole, seeing if I can feel the bullet still in the car. I feel nothing. So I pop the hood and look in the engine. I can just make out the hole where the bullet punctured from the interior through to the engine, but the rest of the trajectory seemed to pass amazingly through a series of small spaces in between essential parts of the engine. The bullet must be lodged in a road somewhere, an unnoticed artifact of some conflict within this car, just another grain of sand in the sediment of human suffering. I reach in, my fingers probing, and feel the prick of frayed wire. I reach further, feeling for the other end of the fray, the matching end, the pair that I could reunify. I turn on the ignition, the engine purrs, but the dashboard remains dark, the meters mute. My mind moves in the familiar ways; wondering if the problem is simply the electrical connection, or some error in the electronic circuitry, figuring out the angle I will need to see the wires, the way to jack up the front of the car.

I take my time, ensuring I do not scratch any part of the car or move anything that will cause me problems. The job is not difficult, as long as I reduce it to a series of the smallest possible tasks, completed in the appropriate order.

Just as I crimp the two wires together, I consider ripping them out by their roots. The Sheikh is not my employer. Whatever offer he might make will certainly suit his purposes more than mine. Who is he to me? Who am I to him? He is Sheikh Omar—a powerful man at the center of some nefarious web. I am Ismail Khan, a simple mechanic. He is the man that gave me my name. In some parallel universe of deception we are related, bound, like family, like father and son.

I restore all the parts, close the hood. After jacking up the rear wheels I turn on the ignition one more time, see the dashboard illuminate, carefully press the accelerator with my foot and see the speedometer register the speed of the travel the rear wheels imagine.

On a whim I press the button to turn on the stereo. The device resumes a melody where it had been arrested the last time someone turned off the stereo. A few notes reach me, amplified through the warm clarity of good speakers. I look around, surprised, disoriented. I know the fingers that pluck these strings, I know this melody as if it were a lullaby I heard as a child. I imagine Sheikh Omar—sitting in this car, just as I have sat on my cot—listening to the music of Hamyouk Hussain. The rubab has soothed us both.

The driver comes close, looks at me with a bemused smile. "You're finished? The speedometer works?"

"Yes."

The driver juts his chin and nods his head. "That's good for you, the Sheikh will be pleased."

As if summoned, the Sheikh appears again from the door. "So?" he asks, holding his hands crossed before him.

"The electrical connection had been severed," I don't mention the bullet, which must be obvious to him. "The speedometer's working, though I can't repair the dashboard casing here. Maybe I could fabricate something, but I'd suggest ordering a new piece from Mercedes directly."

The stereo falls silent, pausing between tracks.

"Turn off the car," the Sheikh says. He glances at the driver then back to me. "Let us talk inside."

I follow him into the ostentatious chill of the house, imagining what he will offer me, sure in that moment of what I want from him.

Chapter 16

Peshawar, Pakistan.
Two years after the bombing

I cannot find a tea shop in Peshawar that plays the broadcast of *My Brother.* The locals do not consume such bawdy humor in public. The austere desperation, palpable on the streets, does not foster the kind of anonymous camaraderie I experienced in Karachi. I find a few DVDs of past episodes, but I have seen them all, and watching them in isolation, the actors seem bleached, their double entendre hollow, the dancing girls garish. So Hamyouk Hussain's rubab expands, fills the holes in my life, becomes my whole life.

The cars come to me often for repair. I watch the local news enough to recognize a pattern; stories of skirmishes and increasing U.S. security actions inevitably portend the arrival of an SUV or a Mercedes at my shop. Sometimes they come on the back of a flatbed lorry, or towed slowly by another car. Occasionally I will hear a story about spare parts, the salvageable guts of some car or another being transported over the Khyber pass on the back of a mule, or in a bullock cart. I never see the conflict that causes these mechanical injuries, the seemingly endless series of bullets from an automatic weapon that rip up the side of a car, the explosives that will shred an engine, leaving burnt and twisted metal in their wake. I have made my deal with Sheikh Omar. I will work on these cars, I will deliver my magic, not from a shop on a public lane, not in a place like the shop in Karachi, where at any moment the ISI or the police might approach, but from a place where I am protected, buffered. I did not want to be holed up again, no more cockroach-style existence. I want the more sophisticated shielding that the Sheikh could arrange.

So I am able to listen to my music in the open air of a tiny courtyard. Occasionally small birds come to visit the blooms of the potted plants I have acquired, sip the water from a little bowl I have placed outside. Three consecutive walls stand between me and the shop. On the other side of the courtyard wall, I spend my sleeping hours in a small, but well-lit room, and when I wake I wash myself from a bucket of water beneath the tap and watch the dirty suds disappear down a drain in the tiles. Beyond the second wall, another room houses a locked metal case with the tools that allow me to repair their cars. The tools I have assembled seem to suggest that I am part mechanic, part electrician, part programmer, and to their eyes, part magician. And beyond the third wall are their cars. They do not see me when they come in. I try to know as little as possible about them or the men who deliver their cars. My assistant, a teenaged boy handles the initial formalities. Only when the drivers are gone do I come out to hear the report from the boy, to make my own diagnosis and plan for the vehicle's rehabilitation.

In the evenings, like tonight, I enjoy the cooling air, I eat the meal that the boy fetches for me and I sit and talk. I imagine her with me. I imagine this courtyard is just a small cabana off the main courtyard in our Moroccan home. In these silent conversations, Kathryn and I talk about the boys, about how they have grown, about how much Michael is reading and how Andrew has mastered the tricycle. I can hear their laughs and shouts just over the wall, I hear the splashing of a fountain. And the jasmine flowers give up their perfume. And sometimes, like tonight, I sit with her until the sun sets and the moon rises and I lay back on the charpoy hearing her whisper in my ear, feeling her hair brush across my shoulder and I remember the curves of her body. I remember them so vividly, can almost feel them so accurately through my fingertips, that my sex responds. And when she opens her legs to straddle me, when I slide my own hand around me, entering her in my mind, my nerves are on a hair trigger. So this hand that coaxes inanimate objects into motion all day, needs only offer the briefest conjugal touch this evening to achieve the release, the desired and dreaded outcome. For as soon as I ejaculate, I see the walls that I allow to confine me. The distance—that seconds earlier had seemed malleable—telescopes out into an impossible expanse.

I wash myself and slide my feet into my *chappals*. I need some air, I need to see other people. I open the door out from my courtyard and follow a maze of narrow passageways through the compound. I can hear the sound of cooking pots and women with coarse voices scolding children to sleep. I hear the slosh of water in laundry tubs, the crack of bed sheets hung out to dry. The rambling path through the servants' section of the compound eventually leads to a small alley where ragged cats hunt for rice or bits of gristly meat from the discarded rinsewater.

I quickly fall in step with a group of men passing by, their Kashmiri-style embroidered caps framing their foreheads. I wish to hear their conversation, to walk for a change with others, not as a lone fugitive.

In town I scan walls and shop windows for advertisements. At last I find it, the reason why I wanted to be in Peshawar. Hamyouk Hussain will play a concert a week from tonight.

Chapter 17

Peshawar, Pakistan.
Ten years after the bombing

Today is my birthday, or the birthday of the man I used to be, Ismail Khan claims a date that means nothing to me. I am a man in my forties. When my father was this age he was expanding his farm, growing his trading business, watching his sons become men. My life is the inverse, the perverse of his. I have contracted the physical and emotional confines of my life so that almost all of my imagining happens within the little domain of my courtyard. The jasmine covers the walls so that I might imagine I am in the setting of some Rumi poem.

Zaid, my assistant knocks on my door to bring me dinner, rice and meat curry cooked elsewhere in the compound.

"Come and sit with me tonight," I tell him before accepting the food as I usually do.

Even though he has grown into a man, he hesitates like the boy he was when I first came here.

"Sit. I would like some company." I motion him to the chair next to me. "Tell me stories of your children."

I attended Zaid's wedding a few years back. He has brought his children to me to receive my blessing.

He smiles ruefully. "They are a gift from Allah, though my wife complains often."

"The oldest is a girl?"

"Yes. The other two are boys, al-hamda'allah."

He twists in his chair, looks toward the door as if he would like to return inside. I have taught him much of what I know. He could go out and start his own shop, he could leave me and start another life. But this is not the Pakistani way. Zaid is loyal to me. I wouldn't dare to call it love, but at least a deep familiarity.

"Maybe you could come for a meal with us outside?" he asks.

"Now? You've already brought the food."

He stands up. "Maybe after Friday prayers sometime."

"You don't want to stay."

He twitches his head. "Brother," he says respectfully, "there are ghosts in this courtyard."

"You mean djinns?"

"No, ghosts. Maybe they come with the broken cars. I don't know, but they aren't from here."

I look around seeing only the same courtyard I have seen these many years now. "So where are they from?"

He shakes his head. "Just somewhere far away. They are angry for being killed, for not being allowed to finish their journey here on earth."

"How do you know?"

"I've encountered lots of ghosts here in the Sheikh's compound. They get trapped in the inside rooms, especially where there's only one door." He takes a step to leave. "Some of the servants blame the Sheikh's work. I don't know about that. I just know he's a good Muslim and he's always taken care of me and my family. Anyway, you should spend less time here. And be sure to clear out the spiders webs. The ghosts get tangled in the silk."

He leaves me alone with my food.

I think, as I have so many times, about calling Kathryn, reaching out in some way. Would she remember today is my birthday? But

I have nothing to offer her, don't yet have the savings or the savvy to arrange a place for us in Morocco. Would she really come even if I did? What would I say to her if she answered?

I eat only half my dinner, cover the remainder with a pot lid to protect it from the flies and rats.

I take the straw broom from just inside the door and return the few steps to the far end of the courtyard. I sweep out the cobwebs in the corners from the ground to the top of the wall. I can't shake the feeling of a chill as I lie down on my cot to sleep earlier than usual.

Chapter 18

Twenty years after the bombing

Zaid and I sit in a tea shop, a dirty cat weaves in and out of the chair legs, hoping for scraps. Today we indulged in a sheesha, both taking long draws from the hose of the water pipe. As we exhale like lazy dragons our conversation grows quiet. I watch the street. Peshawar is a town of men, dominating the streets, driving the cars, making the noise. But I can feel the energy of the women. From behind the walls of every home waft their smells, their sweet sweat, the rose water in their hair, uncovered in the privacy behind the walls. I haven't talked with a woman in years, only imagined Kathryn's words.

"My wife," Zaid surprises me by speaking. "Is every woman like this after too many years of marriage?"

"Like what?"

"Only eating and arguing. No attention to me, no respect for my manhood."

I wait for him to continue.

"Oh, what would you know of a wife anyway?"

I bristle. "I had a wife," I say defending myself. "But…something happened."

He takes another draw from the pipe. "Well, I guess if all the wives were good, we wouldn't need Lucky Lane," he says of the nearby street lined with brothels. "You never go?"

I shake my head.

"Sometimes I wonder if you are really a man."

"Me too." I cast my eyes away. "Me too."

Two weeks later when Zaid brings me my evening meal, I leave the food on a stool and follow him out.

"Would you…"

He turns, curious.

I feel as though we have shifted positions and I am now sub-servient to him. "Would you take me with you…you know…to Lucky Lane?"

He looks relieved. Nods and smiles, "When?"

"Tonight. Before I change my mind."

"Eat your dinner, brother. I'll be back."

I sit with a woman in a cramped room, barely large enough for me to stand next to the bed. I am nervous, like a schoolboy. I wonder if she will like me. I wonder if I will be able to perform. I think for a moment, that Kathryn will know. How could I face her again? Such a string of stupid thoughts.

Wrinkles spread across her forehead like a map of suffering. Without rising from the bed, she begins to unzip her kameeze, her glass bangles tinkling on her wrists. I touch her hand to stop her. Her skin is so soft.

"What's your name?"

"Noor," she says looking at the floor. Light. Like Queen Noor. Like the Koh-e-noor diamond.

I'm sure this is not her real name, but a hopeful moniker for this dark room.

"Where are you from?"

"Here," she says without expression.

"In the city or outside the city on a farm?"

"On a farm."

"What kind of farm?"

"Apricots." Her answers are so perfunctory, I know she must be lying.

"Do you have children?"

Suddenly she looks at me, her green eyes clear. She nods. She holds up two weathered fingers.

"Boys? Girls?" I ask, trying to draw her out.

"They were boys," she practically whispers with a voice that cuts like sandpaper.

I sit down next to her on the bed. "What happened?"

"Landmines."

I wait.

"We are Afghan. The fighters came, looking for men. My husband went with them, thought maybe he could earn some money. The orchards weren't producing much because of drought that year." She holds the hem of her kameeze for comfort. "So he sent us to stay with his brother, closer to the border. My husband didn't come for months. The boys...you know boys...eight and nine years old...they wandered around the farm...trying to stay away from their uncle, he was too strict. One day they went too far, walked down a path where they shouldn't have." She raises the hem of her kameeze to cover her face, as if she were reliving the whole scene. "When my husband's brother brought their bodies back on a cart, I couldn't even see their faces...the mines..."

I place a hand on her shoulder to comfort her.

"Who designs a weapon like that? To blow up a grown man's hip? Don't they know there are children in the world? As tall as a man's hip?" She wipes her face, takes a drink of water from a cup next to the bed. "After that I left Afghanistan. What purpose would I have had there without a husband or children?"

"I'm sorry."

"Well, you didn't come here for this," she reaches again for her zipper.

"No." I reach again for her hand. "I'm sorry."

And she leans in to me. I move closer to her, so she can rest her head on my shoulder. I hold her like that, feeling her silent tears soak through my shirt until a little bell rings to indicate my time is up.

———————

Noor's story stays with me—like salt from her tears on my skin. For a week I imagine every wire I see in a car engine could trip a mine. Every time I sweep out the corners in my courtyard, I wonder whose ghosts I untrap. I cannot sleep at night, imagine I hear the ghosts knocking on my door, scratching at the walls.

Tonight, my third sleepless night, I go to my courtyard again, dark in the moonless night. I lie on the charpoy looking up at the stars, wheeling their way through the sky, dragging time with them. I imagine these ghosts, who they might have been, where they might have been going. And not only the few who may be here, but the millions, maybe billions of people, unable to continue their journey on this earth. Noor's children, my father, the people on the freeway, the Palestinians, the Jews, the Indians and Pakistanis crossing the British line of partition. The stars shine and I think of Cambodia, Yugoslavia, Rwanda, El Salvador. Which country? Which peoples? Which group has passed through history without war and atrocity? Where have people not killed and been killed in retribution? I stare at the night sky long enough to distinguish the stars from the satellites. How do we decide who should die and who should live? Don't we all live under the same heaven? These words catapult across my memory. I sit up, touch my finger where I once wore a ring. I stay here, remembering, suffering, until the fist hint of daylight reaches into the night sky.

———————

I go back to Lucky Lane the next day, pay enough money in advance so I will have several hours with Noor.

When I enter her room, she nods. "I expected you'd come again."

"Why?"

She shrugs her shoulders. "I see a lot of men, you're different. Sit."

I do as she says, don't touch her. I look around the room more carefully this time, taking in the color of the walls, originally a bright orange, now faded, stained, patched in places with plywood squares. I resist the heaviness of the walls, focus on Noor, on the light. "Can I tell you a story?"

She nods, shows me her glass-green eyes.

"You had another life before. I did too. That life ended when my father was killed. An American drone attacked a wedding. He had gone to Dargalabad for the wedding—out of loyalty to a friend."

"Where was your life before?"

"I lived in America. I had a wife…"

"A Pakistani wife?"

I shake my head. "American."

She raises her eyebrows in surprise, the lines in her forehead deepening.

"I killed that life when I took my family's revenge. I had no choice." I look away from her, notice the bare bulb hanging from the ceiling in the corner. "I had children with her. Beautiful boys. The older one was so smart, so thoughtful. The baby was just an infant."

"How long since you've seen them?"

The bulb illuminates a tattered calendar on the wall, displaying a month long past. The year displayed in both the Western calendar and the Islamic calendar. Two worlds living in parallel times, different epochs. "Almost two decades since I have seen them."

"They are still alive?"

I look back at her.

"I think so."

"What are you doing here?" She stands, grabbing at my hands to pull me up. "If they're alive, you have to go to them. Boys need their fathers. If you're lucky enough to still have your children, how dare you leave them?"

"I can't just return, though. I would be arrested."

She pauses.

"Why?"

"We…I…I was involved…with another man…in a bombing."

She sits again. "Where?"

The doors in my heart, hoarding my truth inside, yield to this woman, opening, one after another until this room in a brothel becomes a confessional, this prostitute—my confessor. And when I tell her the whole story, omitting no detail I can remember, she sits, open faced before me.

"Who are you?"

"I am Rashid Siddique."

Her eyes grow wide before narrowing skeptically. "Rashid Siddique? The man who took revenge for the drones? I heard that story. Before I was married, I heard the men say that name, they repeated any story about beating America. But Rashid Siddique is dead. How can you be here?"

I run my fingers across my forehead, feel how the years have eroded lines in my skin too. "I guess it was written for me."

"You have to go to your sons. This must be why you're still alive. What other purpose do you have?"

I think over the familiar contours of my life: the endless string of broken cars, the habit of chatting with my assistant, sitting through an occasional musical performance. What purpose do any of these things serve? What would change if I were to abandon any of them?

"I have no purpose."

"I've thought I have no purpose either," she reaches out and strokes my hand. "But today I think I've endured these years here in Peshawar just so I could meet you and tell you to go back to your family. Al-hamda'allah, you still have a family."

I shift my weight on the cot, a spring creaks, she smiles.

"I'm so glad you came to me, I'm so happy you will be reunited."

She sounds so convinced, her words so determined, as if in this tiny room, her words had pivoted the entire world, a tremendous force unleashed by a powerless woman.

"It is written?" I seek reassurance.

"It is written."

I take her hand gently in mine, raise it to my lips and kiss it. She closes her eyes. "Please," she squeezes my fingers in return, "please before you leave, be with me as if you were my husband."

I close my eyes as well, allow the moments to pass so that we might imagine; the past, the future, the things that were not, but yet still could be. And my hands float, as if recently untethered, up her arms. I feel the contour of her neck, the tender skin of her face, the warmth of her breath on my palm. And this touch enlivens me. My body takes over, moving, acting, in ways so long remembered, so long imagined, now as real as the lightness of this woman next to me.

Chapter 19

Sheikh Omar has aged well. His beard is completely grey, but he still looks fit, his eyes are still clear. As we sit on the cushions of his *majlis*, I see his middle has thickened, but he has avoided the paunch and jowls most wealthy Pakistanis display at his age.

"I wondered how long it would take for you to ask me another favor," he smiles, intrigued to see me.

"I think I'm no longer as essential to you as I once was." I run my hand over my beard. "The cars don't come as often, and the circuitry is so complex now that I can't always restore them."

He nods. "Since the Americans retreated a few years ago the conflict has shifted. Now we must contend with the simple criminals and ambitious clan leaders who try to sabotage the rare earth mines." He strokes the smooth screen of a palm-sized mobile computer. "It's a much preferable business, keeping the world addicted to their phones and networks, easier than running poppies and heroin as we did in the old days."

"And I think I've served you well, I never requested much."

"Yes, Ismail," he speaks the name ironically, "I took to thinking of you as a monk, a Sufi of engines, satisfied with a little grilled mutton and an occasional musical concert. So tell me, what favor do you ask for your service?"

"I want my freedom."

He laughs, somewhere between a disgusted snort and a response to a good dirty joke. "You've never been confined. I never kept you from leaving. I've supported you all these years as a favor, out of loyalty for your jihad."

The word reminds me of Ali, a bit of youthful jargon which never described my intention. But I will not argue the point, my objective is beyond this. "I want to be able to travel, abroad."

The Sheikh nods thoughtfully. "Where? Morocco? Europe? Maybe Australia?"

"America. I want to go..." I stumble over the word *home*. Of course the country is not my home. I want to see Kathryn and the boys, though I am no longer sure they are my family. What I really want most is to go back, the most impossible desire of all. But I cannot express this to him either. So the sentence hovers, open ended.

He exhales, leans back against the cushions, thinking. "This is much more complicated. I cannot arrange for a U.S. visa." He shakes his head to end the discussion.

I press him, "How about Mexico or Canada? I could figure out my own way across the border."

"What about this is in my interest?" the Sheikh asks. "Why would I possibly want you in America with what you know of me and my business?"

"I'm not asking for this as a business transaction, I'm asking for your help as a man, a father. My sons are grown. I would like to see them again before I die."

"You think now that your father-in-law has died, yes, I saw the *Washington Post* obituary, now you think you have the balls to go back." He shakes his head with mock sympathy. "You have grown so pathetic."

I cast my eyes down to the carpet, trace a geometric pattern in the pile with my index finger. "Sometimes," I begin politely, quietly, "a car's ignition can be triggered remotely, sometimes when the speedometer hits a certain speed, something malfunctions, something explodes." I look into his eyes, whispering as if I were revealing a confidence. "I had thought about a kind of trigger like this when I was in Los Angeles. I read a lot about them. I could easily install one."

He reaches for his tea, momentarily unsettled. "You know of course that I would know immediately if you provided any information that might compromise my situation. You know, as well as anybody, that the consequences would touch not just you, but your family," he narrows his eyes, "that American woman you married, and your sons."

"I understand."

He sits back, looks up, closing his eyes, consulting with himself. "I can get you to Spain, Guatemala maybe."

"Mexico. A flight to Mexico."

"Give me some time."

Chapter 20

The word from Sheikh Omar arrives in an envelope, unexpectedly ornate, like an invitation to a wedding. He has invited me to join him for an evening of music *Celebrating the rich cultural heritage and brilliant innovation of the master Afghan rubab player, Hamyouk Hussain and Peshawar's own Masood Zakiri on tabla.* Perhaps the invitation is a ruse, and the Sheikh intends to kill me before the evening is out. Perhaps the invitation reflects his profound understanding of what has kept me alive all these years. Regardless, the invitation is irresistible. I purchase a new kurta, elegant with zahri-work embroidery along the collar and hems. When the car comes to fetch me, I tremble, perched on the cusp of a great shift in my life. I feel as if I am preparing simultaneously for my wedding and my funeral.

I sit on the deep pile of the red carpet, the same carpet on which the musicians sit a mere ten feet from me. As they warm up their fingers and wrists on their instruments, I look around, try to distinguish individual conversations from the low rumble of voices. Someone discusses the routes of East West airlines and their frequency through Dubai, another ridicules the audacity of some small merchant family sending inquiries about his daughter's marriage plans. All conversations discretely stop, though, when the door at the end of the room opens and Sheikh Omar steps in, his arm over the shoulder of another man, who is immaculately groomed and elegantly dressed in a kurta, obviously, but diffidently tailored out of the finest cloth.

The musicians sense the change in the room, express thanks for the host's hospitality and begin to play. In all my years of listening to recordings of the music, I have seen my beloved musician only a handful of times, and never in such an intimate setting. I can hardly contain my excitement to see the plucking of the strings in the very instant the sound is created. But my delight does not, cannot last long. As I feel their eyes on me, I look up. Sheikh inclines his head to whisper into the other man's ear and nod in my direction. The man looks familiar, I try to place him. I close my eyes and feel the music. I remember him, Dawood, from a newspaper caption under a photo, the eldest son of Ibrahim Dawood, the powerful king of the underworld, the Muslim mobster who fled India and took refuge in Pakistan. This son helps him run the family's far flung businesses—hotels, drugs, shopping malls, even East West airlines—from Bangladesh to Morocco.

When the music finishes, Sheikh Omar and Dawood the younger clap politely, I look around the room again, wondering about the dozen or so men, Afghans, Pathans, Pakistanis, but do not approach any of them. And when I turn to look again at Sheikh Omar and Dawood, they are gone. The only person I really care about in the room is *Ustaad* Hussain, Master Hussain. I wait until the other men have expressed their appreciation, their hands to their hearts, nodding, flashing brief smiles. Finally I approach him, unsure what to say after two decades in a one-sided relationship. He looks up at me and I am silent, amazed simply to be looking into his eyes. What pain they must have known, what understanding of beauty they convey.

"You cannot imagine how honored I am to have been here, Ustaad."

He smiles. "The honor is mine. I am indebted to Sheikh Omar."

"Really?"

He smiles again. "My most important patron."

"Here in Peshawar or in Afghanistan?"

"Yes," he says with ambiguous finality.

334

"Can I ask you a question?" I continue before he can refuse me, "do you have any words for a man returning from exile?"

He thinks for a minute, inhales. "No words, but listen," he motions for me to sit down. He plucks a few notes from his instrument, each one seemingly a whole beautiful phrase in and of itself. And then a cascade of angry arpeggios, and long lilting notes of sadness. He looks up, eyebrows raised to see if I have understood.

"Bittersweet," I say.

"Precisely."

———————

I return to my room, my cell in exile, relieved to be alive, bewildered about the meaning of Sheikh Omar's invitation.

Zaid, my assistant, knocks. "A car has come. You need to take a look at it. Range Rover, custom stereo."

I open the door, Zaid stands as he always does, even as he continues to grow older. But today I stand differently, perhaps smaller, but leaning forward into my future. "I'm done with my service. You can repair the car, you have all my tools, you know as much as I do now."

He pulls back, stands taller. "Really? You think you can stop just like that, like turning off a light?"

The word makes me think of Noor. She said it is written that I will leave. Looking at one more car won't make a difference.

I follow Zaid, sit in the driver's seat. I turn the key in the ignition, all of the meters glow to life and the engine hums without error. He didn't mention the problem. With a sinking feeling, I imagine Sheikh Omar has sent the car, somehow booby trapped. I reach to turn off the car, notice an envelope in the compartment between the seats. A small handwritten note inside says, *The path to freedom begins beneath your feet. And the music is for you.* I turn on the stereo and hear the notes of Ustaad Hussain. I recognize the melody from the night before. I relive those magical minutes, without the anxiety of Dawood's gaze. When the music ends, I brace myself, pull up the floor mat. No wire, no trigger, no explosion. I find a passport, the cover carefully worn. Inside, the photo of a Sikh man in a turban with a dour expression gazes at me with my eyes. A small sheet of paper stuck between the pages notes a flight, East West Airlines, Karachi to Dubai to Madrid, scheduled for three weeks from today.

Chapter 21

I run my finger over the new hairs above my lip. After two and a half weeks my mustache has grown in above my beard. My Islamist identity has transformed into another Sikh identity. I unburden myself of the things I have acquired in Peshawar. The tools obviously go to Zaid. My few books I bring to a second hand bookstore. My music collection and the latest of my players I pack into a small satchel and bring to Lucky Lane. I want Noor to understand the Ustaad's message; beauty continues in exile, and eventually exile can lead to homecoming. But more importantly, I need her blessing.

She sits with her back toward the door, the room still smells of male sweat and sex. She turns, her expression of bland fatigue softens into recognition. She respectfully pulls a chunni over her hair, as if our meeting required the manners of the outside world.

I kneel before her, rest my head in her lap. "I'm returning. I need to see my sons, to face my wife." She runs her fingers through my hair. "What should I say to her?" I ask in a whisper.

"Don't say much." She traces the outline of my ear with her finger. "Listen. Tell her you have never stopped loving her. Mostly, you must ask for her forgiveness."

I inhale at the enormity of such a request, lift my head to see her eyes. "Do you think she would give it? Would you?"

She looks past me, seeing beyond this room to some distant

landscape, maybe the apricot orchard, maybe the edge of her brother-in-law's farm. After a long pause she finally speaks again. "She will ask why you waited so long. Why you didn't let her know you were alive." She looks directly at me. "What will you tell her?"

I squirm as I did when once my mother learned I had cheated on an exam. Then as now, I could offer no good answer, I could only recognize some flaw in my character, some selfishness, some weakness. "I've been ashamed, I've felt afraid. I was strong enough to plan and build a bomb, but I wasn't strong enough to face her."

"You've waited long enough. Go and be a man."

Chapter 22

I tell the taxi driver I am going to the airport. He simply nods and shifts the car into gear. For him this routine trip means nothing more than a large fare and perhaps a good tip. He does not know that the airport will launch me into a world of unknowns as dangerous as the dragons cartographers used to draw beyond the contours of the charted world. The car merges onto the street that leads to the ring road, ascending the overpass, swerving quickly to avoid a man leading a bullock cart loaded with his family and their ragged bundles of belongings. Perhaps he is in exile, perhaps he has left his home and garden, his trees and goats on the other side of the Khyber pass. For a moment I envy him the warmth of his wife and children.

Last week Sheikh Omar had called me on my assistant's phone. "Everything is arranged," he had told me. "But you will only come to know the details of each leg of the journey when you need to. Have faith," he commanded me, "and do not fear. Your fear will only arouse the suspicion of others." I close my eyes and recall a familiar melodic phrase plucked from the rubab. I hum the phrase over and over, as others would repeat a mantra.

In the airport, I struggle to understand the bewildering maze of ticketing and security. Two decades out of practice, I ask other travelers which way to go, where to stand, what documents to present.

I may have spent countless hours sitting in luxury cars, but I am less worldly than the illiterate laborers who leave this place, dreams of consumer goods and education for their children fuelling their flight.

And then I am on a plane, rising into the air. Pakistan falls away below. The air host previews the Chinese action film, the complimentary feature which will be screened on the seatback screens. And suddenly the ease of my release stuns me. Without any physical exertion, without any contrived interchanges, I am hurtling toward America. Three and a half hours ago I closed the door on my small rooms for the last time. I could have made these same actions last year or the year before, or many years before. Noor's question haunts me. Kathryn will ask why I waited so long.

―――――――

The taxi turns into a run-down neighborhood on the outskirts of Madrid where storefront signs are lettered in both Spanish and Arabic, two languages I can read but cannot decode. The driver stops in front of a small hotel, turns and speaks to me. I shake my head. He points to the piece of paper where I had written an address. Still unsure, I pay the fare and step out into the smell of fried fish and garlic, diesel and potted rose bushes.

I look for numbers on the building that would match the address in my hand. A Moroccan man, dressed in an ochre-colored *jalabeyah* walks past, answering a tinny recording of the call to prayer. Suitcase in hand, I follow him into a narrow doorway, opening into a small courtyard leading to a mosque, covered in brilliant North African mosaics. I crave the coolness of the mosque, the familiarity of the prayer. I leave my shoes in the antechamber and roll my suitcase up next to them. I wash my hands and face in the communal faucet and pray on foreign soil. Only when another man eyes me on the way out do I remember that my turban marks me as a Sikh, not a Muslim.

I check into the small hotel room and fall into a coma-like sleep. The morning brings a breeze and a new set of fears. I don't know where or when or how I will get to the next place I am going, the next increment closer to America. I sip strong coffee in the hotel café and notice a changing of the guard at the front desk. A dour old man takes over from a young man, perhaps he is the grandfather, for the day shift. Clutching my cup for some kind of false safety, I approach the old man.

"Excuse me," I ask in English, remembering the question Sheikh Omar had instructed me to ask, "do you know where I can exchange Pakistani rupees for dollars?"

The old man laughs, his face suddenly opening like a vision of Santa Claus. "No one wants the Pakistani money," he squeaks. "But maybe I have a friend who can help you with the transaction. Wait here, he will come this afternoon for his tea."

"Thank you," I say discerning a knowing twinkle in his eyes. "*Shukria*," I say in Punjabi, expressing not just polite thanks, but profound gratitude.

I wander a few blocks from the hotel taking in the strangeness of the place. The people dressed in such modern clothes, the women revealing shoulders, hair, cleavage so nonchalantly. I stare at these provocative curves as if they were magnets, the local men hardly seem to notice. Advertisements display shiny cars, sleek mobile computers, clean and beautiful people consuming all manner of alcohol. In all my memories and fantasies of America, I had omitted the brazen sexuality and consumerism of the West. Like a mole deprived of light, I have developed other senses to compensate. I have fallen in love with music, with sounds that reach the most intimate recesses of my heart. I follow the curves of the sublime, understand the seduction of memory and hope, know that riches and lusting after material things are merely strategies for crowding out loneliness. I return to my hotel bed, close my eyes, try to calm my jangled nerves.

In the afternoon a young Palestinian arrives at the hotel, dressed in athletic clothes I find ugly and cheap looking, but suspect reflect the latest fashions. The old concierge directs the young man to my table. He does not sit, or want to linger over tea. He glances every few seconds at his mobile computer sliding his thumb across its screen. "Tell me who you know," he enquires bluntly.

Stunned at his impatience, I say quietly, "Sheikh Omar."

The young man scowls, he reminds me of Ali, a restless misdirected energy brewing beneath his skin. "You cause me a lot of work. But follow me. We'll start with the hawala and the funds."

I avoid thinking too much. I allow myself to be led, directed. I sit on the back of his scooter, close enough to smell his cologne. He pulls up to a small shop selling mobile phones, prepaid calling cards, and a rainbow of frivolous phone accessories.

He speaks to the man behind the counter in a pastiche of Arabic, Spanish, and English. At some point, he looks around the shop, confirming we are the only customers and then opens his palm, motioning for me to hand him something.

When I shrug, he whispers impatiently, "Passport."

I remove the small book from my pants pocket, clutch it for a moment before allowing him to take it.

Once again on the back of his scooter, darting through cars and small lanes, he says over his shoulder, "I'll come back to the hotel in a couple of days, you'll have an Indian passport."

I return to my hotel room and resume my painfully familiar occupation—waiting.

And then I am on a plane to Buenos Aires. Another hotel, another couple of contacts, I don't bother to ask if they are Palestinian, or Algerian, Egyptian, or Lebanese. What do I care about their jihad, their revolution, the illicit ways they move people and money and weapons around the world? I have faith in their abilities.

More waiting.

Then a flight to Mexico City. I take a bus to Tijuana. Woozy with the smell of stale beer and fried corn, I am weary from the waiting. I ask my way to the hotel. As I sit on the bed watching a cockroach wander unafraid along the floorboard, the phone rings. I pick up the earpiece, hold it gingerly next to my head, as if it might hurt me. "Hello?"

"Buy a business suit, you'll travel by Mercedes and need to look like a businessman."

"When?"

"Two days." The line goes silent.

I lie back on the bed and smile, amused. I may not be comfortable with a Western suit, but a Mercedes, any Mercedes, will be like an old friend.

I check the corners of the ceiling, but no arrow points toward Mecca. What do I care? The only direction I want to know is north.

When the car arrives at my hotel two days later, my intestines are in turmoil from the water, but I am pleased to see the car bears California license plates. The driver looks me over as I sit in the passenger seat, he does not linger in the driveway. "Not the most stylish suit, but I guess it'll do." I figure he is Lebanese, maybe Syrian. "And the shoes?" he asks. I lift my foot to show him.

"White socks?"

I am silent. They are new, I bought them at the same time I bought the shoes.

"Don't you have any dark socks?"

I just shake my head. Why does he care about my socks?

"God dammit. We'll have to stop and get you some dark socks. Better be quick, it's nerve wracking enough to cross the border, but sitting here in Tijuana in a Mercedes is just asking for trouble." He swerves to pull into a small parking space. "Wait, I think I have a pair in my bag." He jumps out of the car and I see the trunk open through the rear window. He returns with a crumpled pair of black socks.

"If we're lucky they'll just wave us through at the border, but sometimes they look in and if they see something that strikes them as odd, they'll pull us over for extra scrutiny."

I cringe as I pull on his dirty socks.

He pulls the car back into the street. "You can call me Abe, short for Abdul. Show me your passport."

I pull it from my breast pocket. He holds it in his lap, glancing back and forth from the stamped pages to the cars around us. He nods, pulls a small plastic card from his own breast pocket, slides it into the passport and returns it to me. As I examine the forged green card in the passport, he talks quickly.

"We are with Calexico Equity, meeting with investors in Mexico. We have an interest in beach front real estate, and manufacturing capabilities along the border."

I hope I won't need to repeat any of this.

And before I can think about where I will go in America, we are in the queue of cars, making slow but steady progress toward the border. Abe rolls down the window and hands our documents to a fat woman with bleached blonde hair in a khaki uniform and military style boots. She runs a scanner over our documents, glances at her hand held screen and then at a monitor mounted on the gate above us. She leans in toward the car and looks at us—though not as far down as my feet in dark socks and shoes—and then into the empty back seat. Then she looks up in response to one of her colleagues. "What?" She holds up her hand, signaling for us to wait. Abe keeps his foot on the brake, his index finger taps out an almost imperceptible rhythm on the steering wheel. My breath seizes up in my lungs.

She looks back inside the car and then turns back to her colleague, "Yeah, I brought my lunch, but ice cream, that'd be good." And she hands back our documents and waves us through.

We are in.

I can only look straight ahead. America rolls out along a six-lane freeway. And so simply, I have returned to a country both familiar and foreign. I expect I should feel something, but numbness overwhelms me. I have accomplished the long journey, the series of forgeries and deceits. But just as when I returned to Pakistan after the bombing, no one will be ready to greet me, no one will open their arms with relief that I have arrived safely. As the adrenaline subsides, I realize the most difficult actions of this path are yet to come.

After a few miles, Abe exhales loudly. "So where do you want to go in San Diego?"

I look at him, surprised. "You don't have directions about where to go?"

"What do I look like? A tour guide? My instructions were to bring you into the U.S. Here we are."

"Could you just bring me to a hotel?"

"Which one?"

I shrug my shoulders.

He looks at his watch. "I have to go downtown to drop this car, I'll drop you someplace near downtown. It'll be easier for you to walk places since you don't have a car."

A sudden nostalgia for the car grips me. I don't want to leave my seat, don't want to be separated from the familiar smell of the leather and the dependable hum of the engine. Anxiety tightens my stomach just as when my parents dropped me off at a hill station boarding school for 10th standard, thinking the structure and discipline of the place would curb my problematic success winning girls' affections. My parents did not relent, even when they saw me choking back tears on the drive into the mountains. The driver does not care for my emotional state either. Unceremoniously, he leaves me standing before the automatic glass doors of a Best Western.

Chapter 23

San Diego, California.
Twenty years after the bombing

For three days I wait, tensed like a coiled spring in that hotel room. There will be no more introductions, no more men who will deliver me like some kind of dangerous package to another place. I am waiting only for myself. I need only find the directions to her home. The absurdly simple task inflates in my mind. I watch the television screen in the hotel room, trying, unsuccessfully, to lose myself in other peoples' dramas. I order a pizza, and think about turning back. But I have no one waiting for me, no transport to the border. I have not planned for a return to Pakistan.

Be a man, I tell myself. Finish this thing.

But the days pass.

The front desk calls, I must pay the bill, they do not allow guests to stay for more than a week without paying. I turn over several months' worth of wages for my week-long stay.

I brace myself to step into the hostile friendliness, the toxic cleanliness of America. I spend two hours walking to the address I have for the hawala. In a non-descript low-rise commercial strip, the shop offers both pre-paid phone plans and travel services beneath dusty posters of Dubai and Mecca.

I request the funds that have been piling up since I cancelled the postal mailings to Kathryn. "I had expected you several days ago," the hawala man says in Arabic-accented English. "I thought maybe something had happened to you."

"A whole lifetime has happened to me," I respond somberly, taking the cash in an envelope and walking back out. I stand on the corner watching the traffic, hoping for a taxi to come by. After a half hour passes, the man from the shop comes out. "Do you need something?"

"A taxi."

"Well why didn't you say so? You'll wait all day here. In America everyone has their own car." He waves me back inside while he requests a car for me.

I gaze at the Mecca poster. I never made the Hajj, never suffered through the swirl of crowds and heat to throw stones at the devil and circle the Kabba as my father and grandfather did. But this pilgrimage to my past, I remind myself, is every bit as difficult, will also align my life with God.

The car arrives, and the task I had procrastinated this last week, he accomplishes with a few words into his navigator screen. A red line on a map shows in stark clarity the final leg of my journey to Kathryn.

The red line grows shorter and shorter until he pulls into the driveway of an apartment complex. My heart sinks. The units look small, the building shabbier than what I remember of our condo together in Los Angeles.

The driver turns around. "What are you waiting for?" He points to the meter still running on his screen. "The fare will increase until you pay."

Still I sit, slowly pull out bills to pay the fare. He turns off the meter and still I sit.

"That's it, man. I've got another passenger waiting."

Then I am standing in the driveway. A bead of perspiration slides down my back. My heart pounds. Kathryn could be close enough to be in my arms within moments. I look down at my hands, the darkness of years of mechanics' work lingers in the swirled lines of my fingertips. How could these hands possibly be worthy? A car pulls past me into a parking spot. The driver, a young Latino man gets out and looks at me briefly, his eyes passing over my turban with a momentary interest, but he says nothing as he ascends the stairs and disappears down a corridor. I step toward the bank of mailboxes, consider simply leaving the bills I have picked up at the hawala and leaving before I cause more damage in Kathryn's life.

I can barely focus my eyes to read the names on the individual boxes. I nearly jump at the sound of a woman's voice. "Can I help you?"

I recognize the voice, unchanged after all these years. I turn, take in her face in a moment before averting my eyes. She has aged. Of course I knew she would, but I hadn't considered the ways the years would line her face.

"I'm just looking for a mailbox."

"I can see that," she says. "Whose mailbox are you looking for?"

"Kathryn," I pause, I want to call her by her name, I want to say Kathryn Siddique, but I catch myself. "Capen."

"That's me," a note of curiosity in her voice.

Wordlessly, I offer the envelope bearing the words, *To the Family of Rashid Siddique.*"

She sighs, does not reach to accept the envelope. "Are you the one who delivers these?"

I shake my head. "This is the first time I've come in person." I look up again, allowing myself to engage her eyes. Her pupils grow wide. Her smile of pleasant hospitality gives way to a series of expressions in quick succession, reflecting emotions I can only imagine.

"Are you Rashid Siddique?" she asks, she nearly laughs at the absurdity of her own question.

I inhale, bracing myself for the world of possibilities beyond this question. "I was."

Part Four

The Book of After

Chapter 1

San Diego, California.
Twenty years after the bombing

Kathryn's eyelids close and her knees buckle. Rashid responds instantly, reaching out for her in a gesture part embrace part rescue. Rashid had not expected Kathryn in his arms so quickly, nor had he imagined that he would hold her unconscious. For a few moments he can feel her heat, smell her perfume, follow the graceful line of her hair. When she revives she does not react, simply allows herself to be lifted to her feet, only nods as Rashid motions toward the stairs. He supports her as they walk together toward her home. Inside, he sets her on the sofa. In the kitchen he opens all the cupboards until he finds a glass, then brings her water. She watches his movements. Even in his nervous unfamiliarity, she can see the elegant strength of the man she knew. As he offers her the glass she carefully avoids his fingers, as if he might be a mirage that could vanish with the slightest provocation.

"You cannot be Rashid, he's dead, he blew himself up in a terrorist bombing."

He closes his eyes, wondering how to navigate the wasteland of wounds between them. "I didn't die in the bombing."

"I don't believe you're him." Her rational mind will not allow her to accept what she knew the moment she saw his eyes. "The Rashid I knew would never have stayed away for so long. But I didn't think the Rashid I knew would blow up a freeway either." Quietly, as if to herself, "Maybe I never knew who Rashid was." More forcefully she looks again at him, "But I don't believe *you* are Rashid Siddique."

"The hotel room where we spent our first night together was the Grace Hotel. The chunni you wore when you first met my family was a sapphire blue. When your mother came to Pakistan for our wedding, she could eat the spicy food, but hated the sweet ladoos." He recounts these intimate memories—which had sustained him during his exile—as evidence of his identity.

She holds up her hand, closes her eyes to stop the assault of details from a past she has long since buried. "Then how…why," she opens her eyes lowering her upturned palms to encompass the entire image of the man standing miraculously before her.

He sits in a chair before her, clasps and unclasps his hands. How many times had he rehearsed this explanation? He thinks of Noor's warning not to talk too much, her counsel to listen.

"You owe me an explanation, everything," Kathryn says with steely resolve.

He hesitates.

"I'm waiting." She flares her nostrils in anger.

"Let me start at the beginning, when I returned to Pakistan for my father's funeral."

She nods, prepared to listen.

"My mother was waiting for me. She had already planned that I would be the one to take revenge for his death. She couldn't live with the idea that the injustice of his death wouldn't be answered." He continued in this way, explaining his protests, his brother's challenge to his honor. When the story moved back to America, to the times when Kathryn would have figured into the story, she looks at her hands or closes her eyes. She wills herself to listen to the whole story, the whole absurd distortion he details, before she questions

352

any specific part of it. His description of Ali, the bombing, his flight and his exile are cursory, just a few sentences. He just wants to finish. Her expression is inscrutable.

"And today, I finally took the last step, I came to see you. When you saw me, I was thinking to turn back, to just leave the money and go." He falls silent, his whole story unwound.

She looks down at her hands again, running her eyes across the lines in her hands as if she were trying to read a book in a foreign language. "So why come back? Why now?"

He also looks down, sees the outline of his father's hands in his long fingers. "Because I didn't want to die in that little courtyard in Peshawar like a coward, I didn't want to die without speaking to you one more time, before I had seen my sons as men." His chin trembles, his breathing grows shallow as he realizes the alternative ending, a quiet extinguishing of his life in Peshawar, will not happen.

Kathryn rises, moves to stand in front of him. She lifts his head with a hand under his bearded chin. She brings her face close enough that he can imagine her kiss. A great sense of relief fills him, how easily they are reunited. He closes his eyes, waiting for the warmth of her lips. When he hears the crack of her palm against his cheek he is unguarded, bewildered. But when her blows come again and again, he starts to fathom her silence during his monologue was a deep gathering of rage.

"You have no idea what you've done to me," she delivers another blow, "what you've done to my sons," he turns his cheek and accepts another blow. "And now you come back because you're afraid of your own death as a lonely old man." Another blow. "Some kind of withered terrorist."

He raises his arms to protect his face, so she directs her anger at his chest, pummeling against the cloth of his occupied shirt as she did so long ago against his empty shirts.

"You son of a bitch. You're still dead to me," she gasps, choking back tears, "and the woman who was your wife, that Kathryn, you killed her too when that bomb exploded on the freeway!"

He has no words to respond to her force. He stands, backs toward the door. He steps outside, but holds her gaze. "I still want to see our sons. I'll come back when…when you've had some time."

He closes the door behind him, hears her bang her fists against the inside of the door. "They're not your sons," she screams.

She resists the impulse to open the door and continue her invective.

Both alone now, on either side of the door, they each carry the image, the undeniable reality of the other with them.

She walks to the kitchen for water, to the bathroom to use the toilet. Back and forth through the rooms she walks, not knowing what to do next, what to think, what to fear.

He walks down the stairs and out to the street, not recognizing anything around him from what he had seen on the way in. He walks for nearly a mile before reaching a restaurant where he asks a waitress to request a car. Despite the welts he can feel burning on his cheeks, he feels a glimmer of calm. He has done it.

Chapter 2

Kathryn watches the sun set over the ocean, a second glass of scotch in her hand. She thinks back over a thousand moments, a thousand events that would have been easier with a husband, with a father for her children. She tries to square her memories of the weeks between her father-in-law's death and the freeway bombing, with what Rashid told her today. She has barricaded that time so angrily, that she shakes at the effort required to reach those memories. As the earth swallows the last of the day's light she walks through the darkness of her bedroom into the closet. She turns on the light and reaches into the back of a shelf for a manila envelope. The return address displays the name of the journal where she used to work. They had sent her some of the personal papers from her desk when they finally terminated her employment. She had never bothered to open it, so she pulls at the seal grown brittle from age. Inside, a copy of her university diploma, a photo of her drinking tea with a group of influential Gulf Arab men, a few printouts of personal emails and a few photos. The faces of her sons—Andrew almost unrecognizable as an infant—peer at her from the past. At the bottom of the pile, the photo she thought she might find; an image of Kathryn and Rashid, a man and a woman who no longer exist, arm in arm, smiling and sweaty, pausing mid-dance in a nightclub in Dubai.

Did they really look like that? Who would that woman be now if not for the bombing? Who would that man be if not for the drone attack? She picks up the photos of the boys again. Who would they be if they had not been abandoned? What kind of men would they be now if they had been raised by both their parents, if they had had a man in the house? She thinks of Rashid's parents, imagines his mother demanding Rashid take revenge. What kind of woman does that? What kind of woman condemns her own son for the sake of her honor? No, she thinks, better the boys were raised without that kind of poisonous culture. Whatever could have been doesn't matter now. But how dare he deceive her all these years, as if those weeks before the bombing were not deception enough?

She throws the photos. They flutter with an infuriating grace. She bangs her fist into the wall only to recoil at the pain in her knuckles. "God damn you!" she screams at the man who is once again absent. She goes to the kitchen and retrieves all of the glass bottles she can find and one by one throws them into the bathtub, listening with satisfaction to the shattering crash they make as the glass hits the porcelain. She wishes Rashid would come back so she could direct her anger again at its source. With the bottles exhausted, she storms back to the kitchen, makes fists, looks for something that will assuage the wave of emotions she cannot contain. She pours herself another glass of scotch and throws it back in a single gulp. The alcohol burns. She sits on the couch, as the world seems to tilt. She reaches for the phone and calls Michael.

"Mom?" he answers, "it's late. Are you all right?"

"No. I'm not all right," she says.

He hears her as if from a great distance. "Mom, what is it? Are you sick? Do you have a fever?"

"No…something terrible has happened."

"What? What is it? Should I call 911?" When she doesn't answer he speaks urgently, "I'm coming, stay there, stay on the line with me…OK…OK?"

"OK," she finally says closing her eyes.

Michael rushes to his car, the phone still to his ear. Every few minutes, as he speeds toward her, he asks her if she is still there.

She responds with a word or two. He does not turn off the phone even as he bounds up the stairs to her door, to the place where he spent so many years with her as the man of the house. He uses his key to open the door, calls into the darkness of the room. He hears her call his name from the direction of the couch. He turns on a lamp beside her, touches her forehead, sits down and holds her hands. "What is it?"

She opens her eyes, smiles weakly at the sight of her son, now almost as old as Rashid was in the photo on the bedroom floor. "He's such a bastard," she says shaking her head.

"Who?" Her words catch Michael off guard.

"Your father."

"You finally want to talk about what happened?" He had wondered if she would ever breach this taboo.

"No. After everything, after all these years, he wants to see you boys."

He cannot make sense of her words, smells the alcohol on her breath. "Did you dream about him?"

She opens her eyes, sits up and looks squarely at Michael. "It was no dream, Rashid Siddique is alive. He came to see me today."

"What? Why didn't you tell me he's alive?"

"I didn't know." She opens her mouth to speak, uncertain where to start. When the words don't come she asks Michael for a glass of water. He goes to the kitchen, returns to find her head slumped on the back of the couch, her eyes closed. He touches her shoulder to rouse her, hands her the water.

"Where's he been all this time?" he asks.

She closes her eyes, raises her eyebrows as if they will help her articulate her thoughts. "In Pakistan, living underground with a different name." She retells some of what Rashid told her today. She closes her eyes again, not wanting to see the pain this will cause Michael.

"So where is he now? When can I see him?"

This reaction surprises her, she sits up, suddenly alert. "Why would you want to see him?"

"What do you mean? He's my father."

357

"He's a terrorist."

"And you're his wife."

Before she can stop herself, she slaps her son. After so many years of fighting this identity, of reconstructing her life to avoid being the terrorist's wife, to protect her children from the reality of their father's actions, she cannot tolerate her own son forcing this identity upon her.

He stands up, backs away from her, stunned. "That was uncalled for. I didn't do any of this to you."

She starts to cry, holds out her hand to him. "I'm sorry. Sit down. I don't know what to think, what to do before he comes here again."

"He'll come again? When?"

"I don't know, he just said he would come again."

"We need to call Andrew. We all need to be together."

"No," she says fiercely. "He doesn't know anything."

"You can't keep this from him. Rashid's his father too."

"Some father."

"Andrew can judge Rashid however he chooses, but you at least have to give him the opportunity."

From the freeway they can hear the scream of an emergency vehicle, and then the night is quiet again.

She sighs, closes her eyes. "Call him in the morning, it's too late now. I just want to sleep." She looks up, feels only her own weakness. "Will you stay on the couch?"

"Of course."

Kathryn wakes, walks to the bathroom, opens the medicine cabinet for aspirin. She blinks through a residual alcohol fog. In the bathroom she notices the bathtub is clean, not a single shard of broken glass. Perhaps she only imagined the encounter with Rashid the day before. Perhaps she has only awoken from a nightmare and the sunlight will shine on her life just as it did the previous morning. But in the kitchen she sees Andrew already sitting with

Michael. He stands to kiss her.

"Hi, Mom. What's going on? Michael told me it was an emergency."

"More like a disaster. Michael hasn't told you anything?"

Andrew shakes his head. "What's wrong, are you sick?"

"Is there coffee?"

Michael pours her a cup, adding milk and sugar as he knows she likes it.

"Michael, can you explain this to Andrew? I don't have the strength to tell the whole story."

Michael exhales, puffing out his cheeks at the enormity of the story. "You remember my commencement speech? About the different systems of justice?"

Andrew nods.

"Well the idea of a man from another culture obligated to take revenge for some injustice done to his family, that wasn't…um… that's much closer to our lives than you think. Sometimes a man does something because he has no choice, because his culture demands it, they don't have better systems."

"Michael, spare me the moral lecture, what's happening here?"

Michael tries another tack. "Andrew, our father did a terrible thing when you were just a baby. He didn't die in an accident, we thought he was killed in a bombing in Los Angeles that he had planned. A revenge attack, after his own father was killed by an American drone attack in Pakistan."

Andrew's brow furrows. "Mom, is this true?" She doesn't look up from her coffee cup. "Why are you telling me this now?"

"Michael's telling you the truth. But what I found out yesterday…someone came to see me…your father isn't dead…he was here yesterday."

"What the hell? Why don't I know anything about any of this? I always thought our father was Greek." Anxiously, he squeezes one of his thumbs. "Mom, you lied about this all these years? You broke your precious little code of conduct to me, of all people? 'Tell the truth' you always harped. What's the truth here?"

"I didn't lie," Kathryn says, almost a whisper. "I protected you by telling you nothing. Whatever you heard about your father when you were children, I'm sure Michael told you, not me."

"All right Mr. Storyteller, you better tell me the whole story now. How long have you been lying to me too?"

"Don't twist this, it's not all about you." Michael looks at their mother protectively. "I haven't lied to you either. I found out all of this on my own in law school, I went looking, did some research."

"And you found…?"

"And I found we are the heirs to a very ugly legacy. Mom tried to shield us, but the truth always comes out." Michael takes a gulp of coffee. "It's probably best if I start back when Mom was working in the Middle East."

"Mom, you worked in the Middle East?"

She nods, "A long time ago, before you were born."

And Michael continues the story. The facts Kathryn recognizes. The nuances, the inferences however, seem foreign to her. So invested she has become in protecting herself and her boys with an alternative version of the story, that she can hardly understand the possibility of another perspective. Eventually Michael's story leads to the present. Silently, he places his open palm over the top of the coffee cup, a gesture of finality.

"Oh my God." Andrew runs his fingers through his thick wavy dark hair. "What do I say to all this? You two, my family, now you feel like strangers with all this deception. And some stranger shows up claiming to be my father and wants to know me." He pushes his chair back, stands up. "No thank you, I don't want any of this. You can work out the drama without me."

"Andrew!" Michael scolds. "We need to see him, he's our father."

"I never had a father."

"Mom, don't you think we have an obligation?"

"An obligation?" Andrew snorts. "Since when do you owe him anything?"

Michael begins to answer, but a knock on the door interrupts him. He and Michael both look at their mother, unspeaking. The knock comes again. Kathryn stands up and calls out, "Just a minute."

She steps into the bedroom to change out of her bathrobe. When she comes out again, dressed in dark pants and a sweater, Andrew is sitting next to his brother, hands clasped, knuckles white. Kathryn nods at her sons and calls through the door, "Hello?"

"Hello. May I come in?" a man's voice replies.

She inhales deeply and opens the door. Rashid, bearded, with dark circles under his eyes, appears darker skinned than she remembered.

Andrew unclasps his hands, presses them into his thighs, wishing he had already left, but unable to turn away from this strange looking man.

Kathryn steps aside to allow him to enter.

Michael speaks first. "I'm Michael." He stands, holds out his hand. "You must be Rashid Siddique."

The father reaches out for his son's hand, holds the warmth of his own flesh and blood as a stranger. Rashid wishes he could pull this man close, embrace the little boy, now grown.

Into the pregnant silence, Michael speaks, "And this is my brother Andrew."

Reluctantly, Andrew stands up and puts out his hand, forcing Rashid to move toward him. "Masha'allah. My God, you are such a man."

"That's what happens in twenty years," Andrew says caustically.

After another awkward pause, Rashid tries to be gracious. "Can I take you all out for tea, maybe somewhere we could sit and talk?"

"Not outside," Kathryn says. "I will make you a cup of coffee if you want. We'll sit here."

"Yes, please. I would appreciate it."

The father and his unfamiliar sons sit down around the table. Kathryn brings the husband a cup of black coffee, remembering how he preferred his drinks sweet and milky. She waits to see his grimace, wonders if he will have the nerve to ask for sugar. He only nods in thanks.

"I knew you two in another lifetime, past," he says, the English feeling foreign and clumsy on his tongue. "I don't know you now. Can you tell me what you're doing?"

Andrew looks at his mother and his brother for guidance.

Kathryn speaks for them. "Andrew is studying clean tech at San Diego State University. Michael has studied law and has just passed the bar exam. He's working for the American Civil Liberties Union."

"Do you both live here with your mother?"

"Not anymore," Michael says. "I have an apartment near downtown, and Andrew lives on campus in student housing."

Rashid takes another sip of bitter coffee and tries to conjure up the next question.

Andrew grips the edge of the table, "What do you want from us? I didn't know anything about you until this morning, and now I know only that you've done horrible things not only to us, but you have killed people because of what my brother here calls your... how did you say it...your 'primitive belief in an alternative system of justice'." He straightens his arms, forcing his torso as far away as possible from the table without letting go. "So let's skip the small talk and tell us what you came here for."

"Andrew," Michael hisses, "you don't need to be so rude."

"Really?" Andrew scoffs. "This guy blows up people and then abandons his family for twenty years and you're worried about my manners?"

"Look, I remember him from before. I haven't seen him since I was in kindergarten. I have some questions."

Rashid nods. "Ask. I'll answer every question."

"How did you feel when the bomb went off? Were you satisfied?"

Rashid raises his eyebrows until they nearly disappear under his turban. He pauses, thinking. "I felt terrified. I had wanted to alert the authorities about the plan before it happened."

"But you didn't," Michael says.

"So once I realized I couldn't stop the bombing, I realized this was my fate and I had fulfilled something...something important to my mother, my family in Lahore." He runs his hand over his beard. "Imagine how would you be feeling if your father were killed."

"Um, we didn't have a father, remember?" Andrew says with thick sarcasm. "And if I had known our father was you, I would've been glad if he was killed."

Rashid purses his lips together. "Then imagine if your mother had been killed. The woman who did everything to raise you."

Andrew looks at his mother, sees so clearly how she has aged. She avoids eye contact with all of them. He reaches out to touch her hand. "I would feel terrible, angry, sad, of course." He holds her hand now, tightly. "But I wouldn't go out and build a bomb and sacrifice my wife and children for some stupid sense of grief."

"So you never knew anything about me?" Rashid looks at Kathryn. "You never told them anything about the attack in Pakistan? Anything about who I was?"

She only shakes her head.

He buries his face in his hands, horrified. "Maybe you cannot ever understand," he looks up, "especially you boys. Your world is so different from mine." He halts, resting one hand on top of the other. "Do you have another question?"

"What do you think should happen to you now?" Michael asks, as if he had long ago prepared a set of questions.

Rashid closes his eyes again. For all of his dreaming about this reunion, his preparations now seem woefully inadequate. "What should happen? I'm not sure. What could happen? I could get to know you, see you in your lives as adults. Help your mother, if she will allow me."

"It's a little late now, don't you think?" Andrew says. "I think she did just fine without you."

Michael moves his coffee cup to the side, as if to clear the way to his father. "Really? You don't think that you deserve any punishment? You aren't worried about law enforcement?"

"I've worried about law enforcement for twenty years. But now that I've seen you all, I won't fear them anymore."

"Why won't you answer my question?" Andrew almost whines. "What do you want from us?"

Rashid looks each of them in the eye in turn. "I just wanted to see you again, and—" his stomach turns as it did the first time he saw the bombing on the monitor in the airport "—and I want to say I'm sorry, to ask your forgiveness."

"What? On what grounds?" Kathryn erupts. "We should just forgive you because you come waltzing in here and ask for it?" She stands up. "Get out of here. Leave us," she says with a deep, quiet voice. "You've done enough damage. I don't want you here, threatening everything I've worked so hard to build after you abandoned us."

"Mom," Michael interjects. "We're not done."

She turns to him, asserting her authority. "I'm done and this is my home."

"Capen Code, rule number nine," Andrew whispers to Michael. "Be polite to your host."

Rashid sits paralyzed by his fear of the abyss beyond her door.

"What are you waiting for? You need to go!" she thunders

"Please," his voice constricts, "let me talk with the boys a bit longer."

Unnerved that Michael's expression nearly mimics Rashid's, Kathryn relents for her son's sake. "You have five minutes. I'm going in the other room, and when I come out you need to be gone." She turns and walks into the bedroom, slamming the door behind her. Rashid fixes his gaze on her half-empty coffee cup.

"You can't imagine how painful it was to be away from you, how many times I've thought of you, imagined your lives." He tugs nervously on his beard. "I was always sending my love." He looks up at his sons.

"How?" Andrew asks. "By carrier pigeon?"

"I sent my prayers every night, and I sent money, four times a year."

"Useless. We didn't get either," Andrew replies flatly.

"How long will you be here?" Michael asks.

"Only some minutes I think."

"No, I mean how long will you be in the U.S.?"

"I want to see you both again, I would be glad for more time to know you."

Michael raises his eyebrows, "The longer you're here, the more likely you'll be arrested and tried. You know there's no statue of limitations on acts of terrorism."

Rashid nods in acknowledgment.

Andrew sits mutely, his arms crossed. Michael pulls his wallet from his back pocket and retrieves his business card, handing it to Rashid. "I don't want to aggravate my mother, you should go now."

Rashid stands to go, turns to look again at Andrew who sits impassively. Michael moves to hold the door open. Rashid clutches the business card in his left hand, the only hope preventing his fall into nothingness. He reaches with his right hand to shake Michael's hand again. "Thank you," the words conveying an insufficient, thin politeness to his ears. "Shukria," he reverts to the Punjabi word to express his indebted gratitude.

In the bedroom, Kathryn hears the door open and shut, closes her eyes, and weeps.

Chapter 3

The hostess tells him to sit anywhere. Rashid surveys the restaurant, everything clean and bright, popular music piping through speakers. He chooses a booth in the corner, as far from the door as possible, but with a clear sight line. He sits, stares blankly at the plastic stand on the table advertising a new breakfast dish. Why is America constantly reinventing everything? Even breakfast. A waitress comes with a coffee pot and mug in hand. "Coffee?"

"Tea please."

She frowns and turns around.

Sitting on the smooth vinyl seat, his insides feel ragged, his thoughts blunted. He can accept, even understand if Kathryn rejects him. But if his sons will not see him, his whole life will have been a waste of waiting, he may as well have blown himself up with that bomb. At least then he would have died knowing he was loved. The waitress brings his tea and a menu and still no one arrives. Rashid checks the front of the laminated menu to be sure the name of the restaurant is the one Michael had told him on the phone last night. He pours cream and four packets of sugar into the tea, hoping for a familiar pleasure. He can barely drink the excessive sweetness.

A television perched above the cashier's stand projects a series of silent video clips and a scrolling newsfeed; replays of last night's American football game, then planes taking off from an aircraft carrier. Perhaps this is part of the U.S. Navy build up in the East China Sea, or in the Indian Ocean. The superpowers continue to tour their deadly dance in theaters around the globe. He shudders.

Michael finally appears at the table. Rashid stands quickly, aching to reach out and embrace his son. Michael politely shakes his hand, as if they had met to discuss business.

"You are good to come today."

"I still have more questions," Michael has not come for Rashid's pleasure.

Rashid nods. "Tea first?"

Michael shrugs, allows Rashid to signal the waitress for a second cup.

"Who else knows you're here?" Michael asks.

"No one. An acquaintance in Pakistan knew I was coming only, but we aren't in touch."

"Where are you staying?"

"At a hotel downtown."

"Which one?"

"Why do you want to know?" Would his son turn him in to the authorities?

"Yeah, maybe it's better if I don't know. All right, so how did you do it, I mean how did you manage to live in secret for all this time?"

"I made a small life for myself, a small salary working as a mechanic, and I saw very few people. I had protection from a man…a man with some influence."

"Did people know your name, know who you were?"

Rashid shakes his head.

The waitress arrives with Michael's tea. "What can I get for you?"

Michael orders the hot breakfast dish advertised on the table.

"Two please," Rashid grasps for some commonality.

Michael pauses, running his hands through his hair. Rashid, attentive to Michael's every nuance, recognizes the mannerism as Kathryn's. But his features, his coloring, his build clearly reflect Rashid.

"What would you do if my mother called the police?"

"Is she planning to?"

"Let me tell you something about my mother. She's not like

you. I can't even believe she ever married you. She doesn't like foreigners, doesn't like unknown or unexpected things. She just tried to be normal, an American, a hardworking single mom. She never said a word about you."

"And you didn't ask?"

Michael shakes his head, marveling at what this man doesn't understand. "Imagine me, a five-year old kid. I see my mom almost disappear before my very eyes, she doesn't get out of bed, she doesn't laugh, she doesn't even look like the mom I was used to. I have some idea that she's sick because my dad died. When she starts to get better, the last thing I want to do is remind her of the thing that hurts her."

Two huge plates arrive, piled with eggs and potatoes, onions and peppers. Rashid looks up, the television projects images of a happy grey-haired couple walking on a beach, sitting at a restaurant, strolling in a park—an ad for financial services. If he had stayed, could their life have been like that?

"Do you think I could ease some of her suffering?" Rashid asks.

"Do you really imagine that she wants to see you now? You can't change anything that happened, you can't make any of her past easier for her now. She's struggled to be happy. Her sons are making her proud, she has money for retirement, she has Johannes for company, what would you think you could do?" Michael takes a bite of his breakfast, looks down as Rashid flinches.

"Who's Johannes?" Rashid asks, jealousy unexpectedly flaring his nostrils.

"Her friend. Not sure the nature of their relationship, not my place to ask."

"Do they live together?"

"No. Somehow we agreed I was the man of the house. I don't think I would have liked someone else coming in and taking my mother's attention away from Andrew and me."

Rashid observes his son before him, clean shaven, well dressed in a button down shirt and jeans, handsome and poised. How long did it take? How soon after he left did the kindergartner turn into the man of the house?

"You seem to have done a good job. I knew Kathryn would be strong, but you...I didn't expect...I see you and she didn't need me."

"Oh, we needed plenty for sure. Andrew didn't remember ever having a father, and what did I know about being a father? But Mom always taught us not to dwell on what we didn't have. We had each other and we had Uncle Ted and his family." He takes a sip of his tea. "We still do."

"Do you think..." a ringing sound interrupts Rashid's question. Michael reaches for his pocket, looks at the screen and then gestures for Rashid to be quiet. "Hi Mom...I'm just getting breakfast...yes, I can come by. I'll be there in about a half hour...I love you too."

He sets the phone down. Rashid stares at it. How close she is now, the real woman, still living and breathing. And loving. He doubts he will ever again feel her love directed toward him. Michael eats quickly. "I have to go. You understand."

"Of course. Will I see you again? Do you have more questions?"

Michael puts down his fork, takes a deep breath. "Give me some time. Call me in a couple of days. I'm not sure what the purpose would be for us to meet again."

Rashid closes his eyes and bows his head. "I will." When he looks up Michael is already at the cashier stand, paying the bill. The television displays another commercial, a father and son riding bicycles along a tree-lined path. Rashid looks away.

Chapter 4

Rashid nearly jumps at the knock on her door.

Kathryn motions for him to relax, to stand down, as if he were a frightened animal in her home. "It's Michael," her tone sharpens, "my son."

The words sting, reinforcing the violence she has done to his memory. As she opens the door, Rashid stands again, slowly. Michael greets her. Though still handsome, he looks different than he did a few days ago at breakfast, his eyes darkly circled, his face now shadowed with stubble.

"Rashid," Michael acknowledges him.

"Michael," his father replies in kind, "thank you for agreeing to see me."

Kathryn stands between them, barely comprehending how they could be connected. "I'll get us water."

"Please," Rashid says meekly.

The two men sit in Kathryn's living room, facing each other, not talking, listening to the sound of glasses on the counter, water rushing from the faucet. When Kathryn returns she serves her son first, placing a protective hand on his shoulder. She sets the other glass in front of Rashid on the table.

He feels untouchable.

"Andrew?" he asks quietly.

"Andrew's not coming," Kathryn says. "He told me he wants nothing more to do with you." A desperate chuckle escapes from the tightness in her chest. "What the hell do you expect us to say?"

He presses his lips tightly together. "Nothing. I don't expect you to say anything." He sips from the glass and sets it back down.

Michael holds his mother's hand.

Rashid inhales. "I have come tonight to tell you I won't bother you again. I was foolish to dream I could possibly return to you, that you would allow me back into your lives." He looks at Michael, holds out his hands. "He is such a man, such a very good man, Kathryn. I will be grateful to you all my life that you've raised this son…our son…into this man."

"By myself," she jabs again at his wound.

"Yes, I imagined I was helping with the money I sent."

Kathryn flinches at the memory of those envelopes, sits down on the arm of Michael's chair.

Rashid runs a hand over his clean-shaven face. He has taken off his turban, removed his beard. He no longer needs to hide behind some other identity. He feels exposed, wonders how to start with what he knows he has to say. "I learned to live only in my imagination." He looks from Kathryn to Michael and back again. "For twenty years I imagined reuniting with you, with all three of you, and continuing our lives. I prayed for your safety. I believed God would protect you, would compensate you somehow for your suffering." He presses his hands into his thighs, rests them uneasily on his knees. "But this was not your reality." He resists the impulse to accuse her of murdering his memory, never speaking of him to their sons. "I understand now that I held on to this impossible fantasy for my survival. Not for yours."

She lets go of a deep sigh, closing her eyes against the sight of him, whatever attractive appearance he had once possessed, ground away by the intervening years.

"So after I leave here tonight, tomorrow morning, I'll go to the authorities. I will allow them to decide my fate." He looks out the window into the darkness, unable to bear the distance separating him from these people he loves just a few feet from him. "This world has nothing left for me."

"Don't expect me to feel sorry for your suffering." She shakes her head. "You've brought this on yourself, and now after all these years, you come back like some ghost to haunt our waking lives. Please go."

"What?" Michael blurts out.

Rashid and Kathryn turn, surprised to see Michael leaning forward.

"How can you think that would be acceptable to me?" he demands indignantly. "How can you think that after abandoning us, after all that you've put my mother through, after all the experiences you denied me and my brother, that you can just appear, like you came out of thin air and then abandon us once again?"

Rashid looks helplessly, "What do you want from me?"

Michael utters an incredulous sound, almost a laugh. "What do I want from you? At least some time to let me decide." He stands up, looks down on his father. "I don't know who you are. You might be a monster. You might be some kind of misguided militant, or a victim of some backward tradition. But for some reason my mother married you, at some point you were here with us." He grimaces, resisting the tears shining in his eyes. "I remember who you were. I was a little boy who had a father. And then I was a little boy who didn't. And as if that weren't hard enough to comprehend, for twenty years I was not allowed to admit any of those memories, to anyone." He paces away from his chair. "You may have been underground in fucking Pakistan, but my childhood, my memories have been underground too, afraid of the wrath of her suffering."

Kathryn looks at Michael, cut by his words.

"Sorry Mom, I don't blame you, but you weren't the only one he left." He steps closer to Rashid, towering over him. "So at the very least, you owe me some time to decide for myself about whether or not I want you in my life."

Silence hangs in the room.

She speaks first. "Michael, he can't stay." She turns to Rashid, "You can't stay. Forget the emotions for a minute, he's a fugitive," she raises her shoulders at the obvious fact. "Every minute he's with us, we risk our own innocence. Michael, you should understand the legal implications better than I do."

Michael sits again, now on the arm of the sofa, just a cushion away from Rashid. "Are you still an American citizen?"

"I don't know. I don't have an American passport. I'm traveling on a green card."

"A legitimate one?"

"No," Rashid averts his eyes with the admission.

Michael pauses, thinking. "Well, you were once a U.S. citizen so you have rights to due process under the law and to legal representation."

"For what? I will admit my guilt, why would I need represen-tation for that?"

Michael holds his hand to his forehead, closes his eyes in frustration, then speaks with forced patience, "Because your sentencing could still be negotiated." When Rashid doesn't respond, Michael says very delib-erately, "You could avoid the death penalty or solitary confinement."

Rashid smiles ruefully. "I've already endured both. I'm not afraid of those things."

"But *I* am."

Rashid blinks with surprise. "So what should I do?"

"You will not go alone," Michael commands. "Tomorrow, I'll go with you. I'll provide you legal representation."

"No Michael," Kathryn gasps.

"Mom, I'm a grown man. This isn't your decision."

She flinches at his defiance, the independence she has always instilled in him.

"You will wait tomorrow, until I come for you. All right?"

"You're sure you want to do this?" Rashid looks up into the eyes of his son, sees the reflection of the little boy, wonders at the mystery of how he has become this man.

"I'm sure." Michael does not soften. "You have to commit to me that you won't talk to anyone from the government without me present."

"You have my word."

Michael holds out his hand to confirm the agreement. Rashid hesitates then grasps Michael's hand, pulling tightly, and then he feels the arms of his son around him. Something inside him cleaves, allowing all the years of waiting, all the guilt and fantasy and self denial to swirl into the whirlpool of the past and his horizon fills from pole to pole with the strength of his son's exquisitely paternal embrace.

The sight of these two men causes Kathryn to catch her breath. She feels the years without affection, without her complement. Would she recognize those arms again?

"Michael, you should go home and get some sleep," she speaks as they separate from each other.

He nods to Kathryn, again the obedient son. At the door, he glances at Rashid and then at his mother. "Are you sure you want me to leave you," he hesitates, "alone?"

"I'm OK," she reassures him.

Rashid stands near the door, unsure what to say next, expecting her to ask him to leave.

Kathryn turns back to him. She looks at his hands, avoiding his face. "If you're going to give it all up tomorrow, this could be your last night of freedom."

"Or my last night of exile."

"All of a sudden, I…how do I say this? I have so much to say to you. So much anger, I thought I just wanted you to disappear again so I wouldn't have to deal with you. But now that I know I'll lose you again…"

He allows the silence to linger before speaking. "What can I say to you? What can I give you? Anything I have the power to do."

She covers her face with her hands, drawing inward, vulnerable. Slowly, he reaches out one hand to touch her arm, then the other until their arms form a circuit, an energy flowing back and forth between them. In the space between them, the void, the absence and longing lingers. But she allows him to reach across, to make his way to her. In the hesitation she crumbles, her cheek rests against his chest, the heart inside beating furiously. And his arms are around her. He braces for the end of this moment, savoring her life next to his. Then, directed by a will she cannot control, she presses her palm into the small of his back, holds him to her, wishing she could stay like this, wishing the time before and the time yet to come would fall away, leaving only this feeling of connection.

Rashid speaks the words that threaten to burst through his chest. "I'm sorry."

"For what?"

"For so many things, I don't have enough words to say them."

Chapter 5

Two days later

The phone rings, waking Kathryn from a pleasant dream. In the moment before she remembers that everything has changed, again, she answers the phone.

"Hello?"

"Hello, is this Kathryn Capen?"

"It is."

"This is George Dalrymple, I'm a reporter with the *New York Times*. I'd like to ask you a few questions about your son and his client, Rashid Siddique."

She is suddenly wide awake. "What?" She looks at the clock, 6am. "What do you know about my son?"

"The Department of Justice has released a statement that Michael Capen is representing his father, Rashid Siddique, in a hearing to determine sentencing for the 2010 double freeway bombing."

She pauses, allowing the reality to settle. "I have no comment."

"Are you sure? This will be a big story, if you don't speak for yourself, others will likely write their own interpretations of your position. Likely it won't be pretty. They'll probably speculate that you had some knowledge of Rashid's exile, perhaps you even helped him."

His aggressiveness irritates her. "I will excuse your bad manners.

And again, I have no comment." She hangs up. She wants to go back to sleep, but knows this call will be followed by others. Her mind lurches to Andrew. She calls him. Her heart sinks when he answers not from the fog of sleep, but with an anxious alertness. "They've called you?"

"Yes. What am I supposed to say?" He sounds like a little boy.

"Nothing."

"I mean really, Mom, a week ago, I was just some guy going to school, seeing a girl. I was normal. And now, I suddenly learn my dad is a terrorist, my brother is a sympathizer, and my mother has been lying to me my whole life. I mean...what the fuck am I supposed to tell the reporters?"

She pushes back the sheets to get out of bed, a few black hairs still on the pillow. She cringes at another truth she has refrained from telling either of her sons. "You don't tell the reporters anything. Don't even answer their calls." She goes to the window, looks out to the ocean, an indistinguishable grey under the morning clouds.

"And then what? I just go back to my classes like nothing has happened?"

She sees a van pull off the street and into the driveway of her complex. The news television station call letters and the satellite mast provoke a maternal instinct. "Andrew, listen to me, I think you should pack a few things, it'd be easier if we weren't here for a little while."

"Pack? And go where? What about my classes?"

"Grandma's house has a long driveway and a gate, we can be buffered there."

"Mom, you're not exactly sounding rational here. I'm not running to Grandma like I did something wrong. I'm just doing my thing and my whole family is going ape shit around me. If I'm going anywhere, it's over to my girlfriend's place, at least Hema is who she says she is."

"I really think it'd be better if we were there together, you and me with Grandma."

He lets out a snort. "Better for who? I think you've lost the

right to claim you have any idea of what's best for me." Silence.
He disconnects.

Chapter 6

Kathryn's mother makes her a cup of coffee, adds the milk and sugar in the proper proportions. Even before Kathryn had moved her suitcase in past the door, her mother had set her to peeling potatoes for the evening's stew.

"Life is predictably unpredictable, my dear," her mother says. "That shouldn't surprise you."

Kathryn takes a sip of coffee. "But I'm too old for this kind of upheaval, I've worked too long to order my world and raise my boys."

Her mother lets out a little chirpy laugh. "And I'm not too old to adjust to losing my husband? I'm not too old to give refuge to my daughter?" She points at the bowl of brown-skinned potatoes, "Don't forget to cut out the eyes. Life never guarantees you anything, never owes you anything."

"Maybe life doesn't, but I would think Andrew owes me something. Maybe I should call him for a videochat. Can I call him from your number?"

"As you like, but you know I don't bother with the video. Except for the boys, everyone looks better in my imagination anyway." She chops a tough carrot into bite-sized pieces. "And what would you tell him? How would you convince a smart young man, who still believes in his own immortality, that you were right, that you know better than him?"

Kathryn stops peeling. "Did I make a mistake? Did I do the wrong thing by not telling him anything about his father?"

The older woman doesn't hesitate at the chopping block. "Maybe. Maybe you made a mistake in marrying Rashid. Or maybe I made a mistake in letting you go to Dubai. Or maybe we all made a mistake in electing the wrong government." She reaches into the refrigerator for an onion. "But so what if we did make those mistakes? There's nothing to do about it now. My life these days is about one day at a time, things are what they are. I no longer hope to change the world or to be right. Mostly I'm sure to enjoy the beauty that comes into my life, to be kind to everyone, to understand that everyone around me is fragile with fear and anxious for love."

Kathryn sighs, trying not to show her irritation. "So what should I do about Andrew?"

"Just be patient. He has to process in his own way. And peel some garlic."

Despite the updated furniture, her childhood bedroom seems somehow frozen in time. She remembers looking out the window at the redwoods and the roses her mother tried to coax from under their shadows, and she remembers dreaming of exotic places. She had not yet known the names of Karachi or Shanghai, Marrakesh or Bangladesh, but she had wanted her world to be bigger, more exciting than the suburban landscape of her friends and their school. She had not yet understood the unpredictable and dangerous territory she had carried within her own heart. Perhaps she would have been safer, happier if she had stayed put, married a local boy, or a college classmate. Her mother annually amassed a stack of Christmas cards from friends whose children had raised their families close to home, with updates of winter ski vacations, and spring trips to Mexico. Why had she thought she should have something more, as if their comfortable contentment was somehow provincial and narrow? What good had her adventures brought to her, or her family, or anyone? Only suffering.

She pulls back the covers on the single bed, slides in between the cold sheets and waits for the sleeping pill her mother gave her to take effect.

———————

Kathryn and her mother sit down with their dinner in front of the screen, as they have for the last week. Rajiv Khan, an Indian with a perfectly mainstream American accent, moderates two intentionally inflammatory guests as they debate the implications of a son representing his father.

"The question is whether he can provide honest representation, free of emotional manipulation," one white man posits.

"You're worried about whether or not the representation is good?" the other white man responds. "We should be more concerned about how we're going to find a suitable punishment for Rashid Siddique's admitted role in the 2010 double freeway bombing."

Rajiv interjects. "But surely this is the most unusual legal representation we've seen in decades. A child, who believed his father was dead, a son, just barely out of law school, advocates for lenient sentencing for his father who has suddenly reappeared in his life. Not even any of the Guantanamo Bay prisoners had such unusual representation."

"Don't make either of them into a celebrity. This was a man who attacked his own country," the first pundit counters.

"…his adopted country," the host clarifies.

"…but the native country of his wife and children, and he brutally attacked his fellow Americans."

The newscast cuts to images of the attack, the destruction on the freeways. Kathryn turns off the screen. "Nothing new tonight. I hope Michael isn't watching any of this. He's really put himself in the middle of the stage."

"Are you worried?" her mother asks.

"Wouldn't you be?"

"Well, is there anything you can do at this point? Can you convince him to walk away? Can you protect him from the media, the commentators, from here at the end of my driveway?"

Kathryn looks down at her food, shakes her head.

"Then stop worrying, it doesn't help anyone. You've raised that boy as best you could. Michael is a man now, you've got to let him go."

Kathryn turns her spoon in her hand. "It's so hard. I feel so guilty for putting him in this situation."

"Of course it's hard. Do you think it was easy for me to sit back and watch you make one risky decision after another?"

"Like what?"

"Like moving to Dubai."

"But Dad moved overseas."

"He already had a job when he was leaving, and he was a man. And then you went to Pakistan."

"You never said anything."

"What difference would it have made?" her mother asks without any hint of resentment. "You were an adult, I didn't want to threaten our relationship by being the voice of doubt."

Kathryn's phone rings, Michael's image appears on the little screen. Kathryn rushes to answer it. "Michael! Michael, how are you doing? Are you all right?"

"I'm fine Mom, a little tired, but this is an amazing process. You can't imagine the kinds of people who are calling to talk to me."

"What do you mean? Like who?" Concern tugs in her belly, she imagines international terrorists viewing her vulnerable son as sympathetic.

"Academics, constitutional law types, elected officials, Pakistani businessmen, even a publisher who wants me to write a book. I couldn't have engineered an opportunity like this if I tried. Amazing." He sounds breathless, almost giddy.

"What's happening with you and your...what is happening with Rashid's case? I mean, besides what I'm seeing in the news."

"Rashid. Like I told you last week, he has a very simplistic idea of what we should be doing, I'm glad he didn't go by himself, they would've given him the death penalty in a heartbeat. And he's very old-world in some weird ways. He wants to have every negotiation in person, he doesn't trust phone calls or emails. Sometimes he'll work through a video call."

"How's he treating you? How are you getting along?"

"Oh, he's great usually. He falls all over himself to be grateful, but he says he doesn't care what happens to him, he's only worried about us."

"What do you mean?" Kathryn lifts the curtain to scan the yard from the kitchen window.

"Well, there are some parts of his testimony that're still unclear, like who paid him while he was in Pakistan and how he got back to the U.S. And he refuses to give any information, says it could jeopardize his American family's safety. That makes the feds crazy because they think he can link them to some larger terrorist organization. In fact, some people I've talked to are even suggesting some unbelievable things like allowing him to live free in Pakistan so they could use him like bait to see what bigger fish they could catch. It's infuriating that he won't tell me everything, because I'm his lawyer, but he tells me that I'm his son first."

"You're my son…too. Please be careful, you can't be sure of everything you're dealing with."

"Don't worry. I am careful. Mom…he's asked to talk with you via video. I've negotiated with the judge to allow two minutes, with a federal investigator observing. Are you willing to talk to him?"

Kathryn looks up at her mother, seeing only her inscrutable calm. "What does he want to talk with me about?"

"He says it's strictly personal. Wants to tell you something from his heart."

"Maybe he could just tell you and you could tell me?"

"I told you he's adamant about this face-to-face stuff. I negotiated pretty hard for it Mom, I hope you'll agree."

"When would it happen?"

"Tomorrow, morning. 9am Pacific time."

"Can I think on it a little while?"

"How long?" he asks, obviously disappointed.

"I'll call you in the morning?"

"I have back-to-back meetings starting at 8am. Can you call me back tonight? Doesn't matter how late it is."

"All right, I'll call you back tonight. And Michael…"

"Yes Mom?"

"I love you. Please be careful."

"Of course. I love you too, and send my love to Grandma." She can hear another phone ring on Michael's end. "Gotta run. Call me tonight."

Kathryn's mother cuts another piece of beef for herself, waiting for Kathryn to speak.

"Mom, Rashid wants to speak with me by video."

"Are you surprised?"

"I guess not. I just don't know what the point would be." Through her fear, she feels a longing.

"Remind me of one of your rules," Kathryn's mother smiles gently, "one of your Capen Codes, the one about regret."

"No regrets." Kathryn pauses, almost embarrassed, before repeating one of the rules she taught her boys to memorize. "We live our lives the best we know how. If something goes wrong, change your behavior, you can't change the past."

"Yes. I always liked that one. I actually used that a couple of times, changed my mind about things because I wanted to be sure I wouldn't be tempted to regret my decision later."

Kathryn looks again at her phone. "So are you saying I should take the call?"

"No, just suggesting you think about which decision you might regret."

———

Kathryn sits before a computer screen, waiting. She sees the Department of Justice seal and hears a voice.

"Kathryn Capen, please be advised that your communication with

Rashid Siddique will be monitored by the Department of Justice and the Department of Homeland Security. While your communication cannot be quoted as testimony, the Departments reserve the right to question either of you regarding anything discussed or implied. Do you agree to these conditions?"

"I do."

"Thank you for your understanding Ms. Capen. You will now be connected."

From a small concrete room, Rashid sits in a prison jumpsuit, his wrists and ankles shackled, the chain locked to a metal hook in the floor. He knows beyond the mirrored window in front of him observers will scrutinize his every expression. But he hears nothing, sees only the image of himself, tired and weathered, for long minutes.

Suddenly Kathryn's image appears on the screen, calm but guarded. She waits for him to speak. In contrast to all of the stark hardness of his surroundings, the still beautiful curves of her face leave him grasping for words.

"Rashid, you only have two minutes," Kathryn prompts. "Please, go ahead and tell me what you planned to say."

"Yes...I don't have much time. I need to tell you...I want to say...you...you had hurt me very badly."

Kathryn wrinkles her eyebrows.

"When I realized that the boys knew nothing about me, it was as if you'd killed me."

She flares her nostrils. "How dare you twist this around."

"Wait," he tries to raise a hand to stop her, the clank of the metal chain stops him short. "But I've been thinking about your decision, until now. You protected them. And you did me a very good favor, even. Because Michael didn't know anything about me, he's been able to see me...see me for who I am, he understands me in a way I never imagined when I was dreaming about the three of you all those years."

She nods, unsure how to respond.

"I know I have to finish this quickly. I just wanted to tell you, no matter what happens I hold nothing against you. I have forgiven you. I have even forgiven America. I have no more anger." He looks down, closes his eyes and looks up again. "And I have no regrets. It was all written." He lifts a finger and lowers his head so the finger can trace the line of his forehead.

"Ten seconds, Rashid," a man's voice cuts into the line.

"Please understand that I did what I had to do, and so did you. I wish it could have been different, but I am grateful to you for…"

The line cuts off. The connection ends.

Kathryn slumps forward, suddenly limp, and lets out a whimper.

Rashid exhales, hears the chain again as he adjusts his feet.

───────────

"What fucking business does he have telling me he forgives me? Excuse my French Mother, but for God's sake, what do I need to be forgiven for? What good does that do me?"

Kathryn's mother pours water into the coffee maker, preparing the second pot of the morning. "He isn't doing it for you. He's unburdening himself. Making amends where he can and letting go of everything else. Think about it…he held so strongly to his clan culture and his anger that he was willing to plan a bomb attack. Then he held so strongly to his dream of you that he believed after twenty years he could reunite." She pours in the coffee grounds. "Obviously something has happened and he's given up the dream of you. He's given up his innocence. He's even willing to give up his life, so why should he hold on to his anger, his feeling of injustice?" She opens the cupboard and pulls out a box of cookies. "Your father did something similar when he was dying. He talked about all of the disagreements he'd had with colleagues, the jabs they had made in articles and lectures. It was as if he inventoried every little injury that he still remembered, and then he laughed about them. 'What did they matter?' he said. 'When you were by my side the whole time?'"

"If this is about Rashid letting go of everything, then why bother with dragging Michael into it? Why's he putting my son at the center of the ordeal?"

Kathryn's mother sits down, sets the box of cookies in front of her daughter. "If you ask me, this thing with Michael isn't about Rashid, Michael's doing it because Michael needs to."

"Well, what did he think I would do…" Kathryn picks up an earlier train of thought. "…sing my kids songs about his heroic revenge? Did he think I'd tell them bedtime stories about the bravery of one man against a whole nation? I mean he fucking planned to blow up a freeway." Her hands tremble, she tries to repress the memory of these hands caressing the same man.

Her mother pushes the box of cookies toward Kathryn.

"Mom, can I tell you something?" She takes a cookie, crumbs falling. "I'm jealous, I'm not proud of this, but I raised that boy, I made sure he learned to be a man, and now he devotes himself completely to defending his guilty father." She looks away, bites her lip. "How am I supposed to feel?" she says shrilly.

"You need to feel everything you feel. You can't avoid it, pain, anger, shame, whatever your heart tells you. But you can't hold it here," the older woman pulls her arms in, protecting her heart. "Life goes on."

Chapter 7

Rashid stands patiently in front of a locked door as the guard locks another door behind him. The transfer from his cell to the room where he can meet with his lawyer strikes him each time as unnecessarily elaborate. What would he do if there were less security? Run away? Plant another bomb? Once the guard opens the door ahead of him, Rashid sees Michael's face light up. Could there be anything more exquisite? Could a father ever want for more than his son's love? Would he feel as grateful, would his chest swell with wonder in the same way if he had grown accustomed to this kind of interaction? His life since he decided to surrender has revealed itself like a string of jewels, a series of interactions with Kathryn and Michael, crystalline new memories, separated by long periods of quiet in which to enjoy each facet, to marvel at the complexity of love.

"Rashid, how are you?"

He has no words to adequately express his state. "Fine, I'm fine. And how are you?"

They do not touch. Rashid sits in a molded plastic, prison-safe chair, across a featureless table from his son. The door behind them closes with the sound of a metal deadbolt turning.

Michael leans forward on the table. "The feds are very close to agreeing to our requests. You know that last week I had gotten them to agree to hold you in a minimum security penitentiary, but they wanted you to be on the east coast, one of the facilities where they send people from the D.C. jurisdiction. I argued against it. The D.C. jurisdiction has no bearing, the defendant was from California, the crime was in California. So they're considering locating you in a facility in San Louis Obispo. The weather's fantastic, the facility has a library, you'd be placed with other low security..." he hesitates over the word *prisoners*, "...with low security threats."

"You know, Michael, beta, I'll go wherever is decided. I have no more desires for myself."

Michael shakes his head, rolls his eyes toward the ceiling, which Rashid mistakes as a glance toward heaven. "I know you keep saying that, but *I* want you to be in a place where I could see you. So I'm even trying to negotiate for enhanced visiting privileges. But..."

"But...?"

"They want some additional information about your contacts, the people who arranged for all of your passports, the people who provided the funds for you and Ali." Michael hesitates; he has conveyed the request already, dozens of times, phrased in every imaginable way.

Rashid shakes his head, only once, as he has done with each request. "I told you, the source of most of that information was Ali. He never revealed his contacts to me. I never asked. Were they Al Qaeda? I don't know. I didn't want to know. I knew only he served my purpose."

"And the people who helped you to return to the U.S., you must know who those people were."

"I knew a man, only by a single name, a nickname really."

"So tell me that name," Michael nearly pleads.

"No. No." He remembers Sheik Omar's threat. "It's not worth it."

"Not worth being in a place where you could see us, your wife and children, more? That's not worth a name?"

"It's not safe to give you that name."

"Not safe?" Exasperation elevates Michael's voice. "What could happen to you? You'll be in a secure facility."

"But you won't." Rashid looks his son in the eye, spreads his hands on the table as widely as the shackles will allow. "You...you more than anyone must understand…revenge cannot be stopped. I'm allowing America to have her revenge." He makes a fist with his right hand. "Let her do what she needs to do. To me." He bangs his fist against his left hand. "But I will not give the world one more action which could cause another man to seek revenge." He turns his left hand, palm up, and wraps his fingers around his right fist, embracing the inevitable.

Chapter 8

Kathryn glimpses her reflection in the glass door as she enters the bank, her wide-brimmed hat obscuring her sunglasses and unpainted lips. She feels a tremor of anxiety as she steps inside, maybe she should have called Ted and asked him to come and protect her in her attempt to evade reporters. How many times has she made this trip, an envelope of cash in her purse, an ache in her lower back? But today, she has nothing to deposit, she is not shedding something illicit, but harvesting, harnessing the power of her patience. She sits in the familiar room with her safe deposit box. Instead of the habitual hurry, she sits quietly, pausing to formulate her intention, to gather a little prayer for her son. Michael had sounded like a small boy when he called, requesting money.

She removes all of the envelopes, extracts the bills from each one, makes a stack of cash on one side of the box, and discards the envelopes on the other side. With each envelope she thinks now of the sender, not some nefarious group making martyr payments, but Rashid, sending money anonymously through some local hawala agent. With each set of bills, she begins to understand his sense of devotion, his misguided idea of caring for them. As she closes the cover on the box she hears metal rattle inside. She reaches in, remembering now, retrieving two wedding bands, seeing again the inscription *Beneath the Same Heaven* on the gold band. She pauses, thinking to leave these rings to their darkness. But instead, she slides them into a pocket in her purse. She will return the box empty, close the account, end that chapter.

———————

She rings the doorbell with both relief and apprehension. Her brother opens the door, gives her a feisty smile.

"Never a dull moment in your life, huh?"

Kathryn pauses, uncertain what to say.

"Come in, come in." Ted smiles, "I've almost forgotten what you look like without those red lips."

Janet comes into the hall, hugs Kathryn. "I'm glad you're here. We'll have a good dinner, it's been too long."

"Is Andrew here?" Kathryn puts down her bag, still full with the money.

Ted shakes his head. "But don't worry, he said he'd come, we've seen him a couple of times since…since Rashid returned from the dead." He exhales a little laugh.

In the kitchen Janet has already poured four glasses of red wine. "How's your mother?"

"She's a little older, a little more frail, but she's been wonderful taking care of me."

"And what do you hear from Michael," Ted asks, "aside from what we see in the media?"

"He's fine." Kathryn doesn't elaborate. "I don't know where this is all going." She accepts wine from Janet.

"Doesn't seem to me this has to change your life too much," Ted muses. "Rashid pleads guilty, goes to serve his time, you continue on with your life."

She starts to object, as the doorbell rings.

"That must be Andrew," Janet says moving to open the door.

"Mom," he greets her sullenly. "Hi Auntie Janet, Uncle Ted."

Kathryn winces, resists the urge to reach out to him, goes through the motions of conversation as they sit down for dinner. At last, when she can no longer stand the elephant in the room, she nearly blurts out, "I need to tell you all something. Something about Rashid that no one knows."

"Oh fuck," Andrew mutters.

Kathryn pretends she hasn't heard him. "I have almost a hundred thousand dollars in my purse there. Cash."

Andrew furrows his eyebrow. Kathryn rubs her lower back. "I received unmarked envelopes with cash in them every few months. I realize now Rashid was sending them, this money was for you and Michael. It's about time I gave it to you."

"My God, Mom!" Andrew leans his head back covering his eyes with his hands. "How many secrets are you going to suddenly reveal? Any more lies you've been telling me that you'd like to come clean about?"

"Shit, you got any piles of money in there for me?" Ted teases. Janet suppresses a smile.

"You can take my share, Uncle Ted. There's no way I want anything to do with that money or that man."

Ted scoops a forkful of salad. "I'd love to buy some surf toys with that cash, but it doesn't belong to me. Take a little while to think about it, Andrew."

Kathryn reaches for her wine. "Actually Ted, I was hoping you might make the deposit into Michael's account in small increments, like you were supporting him." She takes a sip. "You know, I just don't want any questions from the feds about where this money came from."

"Wow, now that I'm almost retired I could pick up a new career in money laundering."

"Call it what you like, I'm asking for your help."

"Yeah, I'm used to that."

Chapter 9

Rashid waits in his chair, looking through the glass into the empty visitor's room. He runs a hand over his neatly trimmed hair, reaches—out of habit—to tug on a beard long gone. He can't remember the last time he felt so at ease. He hears the clank of a metal door and Kathryn comes into view, carrying her purse and a manila envelope. A prison guard follows her, standing in the corner where he can observe them both.

"I appreciate that you've come," Rashid says as she sits down in the chair on the opposite side of the glass. "I know it's a long flight from the west coast."

She nods. Fidgets in her seat as she takes in his appearance through the glass.

"It's not bad here," he presupposes her question. "I have time in the library and outside every day."

"And the other people?"

"Mostly they leave me alone. Since I'm not white or black or Latino, I don't have a place in their gangs." He decides not to tell her more than this. She doesn't need to know about the constant possibility of violence in the prison, the taunts and slurs he endures. He doesn't seek sympathy from her. "How is Michael?"

"He's fine. He decided to give up his apartment and he's staying with me temporarily." She pauses as if deciding whether or not to tell him something. "He's planning to use some of your money," she inhales, "to go to Pakistan."

"Really?" Rashid's heart leaps inside his chest. "Finally he'll go back to see where he comes from."

"He'll see where *you* come from." She frowns, looks directly into Rashid's astonishingly clear eyes. With his graying hair, in the wrinkles of his forehead she can see the likeness of Rashid's father, and in the fullness of his lips she sees the familiar curve of her son. "I'm thinking to go with him."

"So you can see my family?"

"I just think it'd be safer if I went with him."

Rashid sets his hands on the table, resting one on top of the other, almost gracefully. "God is great. My family will welcome you both."

She sits quietly, observing the calm in his movements, the gentleness of his voice.

"Will Andrew go as well?" he asks hopefully.

She shakes her head. "Andrew…Andrew will need some time and some space to know what he feels. He's hardly speaking to me."

"Of course. He'll come back to you, don't worry. A son will always return to his mother. He has no choice."

His words, simultaneously soothing and stinging, penetrate the protective emotional barrier she had carefully cultivated on the long car ride from the airport. She lowers her head, sighs. "Somehow I can't believe how all of this has transpired, so beyond my control. What more could I have done? Could I have made it different in some way? I wish we'd just had a normal family life, I wish we just could've raised our sons, been normal people worrying about small things."

She looks up, leans her forehead against the glass. He can see tears in her eyes. He sets his fingers against the glass, as if he could wipe the tears away.

"Kathryn, it was all written. What I had to do was terrible… terrible. So now it's my responsibility to pay the price for that. There must be justice. But there's nothing any of us could've done to make things different." He finally allows himself to reach his other hand through the small opening where the glass meets the table. The guard leans in, alert. And she accepts the gesture, reaching her hand to touch his.

"Almost Morocco," he whispers.

"What?"

"This is almost as sweet as my dream of meeting you in Morocco. At least here I have nothing left to hide, nothing left to fear."

She closes her eyes, focusing only on the sensations in her fingers where they touch his.

"What's in the envelope?"

She inhales deeply and pulls her hand away. "Well, you'd asked me to bring you news of the boys and me," she pulls a stack of printed papers out of the envelope. "It's not exactly news." As she lifts the envelope, something falls out, metal clinking against the table top. She picks up a gold band, triggering a ripple of recognition in his body. Setting the papers aside, she picks up the ring and presses it between her palms. "This is yours, you should have it back."

Wordlessly he opens his palm, with something approaching disbelief.

"No passing objects," the guard barks.

She flinches, nods, slides the ring onto her own index finger.

"Thank you," Rashid whispers. "Please wear it."

She takes the papers in her hands. "This is something I started writing in the last few weeks, trying to…." Feeling exposed, despite the glass, she presses the papers up against her chest. "Do you want me to read you some?"

"Of course."

She sets the papers back on the table, bites her lower lip, takes a breath. "Kathryn answers the phone," she reads. "The man asks where Rashid is. She recognizes the man's voice, her husband's manager. '*You* should know where he is,' she says, 'you sent him offshore for a job.' He tells her she better call him. She sets the phone down, confused. When she hears a knock at the door, she opens it, surprised at the serious expression of a man in a suit. 'Are you Kathryn Siddique?' he asks. 'I am agent Roberts, FBI. I need to talk to you about your husband.' She tries to close the door…"

Kathryn pauses, looking up to see if Rashid recognizes the story.

He presses his eyes shut. "Can you ever forgive me?" He looks again, into her silence.

She reaches her hand to her heart. "It's the only thing I can't…" slowly she sets her hand in the space beneath the glass. "Forgiveness is the only power I have to make things different."

She closes her eyes.

He nods.

Acknowledgements

I am grateful to those who helped me bring this book into the world. I am grateful to the whole Grewal family for welcoming me into their family and sharing with me their culture and their love; to Isvinder Singh Grewal, Arshdeep Jawanda, Sattar Izwaini, Tracy Sterk, and Eric Aamoth who helped me understand other points of view; to Sarah Jane Lapp, Amy Alyeshmerni, Sidney Higgins, Kim Fay, Kris Ruff, Dureen Ruff, Jill Muller, Heather Capen Cox, and Michael Swinney who read early versions; to Christopher Little and Emma Schlesinger who provided expert feedback over the course of multiple versions; to Madeline Baugh, Emmy Harrington, Amy Perry, Holly Prado, Molly Ann Hale, and Charlie Davis who encouraged me and kept me on track; to Barbara Baer who read each step, believed in the story, and showed me the way; to Kelly Huddleston and David Ross who delivered it over the line; to the bus drivers of the Metro 96 line who unknowingly hosted my writing studio; and to family—my children Nirvair William and Sukhdev Josh, and especially my husband Lali—whose love made it all possible.

CPSIA information can be obtained
at www.ICGtesting.com
Printed in the USA
LVHW111529010819
626170LV00002B/328/P